A Man Of Faith . . .

Monsignor Riley hadn't thought so. "Faith above all else, Sean. Faith in Our Father. Without faith, what are you?"

"A man, Monsignor. No more, no less."

"You are not as other men, Sean. When you made the decision to become a priest, you elevated yourself above the ordinary man."

"Yet I am still a man. I thirst like a man, I hunger like a man, I have desires like a man."

"Carnal desire, in my opinion, is one test of our faith. A means by which God has seen fit to judge us worthy in His eyes. You must scourge yourself of all lusts of the flesh, my son. We have all gone through it. You will emerge the better priest for it."

"But I don't know if I wish to be a better priest, or any kind of priest, if it means giving up Nora."

"This woman has been sent by God as the ultimate test of your faith. Triumph over this temptation and you shall belong to God forever!"

"I'm not sure I want to be God's forever. . . ."

"The pleasures of the flesh are transitory. The love of God endures into eternity."

"I love Nora. I love her more than life itself. Perhaps I love her more than God!"

CLAYTON MATTHEWS

THE BIRTHRIGHT

SEVERN
SH
HOUSE

This title first published in Great Britain 1988 by
SEVERN HOUSE PUBLISHERS LTD of
40–42 William IV Street, London WC2N 4DF.

British Library Cataloguing in Publication Data
Matthews, Clayton
The birthright.
I. Title
813'.54 [F]   PS3563.A84
ISBN 0–7278–1511–3

BCll.97

03207718

Printed and bound in Great Britain

To Hoyt and Hubert Baldwin,
whose ancestors fought in the
Battle of San Jacinto

THE BIRTHRIGHT

Part One

1836

1

The sun's rays stabbed, like the devil's breath, through the thin blanket stretched over the sides of the two-wheeled cart.

Pain.

The labor pains were only seconds apart now, the contractions squeezing her swollen belly like some torture instrument. The jostling of the cart didn't help, and the pain was a thousand knives digging, gouging, twisting, causing agony unbearable.

But she was determined not to call out to Sean. The poor man had had enough travail and trouble this past year. As another spasm seized her, she bit down hard on her lower lip to keep from crying out, bit so hard that the brassy taste of her own blood filled her mouth.

A final monster contraction squeezed, and consciousness began to slide away from her. She tried desperately to hold on, but the engulfing darkness offered surcease and she finally gave way to it. Just before she slipped under, she was sure that she felt the pain ease, and warm wetness flooded her upper thighs . . .

Sean Moraghan plodded, leaning into the crude harness he'd improvised from the one he'd used on the mule. The two-wheeled cart carrying Nora and all their worldly goods—precious little—resisted stubbornly, almost miring in the dusty ruts of the trail with every step Sean took. Their mule had drowned fording the Sabine River three days before. Thanks be to the Lord, Nora hadn't been taken with the animal.

Trail!

El Camino Real, they called it, stretching the breadth of Texas. What a grandiose name for such a primitive road!

Lord God, he was tired, bone-tired, mind-tired. For the first weeks of their journey from Tennessee, the arduous physical labor had left Sean so benumbed with weariness at the end of the day that he wasn't able to think, so tired he could sleep where he dropped. But now he had gone beyond mere weariness, until his mind had become a separate entity from his body. At times he was almost in a state of spiritual ecstasy, and he moved like a man in a dream, his mind free to probe the questions of the universe, of the relationship between man and God, questions for which he had no answers, to which there were no answers.

How many times had Monsignor Riley childed him in that gentle voice? "Questions. Always the questions, Sean. True faith requires no questions. Questions reveal a fatal flaw in us . . ."

A faint cry brought Sean's head up. At first he thought it was the cry of some small animal in distress. It came again, and he finally identified it. Panting in his haste, he grappled with the harness until he could step free of it. Lowering the stays to the ground, he hurried around to the rear of the cart and pushed back the blanket.

He stood frozen in astonishment and awe. Nora's

3

swollen belly was flat, and there between her spread thighs was the source of the thin cry he'd heard—a red, feebly thrashing infant! He saw at a glance that it was a boy.

His son!

A year ago, even six months ago, never in his wildest imaginings would Sean have dreamed that he would ever sire a child. Nora had been three months pregnant before she had informed him.

"Lord God," he whispered in reverence. "By the Virgin Mary!"

Nora stirred, responding with that bawdy chuckle of hers. Her voice so weak as to be barely audible, she said, "I hardly think that applies, my darling. It was not an immaculate conception, if you will recall." Then she raised her head, face pale and beaded with sweat, to stare down the length of her body at him. "Don't just stand there like some great oaf, Sean! You have things to do. Quickly! I can't do everything. Heat some water. The baby has to be washed, and the tad's still attached to me, you dunce. You have to cut the cord."

"Nora, I can't be doing that!"

"Men! If there *was* some way an immaculate conception could be carried out, we women could very well do without men."

Stretching her forearms along the bed of the cart, she levered herself up onto her elbows, then propped her back against the side. Before Sean's horrified gaze, she picked the baby up gently in both hands, bent almost double, and severed the umbilical cord with one bite of strong white teeth.

"God above, woman, what are you after doing?"

"Doing what has to be done." Quickly she tied the cord off, deposited the baby back onto the blanket, and sank back with a sigh. "Now, dear man, will you get on with what I asked you to do?"

The urgency in her voice galvanized Sean into action. He was honest enough with himself to admit that he

4

was glad of an excuse to escape. During the past six months with Nora, Sean, who had known as much about a female as he did about a camel in the African desert, had been constantly dazzled and astounded at the ways of women.

Still Nora, he was positive, was an exceptional woman. Even in his abysmal ignorance, he would have been willing to wager that very few women were capable of doing what she had just done.

Sean rolled the cart off the trail and under the shade of a live oak. Other travelers had scoured the sides of the trail clean of all deadwood, and he had to range back into the trees. The August day was sweltering, the air so thick and humid it was like moving underwater. The piny woods had a resiny scent. Insects sang a drowsy melody in the heat. The rich red earth had a fecund odor.

Before he had gathered enough wood for a fire, he came out of the edge of the trees onto the brink of a shallow valley. About two miles distant smoke rose straight up into the still air. It was most likely Nacogdoches, the town he had been informed he would eventually come to along this trail.

For just a moment Sean debated with himself—should he hurry Nora and the baby into the town for a doctor, and proper care?

But he knew that it would be too much of a risk, to both Nora and the baby. Many of these towns, he had learned, had no doctors. He would have to tend to her and the child as best he could himself.

The cart was quiet when he returned with an armful of wood. Apprehensive, he stuck his head under the blanket. "Is the baby after being all right?" He swore at himself for the lapse into brogue, something he was apt to do in moments of stress or anger.

"He will be, Sean, when you get on with it." In counterpoint to her tart reply, the baby yowled lustily.

Hurriedly, Sean built a pyramid of dry wood, whittled

a few curlicues of kindling, and labored with his flint and piece of steel. Sparks flew, and finally one caught.

Then he constructed a tripod of greenwood from which to suspend a kettle, and went to fetch the water keg. Water had been scarce since they left the Sabine, but there was enough to fill the kettle, with a little to spare. He hung the kettle over the flames, then crossed again to the cart.

"Nora, I spread a blanket on the ground. Can I help you out and onto it?"

"You can, and thank heaven for small favors! I thought you were going to leave me in here in my own piss and stink forever! Not to mention the baby!"

"Nora, I do wish you'd watch your language. That's no way for a lady to be talking."

"Who said I was a lady? Not I. If I had been, I wouldn't be here now, birthing the bastard son of Sean Moraghan!"

Sean winced. "Sweet, he's not a bastard."

"Perhaps not, strictly speaking. But considering we've only been wed six months, it's not far from the mark. Now can you deny that?"

Sean sighed. In one respect he was relieved. If Nora could talk like this, it meant she was all right, but it also meant that he would be receiving the rasp of her tongue. Not that he minded all that much; her frankness was one of her attractions, and she usually managed to pretend the proper lady when in the company of others. And God knows, he thought, she wasn't a complainer. If she had been, there had been ample to complain about these past few months.

Gingerly, he helped her out of the cart, handed her the baby, and supported her to the blanket under the tree. She sank down with a grateful sigh, leaning back against the trunk of the tree, and took the boy into her arms.

Sean squatted by the fire, waiting for the water to

heat. He was a tall, lean man by nature, but the hard work and a scarcity of food had gaunted him even more. His hair was long, almost to his shoulders, so black as to be almost blue. He would have been handsome except for a rather prominent nose. His full-lipped mouth customarily shaped a smile, but of late there had been little to smile about, and the dark eyes, usually gentle, had begun to harden.

He stretched his long hands toward the fire, not to warm them, but to examine them. Unaccustomed to physical labor for most of his thirty years, they had blistered over and over on the trail, and calluses had finally started to form; yet they still pained him considerably.

Sean turned his thoughts to pleasanter subjects—to his son. Closing his eyes, he voiced a silent prayer of thanksgiving. Before it was completed, he began to smile wryly. Did he still believe in God? He wasn't sure, but the long habit of prayer was hard to break.

Faith. That was the knotty nub of it. Was his faith still intact?

Certainly Monsignor Riley hadn't thought so. "Faith above all else, Sean. Faith in Our Father. Without faith, what are you?"

"A man, Monsignor. No more, no less."

"You are not as other men, Sean. When you made the decision to become a priest, you elevated yourself above the ordinary man."

"Yet I am still a man. I thirst like a man, I hunger like a man, I have desires like a man."

"Carnal desire, in my opinion, is one test of our faith. A means by which God has seen fit to judge us worthy in His eyes. You must scourge yourself of all lusts of the flesh, my son. We have all gone through it. You will emerge the better priest for it."

"But I don't know if I wish to be a better priest, or any kind of priest, if it means giving up Nora."

7

"This woman has been sent by God as the ultimate test of your faith. Triumph over this temptation and you shall belong to God forever!"

"I'm not sure I want to be God's forever . . ."

"The pleasures of the flesh are transitory. The love of God endures into eternity."

"I love Nora. I love her more than life itself. Perhaps I love her more than God."

"Blasphemy! Rank sacrilege! Fall to your knees and pray. . . ."

Nora's tart voice broke into Sean's thoughts. "Sean! Are you going to let the water boil away?"

He glanced at the kettle and saw that it was boiling merrily. "Sorry," he mumbled, and hastily unhooked the kettle, scalding his hand in the process. A great oath exploded from him.

"Such language," she said mockingly. "And from a priest yet!"

"Ex, Nora. Defrocked. Excommunicated."

Her face grew still as he came toward her carrying the kettle. "Any regrets, darling?"

"None," he said promptly, and stoutly.

How true was that? He had to wonder.

Then he kneeled beside her and clumsily picked up the baby, fingers feeling big as sausages. His face bloomed in a foolish smile, and he said, "How can I feel any regret, with what you have just presented me?"

"No need to handle him like a porcelain doll, dunce head," she scolded. "He's not going to break."

With a cloth and a rough towel, he washed his son with loving if awkward care. Done, he laid the infant on the blanket and stood up.

"Aren't you going to do the same for me?"

Sean felt his face flushing. Despite all the times he had held Nora naked in his arms, he was still agonizingly embarrassed when he came upon her in daylight without clothing.

"I . . ." He swallowed. "Can you manage by your-

8

self? We have nothing to eat but the remains of the jerky, tough as old leather and about as tasty. You must be starved; I know I am. I'll take my pistol and scout around for a hare for our supper."

"Yes, darling." Her mouth curved in that smile he'd come to think of as special, special just for him. "I wouldn't want you any other way."

"What?" he said in confusion.

"Never mind, just run along with you," she said crossly. "I'll manage very well, thank you."

Sean went to the front of the cart and removed his pistol from the wooden holster hooked to the cart, kept there so it would be handy when he was pulling the vehicle. He checked the priming of the percussion fire-arm, called a caplock.

He said, "I won't be far away, Nora. There are some rough types along this trail. If you need me, just call out."

She waved a hand at him, without speaking, and Sean stepped among the trees, the pistol at ready. Until he had started on this trek, he had never fired a weapon in his life; but knowing what might confront them on this trip to Texas, he had spent precious money on both a pistol and a musket. To his amazement, Sean discovered that he had a natural aptitude for firearms, and was now a reasonably good shot.

The supreme irony—a disciple of the Prince of Peace handy with weapons!

He moved slowly, carefully, farther into the woods, his gaze darting about in search of a cottontail rabbit, that tasty animal abounding in this area—a ball of fur on its rump remarkably like a flowering cotton ball.

It was Sean's intention to settle in East Texas. In the small trunk in the cart he had a letter from the hand of an empresario, affirming that Sean's application for land near Nacogdoches had been approved.

Back in Tennessee he had heard tales of 12-foot cotton plants in Texas that renewed themselves each

9

season. It was said that the soil in the territory was so rich that "if you plant tenpenny nails in the ground, you will harvest a crop of iron bolts."

Conceding that much of this was probably the extravagant embroidery frontiersmen loved to weave into their tales, it still opened up exciting vistas for a man who was not averse to hard work. Sean knew absolutely nothing about farming, and he had little money with which to purchase needed farm implements; but he would manage, he was sure of it.

A chattering sound and a movement on the branch of a live oak drew his attention. Sean froze, squinting his eyes in an attempt to penetrate the foliage. Then he saw a blur of brown, and spotted a plump squirrel squatting on its haunches on the tree limb, nibbling on an acorn held in its forepaws. The animal was less than ten yards from where Sean stood, and apparently hadn't noticed him.

He had never eaten squirrel, but he had been told that the meat was most tasty, if not as plentiful as that on a rabbit. Avoiding any sudden move, he slowly raised the pistol, cocking it and sighting down the barrel.

Much of the food they had subsisted on during the long journey had come from Sean's hunting of game. Yet he still had to force himself to kill, using his vivid imagination to conjure up images of Nora starving because he was unable to provide food for her belly. Now there was a third mouth to feed. The baby couldn't eat meat yet, of course, but Nora had to eat to provide milk for him.

Sean fired. Smoke puffed up, and the pistol ball whacked into the limb beneath the squirrel, knocking the animal to the ground, momentarily stunning it. The practice of "barking" a squirrel was favored over a direct hit; a pistol ball could rip all the meat from the small animal. Sean loped over to the fallen squirrel, and delivered the killing blow with a rock.

Before picking the animal up, Sean carefully made

the pistol ready for firing again. Back in Louisiana Territory, a grizzled fur trapper had watched Sean kill a rabbit, then ram his unprimed pistol into his belt in his haste to pick up his kill.

"Nere do that, hoss. Out here, when a man fire his oney weapon, better reload then and there. Your life may depend on it."

Taking the Barlow knife from his belt, Sean squatted and quickly skinned and gutted his prize before hurrying back to camp with it. He grinned when he saw Nora holding his son to her breast. Involuntarily his glance jumped away from the sight of her bared breast, full, blue-veined. Even though he had not touched her in passion for some weeks because of her condition, Sean was ashamed of the quick hardening at his loins.

With that unfailing knack of hers Nora said, "It won't be long now, Sean, until it'll be all right again. A few weeks."

"I don't fathom your meaning, Nora."

She hooted. "Not much you don't, Sean Moraghan!"

Face burning, Sean went about preparing the squirrel for cooking. Then he stoked up the fire, spitted the squirrel with a long, sharpened stick, and held it over the flames, cooking it slowly.

By the time it was nicely brown, dripping grease spitting on the flames, the sun had gone down. Twilight brought, if not a cooling, at least an illusion of it.

When the squirrel was done, Sean dismembered it, arranged the pieces on a board they had been using as a plate, and carried it to his wife. He was relieved to see that the baby had ceased sucking and was asleep in Nora's lap. Her breast was adequately covered, and she had her head back against the tree trunk, eyes closed.

"Supper's prepared, Nora," he said with false cheer.

Nora's eyes fluttered open. She carefully placed the infant on the blanket beside her and sat up straighter. Sean extended the board, and she selected a piece, biting into it.

11

Chewing, she said, "Ah, it's delicious." Her eyes glinted with mischief. "Did anyone ever tell you, darling, that you'd make some woman a fine husband?"

"Not so fine, I fear," he said glumly. "A boy of ten could kill a squirrel with a stick and cook it. So far, I've managed to get us banished from Tennessee, and we're out here in the wilderness, impoverished, with another mouth to feed, and . . ."

"Hellfire and spit, Sean!" Nora said, eyes flashing. "I'll not listen to you bad-mouthing yourself, nor to your Black Irish glooming about! As my grandpa used to say, you'd complain if hung with a new rope! You've fed us, fathered a fine son, got that allotment of 4,428 acres in that Texas land grant, which is fine cotton land, so you've been telling me . . ."

"I've only been telling you what I have been told. But I've also heard some disquieting rumors along the way. I've hesitated to tell you because of your delicate condition . . ." This wrung a snort from Nora. "But you're entitled to know. It's said that some of these empresarios are fraudulent. True, they're empowered by the Mexican government to sell those acres to American families for sixty dollars, but it is rumored that many sell their allotments many times over, and when a man arrives to claim his land, the empresario is gone, and there is no land to claim."

Concern shadowed her eyes. "And you think this empresario is such a man?"

Sean shrugged. "I don't know, sweet. Unfortunately, the world is peopled by the wicked."

"Spoken like a true crusading priest." Amusement brightened her eyes. "Tell me . . . Did it sore try your conscience to have to swear you were a Roman Catholic?"

"I did not lie, Nora. I am still a Roman Catholic."

"Are you now?"

"And besides, it is my understanding that the Mexican authorities do not enforce this rule. It is merely

12

an edict handed down by the central government in Mexico City that an American family taking up land in Texas should swear allegiance to the Church."

"I know, darling, I know." She stretched out a greasy hand. "I'm sorry, Sean. I should be horsewhipped for bedeviling you the way I do. Any other man but my gentle Sean would not tolerate my tongue."

He took her hand absently, his thoughts still occupied with the Church. "There is a problem, however, one that has been in my mind all along. If it becomes known that I was once a priest of the Church, now in disgrace, it could go hard for us . . ."

"And that is my doing!"

"Now stop that, Nora!" He squeezed her hand so hard she winced. "We agreed that we would never mention that again. But we must remember never to breathe a word of it. Since I have taken a new surname for us, there is no reason my past should become known."

"Unless someone from Tennessee who knows us should come here."

He nodded gravely. "There is that chance, but it is such a remote possibility that I think we needn't worry." Privately he was not so confident. If they had migrated to Texas, wouldn't others who knew him do so as well? It was a worry that he would have to live with from this day forward.

He essayed a smile. "We have enough to worry about without adding to it. Do you think you would be safe alone here if I were to ride into Nacogdoches in the morning? It's just up ahead. I don't think you should travel for a day or so, but I want to check on our land as soon as possible."

"I will be fine, darling. Leave your pistol, ball and powder. I'm a fair shot, as you know. If any villain should try to molest me, I'll give him a pistol ball in the . . . What is it they call them here? *Cojones?*" She laughed. "If we're going to live among Mexicans, we have to learn the language."

13

Sean smiled palely. "It's my understanding that the Mexican population is sparse here in East Texas, outnumbered by Americans ten to one."

"Well, whatever. You go ahead, Sean. I'll be fine. Who would bother a woman with a new baby?"

From Sean's journal, August 18, 1835:

Conferred with the empresario this day. A busy individual, and could spare little time for me. But he assures me that our land is there for the claiming. It is the custom, I understand, for the empresario to allow a newcomer 30 days to study the countryside, so he therefore may be content with his choice. Then his selected acres are platted, and he is issued title. But this man, thinking that he might not be present upon our arrival, has already performed this chore for me, and assures me that I will be pleased by his selection.

Since he seems a man of some substance, a Christian man, I put my faith in him.

The land is ours! Although we have yet to set foot on it, I am transported. As is my dear Nora.

The empresario did mention that I was favored by fortune in one respect. The Mexican government had, for a time, rescinded its liberal immigration laws, forbidding any new settlers. But recently, as recently as our departure from Tennessee, the Mexicans again began welcoming us to their country. Fortunate indeed we are!

The empresario did pass on some disquieting news, the reason, I gather, for his imminent departure. Texas is in turmoil, and trembles on the verge of open rebellion against Mexico! A convention of Texas delegates has been called for Oct. 8, in San Felipe. What action will be taken there, no one seems to know. It would appear that we Americans are too long accustomed to freedom, and averse to

14

the strictures imposed on us by the tyrant, Santa Anna, known hereabouts by the derisive name of Santy Anny.

What effect this will have on us I cannot foresee, but it strikes an ominous, somber note for our new life.

In Nacogdoches, a village of some 800 hardy souls, yet the largest settlement in Texas, I am informed, I met a fellow Tennessean, a man of whom I have heard much. Mr. Sam Houston! A man of many parts. A renowned soldier, a member of the United States Congress, once the governor of Tennessee. He is also a known womanizer, a man of vile temper, and an immoderate drinker. By his many friends, he is known as the Raven; by his enemies, Big Drunk.

I met him by chance on the outskirts of the village. What a splendid figure he cuts! Riding a great white horse, with a Mexican saddle and bridle, elaborately ornamented. Wearing a Mexican outer garment, called a poncho, also elaborately embroidered. Mr. Houston is the most magnificent specimen of physical manhood I have ever seen!

I was told that Sam Houston now makes his home in Nacogdoches. Has a practice of law there.

With such a man as Sam Houston abiding here, the omens for the future can only be good!

Nora agrees wholeheartedly.

Another momentous event this day.

We selected a name for our firstborn. Brian. Brian Patrick Moraghan.

It has a strong, yet melodious ring to it.

May the Lord God bless you for all your days, Brian Patrick Moraghan!

2

Their 4,248 acres lay almost a full day's walk north-
west of Nacogdoches. Nora had recovered enough now
so that she could walk alongside the cart, week-old
Brian in her arms. This didn't make it any easier, however, for Sean to pull the cart, since he had purchased a
number of tools in town—a single-bit ax, a handsaw,
pick and shovel, a plow, among others—along with a
supply of food staples, and a sack of seed corn.

Considering that he was a newcomer, Sean was
astounded at the ease with which he found credit at the
general store. He had a horror of indebtedness, yet he'd
had little choice, if they were to build a shelter cabin
before winter, and plant a few rows of corn. It was
really much too late for corn planting, but he hoped to
grow enough to help them through the winter. He had
been told that there was ample game in the area, so
they need not fear starvation.

He pulled the cart atop a small rise, and paused,
breathing heavily. He consulted the crudely drawn map

provided by the empresario, and knew that the valley stretching below him, bisected by a small stream, was the Moraghan acreage. Here, the stream bent sharply, forming a triangle in the shape of an arrowhead, with water on two sides.

The empresario had told Sean that when he saw the river triangle he was on his allotment of land. "The river bottom along there, Mr. Moraghan, is as fertile as any land in that region, and the rest of your acreage will grow lush grass up to your ass, come spring. You can raise cattle, hogs, mules, horses, whatever you've a mind to."

Now Sean gave vent to a sigh of satisfaction. "There it is, Nora darling. Our land!"

"It looks grand, Sean. But look there!"

Sean followed the direction of her pointing finger, and went tense as he saw a ribbon of smoke rising straight up.

"Is the smoke from someone camped there, or what?"

The sun had set and dusk was sweeping across the bottomlands. Sean squinted, and he felt a pulsebeat of anger at what he saw in the grove of pecan trees on the riverbank.

"There's a lean-to! It's squatters, Nora, on *our* land! I was warned that this sometimes happens, people coming in and trying to claim squatter's rights to land somebody else has already claimed. Well, by the Lord God, we'll see about that!"

He swung around to yank his musket from the cart. Plucking the pistol from the cart holster, he held it butt first to Nora. "You stay here, while I roust them out. Keep the pistol handy, in the event some ruffian happens along."

She accepted the pistol, then said firmly, "You're not leaving me behind, Sean Moraghan. I'm going right along with you."

17

"It might not be safe. They might balk at leaving and there may be several of them . . ."

"And so? Would I be any better off if they kill you and come after me? Besides, if I'm along with Brian Patrick in my arms, a poor mother exhausted at the end of her long journey to her own land . . ." She assumed a woebegone, long-suffering expression. "It'll melt their hearts, don't you agree?"

Despite his anger at the squatters and his concern for Nora, Sean had to laugh. Nora had a marvelous talent for playacting, and had once considered a stage career, a dream that had shocked her sister and everyone privy to it—an actress was considered no better than a whore. The first time Sean had seen Nora had been at a performance of *Macbeth* at a schoolhouse in Nashville. She had portrayed a Lady Macbeth despicable in the extreme, the most convincing performance of the role Sean had ever witnessed.

With a sigh he said, "All right, come along. You are a willful wench, Nora Moraghan."

"Out, damned spot! Out, I say!" she exclaimed, with a dark and gloomy countenance.

"Nora, stop that!" He was startled anew each and every time she seemed to read his thoughts.

"Yes, M'lord. Your wish is my command." She tried to curtsy, made awkward by the boy in her arms.

Laughing, Sean fitted himself into the harness and started down the gentle slope. With the empresario's bond, he could have purchased a mule, or an ox, on credit in town, but the indebtedness represented by the contents of the cart was burden enough. Since planting season was past, he had no need of a work animal before spring, if then. He managed to tow the cart, so why not a plow?

Their approach to the lean-to attracted no apparent notice. The crude shelter—a wall of logs for a back, a mud-and-grass roof, animal hides stretched across both ends, and the south side open—faced the river.

18

Wary, Sean didn't approach too close. He stopped the cart when he was near enough to see clearly into the lean-to, and extricated himself from the harness. Musket cradled in the crook of his arm, but in position to be brought to bear at an instant's notice, he advanced a few steps, motioning for Nora to remain by the cart.

The fire was in an open pit before the lean-to, and a woman squatted before it on her haunches. Her arms were crossed over her knees, and a wooden ladle dangled from one hand, dragging in the dirt; a kettle was suspended over the flames. Her chin rested on her chest.

There was no other person visible, but in the dimness behind the woman Sean could see mounds that could be sleepers.

Sleepers? At this hour of the day?

Sean took another step forward. "Hallo, the lean-to!"

The woman shot to her feet, squinting at him with eyes the color of muddy creek water. Her brown hair was lank as string, and when she opened her mouth to call out in a cracked voice, Sean saw teeth missing.

"Boys, we'uns got company!"

Behind her the mounds became three men getting to their feet. No, one was a mere lad, of eleven or twelve, Sean judged. The three ranged alongside the woman, and the four made as scroungy-looking a quartet as Sean had ever seen.

The men had long brown hair, unkempt beards, and slack faces with gaping mouths. They wore buckskins as stiff as boards from filth and grease, and a rank odor reached Sean's nostrils on a puff of breeze. The lad made a better appearance, if only for the fact that his face was beardless.

The woman turned her head and spat. She said, "Welcome, pilgrim. I'd ask you to sup with us, but our vittles are slim tonight."

"We didn't stop by to cadge a meal," Sean said stiffly. "I am Sean Maraghan, and this is my wife, Nora . . ."

"Glad to make your acquaintance. Me, I'm Angel Danker," she smiled toothlessly, "called Ma by them knows me. These here are my sons, Lem and Jed. The young'un there is called Sonny. Never did get around to naming him proper."

"My name means nothing to you?"

"Nope, can't say as it does."

"This property you're squatting on belongs to me, allotted to me by the Mexican government."

"Is that right now? We're white folks and don't hold with greaser laws."

"You don't seem to understand! This land is legally mine!"

"Oh, I reckon I understand, but the way I see it, first come, first served." She spat. "And we was here first. All I can say to you, pilgrim, is tough sassafras. I'd say you and your woman had better sashay back to where you came from . . ."

"Mrs. Danker . . ."

"Not Missus. Ma Danker. Never did get around to being married up proper."

"Madam, I have legal title to this land. I have a piece of paper to prove it!"

"Any piece of paper you got, pilgrim, you can wipe your ass with."

"I could go to the authorities!"

"You just do that." Her eyes danced with glee. "Any law hereabout ain't worth doodley-squat!"

Black rage boiled up in Sean, so thick that he almost gagged. "This, then, shall be my law." In a lightning move he had the musket cocked and pointed at them. "Now be gathering up your belongings and go!" As the one called Lem sent a clawlike hand for the pistol at his waistband, Sean aimed the musket dead center. "Faith and you'll be dead before you can draw and fire, bully boy!"

Lem said in a high voice, "Ma?"

Ma Danker's eyes had darkened to the color of mud.

20

"There're four of us, pilgrim. You can get only one of us."

"True," Sean said. "But my wife has a pistol aimed at you," praying that she indeed had, not daring to glance around, "and she's a good shot. That's two dead. Are you willing to pay that high a price?"

"Ma?" Lem said again, voice rising even higher.

"All right, boys. Put together our stuff." Her voice sank to a whisper, the dread sizzle of a canebrake rattler. "We'uns will go, pilgrim. But you'll be sorry for this day. We'll be back. Vengeance is mine, the Good Book says."

Angry as he was, Sean restrained an impulse toward antic laughter. Voice steady, he said, "If the lot of you come around to molest us, it'll be you, or yours, who will be sorry. My promise on that, madam."

Ma Danker spat again, then turned to direct the collection of their belongings. In a short while, they had everything gathered. With a last venomous glare at Sean, Ma Danker led them away. Sean never relaxed his vigilance until the four had disappeared over the rise to the south.

Only then did he relax, but his controlled rage flared up again.

Behind him Nora said, "Whew! That was a touchy situation, darling, but you handled it splendidly . . ."

Sean took several quick steps to the fire pit. With a flat stick he shoveled out burning coals, and sent them spinning into the lean-to with savage swipes of his boots. When nothing happened, he scooped up coals in his bare hands, ignoring the pain, and tossed them onto the roof.

"Hellfire and spit, Sean! What are you doing?"

The dry roof caught almost immediately, flames racing along the edge until the whole structure was aflame.

As suddenly as it came, his anger was gone; yet he felt a deep satisfaction as he stood back and watched the lean-to burn.

21

"You oaf, why did you do that? We could have made use of the shelter!"

"I want nothing used by that family. I will build our own shelter."

"That's fine, but until then? We could have used a shelter in case it storms, until you build one."

Sean knew that she was right, but the knowledge did nothing to abate his satisfaction.

"I've never seen you in such a state of anger, Sean. You seemed like a different person from the gentle man I know."

Again, Sean knew that she was right, and he felt a beginning shame at his display of anger. At the same time, he felt cleansed; the release of his anger had helped ease the frustrations and humiliations he had suffered for so long.

The Danker clan climbed up the gentle rise and entered the trees, with Ma Danker striding grimly along in the lead.

Now Lem said in a whining voice, "Ma, I'm tired. Why can't we bed down here for the night?"

Ma, thoughts clouding her mind like ink, strode on. But it was dark now, and they had nowhere to go. A wrench of self-pity brought a sting of tears to her eyes. All her life, it had seemed that she had nowhere to go; at no place was she and hers welcome for long. The lean-to back there wasn't much; yet it had been theirs, built with their own hands, and no one close by to plague them—until this pilgrim and his woman came along!

She stopped beneath a live oak. "All right, boys. We'll spend the night here."

Jed said eagerly, "Maybe I could slip back in the night and slit that bastard's throat for him?" He fingered the knife sheathed at his belt.

"No, boy. It's too risky. He's going to be watching, and he's armed, whilst all we got is that one pistol of

22

Lem's. We have to see to stealing us some guns somewhere."

"We going to just let that booger get away with running us off our property that way?"

"Naw, Jed. The Good Book says, an eye for an eye, a tooth for a tooth. Our time will come, never fear," she said darkly, "when we will give that Irish cur his due. But we have to mark our time, when it's safe."

"That woman of his'n, that's a right purty piece," Lem said in a thick voice.

"All right, boys, it's time to bed down," she said briskly. "We have to look for us another place, come morning."

They rolled up in their blankets, the older boys some distance away, Sonny close to his mother.

Ma couldn't sleep. The humiliating scene at the lean-to replayed again and again in her mind. She made a vow to the Almighty that the Moraghans would pay dearly for what they had done.

She tossed and turned. Sonny also seemed restless, unable to sleep. "Sonny," she called softly, "come to Ma."

Sonny scuttled across the ground like a crawdad, squirming under her blanket. And Ma hugged him to her in a hungry embrace, one hand reaching for his already stiffening pecker.

3

From Sean's journal, August 24, 1835:

Walked into Nacogdoches this morning to confer with Sam Houston. Although the Dankers have not returned, I feared to risk leaving Nora and Brian alone, and took them with me.

Nora's health has returned, as vigorous as ever. She told me that she enjoyed the walk into town, and the stay overnight.

Sam Houston confirmed what the Danker woman claimed to be true. The law has little force here. There is an *alcalde* to arbitrate disputes, and he sees that posses are formed to track down evildoers: murderers, thieves, and suchlike.

But squatters are commonplace, and a settler is supposed to handle matters on his own initiative. Since I do have a full and legal title, and any squatter is trespassing, Mr. Houston advised that I am free to employ any methods to repel them.

He has knowledge of the Danker clan. They are well-known reprobates, depraved beyond measure, capable of any crime. Mr. Houston, frank-spoken, advises that I would be applauded should I remove them from this earth.

Mr. Houston conversed at length on the coming rebellion, while we shared a jug of prime Tennessee whiskey.

Sam Houston, in his cups, became loquacious, more profane, and even more frank-spoken.

David Burnet, a well-known resident of Nacogdoches, had left for the convention at San Felipe. I had heard rumors that Burnet might eventually become president of Texas. When I mentioned the rumor, Sam Houston gave vent to a mighty belch that I could only interpret as contemptuous.

"Friend Burnet has bustled off full of self-importance, and in all likelihood will stir up nothing but a big wind!"

I said, "You do not hold Mr. Burnet in good esteem?"

"I do not. He is full of himself, has about as much humor as a swamp turtle, going about with a pistol in one hand and a Bible in the other!"

A man of strong opinions, Sam Houston. I said cautiously, "I have heard that he is an honest man."

"Oh, honest he is, I grant you! I also grant that I may be somewhat prejudiced against the man. He damns me for a profaner and a drunkard. Not that he is not right on both counts, the goddamned Wetumpka!"

"Wetumpka?"

Sam Houston grunted. "Cherokee for hog thief."

I was nonplussed, since Sam Houston had just admitted the man's honesty, but before I could beg further enlightenment, Sam Houston changed the subject. "Did you know that the Nacogdoches Committee of Vigilance has just named me commander in chief of the Army of East Texas Territory? What sublime horseshit! What army, I beg you?"

I had no ready answer, but clearly none was required, since Sam Houston continued, "Not that an army is not sorely needed. Some Cherokee friends of mine, recently from Matamoros, tell me that the Mexicans are gathering their armies, and feeling against Texans runs high. They intend to move against us, Mr. Moraghan! Of that I am confident!"

"Sean, are you coming to bed soon?"

He glanced up, with a guilty start. The flames by which he had been scribbling were dying, and he realized that it was quite late. "Coming, Nora."

"Well, I should hope so! You've been scribbling away for an hour or more. Some day I'm going to sneak a look at that diary, or whatever it is, and see what secrets you're putting down."

Sean smiled to himself, as he put away the journal, goose quill, and precious bottle of ink. Despite Nora's repeated threat, he had little fear that she would ever read the journal; she had too much respect for his privacy to do that.

Standing up, he carefully doused the fire with dirt. He stretched, gazing down at the river—a streak of crooked silver in the light of a quarter moon. A cabin was under construction, one log wall finished. Instead of building near the river, where the Dankers had had their lean-to, Sean was building at the base of the gentle north slope of the shallow valley, facing south. He had chosen that site, not only because the Dankers had been down below, but to be as far as possible from the clouds of mosquitoes swarming along the river.

There was one hardship—he had to haul water up

26

from the river. But he had been assured by his neighbors—the nearest a mile away—that underground water was plentiful here, and sweet. As soon as possible, Sean intended to dig a well.

Walking far enough into the dark so the splash would not be audible to Nora, he urinated. He loved this time of the night best. Quiet and still, only the occasional sound of a nocturnal animal, the distant stars brilliant points of light. The Milky Way—he recalled the tales of childhood to the effect that the Milky Way was the stairway to heaven.

Shutting his mind to such speculations, Sean gave his organ the required shake and discovered, to his embarrassment, that it was thick and ropy, semierect.

He returned to the house—he had already begun to call it that—and unrolled his blanket on the ground a few feet from the mound that was Nora. He pulled off his boots, shucked his trousers and shirt, and prepared to stretch out.

Nora's soft voice halted him. "Darling?"

"Yes, Nora?"

"Would you like to come over here with me?"

Her voice, he abruptly realized, which he had thought husky with sleep, was actually thick from that familiar huskiness he had learned to recognize as her signal.

His member, not yet flaccid, grew into its fully erect state. "The boy, Nora . . ."

"He's asleep, goose. Besides, what will he know? He's not a month old, for heaven's sake!"

He took a step, paused. "But Nora, are you sure it's all right? As you said, it's scarce been a month."

"Hellfire and spit, Sean! If anyone would know, it would be me, wouldn't it? What's wrong with you? Knowing how randy you must be . . ." She giggled. "I saw you while you were still asleep the other morning. Stiff as a poker, you were."

All reservations gone, he crossed the distance to her,

27

eager now. He came down on his knees on the blanket beside her. She was naked as Eve, the blanket thrown back.

Her small fingers danced along the length of his organ, and Sean groaned, fearful he would spurt at her touch. He leaned farther down, seeking her mouth. His hands caressed that full figure. Her smooth flesh felt like heated silk. He cupped the wiry mound, and found her open and wet. Without further delay, he positioned himself and penetrated her fully, at one gentle stroke.

Nora cried out softly. "A-ah, my love, my darling! So good, so good!"

They snapped into rhythmic unison with practiced ease, as though it had only been last night since they had enjoyed each other, and not a matter of months.

Nora was the first woman Sean had known carnally. Pledged to the Church early on, he had endured the almost constant horniness of youth like a hair shirt.

The first time he took Nora in love, she had expressed astonishment that, at twenty-nine, he had never known a woman. "My God, it's a living wonder that your thing hasn't shriveled away to nothing from disuse!"

At any rate, his first sexual congress had released such a welling of sexuality in Sean that he knew he could not endure the rest of his life a celibate—never mind that he loved Nora more than life itself. He had recalled with irony the remark Monsignor Riley was fond of using to the young bucks who came to him for advice about their clamoring sexual needs—"Better to marry than to burn!"

"You're thinking again, Sean Moraghan!" Nora struck his shoulder with her fist. "That's not very flattering at a time like this!"

"It's far better than doing the multiplication tables, as I'm given to understand some men do to hold back . . ."

"Don't hold back, damn you! Now, now!" Her body

28

convulsed, hips bucking, and a keening cry burst from her.

Sean loosened all restraint. Gathering her buttocks in his hands, he raised her off the blanket, and drove into her a final time, his coming a blaze of shuddering ecstasy. A shout of joy broke from him.

Finally still, Nora whispered into his ear, "I love you, Sean Moraghan, do you know that?"

"And I love you, sweet . . ."

He froze, as Brian, on a blanket an arm's length away, squalled lustily.

Laughing, Nora said, "I've taken care of one of my men. Now the other demands attention."

Completely unconcerned, she reached out to scoop up Brian and hold him to her breast.

Sean awoke from a deep sleep to the sting of wood-smoke in his nostrils. He sat up in alarm, disoriented for a moment. It was dawn and a freshening breeze was blowing a wisp of smoke from a stump a few yards away. The spot where the house would stand, and a section of bottomland, Sean had denuded of trees for logs for the house.

Without a work animal, he had despaired of ever up-rooting the stumps left behind.

"Burn them, Irish. Start fires at the base and let them burn until the fire eats down to the roots. You may have to start the fires over and over, since the wood is green, but by planting time they should be burned down until you can root 'em out without too much trouble."

This advice had come from Ty Reynolds, his neighbor to the south. Ty was a lean Kentuckian who was full of advice on how to make farm chores easier. Ty, a widower, lived alone in a lean-to. He had spent twenty of his forty-some years farming back in Kentucky, but had no intention of farming his allotment here.

"I've had my fill of farming, Irish. Ass-breaking labor, sunup to sundown, and maybe you'll grow a crop . . . *If* it don't rain too much at the wrong time. *If* a drought don't hit. *If* the insects don't blight you. Nope, this ole boy's had it with the plow. When my ole lady and boy up and died of the pox, I called it quits. But this is damned fine land, grow pretty near anything. I'm gonna squat right where I am, fish and hunt to fill my belly. When things settle down in Tex-*ass,* I'll sell my allotment for a good profit, and move on to somewhere else."

Aside from Ty's dislike of bathing and his fondness for "Kaintuck squeezings," Sean liked the man well enough; certainly he was grateful for his sound advice, and occasional help, when Ty felt energetic enough to lend a hand. And for his company. Sean was content enough with Nora and Brian; yet he longed for male companionship. The curse of the priesthood, where a man lived in the company of other men, in the main, or with nuns, who might as well be men.

Nora detested Ty, and his filthy habits; yet her practical side admitted to the man's utility. This morning, she was already up, frying a slab of fresh pork over the cooking fire—further evidence of Ty's usefulness. Ty had dropped by two days ago with the news that he had spotted a herd of Arkansas razorbacks roaming the bottom next to his place.

"Bag us a couple apiece, Irish, and we'll have fresh meat for a spell, and the rest can be smoke-cured. Keep you in meat until spring. Usually them razorbacks are skinny as broomsticks, poor pickings, but this bunch I saw were pretty plump and sassy." He nodded to Nora. "Render up quite a bit of cooking lard for yourself, Miz Moraghan."

Before dawn the morning before, Sean had taken his

31

musket and gone stalking the river bottom with Ty. Flushing the herd, about a dozen, they had managed to get a razorback each at the first shot, and Sean had time to reload and bring down a second. Despite his skills in many areas, Ty was a far cry from being as good a shot as Sean.

"Well, hell," Ty said with a philosophical shrug, "you're a family man, two more mouths than me to feed. You can make use of the extra. One porker'll do me fine."

It was an onerous chore getting the hogs back to the house, taking most of the morning. On the spot of the kill, they gutted the three hogs, then dragged them back to the house on crude travois—two trailing poles, with stout wild mustang grapevines lashed across them to form a platform. According to Ty, this was the method Indians used to haul things from place to place.

Ty had asked Nora, politely, to have a kettle of water ready. The carcasses were scalded with boiling water, and then cut up. Slabs of ribs were cut for barbecuing. Ty instructed them in how to smoke-cure hams so they could have ham and bacon for some time to come.

"Be better if you had a smokehouse, but you ain't. The backbone is delicious boiled. Careful you don't eat too much at a sitting. Can give you the trots—scuse me, Miz Moraghan. Also too bad we don't have a meat grinder. Could use these guts to make fine link sausage."

The whole day had been taken up by the hunt and the butchering, but the juicy ribs cooked over an open pit for supper the night before had been well worth it. Now, smelling the mouth-watering odor of fresh pork, Sean considered it doubly worth it.

Feeling a little guilty about Nora being up before him—what morning wasn't she up and doing, given good health?—Sean quickly got dressed, stamping his feet into his boots.

With a glance at five-month-old Brian, asleep in the

32

packing crate serving as a crib, Sean strode over to the fire, welcoming the warmth. The long, hot summer was past, extending into a lengthy autumn. Really cold weather had yet to arrive, although it was now into December, but the mornings were quite brisk. His breath plumed the air.

"Good morning to you, Nora. That smells good. Now aren't you repentant for all those nasty remarks about Ty's character?"

She snorted softly. "My estimate of the man's character isn't altered one whit. He's a helpful neighbor, I'll grant, but I would appreciate him more if he'd either bathe or approach me downwind, and without his thumb stuck in that jug handle."

"A man has few pleasures enough out here, Nora," he said stiffly.

"Seems to me he manages well enough . . . Oh!" She darted a contrite glance at him. "I meant nothing in my remark to reflect on you. God knows, I don't begrudge you sharing his jug. I well know the fondness of we Irish for our little nip." A smile tugged at the corners of her mouth. "Could be I'm just jealous because none was offered to me."

He relaxed, laughing. "I could ask Ty the next time he's over."

"Good Heavens, no! He would be scandalized, a female drinking! The man may be a reprobate in many ways, but his views on what a woman should or should not do are almost as rigid as Monsignor Riley's."

"By this time next year we should have harvested a fine crop of corn, so I can brew up our own version of Tennessee whiskey."

"First things first, right?" she said with that twinkling grin, and turned back to her cooking. She picked up another skillet, heated it briefly, greased it, and broke two eggs into it. On their last trip into Nacogdoches, she had bought six hens and a rooster, and they had been enjoying eggs for breakfast since.

Sean stretched, yawning, and looked around his property, with both pride and dismay. The house was nearing completion now. The walls were all up; all that was left was a door and a roof to add.

But the land . . . !

Much of the bottomland, where he wanted to plant the first crop of corn come spring, was now a field of stumps. Sean despaired of ever clearing them away. They resisted all his efforts, as though they had a will of their own. He had tried digging them out, found that each and every one had thick, tough roots, going all the way to China, it seemed.

He had followed Ty's advice, and started fires; yet he had to spend much valuable time relighting them, and the few stumps that had burned to any extent still resisted him stubbornly. Partly consumed by the fire, what was left had taken on an even harder texture. The fact that it had rained frequently of late hadn't helped; every hard rain doused all the fires.

He held up his hands, ruefully studying the undersides. No longer did he need worry about blisters. Months of swinging an ax all day had layered his hands with calluses, like tough leather.

Then he turned to look up the slope and fell to dreaming again. Up there, he would build a fine house someday, for Nora and the boy. Just below the crest of the hill, snug against the north wind, and shaded by two huge, spreading oaks he had left standing. It would be a well-appointed house, he vowed. Maybe after the crops were in next year, he could start on it, at least get the foundation in. Daily Sean was growing more confident of his ability to perform tasks that needed doing. Constructing the crude log cabin had taught him a lot about building. Many mistakes had to be corrected; yet he had learned quickly.

"Dunce head? Have you lost your hearing, as well as your wits?"

34

He started. "Sorry, Nora. I was woolgathering."

"The fine house again, huh?"

"Yes," he admitted sheepishly.

"And a roof not on this one yet, with winter coming. Good thing it's late this year. I was announcing your breakfast, on the chance that you might be interested."

"Not only interested, but famished."

He hastened to the fire, accepted the platter holding pork slices and two eggs, and hunkered down.

Nora removed the Dutch oven from the bed of coals, and dished out fragrant cornbread.

"What I'd give for fresh butter to go with this," he said wistfully. "We must get a milk cow."

At that moment Brian awoke and emitted his usual morning bellow for attention. Nora gestured. "We need a cow for milk for your son, instead of butter for you. I'm not going to let him pull on my titties forever!" She moved away to tend to the boy.

"I'll see about it this week," he called after her. "I have to make a trip into town anyway." He turned his attention to the food, ate hungrily. It seemed he was always hungry these days.

Sean was on the roof, setting shingles in place that afternoon, when he heard a distant shout. Looking up, he saw Ty hurrying toward the house, waving a sheet of paper. Sean had decided that a sod-and-grass roof would not do, and had painstakingly made shingles by hand. Nails being in short supply, they would have to be weighed down with flat stones.

He climbed down, dipping water from the bucket on the post, drank. Nora, alerted by Ty's shout, had come from behind the cabin where she was cultivating a winter-garden patch.

Sean said, "It's just Ty."

"Hellfire and spit! The man was just here!" With a toss of her head, she marched back around the house.

35

Ty was out of breath when he reached Sean. He waved the paper excitedly. "Look what a passing rider just left with me, Irish!"

Sean took the paper. It was a lengthy document, filled with cramped print, and captioned: "Proclamation of Sam Houston, Commander in Chief of the Army of Texas." Sean sucked in his breath sharply. The proclamation was dated December 12, 1835, Headquarters, Washington, Texas, and addressed to: "Citizens of Texas."

Sean read the document quickly, but here and there a phrase leaped out at him: "Your situation is peculiarly calculated to call forth all your manly energies . . . Invited to Texas, you have reclaimed and rendered it a cultivated country . . . You have realized the horrors of anarchy, and the dictation of military rule . . . Your memorials for the redress of grievances have been disregarded; and the agents you have sent to Mexico have been imprisoned for years, without enjoying the rights of trial, agreeably to law . . . The success of the usurper (Santa Anna) determined him in exacting from the people of Texas submission to the central form of government; and to enforce his plan of despotism, he dispatched a military force to invade the colonies, and exact the arms of the inhabitants . . . Citizens of Texas, your rights must be defended. The oppressors must be driven from our soil . . . Our invader has sworn to exterminate us, or sweep us from the soil of Texas . . . We will enjoy our birthright, or *perish in its defense* . . . By the first of March next, we must meet the enemy with an army worthy of our cause, and which will reflect honor upon freemen . . . Let the brave rally to our standard!" The proclamation was signed Sam Houston, Commander in Chief of the Army.

Sean sighed, looked up at Ty. "So it's come then, what Mr. Houston feared and predicted."

"Why so glum, Irish? I look upon it as my chance!" Ty exclaimed. "I'm joining up right away!"

"That's a noble act, Ty. I applaud you . . ."

"Noble, hell! Look, you didn't read it careful. Read that!"

Turning the proclamation around, Ty stabbed a grimy forefinger at a paragraph in the middle, and Sean read: "A regular army has been created, and liberal encouragement has been given by the Republican government. To all who will enlist for two years, or during the war, a bounty of twenty-four dollars and eight hundred acres of land will be given . . . The rights of citizenship are extended to all who will unite with us in defending the republican principles of the Constitution of 1824."

"When this war is over, I'll have me some six thousand acres of prime land! I'll be rich, Irish, rich!" Ty capered, chortling.

In Sean's opinion, Ty's reason for joining the army could hardly be considered patriotic, but Ty was what he was. Besides, what reason did *he* have to be critical? He said, "I suppose people will think me a slacker for not joining up, but I can't . . ."

"Naw, Irish. Nobody'll think none the less of you for it. Hell, you've got a family to look after. Me, I've got nobody. And you're a newcomer. Me, I've been here nigh onto a year. Won't be much of a war, anyways. Them greasers will run like rabbits the minute we stand up and spit back. You watch and see if I ain't right in that."

5

Winter delayed late enough so that Sean had time to
finish the roof, make the cabin as snug as possible,
and construct a fireplace. When the cold weather finally arrived, it was relatively mild. He had learned
that cold weather, generally, wasn't too severe where
they were, and when a cold spell struck, it usually
didn't last more than a few days.

A norther hit in late February, and it was snowing
lightly when he started a fire in the stone-slab hearth
that evening. As the flames leaped up, Sean hunkered
down and warmed his hands at the blaze.

Nora came with the Dutch oven holding a batch of
cornbread. Sean helped her place it on a bed of coals.

"At least we're not wanting for wood to burn." He
grinned. "We're as snug as two bugs."

"You did good, darling. It's a nice cabin." She
kissed him on the cheek. "But it's three bugs, not two."

"You're right, three it is." He crossed the cabin to
pick up the crate holding Brian. "Come along, little

bug. Let's get you all toasty." He carried the crate over and placed it near the fire.

"Honestly, Sean. You're foolish over that boy."

"And why not, woman? He's my firstborn son."

"You keep saying that like you're expecting another soon."

Grinning, he tickled Brian on the belly. "I expect another one eventually, more than one. Can't found the Moraghan dynasty with only one son." He laughed in delight as Brian gurgled, chubby arms and legs waving.

"Dynasty, is it?" Nora sniffed. "I'll have something to say about that."

"Naturally. Can't very well have another son without your help."

"For a man celibate up until a year ago, no expectations of *ever* having a son, you're sure talking like a stud bull," she said in a grumbling voice.

But Sean turned about in time to see her small smile as she moved off. He stepped to the cabin's one window, pushing aside the cowhide stretched across it. It was night now, and the reflected light from the fireplace turned the softly falling snowflakes ruby red.

Tomorrow, he had to start on the next project— digging a cistern at the end of the house to catch rainwater. It was becoming an onerous chore toting water up from the river, and if the river were to freeze solid, they might have to melt snow for water. He would have preferred a well, but he didn't have the proper tools for that.

Tucking the cowhide back into place, he looked around the room. There was not one stick of furniture yet, but that would come in time. There were more urgent needs. The cistern, for one, and a lean-to for the milk cow, Sean thought, as he watched Nora pour heated milk into a bottle for Brian. He had bought a milk cow a month back, and Nora had named the cow Bossie.

"That's not the most original name I've ever heard, sweet. Most people out here name their cows Bossie."

"I see no reason to try for originality. It's no worse than giving your musket a name, like Ty calling his Betsy. Nothing original there. How come a man gives the female gender to his musket, anyway? If a weapon has any gender, it should be male. At least Bossie *is* female!"

Now, squatting again before the fire, Sean's thoughts turned to Ty. He still felt vaguely guilty about not following Ty's example and joining the Army of Texas. News of the war—if it could be called that yet—was scant, but what reports came back were disquieting. There had been a few skirmishes, and the Texans claimed victory on those; yet the rumors were that the Mexican army, under Santa Anna, was moving into Texas in force, far superior in numbers to the Texans.

"Thinking about the war again?" Nora asked, busy frying a slab of ham over the fire.

"Yes," Sean responded with a sigh. "It's hard not to. Our whole future here may be in jeopardy. If the Mexicans are victorious, they may throw us all out of Texas."

"But how can they do that? Our land claims are valid, approved by the Mexican government."

"History has proven that all governments are notoriously fickle," he said dryly. "If they emerge victorious, they can do just about anything they wish. If the Mexican government decides to invalidate our claim, who can say them nay?"

"You mean we would have to leave our land, leave Texas, after all the work you've put in?"

"It's a possibility." He tried to lighten the moment. "You mean you'd be sorry to leave?"

"Of course I would! Here, we have a new life. When we were married, and you took a new name for us, it was as if we were born again. You think

40

I don't have dreams, too, Sean Moraghan?" She straightened up, eyes flashing. "I'd like to see all this fine land growing cotton and corn, same as you, and that grand house all built, our sons happy and proud!"

"*Sons?*" he said teasingly.

Her face, flushed from the heat of the fireplace, reddened even more. "Yes, sons! I want more sons, too. It's about the only thing a woman can leave behind, to show she was at all important in this life, sons and daughters she's proud of. A man can dream of a family dynasty, a great plantation, called Moraghan Oaks, no doubt, or some such. But all a woman can leave behind are sons and daughters!"

Somewhat taken aback by her vehemence, Sean said lamely, "Well, maybe it'll be as Ty says . . . Maybe we'll win, win our independence, and there'll be nothing to be concerned about."

Nora apparently had had her say. She began putting the meat on their plates, dishing up slabs of cornbread—with a dish of fresh, sweet butter this time.

Not long after their supper, Nora bedded Brian down in the packing crate, placing it by the hearth, and retired to the blankets they shared in one corner of the cabin. Sean went outside to urinate, and to fetch in an armload of wood, knowing that he would get up a number of times during the night to feed the fire. He had made the log walls as airtight as possible; even so, there were still cracks through which the wind whistled.

He heaped a couple of logs on the fire and hunkered down, warming himself.

"Darling," said Nora's drowsy voice from across the room, "come to bed. I want you."

So forthright, so desirable, so . . . *his*. Standing up, he voiced a silent prayer to a God he was no longer sure he believed in: Let nothing happen to Nora; I love her so!

"Coming, sweet."

41

He removed his outer clothing beside their pallet. "The longies, too," she murmured. "I want you to make love to me and I hate those bloody things." The bawdy chuckle. "Don't fret, I'll see to it that you don't get cold."

Still shy, Sean turned his back to the fire to hide his growing erection as he divested himself of the long flannel underwear. Then he ducked quickly under the top blanket. Nora's warm body rolled against him, her quick hands finding his hardness unerringly.

"Darling, I am sorry," she murmured against his throat.

"For what, my Nora?"

"For flaying your long-suffering hide with my tongue again . . ."

He laughed softly. "Without that I wouldn't be sure you still loved me."

"On that, you need never have the least doubt. You are my one and only love, unto eternity." She fluttered her lips against his throat. "I do want more sons, more little Seans."

"How about a little Nora or two?"

"Those, too. And now is the time to start. Let's make a baby now."

She found his mouth, her kiss fierce and demanding. Passions blazed, but before Sean could move, Nora rose up and straddled him, taking him inside her with a gasp of delight.

She rode him, a wild, frantic coupling, rode him until Sean's hips bucked, his ecstasy bursting. Almost immediately, a cry of completion was wrung from Nora. She shuddered, shuddered again, then collapsed atop him, her mouth seeking his once more.

In what seemed an instant in time she turned from a wanton female, demanding and giving, into a boneless little girl, asleep curled up on top of him, her warm, sleeping breath stirring his chest hairs.

Sean held her in his arms, just tightly enough to

prevent her from sliding off, not wishing to disturb her slumber. He was thinking of the weeks ahead. It would soon be planting time. By dint of much hard labor, he had finally cleared several acres of stumps, enough for a substantial corn crop. His first crop! It was an exciting thought, and it held his mind until he finally drifted into sleep himself.

One afternoon a week later, Sean was putting the last stone on the round cistern top, using mud-and-grass mortar, when he saw a horse and rider moving fast along the river bottom. He halted work and stepped to the corner of the cabin where he'd leaned his musket. Although he'd never so much as glimpsed one, rumor had it that Indians were marauding in the area.

Almost before the thought was completed, he realized that the rider was white, not Indian. He was still uneasy about the Danker clan—except they didn't possess a horse, and what little he'd heard about the Dankers hinted that they had left East Texas.

The horse, Sean saw, as it drew nearer, had been ridden hard, and Sean couldn't help but hark back to that last visit by Ty Reynolds. The smell of bad news filled the late winter air like the stench of ozone.

The rider, a grizzled oldster, wore buckskins. He reined in the lathered horse, nodded sparingly. "I reckon you'd be the Irisher, Sean Moraghan? Hard to sort out the names of the settlers I was given in Nacogdoches."

"I'm Sean Moraghan, yes. Would you light and have a drink of water, maybe sup with us?"

"I'm Seth Ormsby, and I'll have that water, thankee. Creek water's muddy from all the rain we been having." The rider slid from his horse and Sean saw that he limped badly. "But can't dally for supper, much as I'd like to. I been sent around with a message for everbody hereabout."

He delved into his saddlebags for a sheaf of papers, plucked one from the top, gave it to Sean. While the rider drank from the bucket of water hanging from a peg on the wall, Sean, his sense of foreboding mounting, read the sheet of paper.

It was another proclamation from General Sam Houston, dated March 2, 1836, badly printed and barely legible. It was shorter than the one Ty had brought, its brevity lending to it a sense of urgency if its contents had not.

Captioned *Army Orders,* it read: "War is raging on the frontiers. Béjar is besieged by 2,000 of the enemy, under the command of General Sesma. Reinforcements are on their march to unite with the besieging army. By the last report, our force in Bejar was only 150 men strong. The citizens of Texas must rally to the aid of our army, or it will perish. Let the citizens of the east march to the combat. The enemy must be driven from our soil, or desolation will accompany their march upon us. *Independence is declared,* it must be maintained. Immediate action, united with valor alone, can achieve the great work. The services of all are forthwith required on the field."

After the signature of Sam Houston, Commander in Chief of the Army, a postscript had been added: "It is rumored that the enemy are on their march to Gonzales, and that they entered the colonies. The fate of Béjar is unknown. The country must and shall be defended. The patriots of Texas are *appealed to, in behalf of their bleeding country.*"

Béjar, Sean knew, was the name for the town most Texans called San Antonio.

"General Sam didn't know when he writ that," Seth said, "but the Alamo fell a few days later, March 6, according to word just came before I left Nacogdoches, ever man jack there slaughtered by the greasers, and Santy Anny is right on General Sam's ass.

The word is he's either going to kill all white men or drive us from Texas soil. General Sam needs all the able-bodied men he can get." As though to make a point of his own inability to serve, as opposed to Sean's being sound of limb and body, Seth took two limping steps one way, then the other.

"It's bad then," Sean said.

"Couldn't be worse," Seth said gloomily. "Oh . . . How do, ma'am." He doffed his fur cap.

Sean turned to see Nora coming around the corner of the house, Brian in her arms.

"I heard voices . . ." Her gaze fastened in apprehension on the proclamation in Sean's hands. "It's bad news?"

"The worst." He handed her the proclamation.

"Thankee for the water, Sean Moraghan." Seth clapped his cap on his head and limped to his tired horse. "I have to be on my way. I got me several days of hard riding, to spread the word to ever able-bodied man."

"I'm much obliged to you for including me on your route, Seth."

Seth eyed him measuringly. "General Sam needs all the fighting men he can get. Pears to me you'd make him a good'un." With that, he whipped up his horse, and rode off.

Sean, thoughts churning, stood staring after him.

"Sean?"

He swung around with a start. "Yes, Nora?"

"What we've feared is happening, isn't it?" Her face was pale and set. "Are you going to join up?"

"How can I?" he said in a tortured voice. "Not too long ago I was a man of God, sworn never to do harm to another human!"

"That was then, this is now. Now, we stand to lose everything we've worked for. Even men of God preach that men must fight for what is right, that thine enemies must be smited. Or something in that vein."

"I don't know, Nora. I just don't know."

Without another word he started off with plunging steps. Nora stood silently, her face sad, as he walked away from her. Her words, she realized, probably sounded like encouragement for him to fight, and that hadn't been her intent. Yet she knew Sean—he had to live with himself.

Sean walked down to the river, then turned south, striding through the trees lining the bank. His mind was a tumble of conflicting thoughts, each one terrifying in its portent.

How could he go to war, bear arms against his fellowman? The very thought of killing, or even maiming, someone was abhorrent. He had no fear for himself, although he suspected that others might consider him a coward if he did not go; he would gladly give his life, if by doing so he could help save Texas. And Nora and Brian.

But to kill?

Yet, how could he not go? He had a responsibility to his wife and son. If someone, the Dankers, for instance, threatened them here, he would kill without hesitation, to defend them. Was his going out to meet the threat any different?

Also, he owed allegiance, and military service, to Texas. Texas was his homeland now. If others fought and died to save her, how could he do less? How, if victory was theirs, could he hold his head up when the men of Nacogdoches returned victorious?

Sean fell to his knees, clasped his hands together, gazed up at the darkening sky. Except for the brief prayer at the birth of Brian, this was the first time he had prayed since shucking the priest's robes. Before that fateful day, he had prayed, prayed until his knees were raw, for guidance to resolve the conflict raging within him—a choice between Nora and the Church.

He had received no answer then.

He prayed now: "Almighty God, I pray to Thee for a sign. What shall I do? Shall I take up weapons and go forth into battle? Shall I slay my brothers?"

Thunder did not roll. The clouds did not part, sending a beam of benevolent light down upon him. No voice from on high spoke, voicing wise counsel.

Sean prayed on, as darkness crept around him with the chill of a shroud.

He received no answer to his petition. Finally he got to his feet, muscles and knee joints aching. He turned back toward the cabin, walking with his head down.

It was fully dark when he reached the house, which was bright with candles and leaping firelight, and redolent with cooking odors.

Nora turned from the hearth. One look at his face and she said, "You're going then?"

"I have no choice, don't you see? If I shirked my duty, I could not live with myself, much less my neighbors. And you. And the boy."

Nora had been reasonably sure as to what his decision would be. She had encouraged him, hadn't she? Although her heart gave a wrench at the finality of his words, she carefully kept any dismay from showing on her face. If it meant Sean's life or death, she would willingly have weathered any scorn by the neighbors, and *she* certainly would not think the less of him. But the thinking of men in such matters was strange, so she wisely held her tongue. Instead she said, "You do what you think is right, my darling."

"I don't know if it's *right*," he said angrily. "But it's what I must do."

"Yes, I understand," she said quietly. "When will you go?"

"As soon as possible. The time is very short. I have to arrange a place in town for you and Brian to stay . . ."

"No." She was shaking her head.

47

He stared. "What do you mean, no?"

"We shall remain here."

"You must be addled, woman! I can't be going off and leave you alone here!"

"I'll not move a foot from this place, Sean Moraghan," she said in that stubborn way of hers. "This is our home now. We've worked our tails off to build this cabin. Vandals could move in and destroy it if no one's here."

"Nora, a house can be rebuilt!"

"I am not moving one inch away from here. Hellfire and spit, it's what you're going to war for, isn't it? To protect what's ours? Suppose squatters move in again, like the Danker brood? Besides, it's soon spring. I've a garden to grow, corn to plant, as much as I can by myself. It'll be our first crop, Sean."

"And suppose somebody, like the Dankers, *does* come along? No telling what they might do to a lone, defenseless woman!"

"I may be alone, but I won't be defenseless. Leave your musket behind. Surely Texas can provide muskets for its fighting men. I'm a good shot, you know that. If some intruders like the Dankers come sneaking around, I'll send them packing with a musket ball across the rump!"

She looked so fierce and determined that Sean was torn between laughter and despair.

At the look of concern on his face, Nora came to him, reaching up to cup his face between her hands. "Now you'll have enough on your mind, God knows, without concerning yourself with me and the boy. But I am staying here, in our home, and on our land. Look at it this way, darling . . . This is a raw, rough country. We knew that before we left Tennessee, and knew there were risks. But you can't stand guard over us day and night. Something dire could happen to us while you're off into town, hunting, down by the river, anywhere. We have to trust in God for a few things!"

48

Sean was silent, remembering how hard and long he had prayed down by the river. If he could not receive a response from that, how could he trust in God? He had renounced God, and if there was a Supreme Being, He was clearly angry at Sean Moraghan.

He said slowly, "Your reasoning is logical, as always, but I doubt that will ease my mind while I'm away."

She stood on tiptoe to kiss him tenderly. "Keep in mind that Brian and I are here, waiting for you to return to us. Always hold that thought."

6

From Sean's journal, March 14, 1836:

Bought a new musket in Nacogdoches, pledging my army wages against the purchase price. Caught a ride on a supply wagon bound for Gonzales on the Guadalupe River, where it is said General Sam Houston is bivouacked.

I left Nora and Brian with great trepidation. Despite my dear Nora's assurances, I fear for their safety. But I have learned that when my sweet wife sets her mind to something, there is no moving her. If fortune smiles, I will not be gone overlong.

Our progress across Texas is slow. I have never seen such rain, turning the road into a bog. It almost seems that Almighty God is showing his disapproval of earthlings warring on each other. Could this be the start of another Great Deluge?

Sometimes I despair of myself. How can I entertain such thoughts, when I no longer believe in the Deity?

The rain continues, and the supply wagon slogs along, the oxen straining mightily. This day, we met a family fleeing from Gonzales. The man told us that families are running in terror before Santa Anna's advance. He also told us of the fall of the Alamo. I have to wonder if Ty was one of the defenders.

The man did relate to us a tale of General Houston, a tale both funny and sad. Probably apocryphal. It is my experience that many myths spring up around great men.

In any event, the general was at a convention at Washington-on-the-Brazos when a dispatch was received from Lieutenant Colonel William Travis, the commander of the defenders of the Alamo, to the effect that 150 men were holding the Alamo against an estimated 6,000 attackers, and could not hold out without reinforcements, ammunition, and provisions. The dispatch was received on March 6.

The general rode toward Gonzales at once, to lead his army to the relief of the brave men of the Alamo.

Accompanied by his personal aid, and three other men, the general stopped several miles west, dismounted, and placed his ear to the ground. It was something he had learned from his long sojourn with the Indians. Even though the Alamo was some 150 miles distant, the general stoutly maintained that he could hear firing at the Alamo —*if* it still stood firm.

Shortly, he got to his feet and said sorrowfully that the cannon at the Alamo were stilled!

His words were proven prophetic on arrival at his army headquarters. The Alamo had indeed fallen!

51

As the supply wagon inched on, the skies remained gray, dripping rain, and the mud deepened. They met others fleeing east—whole families, with what worldly goods they could tote, lone men, walking or riding sorry mounts. Most of them were in too much of a hurry to stop and talk.

One man astride a bony mule did stop to pass the time of the day. Sean lingered to hold a conversation, while the wagon moved on. It was from this man that Sean learned that most of the refugees were from the town of Gonzales. "General Sam decided to evacuate the town, putting the torch to it, and retreat to the Colorado. He hopes that the Colorado, which is at flood with all this dad-blamed rain, will halt the Mexican advance, since they're heavily equipped. Hell, General Sam even sank his only two cannon in the Guadalupe River." The man laughed. "They would only have bogged down in all this mud, anyways." He turned serious. "You know what they're calling this? The Runaway Scrape! The way I hear it, there ain't a white family left along the Colorado. They'll keep running, I reckon, right on out of Texas. I know I'm not stopping this side of the Sabine!"

"How far is it to where the general's forces are camped?" Sean asked.

"Two days' ride, if'n you don't get trampled in the stampede, and he's still there. You're about the only ones I've seen headin' west."

"The supplies are sorely needed . . ."

"That's for damned sure!"

"And I'm going to join up."

"Well, good luck, friend. You're going to need it."

As the man drummed his heels against the mule's flanks, Sean said, "Wait! Do you know a man named Ty Reynolds? He joined up some time ago."

The mule rider considered for a moment. "Nope, can't say as I've heard the name. One thing I do know, he wasn't among those died at the Alamo. We know

52

those names by heart, and it ain't likely they'll be forgot anytime soon!"

The man rode on, and Sean hurried to catch up to the supply wagon, cursing the mud sticking to his boots like black glue.

They found Sam Houston and his ragtag army on the afternoon of March 20, at an encampment at Beason's Ford, on the east bank of the Colorado. They encountered a great number of civilians first, strung out along the trail—men, women, and children, all with glum faces pinched with terror. Sean was told that they were all refugees fleeing the Mexican advance and traveling with General Houston's army for what protection it could afford.

The same man who gave this information to Sean told him that a few more volunteers had joined up that very day, bringing the number of Texans up to some 600 men. His informant also said that the pursuing Santa Anna had at least 2,000 Mexicans at his command.

"Where might I find General Houston?" Sean asked.

"Probably under a tree somewhere," the man said dourly. "He's a great one for striking camp under trees, usually the biggest one he can find, and holding his conferences there. Not that I see any need for conferences, since all he's doing is running. That's what he's best at, retreating. We ain't a chance of beating the Mexicans with him in charge of the army."

Stiffening with outrage, Sean growled, "That's loose talk, friend."

"That ain't just my opinion. Most of his soldiers, and a sorry bunch they are, are talking up mutiny, claiming that they joined up to fight, not run." The man looked Sean up and down, nodded wisely. "Since you seem bent on joining up, I suspect you'll find out the truth soon enough."

He turned away without another word. Hands on

hips, Sean glared after him. But under his outrage was dismay. If this man's attitude was indeed shared by a great many of the soldiers, what chance did they have of defeating the enemy?

Shouldering his musket, Sean went in search of Sam Houston. For the moment the rain had let up; yet the skies were still threatening.

The man had been right in one respect—Sean found Sam Houston under a huge cottonwood tree, the largest in sight. He was surrounded by his officers. Sean was further dismayed. The soldiers he had so far seen were ill-clothed, but he had expected Houston and his officers to be better outfitted. Not so. The officers were almost in rags, and what uniforms they wore were pieced together; the little insignia they displayed was bewildering.

Sam Houston was wearing moccasins instead of boots, and he wore no uniform at all, only plain coarse jeans, and a white wool hat. Sean had to wonder how anyone could tell the officers from the men.

Houston was plainly angry, his florid face flushed. He stumped back and forth, waving a letter.

"That's our fine president for you, gentlemen," he said in a low, furious voice. "Damn him for a fool and a coward! Our government, gentlemen, has fled Washington-on-the-Brazos for Harrisburg. And you know what President Burnet says in this dispatch? I am ordered to move our troops in all haste to Harrisburg, to protect the government personnel. Well, be damned to him and his orders!" He flung the dispatch to the muddy ground, ignoring the shocked murmurs from several of his officers.

Houston turned, pointed west across the swollen Colorado. "How can I flee, with General Sesma camped over there, with at least a thousand men, waiting to close with us? Only the river at flood holds the Mexicans at bay!"

Sean's gaze followed the direction of the general's

54

pointing finger. With a feeling of shock he saw tents and the figures of a great many soldiers in bright uniforms moving about.

"But general," a voice ventured, "if the president commands, how can you refuse? He *is* the commander in chief."

"How can I refuse?" Houston demanded. "The fate of Texas hangs in the balance, and *I* am commander in chief of the Army of Texas, not President Burnet!"

A thunder of hoofbeats caused heads to turn. Sean faced around to see three men gallop up on lathered horses. One of the men jumped down and pushed his way through to Sam Houston. The newcomer wore buckskins, with a shot bag and powder horn slung across his chest. He was past middle age, long hair grizzled.

"I have bad tidings, General."

Sam Houston sighed. "What now, goddammit? Spit it out, Mr. Smith."

Sean had heard of Erasmus "Deaf" Smith. Smith was General Houston's chief scout. Defective of hearing since childhood, it was said of him that he more than made up for it by eyesight keener than any man's, and could detect the approach of animals or people well before other scouts could.

Deaf Smith cupped a hand to his right ear. "Heh, General?"

"Goddammit, Mr. Smith, this is no time for games!" the general bellowed. "What tidings do you have? Couldn't be much worse than I've already heard this day!"

"It's about Colonel Fannin, General. As you know, he has been lingering at Goliad . . ."

"*Ma*lingering, is more like it!" As he talked, Sam Houston took a clasp knife from his pocket and a plug of tobacco, shaved off a big chew and put it into his mouth. Now he spat. "If James Fannin had ridden to Travis's aid, as he was supposed to, the Alamo

55

might not have fallen. What's the numbskull done now?"

"Well, he finally made up his mind to leave Goliad. The thing is, he was a little late. Six miles out of town, he was waylaid by two Mexican divisions, commanded by General Urrea. The Mexicans have fourteen hundred men as against Fannin's four hundred."

Sam Houston closed his eyes. "How are our men faring?"

"They are getting their asses whupped, General," Deaf Smith said laconically. "And if you're thinking of haring off to the rescue, forget it. It's all over by this time."

"That stupid, son-of-a-bitching Fannin!" General Houston turned to one of his aides. "You realize what this means, Hockley? There," he indicated his troops with a sweep of his hand, "there is the last hope of Texas. We shall never see Fannin nor his men again. The poor bastards!" He sighed heavily. "Now I don't dare close with Sesma. This is the only force left to defend Texas. If we were to be defeated, the war would be over. And even if we won, there would still be Santa Anna and the main Mexican army. I can see only one choice. We must retreat again!"

"No, General, we must stand firm. This is the place to make our stand." Sean recognized the voice as that of the earlier dissenter. "In my opinion, and I'm sure the opinion of all your officers, retreating from the Colorado would leave the very heart of Texas undefended. The lives of all women and children east of the Colorado would be the price of retreat . . ."

Sam Houston scowled, said icily, "Must I remind you again, sir, that I am in command? Any decision to stand or retreat will be mine alone!"

"But, General, consider what is at stake here . . ."

"I know goddamned well what is at stake! Probably better than any of you!" He waved a hand wearily. "Dismissed! Every blasted one of you!"

Grumbling, his officers reluctantly dispersed.

Sean stood without moving, until he was all alone. The general sat with his head against the cottonwood. From his saddlebag he took a worn, battered book, that Sean saw was a copy of Caesar's commentaries on the Gallic Wars. Also, the general took a vial from his saddlebag, unstoppered, and sniffed at it.

Fearful that he might stand there all day without being noticed, Sean cleared his throat. "General Houston?"

Sam Houston looked up with a frown. "What is it? Didn't I dismiss you, all of you? Or are you as deaf as Erasmus?"

To Sean's astonishment, he saw the general's eyes leaking water. Was he weeping? He took a step forward. "General, don't you remember me?"

The Raven squinted moist eyes at him.

"Sean, Sean Moraghan. From Nacogdoches. I've come to join up with you."

"Of course I remember you. The Irishman." Smiling, the general motioned. "Hunker down here beside me, Mr. Moraghan."

Sean did as instructed. Sam Houston seemed genuinely delighted to see him, seemed, in fact, to be remarkably cheered by his presence. "I'm pleased by your volunteering, it goes without saying. But don't you think you are being a bit rash, young Moraghan?" Houston's smile was utterly without humor. "Surely you've heard the tales? I'm a toper, an errant coward. Even worse . . ." He held up the vial, unstoppered, and sniffed it, eyes watering once more. "A great many say I also take opium . . ."

"I know you're not a coward, sir." Sean was scarlet with embarrassment. "As for the rest . . . A man's personal habits are his own affair."

"That shows a tolerance that would be remarkable, and most welcome, if shared by the men of my command. But in one respect you are in error, Mr. Mor-

57

aghan. The personal habits of a commander in chief, are *not* his personal affair, if such habits affect his military judgment, but the affair of every soldier in his command." Sam Houston was intense, deadly serious now. "However, the rumors current about me have no basis in fact . . . Oh, I am not referring to slurs on my military judgment. History must weigh me for that. I do enjoy my tot, as you well know, sir, but I can be abstemious when necessary, and I have carried no spirits with me since the beginning of this campaign. And in my heart of hearts, I know that I am not a coward. I fear no man! As for the charge of being a user of opium . . ."

He laughed jarringly and motioned with the vial. "I am prey to damnable chills and fever, and this vial contains ammoniacal spirits, and the shavings of deerhorns. My own special nostrum for warding off colds. It has, I fear, become a nervous mannerism, annoying to others, no doubt. But I do *not* partake of opium!"

"I believe you, sir," Sean said stiffly.

"Goddamned few others do," the Raven grumbled and sniffed the vial. Watery eyes squinted up. "Any military experience, Mr. Moraghan?"

"I'm afraid not, sir. But I am willing, and a good shot."

"All the recruits are willing, perhaps too damned willing," the general said ambiguously—or so it struck Sean. "And every Texan claims to be a dead shot." The general's big shoulders heaved in a sigh. "In lack of military experience, you are not alone. I have been too busy retreating to drill my troops, but I shall. I shall, sir, before we close with Santa Anna. Report to my aide, Colonel Hockley, Mr. Moraghan. He will assign you." Without getting up, he saluted sloppily. "Dismissed."

"Sir?"

"Yes, soldier?" The general's voice was edged with frost.

"A neighbor of mine, Ty Reynolds by name, joined your troops before I did. Do you perhaps know of him?"

"In the name of the Almighty, sir, how am I supposed to know one man among hundreds?" Sam Houston slammed his hand against the ground. "I would suggest you inquire elsewhere." He grinned suddenly, a wry grimace. "I must sit here and decide whether to flee farther, join the Army of Texas to the Runaway Scrape, or stand and fight. I might even pray a little. That should provide my detractors with rumors for their mill, since many claim that I have swapped religions so many times that I have no beliefs I can call my own!"

From Sean's journal, March 20, 1836:

This day, I had word of Ty. From one of our officers, I discovered that Ty is with Colonel Fannin. I suppose *was* would be the proper tense, since the fate of Fannin's men is not yet known.

Most I have talked with seem of the opinion that the men with Fannin have suffered the fate of those poor devils at the Alamo. Total annihilation.

Poor Ty! May the Lord God have mercy on his immortal soul!

In the final accounting, it matters little that he chose to serve for selfish reasons, since he will have died in the service of his country.

The words of the wayfarer I met on the trail are all too true, I fear. The men of the Army of Texas are near to the point of rebellion. Most hold Sam Houston in contempt, and a number, I understand, have already deserted.

And such a ragtag of an army! Discipline is non-existent. The only uniforms belong to the officers, and even those are not consistent. The troops are mostly clothed in buckskins, or whatever garments they wore from home. A few have contrived to make what they consider a uniform. Their efforts would be laughable, were not the circumstances so tragic.

I sorely grieve for our cause!

7

When Colonel George Hockley, Sam Houston's aide, learned that Sean was from Nacogdoches, he said, "What are your views about the general, Mr. Moraghan?"

Confused, Sean groped for an answer. "I'm not sure what you mean, sir. I admire him . . ."

"Many of the soldiers are prepared to desert. Some already have. They call him a coward and a fool. Do you share that view?"

"I certainly do not! I believe that the fate of Texas rests in his hands!"

"Well, about that, you may be right," Hockley said dryly. "The question in most minds is . . . What fate shall it be? But be that as it may, I question you about your loyalty to the general because I wish to assign a brave and able man to be near him at all times, to guard his life . . ."

"You think some of his own men might try to assassinate him?" Sean asked, shocked.

"Melodramatic, it may sound, I grant you, but it is a strong possibility. Feelings run high. I thought that you, from the general's own town, might fill the post. But under no circumstances is General Houston to know this. He has refused a bodyguard, and makes himself available to any man, day or night. I intend to see that he has a bodyguard, whether he wishes it or not. On the roster, if we ever have an official one, you will be listed only as a member of the infantry. Is that clearly understood, Mr. Moraghan?"

"Understood, sir."

"You will drill with the others, if that time ever comes, but at night you will spread your blankets by the general's tent, and you will not be required to stand guard duty. On marches, and during battle, you will strive to be always close at his side. The general pays little heed to the rank of those men around him. To give you some authority, I now make you a sergeant, even though you've just been sworn in, and it is the custom to elect our officers." Hockley's smile was ironic. "Since you will be commanding no one but yourself, Sergeant Moraghan, I misdoubt any will question your sudden elevation in rank. Understood?"

"Yes, sir!" Sean saluted, in what he *hoped* was the proper military manner, feeling ridiculous, feeling even more ridiculous when he saw the tiny smile tugging at the corners of Hockley's mouth as he turned away.

It wasn't until then that the enormity of this sudden responsibility crashed in on him. Sean Moraghan, just sworn in, without uniform, without one second's military drill, appointed sergeant, and given the awesome task of defending General Houston against assassins! What kind of a war was this?

"Hellfire and spit, Sean!" He could almost hear Nora's derisive voice. "An army of clowns and dunderheads, with *Sergeant* Moraghan blundering about like the great oaf that he is!"

At the thought of Nora, a great longing for his wife

and son swept over him. He had tried, without too much success, to keep his thoughts away from them, because every time he thought of Nora and six-month-old Brian, he had to wonder if they were safe, again questioning his decision to leave. He knew that he would never forgive himself if anything happened to them during his absence.

Yet his spirits were higher now than at any time since he'd left Nacogdoches. He was needed; he was being entrusted with an important task. It was a good feeling, even knowing that he had been chosen chiefly because he and Sam Houston shared the same hometown.

Thus it was that Sean was nearby the next day to observe Houston pore over his maps, cutting off chew after chew of tobacco with his clasp knife, wearing a path in the earth as he paced and pondered. When anyone approached him, he sent them scampering with a growl.

Sean kept a safe distance, noting that the general looked his way several times, but with a blank expression, as though he did not see him.

Once, when Sean went down to the willows along the riverbank to relieve himself, he learned that word had gone around camp that the general was planning an imminent attack on the Mexican army, and the men were eagerly awaiting the word to charge. Sean was doubtful about this assessment of the general's intention, but he kept his own counsel.

His surmise was proven correct when, in midafternoon, General Houston summoned his officers and gave curt orders—they were to break camp, pack their gear, and be prepared to retreat at sunset. Several of the officers were inclined to dispute the order, but Sam Houston would have none of it.

Drawing himself up to his full, impressive height, those strange eyes almost red in his wrath, he thundered, "Need I remind you, gentlemen, that I am your commanding officer? Question my judgment, if you must. I cannot prevent that in your own minds or among yourselves, but by God I will not brook open disobedience of my orders!"

Grumbling, the officers turned away to carry out the orders.

The men of the Army of Texas were not so easily silenced, Sean soon discovered, as they began to march at sunset. As though to underscore the mood of defeat the retreat heralded, the skies had opened again and a dismal rain began to fall.

General Houston, attired in an old black dress coat, rode his horse along the column of men, Sean trudging along a few yards behind him. As the soldiers recognized their commander, they voiced disrespectful remarks:

"Where you gonna lead us, Boss? All the way to the Redlands?"

"The enemy is behind us, General! How can we fight for our homes and families, less we turn and face him?"

"Yup, if you ain't the balls for a tussle, resign and let us elect a man who has!"

"It's good-bye for me, Boss. I ain't followin' a man afeared to fight the Mexicans!"

Officers rode up and down the column, shouting: "Close ranks! Close up! Close up!"

Still the taunts continued, and Sean, who believed he had a fair measure of the man by now, was astounded when Houston reined in his horse and stood up in the stirrups.

"No, goddammit to hell and gone, I am *not* going to march you to the Redlands and disband!" he said in a voice like a trumpet. "I am *not* going to march you to the Sabine. I am going to march you to the Brazos bottom near Groce's plantation, encamp you there, and drill your asses off, then give you as much fight as you can eat over!"

Hoots of derision and scorn greeted this pronouncement, as Sam Houston rode on, hunched against the pouring rain. To Sean, it meant that the man was human—he had been goaded to the point where he had to lash out.

The motley band of soldiers continued to complain and curse their leader, but they marched, marched in the cold rain, and mud like gumbo, and night black as pitch.

They did not receive orders to halt until midnight, in a thicket of dead saplings, which they cut down with hatchets and used for making fires. Sean also made a fire—with difficulty due to the rain—but he finally had it leaping high. He reflected wryly that he had come a long way since that day in Tennessee when he set out with Nora.

General Houston had dismounted and stood beside his horse, water sluicing off him in a torrent, a lonely, disconsolate figure, since none of his officers would approach him, avoiding him as they would a pariah. Not even his aide, Hockley, was present; Sean understood that Colonel Hockley had ridden on ahead to accept delivery of two cannons sent from the east.

When the fire was burning about as well as it ever would, Sean hastened to the supply wagon for the general's tent. He quickly set it close to the fire.

"General Houston," he called, "why don't you go into your tent out of the damp?"

Sam Houston tromped over, squinted at Sean in open suspicion. "Moraghan, isn't it? Sean Moraghan, from Nacogdoches?"

"Yes, sir." Sean saluted. "Sean Moraghan, it is."

"You're not my orderly, since I don't have one. I can't spare a man for that duty. Hockley told you to keep an eye on me, didn't he? Goddammit, I told him that I don't need a wet nurse!"

Sean said desperately, "General, somebody has to

see to you. It's not fitting for the commander in chief of the Army of Texas to see for himself, or to cook his own supper. Think how it would look, sir!"

The general gave a bark of laughter. "I misdoubt that the men would think much worse of me than they already do, but you are right, Mr. Moraghan. A general has a facade to maintain, in the face of all adversities."

"All I can fix for your supper, sir, is green beef."

"If the men eat green beef, I can do no less."

With a nod Sam Houston ducked into his tent, sitting at the entrance with the flap folded back. Sean saw him take a sniff from the vial.

"Our brave general is taking his ease with opium again." The words, spoken in a sneering voice, brought Sean's head around. Across the fire stood a squat, bull-necked man in greasy buckskins, with the face of a bulldog. He stood with hands on hips, staring at the general.

Sean moved to block the newcomer's view. "I'd suggest you move along."

The man glared at him out of small eyes, as yellow as a cat's in the firelight. "Who says so?"

"Sean Moraghan says so, soldier!"

"Sergeant to you, Irish," the man said arrogantly. "Another papist among us. You'n him," he jerked his thumb at the tent, "should make a fine pair."

He turned on his heel and strode off. Sean called over to the next fire, "Who is that bully boy?"

"Who knows his right name? We call him Bull," a voice replied. "We're all sorry we elected him sergeant. I'd advise you to watch out for him. He likes to ride roughshod over any man he figures he's got an edge on. Know what he does? He writes letters home in red ink, to show he's shed ever drop of blood in him before he'd run from a Mex."

"Thanks for the warning, friend."

Sean busied himself preparing their meager supper. He had learned that supplies were indeed quite scarce.

66

Each day a foraging party scoured the countryside for what cattle they could slaughter. The slaughtered beefs were clumsily butchered, and distributed among the men. Usually the meat was barbecued before a march, and then could be eaten as a cold supper. This time it had not been cooked beforehand—thus the expression "green beef."

Since Sean had arrived with a supply wagon, he'd been able to get a small bag of salt before it was all gone; most of the time the beef had to be eaten unsalted. He made two wooden rods, each a half-inch in diameter and about three feet long, sharpened on one end. Spearing a slab of beef on one, he held it in the flames until it was scorched black. Then he trimmed off the black enamel, handed it into the tent to General Houston.

"Eat the cooked portion around the center, and I'll cook the raw center again . . ."

"Goddammit, sir, I know!" Sam Houston said irritably. "I have lived among the Indians, and I have camped out on the prairie more nights than you have days!"

Tactfully, Sean retreated. Spearing his own meat, he charred it, scraped off the burned outside, and ate hungrily. Before he was done, Houston emerged from the tent, and held his gnawed meat into the flames.

Sean came up from his squat. "I'll do that, sir."

"I'm not helpless." The general waved him back down. "Eat your supper, Mr. Moraghan."

By the time Sean had eaten down to the uncooked portion of the beef, the general was finished. Seemingly reenergized by the brief rest and a few bites of food, he stamped about, fulminating until one of his officers came hurrying up.

Saluting, the officer said, "Yes, General?"

"Prepare to march."

"But General Houston, the men are too tired to . . ."

"We march within the half hour, sir!"

The troops marched thirty miles in relentless rain, finally bivouacking late the second day, near San Felipe, on the Brazos River.

Sean was staggering with exhaustion, and he was relatively fresh. He felt compassion for the veteran soldiers. But at least their exhaustion put a damper on the grumbling. Some made small fires and cooked beef. Others fell to the ground and slept where they lay.

Sean, after erecting the general's tent under the largest tree in sight, spread his blankets on the ground nearby and decided to rest for a bit before eating, but fell at once into a deep sleep.

He was awakened by a boot slamming brutally into his backside. He sat up, blinking. "What the hell . . . !"

"Off your ass, papist. I'm posting you on guard duty tonight." It was the sergeant called Bull.

"I'm not in your company, sergeant, and I . . ."

"Don't matter what company you're in. You're in this army. Now, get off your ass and do what I tell you!"

". . . and I'm exempt from guard duty," Sean finished.

"Exempt, are you?" Bull's face darkened. He bent down, gathered a handful of Sean's shirt, and hauled him to his feet. "I'll show you who's exempt!" He drew his fist back.

Still half asleep and befuddled by the man's inexplicable behavior, Sean did not react quickly enough. The fist smashed into his face with the impact of a musket ball. He careened backward and landed on his rump. Feeling a trickle of wetness on his lip, he explored with his tongue and tasted his own blood.

Bull stood aggressively over him. "Now, soldier, you doing what I ordered you to?"

Rage burst in Sean. "Damnation, no!" he roared. "I'll be taking no orders from the likes of you!"

Before the other man could move, Sean fastened both hands around the nearest booted leg and gave it a savage yank. With a howl Bull flew sideways, sprawling on his back. A cheer went up and Sean was surprised to see several soldiers watching.

He scrambled to his feet, and stood waiting, loose and ready. A savage, almost primeval joy flooded him. He had not fought with his fists since boyhood, and certainly not while preparing for the priesthood, but now he recalled some of those boyhood scrapes—uncomplicated, right against wrong, and how cleansed he had felt afterward, even when he lost, which was seldom.

"You sorry son of a bitch!" The man on the ground glared up at him. "You struck an officer, and you're going to regret that!"

"I had provocation, bully boy, and I have only your word for your rank. I see no insignia on you."

"This pissant army is too poor to provide insignia. But this," Bull shook his fist, "this is all the insignia I need!"

"Then I guess you're going to have to show me," Sean said, knowing he was being childish, knowing that the whole scene was childish, yet enjoying every second of it. He felt immensely alive; his nerve endings thrummed like taut harp strings.

For a moment a look of uncertainty showed in Bull's eyes. Then, with a roar, he was on his feet and charging.

Recognizing that that flash of uncertainty meant victory, Sean tried none of the fancy stuff—he met the charge head on, not giving an inch.

They stood toe-to-toe, slugging. Bull's blows had little steam, and he was already giving ground. Sean used his fists to literally pound the other man into the ground. He knew, dimly, that he would be filled with remorse later, but now he felt no pity, showed no pity. Within the space of a very few minutes, Bull was on the ground, slumped in defeat, his face lumpy and bloody. Sean stood over him, breathing rapidly, waiting for Bull to get to his feet.

The cheer was louder this time; the spectators had doubled in number. A voice from the throng shouted, "Put the boots to the bastard, soldier!"

The noise brought General Houston boiling from his tent. He took in the scene in a sweeping glance. "What the holy hell is going on here?"

Bull scooted along on his rump for a few feet, then got to his feet. "General, this man struck an officer!"

Sam Houston was chewing tobacco. He measured Bull with a look, then turned his head and spat. He said coldly, "What is your rank, sir?"

"Sergeant, General."

"Is Moraghan in your company?"

"I . . ." Bull hesitated before going on, "I haven't completed filling out the company roster yet."

"That doesn't answer my question. Is he in your company, under your command?"

"He refused a direct order, then struck a ranking officer." Bull's voice was a whine now. "I need men to stand guard duty, and he was doing nothing, sound asleep."

"Since you have no insignia, his confusion is understandable. Be that as it may, Moraghan is attached to me, temporarily serving as my orderly. He is not required to take orders from you, sir."

Sean had been listening impatiently. Now he tried to break in, "Sir, I was told that I did not have to stand watch . . ."

With a weary gesture General Houston motioned him quiet. "I would suggest that you find another man to stand watch, sergeant. God knows we have enough men available."

"But, General, he struck an officer!"

The general's voice hardened. "Enough, goddammit! I have enough on my mind without arbitrating a squabble. Now be off with you!"

Sam Houston turned on his heel and went back into

70

his tent. Bull aimed a venomous glare at his retreating back, then transferred his gaze to Sean.

Sean saw that the spectators had melted away at the appearance of the general. Bull strode toward him. His face was so close that Sean could smell his sour breath. He hissed, "You are going to look upon this as a sorry day, you papist! Our fine general is going to be sorry, too!"

"Why don't you go on about your business, bully boy? Or do you wish another lesson in fisticuffs?" Sean cocked his fists.

Bull backed away hurriedly, then turned, sending another glance back over his shoulder. His look was murderous.

Sean returned to his blankets, but he had trouble sleeping. He knew that the man was a bully, and the threats hurled by bullies were usually so much air. But somehow, he was uneasy about this one.

Before he went to sleep, he saw to the priming of his musket and placed it by his hand. His slumber was restless, and he started awake at the slightest sound. It was late, not too long before dawn, when he was awakened yet another time. He sat up. The camp was dark, all lights out, the fires doused. It was a cloudy night, and ground fog from the nearby river swirled along the earth like weary ghosts. Sean squinted about. He could see nothing, and was about to conclude that the sound he had heard had been made by some night animal, when he heard it again.

It had the sound of something moving stealthily across the ground. A twig snapped, and Sean looked in that direction. He saw a shadowy figure, creeping half-bent in the direction of the general's tent.

Sean got to his feet, the musket in one hand. He moved quietly toward the advancing figure. Wisps of fog spun between Sean and the skulker, lending him an air of eerie menace. Strain his eyes as he would, Sean couldn't see enough to recognize the man. Now an even thicker cloud of fog obscured his vision.

When it cleared again, Sean saw that the skulker had dropped to his hands and knees at the rear of the general's tent. He was lifting the tent wall with one hand, and a glint of light reflected from something in his right hand.

A knife!

Sean was still too far away to grapple with the man, and he realized that the skulker could be inside the tent, the knife plunged into General Houston's heart, before Sean could stop him.

Skidding to a halt, Sean raised his musket to his shoulder and bellowed, "Stop! Move an inch and I'll fire!"

The figure froze, then started to turn his face toward Sean, just as another drift of fog moved in, and all Sean could see was a blur. In desperation, he fired.

The man on the ground was already rolling over and over, in the other direction. Then he was on his feet and running into the night.

Sean thought that he detected a noticeable limp in the running man's gait, but he was not that sure. He ran toward the tent, but by the time he had reached it, the skulker was swallowed up by the darkness and the fog.

A light blazed in the general's tent, and voices were raised all around. Running footsteps were converging on the area as General Houston stepped out of his tent.

"What in the holy hell is all the fuss? How can a man get any rest!" Sam Houston, in his stocking feet, charged around the tent, skidded to a stop when he saw Sean. "Are we under attack by the enemy, Mr. Moraghan?"

"A man carrying a knife was about to sneak in under your tent wall, sir."

General Houston turned and motioned to the soldiers clustered around. "You men, back to your pallets! You're going to need your rest. Nothing here for you."

When the men had all reluctantly drifted away, the general glared at Sean from under lowering brows. "This man you saw . . . Was he Mexican?"

"I . . . I'm not sure, General," Sean stammered. "But I don't believe so."

"Who then? One of our own? Are you accusing one of my men of attempting to assassinate me?"

"That would be what I think, yes, sir, but I can't prove it." Privately Sean was positive that the skulker had been the man named Bull, but he hesitated to say so.

General Houston was studying him closely. "I am curious, Mr. Moraghan . . . How did you happen to notice this man? Everyone else was dead to the world. How did you happen to be awake? Did George Hockley ask you to keep *that* close a watch on me?"

Remembering Colonel Hockley's cautioning words, Sean said, "I couldn't sleep sir. It was just by chance that I was awake . . ."

"You are a poor liar Mr. Moraghan, a goddamned poor liar. If you believe that I am going to thank you for saving my life, disabuse yourself of the notion."

The general's voice had risen, until Sean was certain that everyone within a hundred yards could hear every word. He cringed at the thought.

"I was explicit in my instructions to Colonel Hockley. I will not abide being mollycoddled like a suckling babe, so henceforth, sir, I do not wish to observe you hovering around me every second. I require breathing room. Is that understood?"

"Understood, sir," Sean said in a low, choked voice.

"It had by God better be! That is an order, sir! Disobey it to your sorrow!"

73

8

From Sean's journal, March 31, 1836:

Today, we made camp on the west bank of the Brazos River, opposite what I am told is a cotton plantation belonging to a man by the name of Groce.

We reached here after three days of hard marching, in unrelenting rain. At times rain came down in cascades, causing men to stagger and slide off the trail. Our number is now smaller by some 200 men.

When General Houston gave marching orders at dawn on March 28, the men formed ranks reluctantly. Two captains, Captains Baker and Martin, resolutely refused to order their men to retreat farther.

General Houston capitulated, not wishing to lose them entirely (or such is my assumption). He scribbled special orders. Captain Baker and his

74

company of 120 men were left behind to hold a defensive position along the river at San Felipe, protecting the ferry from capture by the enemy. Captain Martin and his 100 men were ordered to go 30 miles downstream and defend the river crossing at Fort Bend.

I was to learn on the march that Captain Baker also was issued verbal orders to put San Felipe to the torch.

I must confess that my faith in General Houston is badly shaken after the cavalier treatment I received at his hands the night Bull had in mind to kill him.

There is no longer any doubt in my mind that the man called Bull was the culprit. The next morning he was gone. Not only did he desert but took the company roster with him, so no one is certain of his true name. As orderly sergeant, the roster was in his keeping, and it appears that he had given different names to different people, resulting in great confusion.

To my mind, Bull's desertion is proof of his guilt, since I am certain my musket ball struck his leg, and he would have been unable to provide an explanation for the wound. Hence, his flight.

I strongly considered confronting General Houston with my conviction, but in the end did not.

Since his manner to me is inexplicable, I have at times, I am sorry to say, been inclined to believe those who claim that his behavior is the irrationality of a man bereft of his senses.

However, I do not shirk the responsibility given me by Colonel Hockley. I still keep a watchful eye on General Houston, if at a distance.

It was at the new campground that Sean finally learned of the fate of Ty Reynolds.

Shortly after dark on the thirty-first, one of the

pickets heard a thrashing in the underbrush, and issued a challenge. A few moments later he led a party of six, all Americans, to the general's tent. One of the men was wounded, being supported by the other five.

Sean drew close as the sentry called excitedly, "General!"

A scowling General Houston emerged from his tent. "What is it, soldier?"

"These men, sir . . . They were with Fannin at Goliad!"

The general registered slack-jawed astonishment. "By damn, that is good news! Or is it?"

One of the six stepped forward, while the others lowered their wounded comrade to the ground.

"The news is not good, sir. We six are among the few of the colonel's command who have survived."

"And Colonel Fannin?"

"Dead, I fear. He was sorely wounded at the battle outside Goliad, and has since been executed."

"Hell and damnation!" The general loosed a string of oaths, then abruptly calmed down. "I would like the whole story, if you please, sir. But first, someone must fetch the surgeon for this poor fellow." He picked a man out of the ranks and sent him for the company surgeon.

Meanwhile, Sean had edged nearer, trying for a closer look at the wounded man; but the other soldiers had crowded around, and now the spokesman for the survivors began to talk in a low, exhausted voice.

"When we were only six miles out of Goliad, we were attacked on an open plain hung with fog. Although outnumbered four to one, we gave a good account of ourselves. The colonel rallied us, forming a fortress of sorts with wagons and equipment. We fought well for two whole days, killing 250 Mexes, while losing only six men, with 40 wounded.

"But we were out of ball and powder and had to surrender on March 20. In return General Urrea, the

76

Mex general, promised that we would be treated with honor and given parole to the States. We were herded back to Goliad and there treated well for eight days, but on March 27, orders came through from Santa Anna, and we were marched out of Goliad, told that we were to be freed on parole and sent to New Orleans.

"The whole thing smelled bad to me, right from the start. There were 700 Mexicans to our 400, and they wouldn't talk, or even look at us. Usually they talk a mile a minute. Also they were all in parade uniforms, and didn't have any baggage."

"We were marched single file, between two lines of guards. Then, about a half-mile from the fort, we were separated into three divisions. The division I was in was marched to the San Antonio River. The Mexicans formed one line facing us. Naturally, we turned to face them, backs to the river, the bank right behind us.

"A Mex officer shouted an order, and one of ours who understood Spanish screamed that we were about to be executed. Almost before the words were out of his mouth, we heard gunfire from the direction where the others had been marched and we knew they were being murdered. But it was too late for us to do anything, as the Mexes fired a ragged volley at us . . ."

"Dear God in heaven!" General Houston exclaimed. "What vile treachery!"

"It was," the speaker said in a tired voice. "It was treachery of the vilest sort, after all the promises made to us."

The general was slicing off a chew of tobacco. Before putting it into his mouth, he said, "But you obviously escaped death, you and your fellows. How did that come about?"

"They're terrible marksmen, is the way I figure it. And it could be that some just didn't have the belly for killing, and missed on purpose. To give the devil his due.

"Anyways, the man next to me was hit. His blood

spurted all over me. See, it's still dried there." He pointed to brown stains on his buckskins. "Men fell all around me at the first volley. Thick clouds of smoke were rollin' around us, toward the river. I made up my mind in a second, gave a loud screech as though mortally hit, and fell backward into the river. At the time I didn't know if anyone else had the same idea."

He was interrupted by the blustery approach of a stumpy man, carrying a cracked black bag and expelling malodorous fumes from a cigar so stubbed it was a miracle it didn't blister his lips. The company surgeon. He kneeled by the man on the ground. Sean still had to get a good look at the wounded man.

The spokesman was continuing his tale. "The current was powerful, which was probably a good thing. It carried me downriver aways before I could make it to the opposite bank. That, and the fact that musket smoke hung over the water like a fog, was what saved me, I'd reckon. I finally made the other bank and ran like mad. My clothes were wet and heavy, and water sloshed in my boots, causing my feet to slide around in them.

"By then the smoke cleared a little, and I saw a couple of other men legging it into the bushes. Looking back across the river, I saw some Mexicans in the water, swimming after us. They'd left their muskets behind and had only their sabers.

"I just up and outran them. I had more to lose than they did, o'course, and I finally lost them. Before the day was over I stumbled across one of these fellers; then the others came along. The last one was that feller there on the ground, shot in the chest while trying to escape.

"So, we made our way east, staying off the main roads and traveling mostly by night." He finished with an infinitely weary gesture. "And here we are, General."

"Yes, here you are," General Houston said glumly. "Damn that Santa Anna's black soul to hell! Do you know if any of the others made good their escape?"

"Some, I hear, but it's only rumors we picked up along the way, from people we came across. They're all in full flight, General, having heard about Goliad . . ."

"I know, soldier." General Houston cut him off with a curt gesture. "Come into my tent, if you will, and make a full report."

As the general and Fannin's man went into the tent, the soldiers grouped around began to drift away, and Sean was able to get closer to the man on the ground.

He gasped when he got a good look at his face. It was Ty Reynolds! The surgeon had just removed a crude bandage from the wound on Ty's chest, and the wound exuded a stench of putrefaction. The surgeon clucked, shook his head, and carried his bag over to the nearest fire.

Sean fell to his knees beside Ty, who had the appearance of death. Sean instinctively fumbled for his rosary, the Latin words of the act of supreme unction already forming on his lips. Recalling where he was, he sat back with a start, glancing quickly over at the surgeon, whose attention was absorbed with an instrument he was holding in the flames.

"Ho, Irish," a voice said weakly.

Sean's start this time was even more violent. So sure had he been that Ty was gone that it seemed a voice from beyond the grave. Looking down, he saw that Ty's eyes were open, and his mouth was warped in a smile that struck Sean as more a stricture of pain.

"Ty! It's glad I am to see you," Sean said, with forced heartiness.

"Looks like I've earned my 600 acres, don't it?"

"You have done very well. You'll be named a hero, fighting with Fannin, fighting so well for Texas freedom."

"Bullshit, Irish. I ain't been fighting for anybody but Ty Reynolds, and I've got the acres that I wanted, and now I'm dying."

"Don't talk nonsense, Ty." He closed his hand around one of Ty's. The skin was hot, and dry and raspy as desert sand.

"I've always been lazy, the easy way out, no better than I should be, but I ain't a fool, Irish." Ty's chuckle had the sound of rattling bones. "Too bad you ain't a priest, you could give me the last rites. I ain't a Catholic, but the way I figure it, it couldn't hurt."

For the third time in as many minutes Sean gave a violent start, and for a perilous instant he was on the verge of admitting his former calling and agreeing to administer the last rites.

"If you'd be so kind as to move your butt out of the way, soldier," a voice said irritably. It was the cigar-smoking surgeon. Elbowing Sean out of the way, he dropped to his knees. The scalpel in his hand glowed red. Without ceremony he began probing in the wound with the heated instrument. Sean's stomach roiled, and he had to look away. Ty screamed shrilly, and fainted.

The stench from the wound was stronger now, and Sean's lips moved, forming curses that he had never dreamed of uttering. He cursed the rain, the war, General Santa Anna—and came close to cursing God.

With a grunt the surgeon stood up. "This one is a goner."

"Dead?" Confused, Sean stared down at Ty. "But he can't be! I just talked to him!"

"Not yet," the surgeon snarled. "But he's as good as. Maybe if he'd gotten to me sooner, but the wound's infected, the poison's flooding his bloodstream. A day, at the most."

The man sounded so calloused that Sean glared at him. "There must be something you can do! You're supposed to heal people!"

"To heal him would take the hand of God, and I'm not God, young fellow." The surgeon snapped his bag shut, muttering, "Men go around shooting one another, then expect me to perform miracles." At Sean's stony look, emotion momentarily livened the weary face, and he said in a raw whisper, "You think I don't feel for the poor son of a bitch? I can't allow myself to feel for every wounded soldier. If I did, I'd end up taking leave of my senses." He gestured, spoke in a normal voice, "Keep him covered, out of the rain, and full of whiskey, and pray that his dying isn't too painful."

Sean stood for a few moments, despairing, shoulders sloping, rain sluicing down his cheeks like cold tears. Then Ty twitched, moaning, and Sean glanced around desperately. He had finally been issued a tent, but so far had been too weary to put it up.

He got busy. He unfolded the wet canvas and erected the tent, praying that the stakes would have a holding grip in the soaked earth. He found a strip of spare canvas, which he spread on the muddy ground inside the tent. He managed to flag down a passing soldier long enough to help him move Ty inside the tent. Ty groaned loudly, but did not arouse.

Sean dug a trench around the perimeter of the tent to divert as much water as possible. He hurried off to find a bottle of whiskey, and had to track down the bantam-sized surgeon before he could get one.

It was long after dark when he returned to the tent, which was overcrowded with two men in it. Sean lit the stub of his last candle, setting it on a piece of tin. As the light rose, Ty moaned, throwing an arm across his eyes. Uncorking the whiskey bottle, Sean knelt beside him. He cupped a hand behind Ty's head and gently raised it, "Drink this, Ty. The surgeon said it would ease the pain."

Ty's eyes opened, and he stared without comprehension, then smiled weakly. "Irish . . . Reckon I went under when that bone-cutter dug around in me with that shovel, huh?"

"Drink this," Sean urged.

He held the bottle to Ty's mouth. Ty drank, some of the liquor dribbling down his stubbly chin. He shuddered, coughed wrackingly, and turned his head aside to spit, the spittle pinkish with blood.

But a touch of color mounted to his face, and his voice was stronger as he said, "Damn my eyes, but that's a skull-busting brew! First good drink I've had in weeks."

"Another, Ty?"

"In a minute." Ty's hand clamped onto Sean's arm with surprising strength. "I'm dying, Irish . . ." As Sean made a sound of protest, "No bullshit, Irish! There's no time for that. The thing is, I've got that land next to yours, and now I'll have more, due me for enlisting. It's all yours; I'll have no use for it where I'm going."

"No!" Sean was horrified. "I wouldn't dream of such a thing!"

"Why not? I ain't a soul in this world, and you're about as close a friend as I've ever come close to having. Who's the land to go to? The nation of Texas, if there ever is one? I have no kin, you know that."

"No, Ty, I wouldn't feel right about it. Besides, I have no need of more land. I have more now than I can manage."

"You're going to take it, want it or not. Hang onto the land and sell it. If we win this scrape, that land could be worth something someday."

Sean started to shake his head, when a movement at the tent opening brought his head around. General Houston was edging inside. Sean's first impulse was to jump to his feet and salute. Ridiculous, since a man couldn't even stand upright, and even the general was on his knees now.

"Is this Fannin's wounded soldier, Mr. Moraghan?" Although the general spoke to Sean, his gaze was on the whiskey bottle, and he licked his lips thirstily.

Ty's hand tightened on Sean's arm. "Who's this gent, Irish?"

"This is General Houston, our commander. Yes, General, this is Ty Reynolds, an old friend."

"Sorry, General. I didn't know, never having clapped eyes on you afore."

"It's all right, soldier." The general waved a hand. "I have just received a full report, and you are to be commended for your valor . . ."

"Shit! Begging the general's pardon. Fat lot of good it does me now."

General Houston stiffened, eyes beginning to burn. Then he relaxed, nodding. "I can understand your feelings, but hopefully history will value your efforts. Now . . . why the raised voices I heard in here?"

"I'm a dead man, General," said Ty, "and I want Irish here to have my land, both what I already own and my enlistment acreage."

"I was thinking it was foolish talk, General."

"Perhaps not so foolish, Mr. Moraghan. A man should always have his affairs in order. And after what this man has been through, he is entitled to whatever wish we can grant him."

"But General . . ."

"General Houston," Ty cut in, "I've heard that you are a man of the law. Is that correct?"

"That is correct, sir."

"Then if you would help Irish draw up a paper, see that it's all legal and proper, I'd thank you kindly. I can't read nor write, nor even sign my name. I'll have to make my mark, and I reckon that should be witnessed proper."

"I am happy to be of service, soldier. Mr. Moraghan?"

With a sigh Sean acquiesced, delving into his pack for his journal, and the quill and ink bottle. He tore an empty page from the journal.

"All right, Ty, if you insist, let's get it done."

Ty began dictating, giving title to all his property to

83

Sean, including the acreage he would eventually receive for serving in the Army of Texas. He broke off with a pale smile. "You know I once told you I had itchy feet, Irish? Well, the enlistment land I want to claim is located in a place called the Rio Grande Valley, down near the Mexican border, or what will be the Mexican border, if Texas wins this fracas."

"For the love of God, sir, why?" General Houston exclaimed. "Why down there? From what I am given to understand, it's not even settled. No Texans, only a few poor Mexicans."

"But it's good land, General, the best. I've been there. Plant a musket ball and harvest a crop of 'em. No cold or snow down there. Someday, it'll be the garden spot of Texas. Mark me! Oh, General . . ." Ty raised his head in an effort to see the general's face. "Will there be any fuss about my getting my 640 acres down there, and it going to Irish after I'm gone?"

"None whatsoever, sir," General Houston said promptly. "I shall see to it personally. You have my word."

Ty sank back, satisfied.

Sean's mind was only partly occupied with the task as he finished transcribing Ty's words. Ty and General Houston were talking as if Ty's demise was an established fact. Sean had to restrain himself from crying out in protest; then he realized that they were being realistic, while he refused to face the truth. What had happened to his training? A priest was supposed to view death as an integral part of life.

The document written, Ty made his mark, and Sam Houston signed his name to it.

Ty dropped back with a raspy sigh, his features drained of color, his eyes closed. With a curt nod to Sean, General Houston left the tent.

In a moment Ty's eyes opened. He whispered,

"Could I maybe have another tot of that skull-buster, Irish?"

Ty Reynolds died two hours later, with Sean crouched beside him, his hand automatically groping for the nonexistent rosary.

9

Nora missed Sean. She would not have thought she could miss anyone so much. Hellfire and spit, he was just a man, wasn't he?

She laughed at herself. There's one thing wrong with that, girl. He's not just a man, he's *my* man! The only man she had ever been able to call her own, and when she was beginning to despair of it ever happening.

But, as her sister Maggie repeated to the point of screaming boredom: "Did it *have* to be a priest? Holy Mother, Nora! Falling in love with a priest is bad enough, all Catholic girls probably do it, at one time or another. But we never *do* anything about it . . ."

"That makes me different. I *am* doing something about it."

"Always you have to be different. Even as a child, you wouldn't play with dolls. You had to put on a pair of Pa's pants and cavort like a boy!"

Maggie was the only blood relation left to Nora on

this earth, and she loved her dearly, but she could be a large pain in the you-know-what.

Maggie was going on. "Not only making moon eyes at the Father, but being the cause of his leaving the Church to marry you! It's a sin against God. Your soul will be beyond redemption."

"My soul will have to take care of itself. I love Sean, as I thought I would never love any man, and I'll do anything short of murder to get him."

"Sacrilege!" Maggie looked horrified. "I've come to expect anything from you, but not this!"

"I should think you'd be happy to see me married off," Nora said mischievously. "I'm twenty-five and soon to be an old maid. How many times have you reminded me of that fact?"

"You'll never be happy, mark my words," her sister said emphatically. Her voice became hushed. "I don't know how you'll ever be able to go to bed with him. I simply couldn't! It'd be like sleeping with God himself."

"It's hardly that," Nora said calmly. "He is a man, and quite a man in that department, take my word for it."

"Oh, my God! You've already been to bed with him, and him not yet left the Church? Oh, the shame of it!" Maggie swayed, her face draining of color.

Nora was already sorry she'd let the cat out. She'd always delighted in shocking Maggie, but this had been uncalled for. Yet she had ached to shout it to the world. Failing that, Maggie had to do. She said, "If you mean, has he made love to me, dear sister, yes, he has."

It was too much for her sister to accept, and the breach between them became a yawning chasm in the time it took Sean to reach his final decision, and Maggie refused to even see Nora to say good-bye when she left Tennessee with him.

Nora often had qualms about that, a brutal break

with her only blood relative; certainly she cared little what Maggie's oafish husband and six whining kids thought of it. But she had known from the moment Sean approached her after the schoolhouse play to congratulate her on her Lady Macbeth that he was what she wanted. There was a sort of magic between them, a magic she could never explain satisfactorily; like a spark that ignited into a blaze that consumed them. She just knew that she would wander lost and desolate the rest of her life if she couldn't have him.

Perhaps if he hadn't felt the same way, she would have meekly retreated; yet, miracle of miracles, she recognized his instant response, and she fought to get him every inch of the way, every weapon at her disposal firing.

Nora hadn't been sure that she had won until that wonderful night when Sean stopped fighting and took her with a roughness that was hurtful, yet was the most tremendous experience of her life, made even more incredible by his admission that she was his first woman.

Nora hadn't been a virgin. After all, she was twenty-five, without Maggie's fear of the Church's condemnation of sex before marriage, and how else could she know what it was like until she had experienced it. She wasn't about to marry some clod first, and be sorry afterward. The two times before Sean had been disappointing—messy, fumbling, dry, painful.

But she opened to Sean's penetration like the petals of a flower moistened by morning dew, and experienced a sunburst of ecstasy at midnight.

After Sean had taken her home, with the promise that he would leave the Church and wed her, Nora stood in the weedy yard before the dilapidated rooming house where she lived, and lifted her face and arms to heaven.

"How about that, God?" she whispered tensely. "I've won! Are you jealous, God? Do you turn green with jealousy when a mere woman takes away one of yours?"

Sacrilege, the worst kind of sacrilege!

Nora had ceased believing in a Supreme Being who presided over the affairs of mortals, like a chess master, at the age of twelve, when her mother and father drowned in a raging river during a furious rainstorm.

No rhyme or reason for it—her parents devout believers. What had they done, what terrible sins had they committed, that their lives should be terminated before their threescore and ten?

Even so, Nora quaked for several days after her whispered taunt, daily expecting divine retribution. And of course she never breathed a word of it to Sean. The darling man would have been even more shocked than Maggie!

Nora never once regretted what she had done. She was happy as an idiot child in her life with Sean, even in this raw, inhospitable country, and was made doubly happy by the birth of Brian.

And now she missed him like hell.

By day, it wasn't so bad. There was enough work to be done, enough to keep several people as busy as a hill of red ants. She had constructed a canvas-covered basket with legs for Brian, so she could stick it into the wet ground out of the mud. It seemed that the rain would never let up. Maybe God was finally taking his vengeance on her—a second biblical deluge to drown one Nora Moraghan.

She laughed at the conceit of it. If there was a God, he must have a bookkeeper—not even a deity could single-handedly juggle all those columns of debits and credits—and Nora Moraghan would hardly be worth a forty-day, forty-night deluge.

The rains brought one blessing, if it could be named that. The earth had finally softened around the roots of the stubborn stumps Sean had been battling for so long, Nora discovered that now their hold on the ground was so tenuous that she had merely to lean on many of them, and they came right out of the earth with a sucking sound almost like a human sigh.

That, at least, should please Sean on his return.

Nora never allowed herself to consider the possibility that Sean would not return; it was unthinkable. Every time she caught herself entertaining such a thought, she immediately busied herself—washing, cooking, planting, anything.

Little Brian was a comfort and consolation to her. He couldn't talk yet, but his mere' presence was enough; and she kept up a running conversation with him when her loneliness grew acute, giving grave attention to his gurgles and cries, as much attention as she would have to an adult discussing important matters.

She arose one morning, three weeks after Sean's departure and looked out the window at a gray, drizzling morning. Her spirits plummeted. Another day when she would be forced to remain indoors. She would have found something to do outside anyway, if alone, but she dared not risk Brian in the wet, and she would not leave him alone in the house.

She dawdled over breakfast chores as long as possible, then cleaned the cabin. Again. She had cleaned it thoroughly yesterday, another rainy day. She paused frequently to go to the window, push aside the cowhide, and peek out, hoping for a glimpse of the sun.

Shortly before noon she was rewarded with the sight of a bright sun and glittering blue sky. Clapping her hands together, she stood for a moment, planning what she could do.

All at once, she heard a horse nicker nearby.

She froze, only her eyes moving, first left, then right; she saw nothing, but then she heard a muffled curse, and her spine turned to a pillar of ice. Her gaze leapt to the door. The wooden bar was in place, but the door was too flimsy to withstand a determined assault. And the window, without glass, was large enough to admit a body.

Nora raced to the fireplace and snatched Sean's musket; she checked the priming, and ran back to the window. She tore aside the cowhide and poked the musket barrel outside.

The act of an idiot, she realized almost before it was completed.

She tried to pull the musket back. Too late. The barrel was seized from the side and wrenched high. Nora had a glimpse of an evilly grinning face. One of the Danker clan. Lem? Jed?

She fired, a reflex action, and the musket ball discharged harmlessly toward the heavens, and the face cackled at her.

"Ma? I got her musket, and she's fired her load. What do we do now?"

"Pull her outside, Lem honey," said that hateful, remembered voice, "and we'll see if the bitch is as hospit-table to visitors as we'uns were to her and that man of her'n."

Lem gave a powerful jerk, pulling Nora partway through the window. She let go of the musket, and tried to duck back inside. His grimy hand shot out again and fastened around her wrist. He hauled her out of the window frame, with Nora catching at everything she could for a handhold. He pulled and pulled, until she thought her arm would be torn out of the shoulder socket. She didn't cry out, fearful of awakening Brian.

Now she was half out of the window, and she could no longer catch at anything. In a last, despairing effort, she spread her legs wide, disregarding the dress hiking up around her waist, and tried to catch at the window frame with her knees. She felt a splinter drive into one. Then both knees were out, and she tried holding on with her toes.

"Whoo-ee, Ma, she's got pretty limbs!" Lem whooped. "And her drawers are peach!"

With a last brutal yank he pulled Nora clear of the window and released her. She fell to the ground with a thud. Dazed, the breath knocked out of her, she dimly heard Ma Danker's voice, "Shameless wench, ain't she?

91

Limbs uncovered like that, and her drawers showing to a boy as young as Sonny."

Almost without volition, Nora's hands groped for her rucked skirt to pull it down over her nakedness.

"Naw, little lady, we won't want you doing that. Besides, it's too late, ain't it?" Lem chuckled coarsely, and pulled her dress back up, then hooked his fingers in the top of her drawers and tore them away.

The puff of cold air on her privates acted like a dousing of ice water. She reverted to savagery—spitting, knees, feet, and hands thrashing, nails clawing for Lem's eyes.

He recoiled, muddy eyes wild with fear. "Huh, Ma! Somebody help, she's gone crazy!"

Back arched and limbs flailing, Nora rocked back and forth on her back like a capsized turtle for a long moment. Desperately trying to regain her feet and scramble away, she took too long, and hands were on her again.

"Pin her feet down, Jed," Ma Danker squalled, her face upside down over Nora's, her hands on Nora's shoulders.

The woman's breath had a vulture's stench.

With weight both on her shoulders and ankles, Nora was finally rendered helpless.

Rancid breath fanning Nora's nostrils, Ma Danker said, "I once saw Injuns stake a white man out on the prairie, spread-eagled on the ground atop an anthill. Leave us strip her down to the skin, then stake her out, spreading her limbs so her honeypot is open, so you boys can dip your wicks." She laughed a witch's cackle. "That'll pay her back!"

"Me first, Ma, I caught her!"

"Never you mind, Lem, who's first. There's aplenty here for both you boys. Let's get her staked down right."

"Ma, can I go, too?"

92

"Naw, Sonny. You're too young. You can watch, though. Might be ed-u-cation-al!" The obscene cackle again. "You, Jed, fetch some stakes, and ropes. Long stakes now, this ground is muddy."

Nora started to struggle again, as the full import of what was in store for her penetrated her consciousness.

"Hustle it up, sugar. She's hard to hold."

Ma Danker cracked Nora alongside the head with knuckles as hard as stones. Nora fell back, dazed, her head ringing. In a moment the ground began to quiver, and she heard a thumping sound.

"Pound 'em in good and deep, sugar. Don't want her gettin' loose while you're at her. A knee in the balls bag can hurt a man somethin' fierce, I'm told."

Next, Nora's thighs were spread far apart, her legs lashed cruelly to stakes. Then two more stakes were pounded into the ground, her arms stretched wide, the wrists tied securely.

She was more conscious now, conscious enough to realize that, except for her thighs, her position resembled Christ on the cross. Was this at God's contrivance? If true, she thought, Sean should be here to observe what a fitting sense of the ironic has his God! At the thought of Sean, full awareness flooded back, and she screamed, straining against the bonds. Pain blazed as she scraped the skin from her wrists.

"That should hold her, but I can't stand her caterwauling," said Ma Danker. "Take her drawers, Lem, and stuff her yap."

Lem's face loomed over her, yellowed teeth bared like fangs, and he clamped a hand on her neck to hold her head still. Nora didn't try to move, waiting until he had lowered his face. Then, as he started to bind her drawers around her mouth, Nora lashed out and up with her head.

The top of her head struck his mouth so hard that

93

dots of light danced before her eyes. But she was elated when she saw Lem's split lip, and bright blood welling like scarlet flower petals opening.

He yowled like a slapped infant, jerked his head back. "Ma, she hurt me!"

"Aw, shit, Lem, sometimes you're as helpless as a kitty cat!"

Hands like pincers seized Nora's jaws, clamping her lips closed and holding her head still, no matter how much she tried to tear it free. "Now, put the drawers around her yap and tie it behind her head."

The cambric material of her drawers had a sour odor, and Nora found herself, idiotically, trying to recall if she'd put on clean ones that morning.

"Now, you Jed, rip her dress off. You, Lem, think you're going to be able to make your pecker stand at attention?"

Hands shredded Nora's dress until she was naked. The air was cold and the muddy ground under her had the chill of mushy ice; yet Nora scarcely felt it. She was so angry at this outrage to her person that her blood boiled, so angry that the whole world seemed to fill up with it.

Dimly, she heard Lem's voice, "I'm gonna give it to her good, Ma, for hurting me like she did."

"Better drop your pants first, sugar."

A weight settled on Nora's body, and Lem's grinning face blotted out the sun. She clenched her eyes shut, as she felt the prod of his engorged organ. Broken fingernails scratched at her inner thighs as Lem frantically tried to ram himself inside her.

Then he was inside and pounding brutally. Dear God, it hurt! The indignity of it had caused wrenching mental anguish, but there was physical pain as well. No man had ever hurt her like this; Sean, in his more demanding moments, had certainly never tortured her this way. The times with Sean, of course,

94

her body secretions had lubricated her, and this time she was dry . . .

Nora rolled her head from side to side, wishing for the first time in her life that she was one of those fainting women. What a relief it would be!

Once, she opened her eyes, and saw Ma Danker, arms folded over her scrawny breasts, face as self-righteous as a newly repentant sinner. Beside her stood the youngest one, eyes staring, mouth open and wet. His hands were jammed into his trouser pockets, and Nora saw with horror that he was masturbating.

She turned her face the other way and what she saw there was even worse. The one called Jed had his trousers open, his organ jutting obscenely.

Nora didn't faint, but something happened inside her mind, as Lem yelled, his spasm beginning. A part of her went away, separating from her abused body. Pastoral scenes of her childhood unreeled across the screen of her mind—the rolling green hills of Tennessee, dotted with brown and white cattle grazing; fluffy clouds scuttling across the sky like frolicking sheep; the Tennessee River flowing gently in summer, water clear as glass—"Get up, Lem, it's my turn in the saddle!"—the insect noon-song of summer heat; horses' hooves pluming dust on country roads; muted cries of children at play, the gentle drumming of rain on rooftops . . .

"Can I have another go, Ma?"

"No, Lem, Miss High-and-Mighty here has been got back at, and you boys have had your fun. To do it again wouldn't be right in the eyes of the Lord. We'll go now, leave her here like that, to think about them snotty ways of hers . . ."

The voice faded, and Nora realized that it was finally over, and she began to return to herself, like a genie being sucked back into a bottle, and she knew then that she had been slightly mad for a time.

95

She opened her eyes, and saw that she was alone. They were gone, probably had been for some time.

With the return of her faculties, physical sensations also returned. Wind gusted across her flesh like feathery icicles, and her vagina felt as if it had been torn beyond repair. She raised her head with a painful effort, and saw the semen stains on her thighs like dried paste, and her stomach heaved. She twisted her head aside at the last moment to avoid the spew of acid vomit from her mouth.

After the spasm had passed, she sank back weakly, wishing her hands were free so she could cleanse her lips of the sour residue . . . .

A rising wail came from the house. Brian! Dear God, she had forgotten him while wallowing in self-pity. But at least the cry meant that he was all right—clamoring for urgent attention and succor, not from any personal injury. As much as she hated Ma Danker in that moment, Nora somehow knew that the woman would never harm a baby.

Brian squalled again, and Nora lifted her head to examine her bonds. She noticed that the rope binding her right wrist to the stake had frayed somewhat in her writhings, and the stake had a sharp edge.

Determinedly she set about sawing the frayed rope along the edge of the stake. She went about it methodically, forcing everything else from her mind. It took a long time, and her arm was without feeling, her wrist raw and bleeding, when the rope finally parted.

The hand free at last, she worked the numb fingers, biting her lips as feeling returned; it felt like a rain of needles had struck her hand.

After a bit, she clumsily worked at the rope around her other wrist, then freed her ankles. She climbed to her feet. A wave of dizziness assaulted her, and she swayed, almost falling. She stumbled forward, fetching up against the side of the cabin, and leaned against it for support, shivering uncontrollably. Exerting a great force of will, she got the shivering under control, then stiff-armed herself away from the wall, and stood un-supported, battling the dizziness as she would an attacker.

A fresh wail from her son broke through her concentration. Nora looked down at her nakedness, then over at the shreds of her clothing scattered across the muddy ground. She turned, pushed the door open, went inside. Brian's red, accusing face elevated above the side of the cradle as he heard her, and the volume of his wail rose several decibels.

"I'll be with you in a minute, honey."

She looked down at herself again, feeling it would be an offense against God and man to tend Brian naked and stained with semen.

She walked stiff-legged over to the wash basin, laved herself in icy water, then scrubbed the skin with a rough towel until it was red as blood. She hesitated a moment in thought, then nodded to herself in decision, and put on a dress. She crossed to the fireplace, stoked the fire, and hung a kettle of water over the flames, ignoring Brian's cries.

Finally she kneeled beside the cradle, freed one breast, took Brian into her lap.

He suckled happily, pulling at her teat until his eyes drifted closed. By that time the kettle of water was boiling. Nora returned the boy to his cradle, and he went to sleep, his thumb in his mouth.

Nora dipped hot water from the kettle into the basin, and vigorously scrubbed her vagina again, stoically ignoring the discomfort.

Finally, exhausted, she lay back on the hearthrug, closing her eyes, at last confronting what had been lurking in her mind.

Dear God, what if she had been made pregnant by one of those louts? The thought made her ill, and she turned her head aside, and vomited once more.

10

From Sean's journal, April 13, 1836:

Yesterday, we marched!

I am still of two minds about General Houston. That he is a man of courage, determination, and rare humor, I cannot doubt.

During the two weeks we remained camped across from the Groce plantation, the general drilled and redrilled the Army of Texas. He succeeded in instilling discipline in us, I do believe, and we are now a more efficient force. Since I have no knowledge of fighting skills or military tactics, I have no accurate way of gauging how effective we now are. But one unfortunate fact remains: the men, in the main, consider General Houston a coward and incompetent and have at least once tried to nominate a new commander, Colonel Sidney Sherman, threatening to follow only his orders. The general acted decisively, posting notices that promised immediate court-martial and speedy execution for any man committing this "act of mutiny." General Houston's firmness of purpose was further illustrated with the appearance in camp of a rather strange individual with a flamboyant name: Mirabeau Buonaparte Lamar.

I am informed that this man is a poet, a former Georgia newspaper publisher. He made his purpose known at once: to rally the soldiers to his command and march into battle with the pursuing Mexican army. General Houston promptly ordered six graves dug and proclaimed that any man following Lamar would be shot at once. On hearing this announcement, Lamar was deemed too prudent to serve under General Houston.

We only marched three miles this day; yet it is a start. When we made camp this evening, in the pasture of a settler by the name of Donoho, I witnessed another instance of the general's dry wit. When the settler, a rather pompous man, hurried over to admonish the general that his soldiers were chopping down his timber for firewood, General Houston wryly reprimanded the culprits: why go to the trouble of cutting down Donoho's timber when the split rails of his pasture fence would burn more readily than green timber?

April 16, 1836: On this day, after three days of hard marching, we arrived at a point one mile from a fork in the road, and an estimated 50 miles from the town of Harrisburg, where our informants tell us General Santa Anna and the Mexican army await us, having already marched on Washington City. Fortunately, the members of the Texas government had ample warning and managed to flee in time to avoid capture.

After camp was set up, General Houston's officers assembled at his tent, and demanded to be told of his intent. Captain Moseley Baker said:

"One way leads to Louisiana and nonconfrontation, and the other to Harrisburg and glorious battle. Which did the General intend to take?"

General Houston ignored him. His officers were angered, and their men threatened rebellion if ordered onto the road to Louisiana. Fires burned all night, and I heard vile curses heaped on the general's head.

The next morning, with General Houston in the lead, we marched to the fork, and at the fork stood a crooked tree. Halfway up, the trunk twisted right: toward Harrisburg and certain battle. Farther up, the trunk twisted left: toward the trail leading to Louisiana, and sanctuary in the United States.

The general sat on his horse under the tree for several minutes, staring up. I could have sworn that I saw his shoulders shake with silent mirth. Then he turned his head aside and expectorated a brown stream of tobacco juice. Back to his army, he raised one arm and pointed south, in the direction of Harrisburg, without speaking a single word. A disbelieving silence reigned for a few moments, then an uncertain, ragged cheer sounded, and we marched toward Harrisburg with buoyed spirits.

[On the margin of this page in his journal, Sean added a later note, an entry made long after the issue was settled. —This tree at the fork in the road became widely known as "The Which-Way Tree."]

Sam Houston drove his army hard. He marched them over 50 miles in two-and-a-half days, reaching Buffalo Bayou shortly before noon on April 18.

Sean, as well as the other soldiers, was exhausted by the forced march, but he, also like the others, was high in spirits. They had a leader now! He tried not to think too much of the coming battle. It wasn't his own death that he feared, but that he would be forced to kill others.

He had never seen the sea, and still did not, since they were some distance from the Gulf of Mexico, but Buffalo Bayou was salt water, and the countryside was low, flat, and marshy, the air permeated by the salt odor that Sean found not at all unpleasant.

They received a sharp disappointment shortly after encamping. Scouts probing across the bayou found Harrisburg in ashes and deserted. Santa Anna had struck and moved on! Were they to be denied engaging the enemy after all?

Sean saw that even General Houston seemed discouraged. He bent over maps spread across his camp table, muttering angrily to himself.

Suddenly the whole camp came alive as the scout, Deaf Smith, rode in with a Mexican captive. Angry cries erupted as Smith herded his prisoner to where General Houston waited, and the scout had to fend off soldiers trying to seize his prisoner.

Cries of "Kill him! Kill the Mex son of a bitch!" rang out, and Sean soon saw the reason. From the scout's hand swung a saddlebag, and the name "William Barrett Travis" was stamped on the leather.

General Houston sliced off a chew of tobacco, put it in his mouth, and patiently waited for the scout and his captive to reach him. "What have we here, Mr. Smith?"

"A Mexican courier, General. I snagged him across the bayou. He was on his way to Santa Anna with some dispatches I'm certain sure you'll find eye-opening."

General Houston took the saddlebag, frowned at the name stamped on it. "Colonel Travis? Not only does this blackguard, Santa Anna, slaughter Texans

101

without mercy, but he carries their possessions around like trophies! Not even the Indians I once lived with are so barbaric!"

His officers gathered around as the general opened the saddlebag, dumped its contents onto his map table, and quickly went through the documents.

Then he looked up, his face alight. "Good news, gentlemen! Good news indeed! The villainous Santa Anna is at New Washington with about 750 men at his command. He plans to trap and slaughter us at Lynch's Ferry, and will be joined there by 500 replacements. Damn me to hell and back, gentlemen!" He slapped his hands down on the table. "We shall meet the enemy on the plains of San Jacinto and victory shall be ours! That I promise you, by God!" He stood tall, his voice soaring. "You have all been spoiling for a fight. Well, goddammit, now we fight! Trust in God and fear not! The victims of the Alamo and the names of those murdered at Goliad cry out for vengeance. Remember the Alamo! Remember Goliad!"

The soldiers, including Sean, shouted back, "Remember the Alamo! Remember Goliad!"

General Houston grinned broadly, spat a stream of tobacco, said to his officers, "Pick a detail of men to build rafts. On the morrow we cross the bayou."

On the nineteenth Sean boarded a raft on which General Sam Houston also rode, and they floated across Buffalo Bayou. Halfway across, the general's gaze settled on Sean, and he scowled, about to speak. He shifted his position, as though to move closer, then his trousers caught on a nail, causing a huge tear. He cursed fluently, then got to his feet, and turned his back, arms crossed over his chest, scowling at the approaching shore.

Sean recalled a painting he'd once seen of General George Washington crossing the Delaware on his way to a great victory. Although the two generals bore

102

little physical resemblance, the parallel was striking.

A good omen?

On the Harrisburg side of the bayou, General Houston ordered the men, as they arrived, to rest hidden in the trees until dusk. Then, astride a great white stallion he had purchased at Groce's plantation and named Saracen, the general led the way out of the woods and across the wooden bridge over Vince's Bayou.

Shortly after dawn on the twentieth they arrived at Lynch's Ferry, which they took control of without difficulty. The general withdrew his army into the protecting wood along the bayou and sent several men on a scouting patrol toward the plain of San Jacinto.

Although not assigned to the patrol, Sean, consumed by curiosity, went along, figuring correctly that an extra man wouldn't be noticed.

The detail was under the command of Erasmus Smith. The buckskin-clad scout motioned the patrol down to the ground at the edge of the wood. Sean flopped down onto his belly at Deaf Smith's elbow. Their position was on a very slight rise, giving them a limited view of a mile of grass as high as a man's knees stretching before them.

Sean said, "Mr. Smith, do you think *. . . ?"

Deaf Smith glanced around. "You're the Irishman, Moraghan?"

Sean nodded.

Deaf Smith cupped a hand around his ear. "Speak up a little, friend Moraghan."

"You think we're really going to fight?"

"Yup. General Santa Anna, he's up there," Deaf Smith indicated the small rise across the plain, "not knowing yet we're here, but he'll find out soon enough. Before the day's over, the general will be sending a patrol back to burn the bridge over Vince's Bayou. When that happens, the only way out of here is to fight our way out. We can't go back the way we come.

We've captured Lynch's Ferry, sure, but you'll notice that the ferryboat is across the river, and likely in Mex hands. Over there," he pointed to his left, "is Peggy Lake, surrounded by marsh. And over there," now pointing right, "is nothing but more marsh and bog. Yup, Irish, we have to fight our way out."

Sean felt a chill.

Then Deaf Smith punched him lightly on the shoulder. "But don't fret. General Houston is a better fighting man than people give him credit for. I've known the Raven for a long time."

"People say that his friends call him the Raven, but his enemies call him Big Drunk."

"Yup, the general likes his jug, but he's smarter, a better general, drunk than most men are sober."

At that moment the scout's words were cheering, but Sean forgot them at the sound of cannon fire from the south. Looking up, he was astounded to see a cannonball whistling over his head toward the wood behind them.

"A six-pounder, I'd reckon. Seems the Mexicans have finally caught on we're here," Deaf Smith said cheerfully. "We'd best get our tails back under cover."

By the time they reached the moss-draped oaks, one of the Twin Sisters, the cannon Colonel Hockley had brought along, had been fired back in answer. Sean stood up in time to see the cannonball knock down several charging Mexican dragoons. A cheer went up from the Texans.

Deaf Smith muttered in Sean's ear, "A lucky shot. And looky there! Old Santy Anny himself!"

Sean followed the scout's pointing finger, and saw a man in full gaudy military regalia, riding back and forth among the Mexican gunners.

Deaf Smith said, "Trying to draw us into charging. It'd be pure-dee slaughter, should we go blundering out there in the open."

The Texans clearly did not share the scout's opinion. They set up a clamor, demanding to be given the order to charge. General Houston, on Saracen, stood up in the stirrups and shouted, "Quiet! Any man charging out there and not killed by enemy fire will face a firing squad, and his officer will answer personally to me!"

The men subsided, grumbling; again muttered charges of "Coward!" were voiced against their commander. Meanwhile, the Mexican artillerymen retired to the woods on the opposite side of the plain, and kept up repeated volleys of musket fire, falling far short of the trees sheltering the Texans.

They bedded down, fully expecting to march into battle at dawn. But Sean, spreading his blankets near the general's, knew differently, since he overheard Houston giving orders not to be disturbed. "I have not had a good night's sleep in weeks. Tonight, by God, I intend to make up for it."

Yet, after his unhappy officers had dispersed, Sean heard the general order Deaf Smith to ride out with a patrol in the morning, at dawn, and burn Vince's Bridge.

Sean awoke once after sunrise, saw that the general was still rolled up in his blankets, and went back to sleep. He awoke a second time when Deaf Smith hurried up to General Houston, who was now sitting on his bedroll, fully clothed, carving off a chew of tobacco.

"General," the scout said urgently, "General Cos came across Vince's Bridge this morning with about 500 men. Reinforcements of Santa Anna's main force."

"Did you fire the bridge, Mr. Smith?"

"Yes, sir, that we did."

"Good. As for Cos and his reinforcements, I've been expecting them. It's better they arrive now, instead of unexpectedly in the middle of battle, probably climbing up our asses. Besides . . ." The general spat tobacco juice. "They've marched long and hard. Likely

105

they're ready for a little siesta, wouldn't you say, Mr. Smith?"

The scout nodded. "Santa Anna has been busy all night, erecting barricades from anything at hand. Saddles, supply sacks, underbrush, things like that."

General Houston laughed. "Looks like he and his men will be all worn out, too, wouldn't you say, Mr. Smith?"

A slow grin split Deaf Smith's face. "I'd say so, yes, General."

"Then I guess we'll just wait a bit."

All morning Sean watched, as the men grew increasingly restless, the officers besieging their commander to order the attack. General Houston wandered about, seemingly at leisure, paying little heed to the complaints.

Shortly after the noon hour, the general gathered his officers around him. "Gentlemen, I seek your able advice. What shall be our tactics? Do we carry the battle to the enemy, against his position, or do we wait here for him to attack us?"

The officers immediately broke into a noisy squabble, apparently about evenly divided as to which action to take. Quietly chewing, Houston listened gravely. After a moment he caught Sean's eye, grinned broadly, winked, strolled away. As far as Sean could tell, not a single one of the officers took note of their leader's leave-taking.

They were still debating, some so hotly defending their position that they seemed near blows, when the general came back. He stood among them, motioning for quiet.

Then, in a loud, firm voice, he announced, "We attack, gentlemen, on the moment! Across the plain of San Jacinto!"

It was 3:30 P.M., April 21, 1836.

The infantry moved out first into the tall grass,

106

maneuvered toward the enemy breastworks a mile distant across the plain. They marched in two rows, the double lines stretching for almost a thousand yards across the front of the sheltering woods. The men in each row were about a yard apart. The Twin Sisters were being brought along with them.

Sean was in the front row. Although the day was far from warm, sweat stung his eyes, coated his hands holding the musket. Except for the swishing of bodies through the tall grass, an almost eerie silence reigned. Sean's senses seemed more acute than he could ever remember: he could hear a crow's caw somewhere back in the trees; the salt smell of the tidal ponds was pungent, burning his nostrils like an astringent; the lowering sun blazed like a ball of fire.

Wiping the sweat from his eyes, he glanced back over his shoulder in time to see the cavalry, led by Mirabeau Lamar, moving out on the right wing to prevent the enemy from retreating to the southwest, their only escape route. Next to the cavalry were the artillerymen, and the company musicians: three fifes and a drum. Twisting his head even farther, Sean saw General Houston, on Saracen, now emerge from the woods. He rode at a canter until he was about thirty yards ahead of the First Regiment.

In a low but clear voice, the general said, "Trail arms! Forward!"

Despite his distaste for the proceedings, Sean felt a shiver go down his spine. His heart thumped fiercely; whether from fear or the pump of adrenalin, he did not know.

They were now more than halfway to the enemy barricades, and there had been no shouts of alarm, no gunfire. It seemed incredible to Sean that their approach had so far gone unnoticed.

They continued to advance. At approximately two hundred yards from the barricades, the general swept off his campaign hat and waved it over his head. The gunners, awaiting the signal, fired their cannon. The musicians played—a rollicking version of "Will You Come to the Bower?"

And suddenly the Texans broke ranks and charged at the barricades, waving muskets and screaming: "Remember the Alamo! Remember Goliad!"

Sean, caught up in the hysteria, pounded ahead with them, screaming the battle cry until his throat burned.

A command rang out: "Halt and fire! Halt and fire, then charge!"

Unheeding, the main body of the soldiers ran on. Abruptly the white horse thundered across their line of charge, and General Houston roared, "Halt, goddamn you! Halt and fire!"

Sean, hearing the general's words and knowing that it would be mass suicide if they stormed over the barricades and found the enemy coolly waiting, dropped to one knee and raised his musket. But he couldn't fire—all that was in his line of sight were the backs of the charging Texans. A few others had heeded the order and were prepared to fire, but frustrated in their attempts. The majority charged on, breaking around the rearing white charger of General Houston like waves around a sea rock.

The general turned his mount about and galloped after his men, now about 40 yards short of the breastworks. All at once the enemy soldiers were firing—a ragged volley, true, but musket balls whistled through the air like hail.

Sean was also up and running again. To his horror he saw Saracen stagger under a barrage of musket balls, and fall headlong. General Houston stepped off just in time. By now the Mexican cavalry had ridden out and were met by Lamar's riders, who shot most of the dragoons out of their saddles. Riderless horses, terrified by the great din, dashed madly about. A soldier reached out to snag one by the trailing reins, and led it to the general, who vaulted astride the animal, and rode once again at the barricades.

It seemed, to Sean, running flat out again, that the general's new mount had taken only a half-dozen strides before it bellowed in pain and collapsed, throwing the general headlong.

Racing up, Sean fell to one knee beside the prone general, ignoring the musket song all around him.

General Houston raised his head, blinking, face tight with pain. "Moraghan? I think a ball shattered my ankle . . ."

"I'll find help and get you back out of range, sir . . ."

"No, goddammit! Get me a horse so I can ride into battle. Texans are dying here. I can do no less!"

"But sir . . ."

"A horse, I said!" General Houston gritted his teeth, then smiled suddenly, seizing Sean's arm. "The men came to hate my guts, didn't they, Mr. Moraghan? That was my intent, you see? To have them angry at me, spoiling for a fight, and not knowing if they'd ever close with the enemy. But now look at them, fighting like demons boiling up from the depths of hell!" His fingers closed cruelly on Sean's arm. "A horse, dammit!"

Sean stood up, looking around. An empty horse was speeding toward him, foam flying from its open mouth like soapsuds. The reins were looped around the saddlehorn. Dropping his musket, Sean launched himself at the careening animal, throwing his arms around the bobbing neck, digging his toes into the dirt. The horse ran on for a few yards, but finally slowed to a stop, trembling. Sean patted the sweat-slick neck, and speaking nonsense words in a soothing voice, led the animal back to General Houston, who had propped himself up on his elbows.

For the first time Sean saw the mass of blood and torn boot leather that was the general's ankle. His belly lurched. As he hesitated, General Houston roared, "Help me into the saddle, you damned Irishman! Disobey at your peril!"

Sighing, Sean stooped, caught the general under his arms, hoisted him almost bodily into the saddle. General Houston seized the reins, whirled the horse about, sent it plunging toward the barricade. Sean snatched up his musket and hastened after him. The horse soared over the flimsy breastworks, Sean scrambling behind.

The scene behind the barricade was utter chaos. And awesome slaughter. Sean was shaken to the core as he observed Texans killing Mexicans everywhere he looked. The Mexicans, clearly caught by surprise, were disorganized and running about wildly. The range was too close now for rifle fire, and most Texas pistols had been discharged, so the attackers were using whatever weapon was at hand—clubbing heads with musket stocks, slashing throats with Bowie knives. In many instances, Sean saw, Texans were ripping muskets from dead Mexicans and turning their own bayonets against them.

It was a rout; what Mexicans could flee, were fleeing, across the plain with Texans in hot pursuit. Yet there were still pockets of resistance here and there, the enemy rallying in clots around a determined officer, and fighting back.

Sean had yet to fire a shot. His initial shock and fear receding, he started toward a group of enemy soldiers still resisting fiercely. Then, out of the corner of his eye, he saw General Houston riding back and forth on his horse, saber flashing. Now a musket ball struck the saber, knocking it from his hand. The general reined his horse in, looking about for a weapon. A Mexican infantryman, observing his unarmed state, kneeled a few yards away, his rifle aiming dead center. The general faced his impending death unflinchingly, but he seemed incapable of spurring his mount into movement.

Without hesitation Sean centered his musket on the kneeling infantryman and fired. The ball struck the man in the chest. A powder puff of dust billowed up, and the Mexican tumbled backward, his musket discharging harmlessly over the general's head.

Sean ran to where the general's saber had fallen, scooped it up, and handed it to him. Grave-faced, General Houston dipped his head in acknowledgment, and rode off, shouting in that thundering voice, "Take prisoners, men! Accept their surrender!"

The Texans, still screaming "Remember the Alamo!" in banshee voices, paid not the slightest heed. As he stood looking around, Sean saw Texans killing the fleeing Mexicans as they would slaughter cattle. Having avoided it as long as possible, he glanced toward the infantryman he had shot. The man was dead without a doubt, his bright jacket even brighter with his lifeblood.

Nausea boiled up in Sean, and he turned aside, turned just in time to see a fleeing Mexican, eyes wild and staring, coming at him with bayonet thrusting, the steel smeared with blood. Sean reacted without thinking, bringing his musket up and around in time to parry the bayonet thrust. Thrown off-balance, the Mexican staggered. Sean brought the musket butt down in a glancing blow alongside his head. He sprawled on the ground, dazed but still conscious.

Sean drew and cocked his pistol, stood over the fallen man. As he hesitated, the enemy soldier, hardly more than a boy, reached out to grasp him around the ankles. Spanish words flowed from him in a flood. Sean couldn't understand a word, but there was no doubt in his mind that the youth was pleading for his life. Sean stepped back, kicking out of the youth's grasp, and returned his pistol to his belt.

111

"Stand aside, friend," growled a voice in his ear. "If you ain't the belly for it, I'll take care of the murdering greaser!"

A buckskin-clad Texan, smoke-blackened features mad with bloodlust, fired his pistol point-blank. The Mexican soldier's face disintegrated before Sean's eyes, and blood and gray matter splattered his boots.

"Lord God Almighty!" Sean gasped, "there was no need for that!" Black rage boiled up in him.

Musket up and swinging, he pivoted, and almost fell. The Texan was already gone, howling after another fleeing enemy soldier. Sean's gaze was drawn to his boots, and at the sight of the obscene splatter, he vomited, falling to his knees and heaving until he was positive that his stomach was turned inside out. Then, in a frenzy, he ripped up handfuls of mud and grass and cleaned his boots.

Only when the last smear was gone did he remember where he was and what he was doing. Still on his hands and knees, he glanced up, cringing away from expected hoots of laughter at his squeamishness.

He need not have bothered.

It was all over, the Mexican soldiers were either dead or in complete rout, and those in flight under grim pursuit by the vengeful Texans.

11

From Sean's journal, April 21, 1836:

This day will undoubtedly be long remembered
in the history books. Santa Anna and his army
have been thoroughly defeated, and Texas has her
independence!

General Houston estimated the length of the
battle of San Jacinto as 18 minutes from the moment the first shot was fired until victory was
ours! An incredible time span, but I must confess
that it seemed far longer to me!

Another incredible statistic: Only two of our
men were killed and 23 wounded, while the Mexican dead number over 600, with an equal number taken prisoner.

Now that the battle is over, the victory ours,
and I am writing this by the fire, I try to assess
my feelings. I killed a man today. True, it was in
a good cause; General Houston credits me with

saving his life. But my heart is heavy and I know not if the passage of time will ease my guilt. At least I took no joy from it, and was not seized by bloodlust, as was the wretch who unnecessarily slaughtered that unfortunate youth.

But enough soul-searching!

The day was not without its unfortunate aspects. General Houston is sorely wounded, his ankle shattered by the musket ball, and General Santa Anna has escaped.

The day following the battle of San Jacinto, Sam Houston, in pain, his shattered ankle swathed in bandages, held forth from his blankets under a moss-laden oak. "If Santa Anna is not captured, goddammit, the war is not over! He can rally troops to him. Find the son of a bitch! From what I know of the Hero of Tampico, he has crawled away from here in high grass, and likely will be dressed as a common soldier. Find him and bring him to me!"

Search parties were sent out to scour the surrounding countryside, while Sam Houston dozed on his blankets, moaning with pain in his sleep.

Sean was not far away from the oak under which the general slept, when a search party rode in, herding a Mexican before them.

As the Texans crowded around, a member of the search party said, "Don't know who the booger is, but he's a Mex officer, that's for sure. We found him wandering around out there. He said he was an infantryman, but that damn sure ain't so." The Texan slid from his horse and took the Mexican by the arm, pushing back his blue jacket. Underneath was a fine linen shirt, and the noon sun winked off the jewel studs on his wrist. "No infantryman can afford duds like that!"

In that moment, a voice rang out from the prisoner compound nearby: *"El Presidente!"*

Colonel George Hockley had walked up beside Sean.

114

Now he exclaimed softly, "General Santa Anna, by God! Come along, my fine general, Sam Houston desires a few words with you."

By the time they had reached the oak, word had spread, and Texans came hurrying up. At General Houston's blanket, Santa Anna broke away from Hockley's grip, leaned down to seize the general's hand, and pumped it. He announced, in stumbling English: "General Santa Anna, Commander of the Army of Mexico!"

Sam Houston raised his head. He blinked, then began to grin. "I'll be goddamned!"

Seeing the general's struggle to sit up, Seán quickly stooped and helped him up against the tree, his saddle behind him, so he could prop himself on his elbows.

The Texas soldiers crowded closer, brandishing pistols, and from some came cries of "Hang the murdering bastard!"

General Santa Anna cowered back in fright. He muttered a few words in Spanish that Sean could not understand. An eighteen-year-old sergeant that Sean knew to be Moses Bryan, the nephew of Stephen Austin, stepped up to interpret Santa Anna's words.

General Houston laughed. "Our brave general is ill, he wishes his medicine chest. Have someone fetch it, George." He raised his voice. "The rest of you men, back off! There will be no hanging today. General Santa Anna is our prisoner of war, and will be treated as such. Sergeant Bryan, remain close at hand to interpret."

The mutters slowly died, but the Texans remained clustered close, their weapons ready. When the man General Hockley had sent came running up with a small medicine chest, Santa Anna seized it eagerly, opened it, and took a bit of white powder. Sean surmised that it was opium, since rumors were prevalent that the Mexican general used the drug liberally.

Emboldened by the opium, Santa Anna drew him-

115

self up arrogantly. "You, sir, are a man of uncommon destiny. Only such a man could have conquered the Napoleon of the West. Consequently, it behooves you to be merciful to the vanquished."

Sam Houston's face flushed, and he thundered, "That, sir, is horseshit, pure and simple! You were not merciful to the gallant men of the Alamo!"

Santa Anna's arrogance drained away. "The necessities of war, General Houston. Your soldiers at the Alamo refused to surrender."

"And the men of Goliad?" General Houston roared. "They had surrendered to the terms offered by your general; yet they were afterward perfidiously massacred. How say you to that, Napoleon of the West?"

Santa Anna began to tremble with fear, unable to speak. His eyes rolled wildly, and he looked about as though searching for an escape route. The Texans, when given the gist of the conversation, closed in threateningly.

Sam Houston slumped back tiredly. "You need not fear for your life, sir, if you do as I ask. A halt to further bloodshed is vastly more important than revenge for your vile deeds. If you wish to save your miserable life, sir, you will order all your forces from Texas forthwith. Is that agreeable?"

General Houston's voice was softer than was his wont; yet there was a tone to it that said, "It had damned well better be agreeable," and it was clear to Sean that he conveyed his message. General Santa Anna quailed, nodded dumb acquiescence.

Sam Houston said briskly. "Excellent! Colonel Hockley, would you fetch paper and pen, so we may prepare the necessary dispatch at once? I shall dictate the wording, if that is agreeable to you, General."

Again Santa Anna nodded without speaking.

Pen and paper were fetched, and General Houston dictated the dispatch in a firm, carrying voice. The message ordered all Mexican troops to depart from

116

Texas at once. The dispatch ended with an unequivocal sentence: "I have agreed with General Houston upon an armistice, which may put an end to the war forever."

When the dispatch was read back to him, Sam Houston said, "Excellent! Now, if you will, pass pen and document to General Santa Anna, so that he may affix his signature."

After the Mexican general had signed, Sam Houston motioned to Deaf Smith, who had been sitting on a log nearby during the proceedings. Sam Houston gave him the dispatch. "Ride with all haste to Fort Bend, Mr. Smith, and deliver this dispatch to the commander of the Mexican forces there."

The scout nodded, and went for his horse. General Houston turned to the downcast Mexican general. "You, sir, will remain with us as a hostage, to ensure that your troops shall not mount an attack on us. You will be treated as an honorable prisoner of war, whether or not you deserve to be so treated, and will be released when I deem it prudent to do so."

The general sank back against his saddle in exhaustion. As Santa Anna was taken away, the Texans also began to drift off. As Sean started to leave, Sam Houston caught his eyes, and motioned for him to stay. The short-tempered surgeon who had tended to Ty Reynolds bustled up in that moment with his bag.

He looked at the general's gray, drawn face, the blood seeping through the bandage on his ankle, and clucked. "I warned you, Sam, that you shouldn't exert yourself, or I wouldn't be responsible."

Without opening his eyes, Sam Houston grunted. "Be responsible? In my opinion, army surgeons have been responsible for more battlefield casualties than the powder and ball of the enemy!"

"I'm not a miracle man," the surgeon said in his grumbling voice.

"In that, sir, you are goddamn right!" Opening his

117

eyes, the general beckoned Sean closer. The surgeon perched on a convenient box and, using a pair of scissors, began to clip away the bloody bandage. Ashes from the stub of his cigar dribbled down onto the general's ankle.

"Careful of that damned cigar!" Sam Houston bellowed. "What kind of a surgeon are you? You should be doctoring horses!"

Unperturbed, the surgeon said, "I'd much prefer treating animals to squalling generals."

"A little respect, if you please. I am your commanding officer."

"I return respect when I receive it." The surgeon took the cigar stub from his mouth and flicked ashes to one side. "These ashes are more sanitary than many things that I can mention."

General Houston switched his attention to Sean. "Again, Mr. Moraghan, you have my gratitude for saving my life."

"It was nothing any soldier under your command wouldn't have done, sir, in my place," Sean said uncomfortably.

"*Now,* perhaps. But not before we went into battle . . ." The general broke off with a groan of pain. Through gritted teeth, he snarled, "That's not a tree limb you're sawing on, sir!"

In a softer voice than usual, the surgeon said, "Would you care for a bit of opium, Sam? It might help ease the pain. I *do* have to keep the wound clean."

"I'll do without the opium, thank you. That is all I need to confirm the rumors."

He turned back to Sean, his effort to ignore the pain obvious. "The battle for Texas is over, Mr. Moraghan. I know you have a wife and child waiting for you, and a crop to get in. You have my permission to return to your family."

Flushed with pleasure, Sean was hesitant. "But shouldn't I wait until the general mustering-out, sir?"

118

"No need for that. I know you have little heart for battle, and I consider you a braver man than most because of that. The others are still spoiling for a fight. I doubt their wish will be granted, but they'll be happy to remain awhile in the hope that . . ."

"You'll not be remaining long, either, Sam," the surgeon said. "I'm shipping you out to New Orleans, or someplace where you can get proper medical care."

"By God, a sawbones who admits he doesn't know what he's doing! I never expected to hear such an admission." Again, he turned to Sean. "You may leave anytime, Sean."

Sean flushed with pleasure again. Sam Houston had called him by his first name! It was a rare accolade, that he well knew.

The general was continuing. "If I recall correctly, you arrived at the Colorado without a horse."

"That's correct, sir. I couldn't afford to purchase one."

"Take one belonging to the Mexican cavalry." He smiled painfully. "The spoils of war. Take it, with my blessing."

"There is one thing, General," Sean said hesitantly. "I dislike mentioning it, but . . . The man named Bull, when he took off, he stole the company roster. I doubt that my name is even on the rolls."

"Bull?" Sam Houston reflected for a moment. "He's the gent tried to crawl into my tent that night, wasn't he? Probably with a knife for my guts."

"I believe that was his intent, yes, sir. I think I wounded him, and that was the reason he deserted."

"I never did properly thank you for that, did I, acting rather churlish, as I recall. At that time, Sean, I was playing the bastard. So, you have my belated gratitude for that as well. And you are wondering, since your name may not be on the roster, if you're going to get the six hundred and forty acres promised you for serving in my army. Is that correct?"

119

Sean shuffled his feet, embarrassed. "I suppose it sounds mercenary of me . . ."

"Not at all, sir! You are entitled to your two certificates. I say two, because I promised your friend, Ty Reynolds, that I would see to it that you received his as well. And you shall. Knowing governments, it will take some time. Since ours is new, it may take longer than usual. But I will see to it personally. And see the paymaster before you leave for your enlistment pay. All who served with me shall receive their proper due. My hand on it, sir!"

Sean accepted the outstretched hand, and choked out, "I thank you, General Houston. I don't enjoy war, and I believed that I'd never enjoy combat." He smiled with an effort. "And I didn't, but it was a pleasure serving under you, sir."

Two hours later, Sean rode a Mexican pony across the plain of San Jacinto, bound for Lynch's Ferry, and the road to Nacogdoches, and Nora and his son.

12

It was close to dusk when Sean galloped the winded Mexican pony over the rise and reined in to look down onto the river bottom. Smoke spiraled up from the cabin, and diffused light filtered through the cowhide stretched across the window. It was as peaceful a scene as he could possibly have imagined.

He heaved a vast sigh of relief. Fears had plagued him during the long, hard ride from the plain of San Jacinto, fears for the safety of Nora and the boy. Now he scolded himself, scoffing at the gloomy Black Irish side of his nature.

Drumming his heels into the sides of the horse, he rode down the rise and across the bottom. Since he'd had no way to send a message ahead to Nora, and not wishing to alarm her, he stopped the horse a few yards away and called, "Nora! Sweet, I'm home!"

There was no sound from within. Sean's heart gave a lurch, and he called again, more urgently.

The door flew wide. Nora stood framed in the

121

lighted doorway for a moment. Then she was running toward him, skirts flying, calling his name over and over. He barely had time to slide from the saddle and catch her in his arms, holding her so tightly she cried out.

"Sean, Sean!" she said in a muffled voice. She fought free of his arms and stood back a step, gazing up, searching his face. Tears glittered in her eyes. "Are you all right? You're not wounded?" Her hands touched him here and there.

He smiled. "I'm fine, sweet."

"But you haven't been gone all that long!"

"The war is over, Nora. Texas has won her independence." His glance skipped toward the cabin. "But are *you* all right? And the boy?"

She looked away, knuckling tears from her eyes. "What could have happened to us? We've just been lonely for you."

"I'm anxious to see my son. Let me put the horse away first."

"You left on foot and came back ahorseback. How did that come about?"

"Like General Houston said, the fortunes of war, Nora." He laughed, full-throated laughter for what seemed the first time in weeks. "That is not all I have profited from the war. Wait until I tell you!"

When he entered the cabin a short time later, Nora was just putting supper on their plates. First, Sean crossed to the box cradle and kneeled to gaze down at his son. Brian was asleep. Sean frowned. "He's still sucking his thumb. Shouldn't he be broken from that?"

Nora laughed. "He's just been weaned from my teats, dunce head. Give the boy time, darling. Come, eat your supper. You must be hungry, unless army food spoiled you for my cooking."

Standing up, he made a face. "Sweet, you wouldn't believe how foul the food was!"

"Then you're a lucky man, Sean Moraghan. I killed

122

two squirrels along the river this morning." She beamed proudly. "I'm becoming a good shot."

"That you are, Nora, that you are."

Sean washed in warm water in the basin. There was something about Nora's behavior that rang false to him. She was overjoyed to see him, there was no doubt in his mind about that; yet some of her joy struck him as forced. Could something have happened in his absence? It couldn't be too serious, if true. Certainly there was no indication of anything amiss. He shrugged, dismissing it. Knowing Nora, he was confident that she would eventually confide in him. It could be just a strangeness brought on by his absence; he felt a certain constraint himself. It was the first time since leaving Tennessee that they had been separated for more than a day at a time.

As they ate, Nora kept up a running chatter. "You'll be happy to know that many of those damned stumps came free from all the rain we've been having. I dragged them out of the way, and planted our seed corn. It should be coming up any day now, and I've got a good garden in. We'll have plenty of fresh vegetables, come spring. And Brian, he's been a good child, you wouldn't believe how good. I take him into the field with me, and he enjoys it, hardly ever complains . . ." She broke off, slanting a guilty look at him. "Here I'm talking up a storm, and you've hardly had a chance to get a word in. I'm dying to know all that happened to you, darling."

"I killed a man, Nora."

"That's what war is about . . ." She broke off, her face going still, and her eyes darkened in compassion. "I am sorry, Sean." She touched his hand. "Tell me about it."

He told her about the battle of San Jacinto, and found the telling easier than he would have thought.

"You saved General Houston's life, Sean. You can be proud of that. I know how you must have felt, kill-

123

ing another human being, but there are times when it seems necessary . . ." A shadow darkened her eyes, then was swiftly gone.

Now that he had begun, Sean found that he could talk freely about his brief war experiences. He told Nora all of it, ranging back and forth—Bull, the fight, and the attempt on the general's life, the death of Ty Reynolds, and the additional acreage that was now theirs.

"Hellfire and spit, Sean!" she exclaimed. "What will we do with so much land?"

"Keep it. I have been thinking about it. Ty's acreage south of here, I'll work, of course. But the other two allotments coming to me will be located in other parts of Texas. Sam Houston told me that I could choose acreage in any area of Texas not already claimed. One spot will be where Ty told me he had already picked out, a place called the Rio Grande Valley. The other acreage, I will decide later. In time the land will be valuable, a heritage for Brian perhaps, and any other children we may have."

Under his intense gaze Nora's eyes slipped away. By this time the fire in the hearth had died down to a glow. Sean stood, drawing her up with him. He said huskily, "It's time for bed, sweet."

Face still averted, she went along with him to their pallet in the corner. Sean said, "One of the first things I intend to do is make us a proper bed. We've slept on the ground long enough."

He turned aside for a last, lingering look at his son. Brian was sleeping quietly, cherubic face forming a smile. By the time Sean reached the pallet, Nora was already under the blanket. He quickly undressed, his erection springing free as he shed his long underwear.

Under the blanket he took Nora into his arms, whispered in her ear, "I've missed you, sweet." He laughed. "You can see how much."

124

He guided her hand to his organ. Nora sucked in her breath, seemed to draw back for just a moment, then she relaxed with a sigh. "It would seem that becoming a war hero makes you more bold, Sean Moraghan! Before, you wouldn't even undress where I could see you!"

"During the battle I thought of being killed, and never being able to hold you like this, ever again. Thoughts like that tend to change a man."

Nora shivered suddenly. Sean thought it was due to a rise of passion, or perhaps the prospect of his being dead.

He pressed his mouth to hers and her response was warm and loving. His hands explored the familiar contours of her body. Cupping her breast with his hand, he rasped his tongue across it. Nora moaned, twitching. The long separation from her fired his passion.

"Sorry, sweet, I can't wait."

He spread her thighs and prepared to mount her. Unexpectedly Nora cried out, clamped her thighs together, and rolled away from him.

Dumbfounded, Sean remained as he was for a long moment, feeling ridiculous, propped in the air on his hands and knees. He said tentatively, "Nora? What on earth . . . ?" He calculated swiftly. "It's not the wrong time of the month, unless I've lost all track of time."

"No, it's not that," she said in a muffled voice.

His manhood softened, retreated into itself. Anger stirring now, he said, "Then what is it?"

He turned, sat down, reached over to put a hand on her thigh. Nora rolled toward him, clinging fiercely, her face buried in the curve of his hip. He felt the warm wetness of her tears.

"Sean, I swore to myself that I wouldn't tell you. But I have to! I *must!*"

"Tell me what? Great God Almighty, woman! What *is* this all about?"

She sat up, snatching a blanket to pull around her,

and hurried over to the dying fire. In a frenzy she threw logs onto the hearth and poked at the fire until it was blazing high.

Slipping on his trousers, Sean approached her, at a loss to understand. A sudden thought blazed through his mind. A man! Had Nora been with another man while he was gone? Not Nora, it wasn't possible! Still . . .

He said tightly, "Did you bed down with another man, while I was away?"

"A man?" She flashed an incredulous look at him. "How could you think . . . ?" She broke off with a laugh that was like no other laugh he had ever heard. "Yet, in a way, you're right."

Sean, more baffled than ever, sat down beside her, but not close enough to touch her.

Nora, staring into the fire, arms around her legs, never once looking at him, told him then of the Dankers and the outrage they had inflicted on her.

Listening, Sean felt a coldness spreading through him, like death. It wasn't rage, not even outrage; it was far more than that. How could a man feel rage at an unfeeling universe, at a God who would allow such a thing to happen?

When the last words had fallen from Nora's mouth, they sat without speaking, without moving, for a long while. Sean felt dead inside; only his mind was alive, filled with a purpose that swelled until it seemed his head would burst with it. He knew what he was going to do, what he *had* to do, but he said nothing to Nora.

Nora spoke first, in a small voice, "Sean?"

"Yes?"

She sighed, as though she had feared he had lost the power of speech. "Perhaps I shouldn't have told you. I may regret it, regret it for the rest of my life. But if I hadn't told you, it would have been between us, even if you didn't know, and I knew that the longer I waited to tell you, the harder it would become."

126

Sean nodded mutely, unsure in his own mind if his nod indicated agreement or not.

She ran her fingers into her hair, face contorted. "Say something, for the love of God! Tell me to leave, tell me anything! It's not as if I'm asking for forgiveness!"

He wanted to tell her that there was nothing to forgive; she had committed no sin. He should be the one begging forgiveness. He couldn't speak; his lips seemed frozen.

All at once her eyes swam with tears. Turning her head aside, she got to her feet with the painful slowness of an old woman. "I'm wrung out, Sean. I'm going to bed. You coming?"

Again, he shook his head, in the negative this time.

He sat on before the hearth, not bothering to pile on more logs. He scarcely felt the cold creeping into the cabin. Nora cried for a long time, each muffled sob a wrench of his heart. He desperately wanted to go to her, comfort her. He could not.

Sean already knew what he was going to do; he had no choice in the matter. Yet he didn't move until dawn seeped into the cabin. Then he got to his feet creakily. He had ridden since sunup the day before, ridden hard all day to get home, and he'd certainly had no rest this night. However, he had passed beyond weariness, into a sort of limbo that gave no physical sensations.

At the pallet he shucked his trousers, then began dressing from the skin out. He was as quiet as possible, not wishing to wake Nora. But as he pulled on the first boot, he saw that she was awake and staring at him.

She said, "You're going after them?"

"I must. If I let them go free after what they did, I could never live with myself." It was, he realized, the first time he had spoken to her since she had told him of it. Now a dull anger entered his voice. "Don't you want me to go after them? What they did was unspeakable, Nora!"

127

"I'm not sure," she said thoughtfully. She sat up, leaning back against the wall. "I know I could have gladly killed both of them if I'd had the means at hand. It's even possible that's the reason I told you, knowing full well what you would do. At the moment, I'm not sure of anything."

In sitting up, the blanket had fallen to her waist, and her full breasts were exposed. Somewhere, in a distant part of his mind, Sean made note of the fact that this was the first time he had seen her breasts bare without feeling arousal.

She said, "But you were just going off without letting me know?"

"I figured that was the best way," he said, occupying himself with the other boot. "You would know where I had gone."

She fell silent, but he could feel her gaze on him as he finished dressing. She didn't speak until he had collected his musket, pistol, and saddlebag, and finally faced her. "I don't know how long I'll be gone, Nora. I'm not coming back until I settle with the Dankers."

"All right, Sean . . ." As he opened the door, she called, "Sean?"

He looked back over his shoulder. "Yes?"

"Be careful, please. Remember that you still have a wife and son . . ." She swallowed, her eyes closing. "At least remember that you have Brian to come back to."

"One lesson I learned these past few weeks is how to survive," he said grimly. Then he softened his voice a touch. "I'll be back, Nora, to both of you."

He went out. At least the Mexican pony had had a good night's rest, and was frisky in the morning chill. The horses belonging to the Mexican cavalry were of sturdy stock, accustomed to long, hard riding.

The horse saddled, Sean sat for a moment on its back. He had not given any thought to what his first move would be. How would he go about tracking down the Dankers? It was unlikely they would linger in the neighborhood, after raping Nora. But one thing Sean had learned—the settlers of Texas, though widely scattered, had a mysterious grapevine. No one could move about in the vicinity in secrecy; someone always seemed to know. He was sure that would be the case this time, since the Danker clan had a smell of evil about them, a miasma that hung about them like a foul swamp fog.

He ranged in an ever-widening circle, the cabin as the center. For most of the first day he had no word of the Dankers, but late in the afternoon, a settler to the west admitted to seeing the Dankers. "They rode by here three, four weeks ago. I say rode, but only two was riding. The woman and the younker. On mules. The other two walked. A worse-looking bunch I've never seen, Mr. Moraghan. They smelled to high heaven, and they whined, crying bad times. I gave them some cornmeal, salt, and sent them on their way, considering it a good price to be rid of them."

"Which way did they ride?"

"West. The woman asked what lay that way, if people lived to the west. I told her damned few."

Sean thanked the man and rode on, following the trail west. He rode until long after dark, before striking a cold camp. He had been in such a hurry to leave that he had few provisions with him, but he did have a little money that Sam Houston had seen to it he received as mustering-out pay, with the promise that the rest of the money due him would be sent along in time. Sean had planned on using the money to buy a few things for Nora and the boy, a few simple luxuries. But the matter before him was more pressing. He would live off the land if he had to. But whatever it cost he would follow the Dankers until retribution was his, if he had to trail them all the way to the Pacific Ocean!

He rode for a week, two weeks, always bearing west.

129

He had no trail to follow, as such, but his hunch had been correct—the Dankers did not pass through the countryside unnoticed. Just when he thought he had lost them, Sean would find another settler who had seen them. At one place he found a man barely able to hobble about.

"That goddamned family of renegades rode in here, and I was fool enough to offer them a bite to eat. They repaid me by beating the tar out of me, and riding off with what little money I had *and* my horses!"

"How many horses?"

"I had a pair of fine mares and they got 'em both!"

So now they were all mounted, Sean thought grimly, and would be able to travel faster.

The settler said, "Whatever you're after them for, I hope you catch 'em, stranger, and give 'em their just due. I'd be almighty obliged if'n you could return my mares on your way back."

"I'll see what I can do."

Sean rode on. Mounted or not, he would still catch up with them. Since they seemed to stop to loot now and then, they would not be traveling too fast, and there was no reason they should suspect he was behind them.

The land had flattened out now, the piny woods behind him, and the area was mostly covered by what he learned were mesquite trees. Settlers were much fewer where he was, but fortunately game was plentiful, so he did not go hungry, although he begrudged the time spent hunting. There were no trails as such, but he was close enough behind the Dankers now that he could track them, and one of the horses stolen from the settler had a flaw in her right rear hoof, like a scar in the shape of a half-moon. Since there was relatively little travel, Sean had no difficulty following the trail left by the mare.

He always started at dawn and, on one of those mornings, after an hour's riding, he came upon the remains of a campfire. The fire was still smoldering. He was close now, very close.

He stood for a moment, looking around at the campsite. If he had not known beforehand, the evidence left behind showed clearly that the Dankers were a blight on the countryside. For one thing, it was criminal to ride off and leave a fire burning. Although it was not yet summer, the heavy rains had ceased, and the land was drying out. A smoldering fire could easily ignite a forest; Sean had learned that mesquite, even green, burned readily. Scraps of food were scattered about, already drawing flies and red ants, and only two feet from the fire were two piles of human excrement. Didn't they even move out of sight of each other when emptying their bowels?

Grimacing with disgust, Sean scraped dirt over the fire, then mounted and rode on, more carefully now, always watching far ahead. He knew they were armed, and he wanted to come upon them unawares.

He finally saw the Dankers one month from the day that he had started on their trail.

He spotted smoke first, a greasy column that burning mesquite made, and he knew it was the Danker clan. The land dipped slightly ahead, forming a shallow draw. Sean dismounted, tied the Mexican pony, and moved forward quietly. It was about two hours before sunset, and he was heading directly into the sun. A few yards short of the draw, he got down on his belly and wormed forward, poking aside the branches of a prickly pear to peer down.

They were gathered around the fire. The woman squatted on her haunches, the hem of her dress in the dirt, poking at something in a skillet on the fire. The boys were all sprawled on their backs around the fire, seemingly asleep. The animals, hobbled, grazed nearby. A pair of mules and the two stolen mares.

Sean sighed softly, studying the situation. The draw had been made eons ago, by water slashing along the earth, and it was actually a dry stream bed. To the south, it twisted left, out of sight of those around the fire.

He crawled back until he could stand up; he checked the priming of the musket, and the pistol in his belt, and eased the Bowie in and out of the leather holster strapped to his boot. Then he worked his way south until he could go down into the draw and across to the other side without being seen by the Dankers.

Once on the west bank, he made a wide detour and approached the edge again, looking down on them. They were closer to this side, and insofar as Sean could see, they hadn't moved since his last look. It was as though they were frozen forever in a tableau.

Sean took a deep breath and walked down the slope, musket cocked and ready in his right hand, the pistol in the other. He knew that, with the sun setting directly behind his back, they would not recognize him immediately. He was more than halfway to the campfire before the woman became aware of his approach. His boots dislodged several small stones. At their rattle Ma Danker glanced his way, eyes squinting against the sun's glare. He saw the uncertainty on her face, and came on slowly.

"Who is it? Speak your name and business, pilgrim." Then she recognized him, and fear pinched her face like a vise. "Boys, come alive! It's him! It's that bitch's husband!"

Lem and Jed lunged awake, hands snatching at the pistols by their sides. Sean had come to a stop only yards away. Coolly he raised the musket and, without even aiming, shot Lem through the heart. The other Danker was swinging around toward him, his pistol coming up, but he was caught in an awkward position, on his knees, teetering for balance. Sean had already dropped the discharged musket and switched the pistol to his right hand.

He raised it, holding it steady in both hands. They

132

both fired almost at the same instant. Sean's bullet struck the kneeling Jed between the eyes, and the other's pistol ball whistled past Sean's arm, plucking at his sleeve and whining off into the distance.

It was all over, that quickly, and Sean had killed again. A total of three now. He was empty of all feeling; he didn't even feel triumph.

His glance skipped to the woman. She was on her hands and knees, staring in horror at her dead sons. Now her eyes moved, bleak in their sudden grief. Her face contorted. "You! You murdered my boys!"

She moved then, scuttling across the ground on her hands and knees toward the pistol by Lem's dead hand. Sean took two steps and kicked it out of her reach.

"I should kill you as well, woman. It was at your bidding that those devil's spawns raped my Nora. But I have not yet sunk so low as to kill women. I'm after thinking that you will suffer more living with the thought that your sons are dead because of you." He looked at the young one for the first time. Sonny was sitting up on his blanket. His face was bleached of all color, and his eyes crawled with terror as Sean's gaze found him. Sean said, "I shall let you live, too, boy, perhaps to my sorrow. But if you have the sense of a gnat, you'll let this be a valuable lesson to you, and run like the very devil from this evil mother of yours!"

Still crouched, Ma Danker spat at him, the spittle splattering on his boots. "You'd better kill me, murderer. If I live, I'll see that you and yours pay for this!"

"I think not, madam," Sean said calmly. "You're like a rattlesnake with its fangs pulled. Your sons were *your* fangs."

He moved then, scooping up Lem's unfired pistol and the one Jed had discharged. "I'll take these along with me, as well as the two horses you stole. My advice to you both is to keep going west, as far in that direction as you can travel."

133

He turned his back on her, and walked toward the two tethered mares.

Ma Danker got to her feet, hands dangling at her sides, and watched Sean Moraghan lead the mares up out of the arroyo and out of sight to the east. There were no tears in her eyes. She had never been a crying woman. But hate boiled up in her, until her blood raged with it. Hate was a familiar emotion to her; hate she had known all her life. Never before had she felt such hate as she did now for this man who had wantonly slaughtered her two boys.

"Ma?"

At Sonny's stricken cry, she turned, opening her arms to him. Her son, the last son she would ever have, rushed into her arms, burrowing his face against her bosom. She smoothed his hair, her burning gaze still fixed in the direction in which Moraghan had disappeared.

"Ma?"

"Yes, Sonny?"

"Are we going to do like he said? Are we going on west as far as we can go?"

"No, Sonny, we ain't. We're going back. That man must pay for his crime. An eye for an eye, a tooth for a tooth, the Good Book says. Retribution is mine, says the Lord. It's up to us, Sonny, to get back at him. None else will do it for us. It's up to you, Sonny. You're the only one left to me."

Hands on his shoulders, she pushed him back, stared into his wet, frightened eyes. Tears had carved runnels in the dirt on his face.

"You have to get even with him, if it takes the rest of your life. Do you understand?"

"I . . ." Sonny gulped. "I think so, Ma."

"You ain't old enough yet, but you will be." She nodded grimly. "Soon you'll be man enough. We can wait. Us Dankers always was patient." She looked at

134

the bodies of her sons. "Now, we have to put your brothers into the ground, and speak a prayer for their immortal souls. They'll rest easier, if they know we aim to revenge their murder."

13

Sean had been gone seven weeks when he once again rode the Mexican pony over the rise onto his own property. It was late in the afternoon. He drew the pony to a halt. Down below, Nora was pushing a plow, making a reasonably straight furrow.

He estimated that close to ten acres of land had been plowed and planted; already green shoots of corn were coming up in some of the rows. Nora was pushing the plow away from him, and apparently had not heard his approach. For the first time since she had told him about the Danker brothers attacking her, Sean felt something break loose inside him, and tears flooded his eyes.

And also for the first time he faced a fear that had been lurking far back in his mind during his absence. There had been the possibility that Nora would be gone when he returned, along with his son.

Now that he knew she was waiting for him, he felt easy again, and the death of the Danker brothers had purged the festering bitterness from his soul. It was behind them now; now they could pick up their lives again!

And while he had been away all this time, Nora had been here, plowing, planting, cultivating—doing a man's work. Well, at least that would change, as of this moment.

He nudged the pony and rode on. Nora had reached the end of the row and heaved the plow around, stopping to use her skirt to mop her brow. Into June now, the day was quite warm. She saw him and dropped her skirt hurriedly, then stood, face still and empty as she recognized him. Sean saw the portable cradle halfway along the edge of the field.

He reined the horse in and slid off, to stand staring down at his son. Brian was asleep, and Sean was pleased to see that his thumb wasn't in his mouth. Looking up, he saw Nora coming toward him. Her eyes were alive and glad to see him; yet there was an uncertain slant to the welcoming smile on her face.

"Nora," he said gravely.

"Sean . . ." She began to hurry now. "Darling, are you all right?"

"I'm fine, sweet."

Running the last few steps, she threw herself against him. Sean held her tightly, one hand cupped behind her head. After a moment she looked up, eyes misted with tears. "Did you . . . ?"

He nodded. "I found them. The Danker boys have paid for what they did to you."

"The woman. And the younger one?"

"I didn't harm them, merely told them to keep going, and warned them to never return to this part of Texas."

"The older two . . ." Her eyes flickered. "They're dead?"

"They're dead."

Her eyes closed and she swayed. Sean caught her by

the shoulders. "What's wrong, sweet? I should think you'd be glad they're dead, for what they did to you. The morning I left you said you would happily have killed them yourself."

"I know, they were terrible men. Still, it seems . . ." She broke off and forced a smile. She half-turned, motioning with pride. "I have been busy while you were away, darling! Our first crop!"

"I see, and I'm proud of you, and just sorry that you had to do all the work. I'll take over, now I'm back. At this moment I'm starved, woman. How about some supper?"

"Not expecting you, there isn't anything cooking, but it won't take me long to whip up something."

Sean reached down and scooped Brian out of the cradle. The boy opened his eyes, letting loose a wail. Sean held him tenderly in his arms.

"Hey now, big fella, it's your daddy home and for good this time. Is that any way to greet your father?"

With a full-throated laugh, Sean strode toward the cabin, Nora following along with the cradle.

But after a solid supper, with Brian bedded down for the night and they retired to their pallet, there was a diffidence between them. Sean was dismayed, yet not too surprised. It was natural there should be a certain restraint, after the long separation and with all that had happened.

He wanted her, God, how he wanted her! Even with the constraint he felt, his tumescence was complete; he was so hard he ached. He had been afraid that he might still feel a reluctance to touch her carnally, after the violation by that pair of villains; but their death seemed to put all that behind him.

He reached out for her. After a brief stiffening, she sighed softly, and came against him.

"I love you, darling," she said. "Don't ever forget that."

"I love you, too. But whatever makes you think I'd ever forget? If it's what happened, it's behind us now, and it certainly causes me to think no less of you," he said, wondering just how true that was:

Before he could speak further, Nora put her hands on his face and pulled his mouth down to hers. At the same time she drew him into her with an adroit roll of hip. He thrust deep into her moist heat, and she cried out in rapture.

Hungry for each other, their long-denied passion broke quickly. Sean did not disengage himself; in only a few moments he was hard again, and thrusting.

The next morning Sean went happily to work, taking over the plowing. The weather was warming up, and Sean relished the sweat brought on by the hard labor. It was great growing weather, and the corn seemed to shoot up as he watched. Within two weeks, he could walk down the rows of early corn that Nora had planted, now ankle-high, and listen with pleasure to the soft, almost seductive rustle of the green leaves.

It was a grand feeling, watching his first crop reach greedily toward the sun. And his son was also growing apace; Brian had even taken a few toddling steps. Sean was a happy man.

Wasn't he?

There was a nubbin of worry—Nora. Most of the time she was her old self, but at odd moments he would catch her standing perfectly still, staring off. Perceptive enough not to interrogate her, Sean had to wonder what was in her thoughts. Was she thinking of the Danker louts?

One morning, almost three weeks after his return, Sean awoke to the odor and the crackle of bacon frying. He had no urgent chores this day, so he luxuriated in a few moments of unaccustomed idleness.

Suddenly a retching sound brought his head up. Nora, hand to her mouth, was hurrying outside. He got up and went to the window. Nora was leaning against the cabin wall, throwing up.

"Nora . . . Sweet, what's wrong?"

She shook her head mutely, turning away from him. After a little she straightened up, smiled palely at him. "It's just a stomach upset, Sean. Maybe a touch of the grippe."

He thought no more of it until that evening on their pallet. He was leisurely caressing her. Knowing that she liked it, he rolled his thumb over her nipple. She cried out, flinching away.

"What is it, Nora?"

"They're a little tender, it seems."

A suspicion wormed its way into Sean's mind, then was gone as quickly, the ache of wanting her driving all else from his thoughts. He continued to stroke her body, so far gone in desire that he didn't notice that she lay almost without moving.

But when he took her hand and guided it to his rigidity, she recoiled. He paused. "What's wrong, Nora? Are you ill again?"

"No . . ." She pushed him away with her hands flat against his chest, and scooted up until her back was against the wall. "There's something I have to tell you, Sean. I've put it off too long as it is."

He sat up beside her, took her hand. "I don't understand . . ."

"I know you don't, and I would gladly give anything in the world not to have to tell you . . ." She broke off, her face stricken in the light of the dying fire.

"Tell me what?" He laughed uneasily. "It can't be all that bad."

"I'm pregnant, Sean," she said in a rush.

Joy burst in him. "Lord God Almighty, what's so terrible about that? I'm delighted . . ." He broke off, as belated knowledge struck him like a blast of arctic air. It didn't take a mathematical genius to figure out

140

that he couldn't possibly be the father. "One of the Dankers?"

She nodded mutely, eyes huge and questioning.

"Which . . .? A stupid question." He stirred. "Why didn't you do something about it, Nora?"

"What? There's little you *can* do, except an abortion. When you're pregnant, you're pregnant. I reckon, once I knew, I sort of put it out of my mind, hoping it would go away."

"How long have you known?"

"I suspected, when I missed my time of the month shortly after you came home the first time. That one night you were home, I thought of letting you make love to me, and you wouldn't ever have known the baby wasn't yours. I just couldn't bring myself to do it."

He said urgently, "You have to do something, Nora! I have little knowledge about such things, but there must be *something* you can do."

She was shaking her head. "No, Sean. It's too late, anyway."

"What do you mean, too late? You say you're . . . What? Three months pregnant? I've heard of women aborting much later than that."

"I didn't mean that exactly . . ." She had folded her hands across her stomach, cradling it. "When I said it was too late, I meant it's too late because there's life inside me, Sean. By now it's a part of me, it's of my blood and flesh. I can't kill it!"

"It's also the flesh and blood of that carrion family!" he said harshly. "I won't have it, Nora! I will not have you birthing a bastard, and one spawned of ravishment! God Almighty, woman, I should think you would be revolted, thinking of what is in your womb!"

"At first I was, but no more. It's a part of me, Sean, and I will not kill it," she said, smiling gently. "I don't expect you to understand. No man ever could."

141

"But what about me?" Sean struck himself on the chest with his fist. "How do you expect me to ever reconcile myself to this child?" He made an agonized sound. "Nora, I don't understand you!"

"I know you don't. Poor Sean." She reached out to stroke his cheek. "I am sorry. I hope that, in time, it will become *our* child. But if not . . . Well, it will always be mine."

"There must be a midwife around, one who knows what to do. You must rid yourself of this fetus, Nora!" Sean said frantically. But he knew, even as he stormed at her, that she had made up her mind. No matter what he did or said, she was determined to have the child.

He flung himself back onto the pallet with a groan, throwing an arm across his eyes. How could he stand to have a bastard offspring of the Danker clan around him? And be expected to rear it as his own? It would make his life a hell! Was this God's punishment?

He smiled without humor. How long was he going to blame everything on God? It was the first time he had even thought of God since the Battle of San Jacinto.

He made an impatient sound, and glanced over at Nora. She had slipped down onto her back and was asleep, a dreaming smile on her lips. She hadn't bothered to cover herself and her full breasts were exposed. Sean looked at her without the slightest arousal.

Sighing, he covered her, quietly got into his clothes, and went outside. It was a balmy night, and a new moon cast a benign light over the valley. He walked to the river and trudged along the bank, deep in thought.

How could Nora accept the fact that a monster was growing inside her? And how would he ever be able to accept this same monster when it came squalling out of her womb?

Sean shuddered, and tears streamed down his cheeks.

142

From Sean's journal, November 27, 1836:

The land has been good to us this year. The crop Nora planted back in March and April yielded a bountiful harvest, enough to sell for some cash and enough to feed us through the coming winter. Today, we celebrated Thanksgiving Day with a table laden with food, including a wild turkey I shot along the river.

We had guests for our feast. Our new neighbors from the farm next to ours to the north. Joe Lyons and his pretty young wife, Anne, are recently arrived from New York State. They have a month-old baby, a girl they named Kate. They will, I believe, make good neighbors, and will help ease our loneliness.

This new nation of Texas held its first election September 5, of this year. All Texas males over the age of twenty-one were made eligible to vote, and this electorate ratified a constitution drawn up by the convention of last March. Texas is now a republic, with a government patterned after that of the United States: a president, a two-house congress, and a supreme court.

I was gratified that Sam Houston, now recovered from the wound received at San Jacinto, was elected first president of the republic by a vast majority. We now have the home rule so long denied us by Mexico!

Sam Houston returned to his home in Nacogdoches for a brief period before his inauguration, and I was privileged to visit with him. He has the same vigor, the same command of profanity, a great store of energy, and he pontificated at great length to me on his plans for Texas.

Brian is walking—toddling would be more accurate. He now speaks one word, a word that Nora says is Pa-Pa.

Three days ago, November 24, 1836, Nora gave birth to a boy. She has named him Kevin, after her maternal grandfather.

Part Two

1853

14

Jaybird naked, the two young men raced yelling into the shallow water of the river. After the water had cooled their sweaty bodies, they floated a few yards apart. Clouds of mosquitoes settled around their heads, and in a moment the sounds of their hands slapping at the whining insects broke the stillness around them.

"Goddamn fucking mosquitoes!" Brian said in his deep, ringing voice.

"Daddy wouldn't be very happy with you cussing like that," said Kevin. "You know he doesn't approve of foul language."

"Hell, Daddy doesn't approve of a lot of things. What he doesn't know won't hurt him. Unless . . ." Brian raised his head, scowling at Kevin, "you go carrying tales to him."

"Have I ever done that?" Kevin said indignantly.

"I don't know. Seems to me he always finds out soon enough, when I've done something he thinks is bad."

"That's because you never bother to hide it. Seems to me that you'd be better off staying on the straight and narrow."

"Hah! Where's the fun in that? Besides, Sam Houston cusses like a sailor. Many of the swearwords I know I've heard from him."

"Sam Houston is a man grown, and you're not."

"The hell I'm not, I'm eighteen! Besides," the white-toothed grin flashed, "they told us at school that the time before twenty was our 'learning period.' So, I'm learning, ain't I? Sam Houston was president of Texas, so cussing sure as shit didn't hurt him any."

"You expect to be president, do you?" Kevin said dryly.

"That'll be a little hard to do. Since Texas has joined the Union, we no longer have presidents. But I could be elected governor," Brian said breezily. His joyous laughter rolled over the water, sending birds fluttering up in flight from the trees on the riverbank.

Kevin floated, reflecting on his brother. He had heard neighbors remarking more than once that the two Moraghan boys were different as day and night. That was true enough, he supposed. Brian was brash, as open as sunlight, adventurous of spirit, daring enough to try anything that he thought would be fun. As a result, he was constantly into mischief, and Sean Moraghan had used the strap freely on him, up until recently. What puzzled Kevin, as well as hurt his feelings, was that Sean had sometimes blamed him, for no reason whatsoever, for the scrapes that Brian got into, and often as not gave him a few lashes with the strap—usually over the strenuous objections of his mother.

In contrast, Kevin himself was quiet, shy, introspective. Brian would charge willy-nilly into any situation that intrigued him, without giving the consequences a moment's thought, while Kevin went over and over it in his mind before acting.

147

There were physical differences as well. They were both tall, slender, and quick, but there the resemblance ended. Brian was almost classically handsome, with fine features, flashing black eyes, and a thatch of thick, wavy black hair, while Kevin's hair was a sort of mousy brown, his eyes a somber gray, and he had a rather prominent nose.

Yet, in spite of being a sobersides, Kevin had his mother's quick wit and sense of mischief, which surfaced at unexpected moments, an outpouring of good humor that even astonished him.

"Hey!" Kevin came to himself abruptly as water cascaded onto his face. He spluttered, splashing around until he stood upright in shallow water, dashing the water from his eyes.

A few yards away, Brian shouted with laughter, and using the heels of his hands, he sent another fountain of water splashing over Kevin. For a few minutes the pair engaged in a furious water fight.

Kevin stopped first. "Come on, Brian, we're acting like a couple of kids!"

Brian slapped one more splash of water at him, then said abruptly, "You walk Kate home from the play last night?"

"You know I did." Kevin felt heat rise to his face at the thought of Kate Lyons.

"She let you pull her drawers down, brother?"

"Of course not!"

"I'll bet you didn't even try," Brian said disgustedly.

"Kate's a nice girl."

"Nice girls do it, too, Kev," Brian said lazily. "I've found that many do, when it comes to taw. They may act like Nice Nellies, and all that, but they're built just like the tarts down at Bunker's Landing."

Kevin said hotly, "You keep your hands off Kate, you hear! When you want to fuck something, go down to the Landing!"

"Why, brother! Now, who's using foul language?"

148

"Well, you make me mad, the way you sometimes talk about Kate."

"You're not fooling me, Kev. You're not all that goody-goody. You'd like to get into her drawers, too."

Kevin was silent, knowing that it was futile to continue this discussion; he would lose in the end, as he always did. Also, he knew that Brian was right. Kate Lyons, at seventeen, was ripening into a beautiful young woman. Affectionate by nature, she seemed to always be touching, getting close to him. It was inadvertent, Kevin was certain; yet he often had to turn away, his erection like a bone jammed into his breeches pocket. Sometimes, from the rather strange expression in Kate's green eyes, he wondered if she realized his reaction. Or, even worse, if she was deliberately causing it . . .

"Kevin," Brian said in a hushed voice, "look over there."

At the nod of Brian's head, Kevin looked toward the opposite bank. Leaning against a sycamore, staring at them speculatively, was a rather short man in dirty jeans, torn shirt, scuffed boots. Yet there was one of those new Colt revolvers holstered on his hip, and he was smoking a Mexican cigar.

"Who is that galoot?" Brian whispered. "You ever seen him around?"

Even whispering, their voices carried, skipping across the water like flat stones. The man straightened up, stepped to the edge of the stream. The westering sun glinted off his eyes. They were brown, and Kevin thought they had a strange muddy look, and lent to him an air of menace. His brown hair was lank, stringy.

Without warning Brian stood up. Even in his nude state he managed an air of arrogance. "You're on private property, stranger, and you got no business here without permission!"

With a lazy motion, yet with a quickness that was deceptive, the man across the way drew and fired the

Colt. The bullet struck the water between Brian's legs, sending up a miniature geyser. Brian did not move, but Kevin saw a tremor pass over him.

"You the Moraghan boys?" the stranger asked.

"What of it?" Brian demanded, still defiant.

"This is what of it, kid . . . Tell your old man that Sonny Danker said to tell him hello."

"Who's Sonny Danker?"

Sonny Danker grinned, showing discolored teeth. "Never you mind, kid. Your old man will know."

Jamming the gun back into his holster, Sonny Danker turned away into the trees, and was out of sight within seconds. In a moment Kevin heard the drumming of hoofbeats, rapidly fading into the distance.

Brian let his breath go with a whoosh, and Kevin stood up beside him. Brian said, "We'd better go tell Daddy."

They splashed their way to the bank and began throwing on their clothes, not bothering to towel off. It was August, and the weather was so hot, and so humid, that they would be wringing wet again within minutes anyway.

Kevin said, "Have you ever heard the name Danker?"

"Yeah, a few whispers here and there. Seems there was a family around by that name, back when our folks settled here. Daddy tracked down and killed two of the Danker boys . . ."

"Killed!" Kevin stared. "What on earth for?"

Brian shrugged. "As to that, I've heard several stories. Some say the Dankers squatted on our land here. Others say the Dankers insulted either Daddy or our mother, and Daddy killed the brothers because of it. I even heard one story that says the Danker brothers molested Mom."

Kevin shook his head in wonder. "I reckon I'll never be able to figure out how you learn all these things."

150

"Folks tell you things," Brian winked, "when you're as natural mean as I am."

Kevin had to laugh. "I can well believe *that*."

Dressed, they left the river bottom, crossed the fields of knee-high cotton, heading toward the big house on the side of the hill. Along the way they had to pass the old log cabin, the original Moraghan residence, which was still kept in good condition, although unoccupied now—except that Kevin knew that Sean Moraghan, when troubled, came here two, three times a year, barring the door behind him and spending the night.

The new house had been painted this year after spring planting and was now white as new snow. The house had been completed five years back. It faced south, with a long, roofed veranda running the length of the front and several rocking chairs placed at intervals, like tethered horses. A breezeway—the dog run— divided the house, with the four bedrooms and a small office at the west end, and the kitchen, dining room, and a parlor on the east.

It was to Sean's office that they hurried now. The door was open to admit what breeze there was, and Jared Whittaker, the overseer of Moraghan Acres, was inside with Sean. Sean glanced up at the racket Brian and Kevin made. "What is it?"

"Daddy," Brian said, "we need a word with you."

"You can wait just a minute, I hope," Sean said with a scowl. "Jared and I are about finished here."

They hunkered down against the wall of the dog run. Kevin listened to the insect sound of Whittaker's droning voice. Sean, not believing in the institution of slavery, hired freed black men, or itinerant white workers, to harvest his cotton crops, keeping a small crew the year round. Kevin didn't like Jared Whittaker. He was originally from Georgia, and the overseer of a large plantation there, and Kevin knew that the man abused

151

the blacks working on the place. But after going to Sean about it once and receiving a severe scolding for telling tales, Kevin had kept quiet from then on. He could hear a little of what was being said in the office, and gathered that Sean and Whittaker were talking about an exciting event that was to take place this fall after the cotton was in—a hog drive to New Orleans. And Sean had promised to take Brian and Kevin along.

Dreaming of the prospect now, Kevin jumped, wincing with pain as a weight crunched down on his foot.

He looked up into Whittaker's pinched face. The overseer turned his head aside, spat a stream of tobacco juice, drawled, "Sorry, boy. Didn't see you hunkered down there."

There was a gleam of malice in his small black eyes, and Kevin realized, for the first time, that the man somehow knew that he had been reported for abusing the field hands.

Whittaker extended a hand. "Here, let me hep you up, boy."

Kevin tried to duck away from the hand—Whittaker's flesh had the dry, scaly feel of a snakeskin—but the overseer already had him by the hand, jerking him up. "Hurt much?"

"No, no, it's nothing," Kevin said and pulled his hand out of the other's grip.

From the office Sean said irritably, "Well, boys, what is it? I'm busy as the devil today."

They hurried into the office, Kevin gamely trying not to limp. Brian, as always, was the spokesman. "Daddy, we were swimming, and a man with a gun came upon us. He fired a shot at me . . ."

Sean bolted to his feet. "What? Who would dare do that to a son of mine? Were you hit, son?"

"Nah, I guess he's just a lousy shot . . ."

"Or just wanted to frighten us," Kevin muttered.

"Daddy, he said to tell you that Sonny Danker said hello!" Brian said.

152

Sean's glance jumped to Kevin, and as quickly away. He paled visibly under the leathery Texas tan. In a low voice he said, "And that's all he said?"

"That's all, Daddy. Then he just walked off into the woods."

"Must be somebody's idea of a poor jest," Sean said.

"But I've heard of the Dankers. You killed two of the boogers once . . ."

Sean's eyes hardened. "Where'd you hear that, Brian?"

Brian mumbled, "I don't know, just around."

"How many times have I told you not to listen to gossip?" He waved a hand. "Now get along with you; I have work to do." As they started out, Sean raised his voice, "But don't wander too far afield, you hear?"

Sean gave up all pretense of work when Brian and Kevin were out of sight. He leaned back with a sigh, running his fingers through hair still black as a raven's wing.

One evening last week, as they prepared for bed, Nora had said, "I don't know how you manage it. Hellfire and spit, you're six years older than me, and not a gray hair, while I'll soon be the color of the old gray mare."

"Age sits more gracefully on me, being purer of heart than the female of the species."

"That's not it. A woman has more things to worry about in this country, that's the most likely reason."

He had stretched across the bed to give her a swat on the rump. For a time, a long time, after the birth of Kevin, they had been estranged, and Sean had feared that he would never feel the same love for Nora again. But time had a way of growing scar tissue over even the rawest of wounds, and they gradually became close again, becoming not only lovers once more, but friends as well, and over the years Sean had adopted Nora's style of raillery and had even grown comfortable in it.

153

The fact that Kevin had been sired by a Danker, and in dark and evil circumstances, was still there; Sean was reminded of it every time he saw the boy; yet he had learned to live with it—most of the time.

He would never come to love Kevin; it was inconceivable that he would. Still, Sean had to admit that Kevin displayed little of the Danker traits, and he watched. Oh, how he watched! The only indications he had seen were those times when Kevin led Brian astray, and even then Nora scoffed at him, saying that he was imagining things. Sean knew differently. He tried to be fair to Kevin, but there was none of the love he felt for his own flesh and blood. It might have helped if Nora had given him more sons, or more children of either sex. But the birth of Kevin had been painful for her, and must have injured her internally; she was never able to conceive again.

The years since the birth of Kevin had been busy ones for both Sean and Nora. His glance strayed to the two framed land donation certificates hanging on the office wall, stating for all to see that one Sean Moraghan, having fought at the Battle of San Jacinto, was entitled to six hundred and forty acres of land. Sam Houston had been right about one thing—the Texas Congress did not get around to making the land certificate bill a law until December 21, 1837, a considerable time after the Battle of San Jacinto. The second certificate was made in the name of Ty Reynolds, with Sean as his assignee. Sean had followed Ty's wishes and taken those 640 acres in the Rio Grande Valley, land he had never seen. His own 640 had been taken near the newly founded town of Beaumont, not too far east of San Jacinto. It was swampland, not good for much of anything, but Sean had a vision of the area becoming a booming port town eventually, like Galveston.

His own, and the nearby acreage Ty had willed him, was certainly enough to keep him busy. The years had been good to him financially. The land was as fertile

154

as it was reputed to be, and each year Sean cleared away more bottomland for the planting of cotton; and in this year of 1853 he had over 700 acres under cultivation.

Cotton culture had flourished along the rivers of Texas. The estimated cotton crop in 1849 had been 58,000 bales, and now, in the 1850s, the yearly yield was close to a half-million bales. Another of Ty's predictions had come true—the land along the river bottom was now worth ten dollars an acre.

Sean had weathered bad crop years—drought, flood, blight, and a severe depression in the early 1840s—and he continued to prosper. It cost him about five cents a pound to grow cotton, which he sold, depending on the state of the market, from eight to ten cents a pound, which gave him a tidy profit. Although he couldn't take credit for the foresight, the location along the river was fortunate, solving transportation problems. Flatboats plied the river during harvest season and collected the cotton in 500-pound bales and carried it to market in Galveston. From there it was shipped via seagoing vessels to the manufacturing centers on the east coast, and to Europe.

Unfortunately the richness of the Texas bottomland was a two-edged sword. Some years the yield was so heavy, producing such an abundance of cotton, that the market was glutted, sending the prices down. The preceding year had been just such a time; cotton had plummeted to four cents a pound, and Sean had lost money. He had learned to anticipate this, and always had a cushion to fall back on. Also, for several years he had been seeking an alternative—another means of making a yearly profit. So far, none of his schemes had been profitable.

This year, he had a new plan. Unlike cotton, animals could not be baled and shipped to market; yet there was a great demand for meat in New Orleans and other large cities in the east. The cattle industry was becoming important in Texas; every year Sean witnessed a number of cattle drives pass along El Camino Real, heading for New Orleans. East Texas wasn't good cattle country; the land was more valuable planted in a money crop than it was employed for the grazing of cattle. Sean had remembered the early years, and the abundance of wild razorback hogs along the river. Pork was as coveted for the table as beef. Why wouldn't a hog drive to New Orleans be profitable?

He had determined last year to undertake it, leaving during the present fall after the cotton was picked and shipped. Toward that end he had been buying and breeding swine for over a year, and had close to 200 head along the river. He'd had to endure a great deal of complaining from Nora concerning the odors wafting up from the pens, and he had to admit that she had a point—the fragrance was rather overwhelming when the breeze was right. Also, he'd been the target of much derision from his neighbors.

"Who ever heard of a *hog* drive?"

"Sure, back east they had hog drives. But, in Texas?"

"And you know what they call hog drovers back there? Pig pelters!"

"Cattle drive, sure, but hell, Irish, porkers are far more stupid than cattle!'

"And cattle can live off the land, graze, but hogs have to be hand-fed."

Sean had tried in vain to remind the scoffers about the wild razorbacks that had once roamed the bottomlands along the river, but most of his neighbors had never seen one. The only neighbor with him was Joe Lyons, and Joe had a herd of swine of his own that he was joining with Sean's.

There was a strong razorback strain in the swine he had penned along the river. There would be problems, he didn't deny that. For one thing, he would

156

have to haul corn along and buy more en route. Of course, being Sean, as Nora often reminded him, the more opposition he encountered, the more scorn heaped on him, the more determined he became.

But now, now things had changed. With Sonny Danker lurking in the neighborhood, dare he go off and leave Nora behind? Nora had never been to New Orleans, so he had asked her if she wanted to accompany them.

"Hellfire and spit, Sean, you must be daft! Me, go all that distance with that herd of swine? I could bathe from now until Judgment Day, and never get rid of the stink!"

If Nora felt any sorrow for not being able to bear more children, she kept it concealed. Of course, in a way, she was surrogate mother to a great many children. Over the past fifteen years, the land along the river had been taken up by settlers, resulting in a large number of children. Naturally there were no public schools; the nearest school of any kind was in Nacogdoches, much too distant to travel. As Brian and Kevin came of school age, Nora taught their early years herself, but she wasn't satisfied until she had badgered, scolded, pestered, and finally shamed the families along the river into agreeing to a schoolhouse, and into providing the pay for a teacher.

As the wealthiest landowner, relatively speaking, Sean had built the one-room schoolhouse, and boarded the teacher, while the other settlers paid the teacher's small stipend, and the few other necessary expenses.

Nora saw to it that the schoolhouse was on Moraghan property, and only a few minutes' walk from their home. "Why not?" she said slyly to Sean. "We'll be boarding the schoolmaster, won't we? And we're building the schoolhouse; so it's rightful it be on our land, and close by."

The fact that it was to the advantage of the Mor-

157

aghan boys, and also provided Nora with something she had long been seeking—an outlet for her flair for dramatics—was never mentioned.

"I doubt that these good folks have ever been so dosed with William Shakespeare," Sean told her, laughing. "In fact, some probably never even heard of the man."

"If that is the case, then it won't hurt them," she retorted.

However, they did respond to the works of the bard in a manner that at first astonished Sean. It didn't take him long to catch on as to the reason—at least part of the reason. In her productions, Nora performed the unexpurgated versions, the bawdy Shakespeare, filled with lusty humor that had the schoolhouse audiences guffawing.

When Sean commented on this, Nora bristled. "Hellfire and spit, that is the way Shakespeare wrote, but the bluenoses have tried to clean his plays up, emasculating them."

Prudently, Sean did not contest her on this. He knew that in the usual manner of settling frontier country, the churches came along first, the schools later. The churches were often used for the first few years of instruction. In that respect, Nora had gotten the jump on the church. The first church was erected only a few years before, and Nora's "entertainments" already had too much of a hold on the river valley; no matter how much the newly arrived ministers fulminated against the bawdiness of Nora's plays, she had too much of a head start.

Recently, she had added something new—plays she wrote herself. They were amazingly good—filled with rough-and-ready frontier humor, low comedy, with a country bumpkin for a main character, and the unsophisticated settlers found them uproariously funny . . .

At a sound in the doorway, Sean glanced up, blinking at Nora. She came on into the room, frowning. The

158

years had been good to her, despite her few gray hairs. The sun in Texas and the hard labor required of a settler's wife usually turned a woman into a leathery, hardened creature after a few years. Not Nora. If anything, she had softened, with the addition of a few pounds, and the curves of maturity. Of course, after the first few years and his prosperity began, Sean had seen to it that her labor was eased by the employment of household help, to which she protested vociferously at first. But, he had noted with some amusement, she had not complained for some time.

She said abruptly, "I understand that the boys saw Sonny Danker down by the river?"

"Damn that Kevin!" He slapped a hand against the table. "Why did he have to go and tell you?"

"Kevin isn't the guilty party," she retorted. "It was Brian, and why shouldn't I be told? I have a right to know if any of my family is being threatened."

"What threat, Nora?" He batted a hand at her. "That woman and her son have been lurking about all these years, and nothing has come of it. Why should anything happen at this late date?"

"Then why is Sonny showing his face here, sending messages to you through the boys?"

"I don't know, sweet. Who can figure out the workings of his moronic mind?"

"He may be a moron, but he has a reputation as a deadly killer. They've long ago lost count of how many men he has killed. You know what they call him?"

"I know what they call him, but Lord God Almighty, Nora, it's been seventeen years!" He sighed, spread his hands. "If you're worried about staying behind here, you can come along with us to New Orleans."

"Travel all that distance with those filthy, disgusting animals? Not on your life, Sean Moraghan! Anyway, it's not for me I'm concerned. It's Brian and Kevin that worry me. What if that terrible woman wanted to

159

wait until they had reached a certain age before harming them?"

"Oh, come now, Nora. That's being melodramatic, isn't it? I can scarce credit her with such a devious mind. Besides, there's nothing to worry about on the drive. We'll have enough along, with the Lyons men with us, to guard against anything dire happening. It's you, left behind here, that concerns me. So, if you won't go with us, I'll just cancel the drive, stay here."

"And what is to happen to those odoriferous animals?" she asked acidly.

He shrugged. "We'll get rid of them some way. Butcher what we can use, sell the rest . . ."

"At a loss?" Nora was shaking her head. "No, the drive will not be canceled. The boys are looking forward to the trip, and I don't wish to disappoint them. And Joe Lyons has an investment in the drive. Anyway, what can happen here? It won't be like the other time, when I was all alone. And there's no need to worry, Sean." Her face twisted in an unexpected burst of bitterness. "No matter what happens, there'll be no bastard sons. No more sons of any kind for Nora Moraghan.

"Ah, Nora!" He was on his feet and coming around the desk. "It tears me apart to hear you talk like that!"

He reached out to her, but she eluded his grasp, darting out the door. She poked her head back in to say, "Just get on with your swine drive." Now she smiled, that familiar, dryly humorous smile. "I would gladly face Sonny Danker any day than suffer long in their presence!"

Nora had been uncannily accurate in her assessment of Ma Danker's thinking on the matter of the Moraghans. When they returned to the Nacogdoches area after Sean Moraghan had killed Lem and Jed, Ma had said, "We'll just bide our time, Sonny, until you get a little more growed up."

160

When they learned that the Moraghans had another son, she said, "Now they got two sons. It's equal now. Two of theirs for Lem and Jed."

Yet time passed, and Ma gave no orders to move against the Moraghans. "We got to make you ready first, Sonny."

Making Sonny ready meant teaching him how to handle guns. After their return, Ma took up with a grizzled Indian fighter by the name of Wade Duncan. Duncan spent most of his time drunk on home-brewed whiskey, but whenever Ma was able to browbeat him into a few hours of sobriety, Duncan instructed Sonny in how to handle pistols and rifles. "Even soused as he is most of the time, Sonny, the sumbitch can pot a gnat in the ass at a hundred yards."

Ma's comment was true enough. Duncan was a dead shot, and knew about all there was to know about guns, and this knowledge he passed on to Sonny. Sonny was frightened of guns at first, vividly remembering the deaths of his brothers: guns were instruments of death. But he discovered that he had a talent for handling guns, and under Duncan's tutelage, he became an expert. He had yet to face another man, but as his confidence grew, his fears lessened.

Wade Duncan expired before the Shelby County war began in the 1840s. The bloody feud lasted for four years, raging across half of East Texas. Both sides used hired gunmen to staff their armed bands, which were given fancy names—the Regulators and the Moderators. Sonny hired his guns out for good pay; he was never exactly sure later which side he hired out to.

But Sonny had found a niche for himself, a way of life. He rode and killed for three years, until six thousand militia were sent into the area, finally bringing an end to the feuding. Sonny got out of it with a poke full of money, six dead men to his credit, and a budding reputation as a hired killer.

Twenty-four now, Sonny rode back to the place out-

161

side of Saint Augustine, where Ma had claimed squatter's rights.

"Ma, I'm a man growed now," he said proudly. "I can handle myself bettern'n the next man." He blew smoke from the Mexican cigar—a newly acquired habit. "Whyn't I ride over and take care of them dad-damned Moraghans for good and all?"

"Not quite yet awhile, Sonny," Ma said. Since the death of Wade Duncan, Ma had aged some. There was still the old fire and snap to her spirit, but she had shrunk physically. "I want that pair of brats to grow to man-size, or nigh to it. Then, when you ride in and smite them, the Moraghans will know what it's like to lose two fine boys . . ."

She broke off as a voice called from inside the shack behind her, "Ma?"

"Yes, girl?" Ma leaned toward Sonny, hand cupped around her mouth. "Som'un I want you to meet, sugar." She called back over her shoulder, "Come on out here, girl."

Sonny's eyes widened in astonishment as a red-haired girl of seventeen or eighteen popped out of the shanty. She was barefoot, and the dress she wore was old and rotten, her lush body splitting it at the seams. She skidded to a stop when she saw Sonny, her gray eyes going wide. She stood on one foot, rubbing the toes of one against the other leg.

"Ma?" Sonny said in question.

"That there's Molly, sugar. I figured it's high time you had a woman of your own. She's a good ol' girl. She'll do whatever you say. If'n she don't, cuff her a good one now and again." A lascivious light flared in Ma's muddy eyes. "Juicy piece, ain't she, boy?" She beckoned. "Molly! Come here, meet Sonny. He's your man now."

Sonny took Molly by the hand and led her back into the shack. Cock already rock-hard, he ripped the dress from her body and took her, took her again and again.

162

Molly gave as good as she got. They rolled over and over on the hard-packed dirt floor of the shack, rutting like animals.

For two whole days, Sonny kept her naked in the shack. Ma slept outside, pushing food to them from time to time. It was the first time Sonny had ever had a woman of his very own. Aside from Ma and a few whores, he'd never even coupled with another woman. Now it was there, right there under his hand whenever he wanted it.

Finally, on the morning of the third day, Ma put a stop to it. Sticking her head into the shack, she watched for a moment as Molly tried vainly to resuscitate Sonny's exhausted manhood.

"Sugar," Ma said, "you're going to fuck yourself, and that gal there, to death. Didn't anyone ever tell you that you can't wear it out? Now, put that pecker in your breeches and come out here. We got us some decidin' to do."

At the fire a few minutes later, Sonny gobbled hungrily at a plate of beans. "What decidin' we got to do, Ma? Want I should go gunnin' for the Moraghans now?"

"Naw, I told you, sugar. Not now. I'll decide when. Thing is, we got to move. I was counting the money in that poke of yours. Right smart bundle of cash. I'm thinking we should maybe use part of it to buy us a place of our own . . ."

"We going to farm, Ma?" Sonny said in disappointment. "I ain't much for farmin'. Sides, it ain't necessary. A man over in Derby County told me that good as I am with a pistol, I won't never have no trouble hiring it out. He says there's always somebody around who'll pay well to have some galoot killed."

Ma was shaking her head. "Wasn't thinking of farming. Just a place to call my own. You know, Sonny, I never had a place in all my borned days all my own, with legal title and all. I'd like that just once in my

163

old age. And you got a family now. What if Molly in there drops a kid? Way you two been goin' at it," Ma grinned, "that'll happen soon, less somethin's wrong with her." She added piously, "The Good Book says be fruitful and multiply."

"Oh . . . Sure, Ma. That'd be real nice, having a place of our own. You pick it out, and I'll buy her."

They found a small place north of Nacogdoches. It was not a farm, just a cabin and a few acres, enough to support a garden patch. But they lived there, Sonny and Ma and Molly, and the children that came along regularly as clockwork. Molly was indeed fruitful.

Sonny was away a great deal. He had an unsavory reputation now, and his guns were much in demand. Texas law was still largely ineffectual. The only time the force of the law was brought to bear was when trouble involving several people broke out. Then, the militia, or the rapidly growing Texas Rangers, were used. But disputes between individuals were usually left to the individuals involved to settle, and that was often where Sonny came in, hiring his services out to the party offering the most money.

Someone, someone clearly with a wry sense of humor, dubbed him the Arbitrator. "When Sonny Danker steps in to arbitrate, you can be damned sure that whatever fuss there was is over when he's done, never mind the dead bodies strewed around!"

This had a rather strange effect on Sonny. Not only was he proud of the moniker, he came to view himself eventually as an instrument of justice. And there were two side benefits to his career. Since he had never encountered anyone as skilled with a gun as he was, he had never known fear, not after he had killed his first man; and from the money earned, he could live a life of comfort—at least he didn't have to labor hard like most to get ahead.

It was a good life, and for long stretches of time, he would forget about the Moraghans, and the deaths of

164

his brothers seemed far back in the past. Consequently, it came as a rather rude shock one afternoon when Ma said, without preamble, "It's time, Sonny."

"Time?" He stared at her blankly. "I don't understand, Ma. Time for what?"

"Time to see that the Moraghans are paid back for what that man did to your brothers." She leaned forward and cuffed him ringingly across the side of the head. "Have you forgotten your brothers so soon?"

"Aw, Ma!" He rubbed his stinging cheek. "O course I ain't forgotten. You know how many times I wanted to go after them, but you always said it wasn't time. I thought you'd forgotten about it!"

"Forgotten! Forget the murder of my own flesh and blood?" Those muddy eyes glared at him. "Never! And if you can forget, you ain't no son of mine!"

"I ain't forgot, Ma, but Jesus Christ, it's been so long! Why did you decide that now was the time, and not before?"

"Don't be using the Lord's name in vain, sugar," she said absently. She was staring off now. "I been waiting for just the right time. They're mighty prosperous these days, I hear. All that land, and a good cotton crop every year. Livin' high and mighty, they are. And now, I hear they're gonna drive a herd of hogs to market down to N'orleans. Them two brats are eighteen now. Leastways, one is. That's what I been waiting for. Not quite as old as Lem and Jed was when they was murdered, but they've been around enough years so those Moraghans will know what it feels like to lose two sons, and right when they think they're settin' on top of the world."

Sonny was startled and a touch dismayed. "I'm to kill the two boys? But Ma, I ain't never killed anyone wasn't a man growed!"

"You'll do as I say! You hear me, boy!"

She reached over and seized his wrist in a viselike grip. Ma had grayed considerably over the years, and

165

had grown scrawnier; yet she was still wiry and strong, and her grip hurt. Wincing, Sonny said, "Yeah, Ma. I hear you!"

"That's my sugar. Sides, eighteen, that's growed up." Smiling, she relinquished her grip. "Now this hog drive, that's the perfect chance. You can see to their deaths out of Texas. Around here, it might cause more of a fuss, them Moraghans being so well thought of by Sam Houston and all them," she sneered, "high and mighty folks. But one thing, Sonny . . ." She leaned toward him, and Sonny involuntarily turned his head aside to escape her bad breath. "I want that Irish puke to know who's responsible, him and his woman. You see to it that they know it's Dankers' doin', you hear?"

"Yes, Ma, I'll see to it."

15

"Hoo-o-yuh!"

A huge sow, suddenly taken with a case of the stubborns, sat down right in the middle of the road; other hogs behind her began to mill about, and the whole rhythm and thrust of the drive was broken.

Kevin Moraghan yelled again, "Hoo-o-yuh!"

The sow refused to budge. Kevin wiped at his sweaty face, which was covered with dust from trailing this herd of two hundred porkers all morning, and swore under his breath.

Footsteps sounded behind him, and Brian said, "Let me, I'll get the bitch moving!"

He carried a long, black-snake whip in his right hand. He drew it back over his shoulder, then slashed it forward. The very tip of it struck the sow on the rump with a sound like a pistol shot. She lumbered to her feet, squealing, and began to forge ahead. Within a few moments the hogs were all moving along again at a good pace, sending up a cloud of choking dust, permeated by that odor peculiar to porkers.

Brian grinned at Kevin. "You have to treat 'em a little rough sometimes."

Kevin just grunted, taking another swipe at his grimy face. Brian wandered away, whistling, the black snake recoiled around his arm.

They were into the second week of the hog drive to New Orleans now. When Sean had first mentioned the drive, Kevin had thought it would be a romantic journey. Well, maybe New Orleans would be romantic, if they ever got there, but there was nothing at all romantic about herding two hundred squealing, filthy, obstinate hogs along this poor excuse for a trail.

The few houses they passed produced people boiling out to observe them, incredulously at first, a disbelief that quickly turned into derision. They were accustomed to cattle being driven to market in New Orleans. But *hogs?*

The first time this happened, Brian had charged at the man laughing at them, the black snake ready to come into play, and he had to be forcibly restrained by his father.

Around the cooking fire that night, Sean had said, "Never mind the sport they make of you, son. It's just that they've never seen a hog drive before, and people have an unfortunate tendency to scoff at anything new to them. But remember this . . . If we get these hogs to market in reasonably good shape, they'll bring us about eight cents a pound. That's more than beef cattle usually bring."

Joe Lyons, sitting across the fire, flanked by his son, Hank, whistled. "You think we'll get that much, Irish? That's better than a cotton crop!"

Joe Lyons was a cheerful man, with graying red hair, merry green eyes, and a short figure that was inclined to chubbiness. Every time Kevin looked at him, he saw Kate's merry green eyes and flame-red hair. He

168

was so desperately in love with Kate that he came near to swooning every time he was in her presence.

Sean was saying, "In a way what you say is true, Joe. But from what I know of hog drives, a drover can encounter a lot of obstacles along the way, and we may lose a lot of porkers before we hit New Orleans. In the east and midsouth, they're accustomed to hog drives, and set up to accommodate them, with feed lots along the route, and taverns where the drovers can stop for food and drink. Along this trail, taverns are few and far between, and we may run into trouble getting corn for feed. That's the reason I brought along a wagon-load. The hell of it is, that's going to run out soon."

Joe was grinning. He took a pull on his corncob pipe, said, "Black Irish Moraghan, the eternal doomsayer."

Sean laughed. "I know, but sometimes it pays to expect the worst. Then you may be disappointed, but never too surprised, when it happens." He stood up, stretching. "I think we'd all better bed down." He cocked his head, listening. The hogs had been fed at the end of the day, approximately eight ears of corn per hog, and they were now bedded down contentedly, with only an occasional grunt or a snuffle to announce their presence. That was one advantage to a hog drive over cattle—hogs were content to settle down after feeding, whereas cattle were often restless and jittery, with a tendency to stampede. Of course, Sean thought with a wry grin, cattle feed off the land, and can travel at a rate almost double the distance of hogs, which could be driven only from five to ten miles a day.

He looked around. Brian and Kevin were already rolled up in their blankets, and Joe Lyons and his son were removing their boots, preparatory to settling in for the night. Joe was a good man, a good friend, and Sean was glad he was along. Within a matter of a few days, he was going to have to start ranging ahead, looking for corn to buy, and it was a good feeling to have somebody like Joe to leave in charge of the drive.

169

* * *

It was late in the afternoon when they came to the Sabine River. Sean was happy to see a tavern on the bank of the river. He knew that a river crossing was one of the worst perils of a hog drive. Unlike cattle, which could be lured into swimming rivers, hogs had to be ferried, and the animals became nervous and unruly on an unfamiliar, pitching ferry.

Consequently, it would be a welcome change to be able to spend the night in a tavern, with good food, drink, and male companionship, before making the difficult crossing.

They fed the last of their corn to the hogs, saw that they were bedded down, and then slicked up preparatory to going to the tavern. Joe Lyons volunteered to remain behind to stand watch over the hogs. Joe was plagued by a drinking problem. "The problem being," he said with that grin that so reminded Kevin of Kate, "that I can't hold my liquor. Never could. The only way I can lick it is to stay so far away I can't even smell it."

"Can I go, Pa?" Hank asked eagerly.

Joe grinned at his lanky son. "Sure, boy. If they'll serve you, get a bellyful. Maybe you'll learn early about what the old woman called, 'the evils of Demon Rum.' Take care of him, Irish."

"I'll do that, Joe." Sean motioned. "Ready?"

Brian and Kevin nodded agreement. It would be Kevin's first time in a tavern. The few taverns in Nacogdoches, and the two at Bunker's Landing on the river, were considered off limits to decent folk, but Kevin had a sneaking suspicion that Brian had patronized taverns. Why not? He had done everything else!

Their arrival had been noticed earlier, and a few of the tavern patrons had stood around outside observing the two hundred hogs with equal parts of astonishment and scorn. But now that it was dark, everyone was in-

170

side as they approached the crude, two-story structure, set high off the ground on flat stones to allow a breeze to pass underneath and, occasionally, water, since the Sabine flooded its banks now and then.

The sounds of laughter and raucous voices floated out the open doors. Several wagons and horses, and one stagecoach, stood outside. They mounted the steps and went into the enormous barroom. The room was packed with men, not a woman in sight, and smoke from cigars and pipes billowed; the air was redolent with the odor of roasting pork, the yeasty smell of ale and whiskey. At one end was a great fireplace, at least seven feet wide; a fire roared in it.

A brief silence greeted their entrance, and heads turned their way. A tall, shaggy man, with a great belly covered by a leather apron, bulled his way toward them. "Well, if it ain't the pig pelters!"

His voice was good-humored, and Sean said just as good-naturedly, "Does that mean we're not welcome here?"

"Friend, if you have money to spend, you're welcome!" the innkeeper roared. "Set yourselves down and name your pleasure."

There was an empty table along one wall, flanked by empty wooden benches. Sean and the boys took it. The rumble of voices had already resumed. Sean leaned back with a sigh, smiling at the easy camaraderie of the barroom atmosphere. He thought rarely of the Church these days, and his defection from it, but whenever he went into a tavern for drinks and food, he thought, incongruously perhaps, of his early days in the priesthood. Women, except barmaids, were a rare sight in a tavern, and those few who did venture in were not welcomed with any warmth. It was the male banter and roughhousing that Sean liked on occasion; he was not a tavern frequenter, certainly, but it was nice to spend an evening in one, letting all female con-

171

cerns be swept out of his mind for an hour or so.

The innkeeper approached their table. "Now what may I be serving you, sirs?"

"You have good whiskey?"

"The best, good sir," the innkeeper boomed. "Four cents the glass."

"Well then . . ." Sean measured the three eager faces with his glance. He grinned. "We will have four glasses, innkeeper."

"The boys then? They are old enough?"

"If they are old enough to drive hogs from Nacogdoches to New Orleans, they are old enough to handle a tot or two of whiskey. I will vouch for them, innkeeper."

"That is good enough, sir."

"Thanks, Daddy," Brian said.

Sean's glance moved to Kevin. He remembered the reputation the Danker boys had for drinking. For most of the time he was able to block from his mind all thought of Kevin's bad blood, but at moments like this, it came unbidden into his mind. He said, "Kevin? Think you can handle it?"

Kevin sat up straighter, tossed his head. "If Brian can do it, so can I."

Sean shrugged, sitting back. "Either of you ever had a taste of strong liquor?"

Kevin shook his head without hesitation, but Brian looked away, before answering, "Not me, Daddy. Nope."

Sean stared at him for a moment, wondering, but not really. He said, "How about you, Hank?"

"Naw. Ma, when she was alive, would have killed me. She hated anything to do with drinking, and since she passed on . . ."

The innkeeper came with four brimming glasses of whiskey, which he set before them. Sean asked, "What's for supper?"

"Roast pig, fresh cabbage, Irish potatoes, hot corn

172

bread, milk and coffee. A fine repast sir, only twenty cents the serving."

"Pork again." Sean sighed. "Lord God Almighty, by the time we get back home the sweat from our pores will smell like pork. But at least we'll have fresh vegetables." He nodded to the innkeeper. "Bring on your roast pig, man."

He picked up his whiskey glass, gestured for the three to do the same. "A toast to the success of our drive, lads! Now, let me warn you . . . Since you're unaccustomed to strong spirits, sip, do not throw it down, or you'll think a charge of gunpowder has gone off in your belly."

They heeded his cautioning and sipped it gingerly. Sean did notice that Brian had about him the air and manner of a regular drinker, but he ignored it, putting it down to his imagination.

The whiskey relaxed them, and the three younger men struck up an animated conversation between themselves, mostly about what they wanted to see in the fabled city of New Orleans when they arrived there.

Sean ordered another whiskey for himself. When Brian mutely held out his glass, Sean shook his head. "No more for you three. You'll have to wait and put a year or two on you. Until that day arrives, *I* will decide."

The food came, and they all fell to with hearty appetites. Scarcely were they finished eating when from across the room came the sounds of a fiddler tuning up. A stringy, gray-haired man stood on an upended keg, sawing at his instrument.

Then he began to stamp his foot, and play a lively tune on the fiddle. Two by two men got up from the tables and paired off into dancing couples. The worn puncheon floor creaked and groaned under the stamping of some forty feet, as they danced a raucous, shouting hoedown.

It was a rather strange scene, but one Sean had often

173

witnessed before. When men gathered in a tavern, with a bellyful of liquor, they liked to dance, and with the shortage of women, they had no choice but to dance with one another. Sean watched with a musing smile as a bearded wagoner in faded dungarees danced past with a trapper attired in fringed buckskins and coonskin cap.

Brian said, "Kev, let's join them!"

"No! I can't dance, you know that! Even if I could, I wouldn't dance with you."

Sean said, "I didn't know you could dance, either, son. Where'd you learn?"

Faint color stained Brian's cheeks. He laughed, his glance skipping away. "I don't know, Daddy. I was just born knowing, I reckon."

Sean nodded, accepting the explanation at face value. Nora had a natural ear for music and loved to dance. She had told him once that she'd never had any sort of lesson, but had learned all by herself. Brian must have inherited this particular talent from her. Certainly he didn't get it from him, Sean thought wryly.

Brian turned to Hank Lyons. "How about you, Hank-o?"

"Sure, why not?" Hank said, grinning loosely, and Sean realized that the one drink had made him tipsy.

He sprawled back against the wall, watching amusedly as his son and Hank Lyons, both laughing like a pair of fools, took to the dance floor.

On a wooded knoll back from the river a quarter mile, but within sight and earshot of the tavern, Sonny Danker squatted on his heels, chewing on a piece of hardtack.

He could see the warm, buttery light spilling out through the tavern windows, and the sounds of a fiddle scraping, and loud laughter floated to him on the faint breeze.

He had been following the hog drive at a distance since it passed through the outskirts of Nacogdoches. He had been a little taken aback when he learned that there were two others along beside the Moraghans. That complicated matters. From ambush, with the Colt and his rifle, he could easily kill all five, but Ma had been firm about that. His target was the two Moraghan boys; the elder Moraghan was to be spared. The death of his two sons would be a more painful punishment than his own death.

Sonny had finally come to the conclusion that he would wait until the drive was finished, the hogs sold, and the drovers left New Orleans for home. Over the past few years, Sonny had grown accustomed to being paid for killing, and if he just killed the two boys now and rode away, there would be no profit in it for him. On the other hand, they would be carrying a fat poke on the way back. If he waited, he could take that poke along with him, thus doing Ma's bidding, but making a profit as well. And done that way, the other pair on the drive would think that it was robbery pure and simple, and would only have Sean Moraghan's word that there was vengeance involved.

Sonny had been a mite troubled all along by Ma's demand that it be made clear to one and all that it was a reprisal for the deaths of Lem and Jed. She didn't understand that the old free-and-easy days were vanishing. Sonny wasn't afraid of Sean Moraghan; he was confident that he could handle him. But there was some law in Texas now, and the prospect of two families feuding, as had happened in Shelby County, might attract more law notice than two boys killed in the course of a robbery. Sonny had the feeling that Ma wouldn't approve of his plan, but there was no reason she ever had to know that he not only killed the young Moraghans, but robbed the old man as well.

Cupping his hands around a cigar to shield the flame, he lit up, wishing that he was in the tavern, where it was warm, where he could fill his belly with hot food and drink. He had been strongly tempted to march boldly inside, sure that Sean Moraghan wouldn't recognize him after all these years.

At the last minute it occurred to him that, while Sean might not recognize him, the two boys sure as hell would, for he had just introduced himself to them not too long ago.

It had been a foolish thing, that, and something that he knew better than to tell Ma about. She would likely beat on him pretty good if she ever found out he'd done a stupid thing like that.

When he was paid to kill some gent, Sonny got the job done any way that came to hand. From ambush, if it was at all possible. A bullet in the back was the easiest way, with no risk to himself. Yet he wasn't afraid to face a man if it became necessary. He knew in his heart that he was better with a pistol or a rifle than any man alive, and so far nothing had happened to prove him wrong.

In this instance, since Ma wanted the Moraghans to know who had killed their two boys, Sonny figured that showing himself to them, knowing they would carry a warning back to Sean, was the best way to do it.

In a sudden spurt of anger he threw the cigar into the night. Fucking Moraghans! It seemed to Sonny that that name had dogged his footsteps since he could remember.

He brought the rifle up to his cheek, the cold stock warming, becoming an extension of himself. He sighted down the barrel, centering the tavern door with the sights. He was strongly tempted to shoot the first Moraghan to come through the door.

16

"Suboy, suboy!"

"So-ee, so-ee!"

The obstinate porkers were not happy about being herded onto the rickety ferryboat. While Joe and Hank Lyons kept the main body of the herd corraled, Sean and the Moraghan youths pushed, kicked, shouted, and black-snaked about fifty of the animals on board the ferry.

The ferry operator stood by his sweep, chewing tobacco and staring off. He had agreed to ferry the hogs across the river for two cents a head. "But don't be expecting me to help load or unload them nasty critters. I ain't lifting a finger. And don't argufy with me none, or I won't ferry a damned one of your porkers!"

Sean and the others had even had to spend much of the morning putting up a removable railing around the four sides of the ferryboat, forming a sort of pen. The ferryman, true to his threat, hadn't raised a finger.

Finally the first load was on board, the removable gate lashed shut across the end. Sean shouted to the ferryman, who untied the boat, and using a sweep, pushed it away from the muddy bank and into the stream. The Moraghans waved to the Lyons, father and son, still on the riverbank.

At Sean's instructions Brian and Kevin stationed themselves at the railing, one on each side. A canoe was lashed to the side of the ferry. But nothing untoward happened on the first trip across. The boat bumped against a makeshift wharf, Sean removed the gate, Brian cracked his whip, Kevin yelled "Whooah!" and the hogs pushed and shoved at each other in their haste to be quit of the ferry.

The ferryman wrinkled his nose at the excrement left behind by the hogs. "Look at that, will you! You folks are going to have to wash down my ferry afore you go!"

"We will see to it, sir," Sean said, his voice biting with annoyance. "Perhaps if you would return for the next load, it might hasten matters somewhat."

Leaning against a wharf post, he gave the cumbersome ferry a shove, sending it out into the stream. He was staying behind with the hogs already ferried. He called, "Mind now, Brian! Be ready to give chase should one of the hogs hop overboard."

"Yes, Daddy," Brian replied.

And this time it happened, what Sean had warned could easily happen. When the second load was halfway across, one boar gave a squealing grunt, and pushed against the temporary railing. It snapped, and the hog splashed into the river.

Following prior instructions, Brian and Kevin quickly unlashed the canoe, launched it, hopped in, and paddled after the hog. The hog was rapidly being left behind by the moving ferry. "They don't take to water too well," Sean had said, "and often drown, either from fear or stupidity, I don't know which."

The hog was going under for the second time when they finally caught up to it. Kevin reached down and seized the porker by the ears and yanked his head above water, while Brian paddled furiously toward the far shore. He nosed the canoe in toward the bank. Sean, who had seen the whole thing, waded out to take the prow of the canoe, guiding it onto shore.

When the hog's feet hit the muddy bottom, Kevin let go his grip and the hog ran squealing up the bank to join the others milling about on high ground.

Brian was laughing uproariously. "Daddy, you were right as rain! That's the funniest damned thing I've ever seen!"

At the profanity Sean looked at him sharply, but didn't comment, moving along the riverbank to where the ferryboat was docking. But he was uneasy in his mind. It had been some time since he had taken the strap to Brian; the lad was a little old for that sort of thing. Yet there seemed a wild streak in him, a wildness that threatened to get out of control.

A dash of high spirits was good for a growing boy; yet Brian sometimes frightened him. A large amount of it was due to Kevin's influence, he was certain. When he mentioned this to Nora, she always became angry. "Hellfire and spit, dunce head! When it comes to Kevin, you have a blind spot. If there's any influence exerted, it's the other way around. Brian is a born leader; there's something about him that attracts followers, like molasses attracts bees. So don't be blaming Kevin for Brian's shenanigans!"

"I do blame Kevin. It's his bad blood that keeps coming out . . ."

"I swear you're addled in the head when it comes to Kevin, Sean! You've blinded yourself to him. I know his antecedents better than you do, but I see no sign of his bad blood, and I've watched him closely. He has no evil traits. He's well-behaved, he's bright, he's gentle. All he lacks is a father's love, and I reckon

179

it's useless to ever hope he'll receive that from you!"

"Bad blood will out."

"That, in my opinion, is another old wives' tale, and so much horse apples! Upbringing is just as important as blood, maybe even more so. Besides," grinning fiercely, "he's half my blood, and I say that's stronger than Danker blood, any day."

A day out of New Orleans they were met by a rather seedy looking individual by the name of Jesse Karnes. Karnes was scruffy, with a beard like charcoal strokes, and clothes badly in need of a wash. The only prosperous thing about him was the big jack mule he rode.

Sean rode out to meet him. He knew that the man was a speculator, and that word of the hog drive had preceded them. It was nothing unusual for some man with money and a knowledge of the market to ride out to intercept a hog drive, or a cattle herd, and to dicker for the animals, hoping to buy them at a few cents a pound below the market price.

Karnes's gimlet eyes lit up at the sight of the hogs, and as quickly he tried to mask his avarice. Sean knew that the hogs looked good. He had not driven them too hard, and had been generous with their feed. On this long a drive it wasn't unusual for a hog to lose ten to fifteen pounds, but he would have been willing to wager that these had gained, instead of lost.

After introductions were over, the dickering began. At one time Sean had detested the long-drawn-out process of dickering necessary for the buying and selling of any product in frontier country. Why couldn't a reasonable price be agreed upon at once, instead of repeated counteroffers? But after a few years, he realized that the entire process was a game, an amusement for entertainment-starved people. Of course, if one party to the dickering was green enough, or stupid

180

enough, to be taken advantage of, to the profit of the other party, so much the better.

Sean liked to believe that he had become quite good at the game. At times like this he even enjoyed it.

Karnes looked at the hogs with a shrewd eye. "Driving them porkers to market in New Orleans, are you, Mr. Moraghan?"

"That is my intent, yes," Sean said easily.

"How long on the road?"

"A while," Sean said tersely.

Karnes nodded, assumed a long face. "Reckon you ain't heard the bad news then?"

"What bad news might that be?"

"Price of cotton dropped to below ten cents a pound. Lowest it's been in a couple of years."

Sean wasn't surprised at the news. He had sensed that this would be a sorry year for cotton, which was one reason for the hog drive. He also knew that the price of both cattle and hogs was pegged to the price of cotton.

"Reckon you know what that means, don't you, Mr. Moraghan?"

"Suppose you tell me."

Karnes said, "It means that the price probably won't be what you expected."

"Last I heard, the price of pork on the hoof was eight cents the pound."

"Man, you're daft!" Karnes gasped in disbelief. "None in New Orleans or elsewhere will pay you that price."

"What price did you have in mind, Mr. Karnes?"

"Four cents a pound, sir, and at that price I may end up losing money."

"Then I don't believe we can do business. I'll take my hogs on to market in New Orleans." He turned in the saddle. "Boys, get ready to move out."

"Mr. Moraghan, you sell to me, it'll save you a

181

whole peck of bother, bother of hunting up a buyer, bother of finding a place to bed down your porkers while in town. And even then, you may end up taking the price I'm offering."

"It's a chance I'll have to take then," Sean said calmly. "My boys have never seen New Orleans. I promised them a look."

"Four and a half, and that's my last offer, sir!"

They dickered back and forth for another half hour, and finally settled on six cents a pound. Since he and Joe Lyons had raised all the hogs themselves, instead of purchasing them for the drive, they would end up with a tidy profit at that price, and Sean hadn't really expected to get much more anyway.

Sean said abruptly, "Agreed, Mr. Karnes?" He leaned forward in the saddle. "Shall we shake on it?"

They shook hands.

Behind them, Brian said in dismay, "Daddy, does this mean we won't see New Orleans?"

Laughing, Sean turned. "Don't fret, son. We'll see New Orleans. Do you think we'd come this far, then turn around and head back?" He didn't add that he, having never seen the city himself, was not about to pass up the opportunity. Of course, he recalled, that some, the priests back in Tennessee for instance, called New Orleans the City of Sin—the new Sodom and Gomorrah.

Karnes was speaking, "If you will stop by my bank two days hence, there will be a bank draft waiting for you, Mr. Moraghan."

The approach to New Orleans was unique. For days, before Karnes had intercepted them, they had been moving through cattle country; now they were in the area of sugarcane and cotton plantations, a country of moss-draped live oak and magnolia; of white-columned plantation houses set back from the road; of endless fields where slaves were still picking fluffy white cotton;

182

of slow-flowing rivers; and finally, the Father of Waters, the mighty Mississippi.

Sean, of course, had seen the river on that long-ago trek from Tennessee, but the boys had not, and the width and the fast-flowing, chocolate-brown water, was a source of awe and wonder to them, as well as the stately side-wheelers churning their way north and south. They had seen a few small steamboats along the rivers back home, but none even approaching this scale.

Then, as they entered the city proper, the great river vanished, diving behind high dirt levees. Sean had heard that the city was below the level of the river, and was flooded almost every year. It gave him an uneasy feeling, riding along with the knowledge of all that weight of water held at bay by only a thickness of earth fill.

But as they traveled along the narrow streets, in the lacy shade of ironwork balconies, the warm air so soft it might have been washed by a rainbow, he gave himself up to the beguilement of this great city. From the wharves drifted the rich aromas of sugar, coffee, bananas and other exotic tropic fruits from distant ports. The years rolled back and he basked in the delight of being in a civilized city for the first time since leaving Tennessee.

It was evening when they reached the fabled French Quarter and the hotel where Sean got three rooms for them—one for himself, one for Brian and Kevin, and one for the Lyons. From the supercilious tilt of the room clerk's nose, Sean knew that about them lingered the aroma of two hundred hogs. Grown accustomed to their own odors on the drive, they had bathed rarely, only in the rivers they crossed; and their clothes were stiff with dirt, and certainly rank with porker stench.

After signing the register, Sean bounced a coin onto the desk. "We would like hot water and a tub brought to our rooms, if you please," he said grandly. "There will be coins of like denominations for the men who serve us, and you may keep that one for yourself, my good man." Turning away from the desk, he winked at Brian.

Once inside the room they were to share, Brian said, "I've never seen the old man in such a grand mood. Back home, he's usually proper as a church deacon."

"He's not all that old, Brian," Kevin retorted. "Daddy's . . . What? Forty-something."

Brian leered. "You mean he's not too old for his rod to stand at attention?"

"That's a terrible thing to say about your own father." Kevin flushed. "New Orleans seems to have an effect on you, too. Back home, you're not this . . . this lewd!"

"Lewd?" Whooping with laughter, Brian fell back across one narrow bed. "I don't know about lewd . . . Fancy word for me. But I'm horny, that I know. And this is just the place. So I've heard."

Kevin had his pack open on the bed, and was taking out his one good suit of clothes he had brought along. He straightened up, frowned over at Brian. "The place for what?"

"It's said that New Orleans is the sporting-house capital of the United States, brother. It has more whores than any other city, and I'm going to get me a taste of it. I'm about to romp like a billy goat! There's a place north of here about a mile, called The Swamp. That's where the flatboatmen and the steamboatmen go to drink, gamble, and buy a wench to lie with."

Kevin gaped at him. "You're not going there!"

"It all depends." Brian shrugged. "Depends on what money Daddy gives us. If he gives us enough, I'll go to one of the places I hear are on Basin Street, not far from here."

"You mean you're actually going to a fancy house? Have you been to one in Nacogdoches?"

"Hardly a fancy house, not in Nacogdoches." Brian

184

laughed, that full-throated laughter of his that was so much like his father's, in those rare moments when Sean roared with laughter. "But if you mean have I been with tarts, yes, Kev, I have. Many times. Hell, I got the natural itch when I was around thirteen." He cocked an eye at Kevin. "I know without asking that you're a virgin."

Kevin felt his face burn. "I've never been with a whore."

"Nor any other wench, I wager. Not around Nacogdoches. And I'm sure not with Kate Lyons."

Involuntarily, Kevin's fists doubled. "I'll thank you not to speak so of Kate."

"Why not?" Brian asked. "She's female, with the same equipment as a whore, you damn fool! If she hasn't used it yet, it's because some bullyboy hasn't been persuasive enough to get her to lower her drawers."

"Brian! We do Kate dishonor talking of her this way!" Kevin was torn between anger and excitement at the thought of Kate in a sexual context; all too vividly he recalled the many times he'd lusted after her.

"Sorry, brother. I'll keep my lip buttoned about your precious Kate." Brian shrugged. "But I am going to a sporting house, you can wager your boots on that! How about it, going with me?"

Kevin started to spurn the offer, but he knew, even as the words of refusal formed in his mind, that the prospect appealed to him enormously. He had been wrestling with his burgeoning sex drive for some time. Actually there was nothing all that shameful about patronizing whores; he had the suspicion that even Sean would tacitly approve, so long as he didn't have to *know* about it.

"But isn't it expensive?"

"Yep." Brian grinned. "But I'm sure Daddy will give us enough. He's not tightfisted."

185

"Won't we be expected to go with him and Mr. Lyons tonight?"

"I overheard the pair of them talking about trying their luck at one of the gaming places. They won't welcome us along for that, you can be sure."

"How about Hank?"

"How about him? He'll be all for exercising that pecker of his, bet on it, brother. From things he's told me, he's a pretty randy fellow."

But would Hank tell his sister about their visit to a fancy house? The thought of that happening made Kevin squirm; yet he knew better than to mention this to Brian.

"Well, Kev? You with me or not?" Brian gave a negligent shrug. "It's all the same to me."

Somehow Kevin intuited that Brian, despite his brave front, was not all that sure of himself, and the thought that his more sophisticated brother wanted his company to invade a whorehouse amused him. He said with a straight face, "Yes, Brian, I'll accompany you."

It went pretty much as Brian had predicted.

Sean had agreed several days ago to accompany Joe Lyons on a gambling fling. If Sean had a singular vice, it was gambling. Even during his days in the priesthood, he was often tempted. Of late years, he had kept it under control. Partly because he could not afford it, and partly because the opportunities in East Texas were rare. There were occasional horse races in Nacogdoches on which bets were placed, and the taverns sometimes saw dice being tossed, but the players were usually low types. Here, in New Orleans, Sean knew, the clientele of the gambling palaces mostly consisted of swells.

They supped at perhaps the most famous restaurant in all the south—Antoine's, on St. Louis Street. It had been established by a Frenchman in 1840—a

186

boardinghouse in the beginning; but the man's fame as a chef became so widespread, his cuisine so in demand, that he soon turned the ground floor into a restaurant, and it was here that the Moraghans and the Lyons ate their supper.

They ate that exotic, tangy dish New Orleans was becoming known for—creole gumbo. It was a dish that none of them had ever eaten, and the opinion was unanimous. It was the most delightful meal they had ever eaten.

As they dawdled over a goblet of brandy and pungent chicory coffee, Sean lit a rare cigar, and said in a broad brogue, "I'm after wondering how the poor folks are doing?" Over the past years he had pretty much cured himself of the brogue, even in moments of stress, and when he spoke it now, he did it satirically.

He looked over at the three young men. "Joe and I are going to try our hand at cards tonight. I hardly think it's fitting for you lads to tag along. Might teach you bad habits. Do you think you can amuse yourselves for the evening?"

"I think we can manage, Daddy," Brian said with a straight face. He added quickly, "There are many things new to us to see here in the Quarter."

"That's true enough. Just don't wander too far afield. Here, in the Quarter, you'll be safe from harm, but there're some places, like The Swamp, dangerous even for a grown man."

"Oh, we wouldn't go to a place like that," Brian said virtuously.

"Fine then." Sean took a small poke of coins from his pocket and clinked them down before Brian. "You're the eldest, Brian, you tote the money. I don't know when we'll be back, but see to it that you three are back in the hotel and in bed when we return."

Outside the restaurant, the men left them. When they were out of hearing, Hank rubbed his hands to-

187

gether. "What say we find us a girl or two? I hear tell there's many walk the streets here at night; they'll do anything for money."

"Street girls? Naw, that's for country clods come to town for the first time," Brian said disdainfully. " 'Sides, a man could pick up the French disease that way. Kevin and me, we're going to a sporting house."

"A sporting house!" Hank looked at Brian, awed by his sophistication. "You think they'll let us in?"

"They'll let us in. We have the money, and they're in the business. Come with me, men. Just follow my lead."

Brian struck off confidently. Hank trotted to keep up, eyes dancing with excitement and anticipation. Kevin went along more slowly, still reluctant, yet determined to brazen it through. Brian had been right—he was still a virgin. The prospect of finally being allowed to indulge in the secret delights that men, and boys, talked of in such hushed tones heated his blood, and he was hot and cold by turns.

Brian finally stopped before an unpretentious structure, two stories high. It had the appearance of an old warehouse, except the front was painted a bright red, and when the massive front doors opened and closed, sounds of music and laughter poured out. Over the door was a small sign, with the words: "Queen of Hearts."

Without so much as an instant's hesitation, Brian rapped on the door. After a moment a towering black man opened it. He looked at the three boys and shook his head, frowning. "You boys come back when you get a few years on you."

As the big door started to swing shut, Brian braced his knee against it. "We're old enough, nigger, and we got two things that says we go in . . . Hard peckers and a fat poke." He held the purse of coins up and shook it, causing the coins to clink together.

The black took the edge of the door in both huge

hands and began to push it inexorably closed. He paused as a voice behind him said, "What is it, Jim?"

"Three young'uns hardly weaned yet, Miss Queenie."

"Let me see for myself."

Reluctantly, he swung the door inward. Before the woman who spoke stepped into the doorway, Brian had the purse open, and was pouring coins into his palm.

He said breezily, "We can pay. Probably better than most of your grown-ups."

The woman was a sight to behold—tall, stately, with bright red hair to her shoulders, and wearing a white satin dress flowing to the floor and tented out over an amazing bosom. But what wrung a gasp from Kevin were the diamonds. Diamonds everywhere. In her hair, around her neck, on her fingers, including thumbs, and on bracelets on her arms. Now she tossed her head, roaring with lusty laughter, and a diamond set in one tooth threw off light.

She said, "I like your style, kid. And Queenie Hart ain't one for turning away a profit." She stepped back. "Come in."

They stepped inside, Brian boldly, Kevin and Hank hesitantly. When the heavy door closed behind them, Queenie said, "Where you pissants from?"

"The great state of Texas," Brian said.

"Texas, huh? A moment ago I heard you call Jim here nigger. They teach you that in Texas?"

Brian twisted his head around to stare at the impassive black man. "What's wrong with that? That's what he is, ain't he?"

"Not in my place. His name is Jim. Now you call him that, if you have a need to, or you pissants leave right now!"

Brian looked truly bewildered, but clearly he was also somewhat intimidated by this formidable woman. He said lowly, "Yes, ma'am."

"That's better. Give me." She held out a beringed

hand, and Brian gave her the purse. "This the first time in a sporting house for you pissants?"

"Not for me. Not new for me at all."

Kevin was paying little heed to the exchange. He was gawking about in awe. The interior of the place was spacious and plush. Lighting was provided by statues holding glittering flambeaux. Pale mirrors glittered everywhere he looked. There were Oriental rugs in bright coverings on the floor, and several paintings of buxom nudes on the walls of the large entryway. Now, looking closer, he saw that the statues were also nude, the privates of both men and women baldly exposed. Face flaming, he tore his gaze away from a voluptuous female of pink and white marble. A useless maneuver, since the entryway was heavily populated by the statues.

"Follow me, boys." Queenie Hart gestured grandly, and swept down the short hall. As she opened a blood-red door, the sounds of a tinkling piano and the hum of subdued voices poured out.

The room they entered was like an erotic dream come to life. The lighting was softer, the candles hidden behind pink shades. The carpet was lush, like walking on deep moss, and the large room was filled with women, sitting at tables and reclining on couches lining the walls. The women were scantily clothed. A few wore wrappers, but the majority wore wisps of silk to cover breasts and loins.

At the far end of the room, at the foot of a stairway going up to the second floor, a black man, hair white as cotton bolls, played a piano. At several of the small tables were men. At each table was at least one girl, and Kevin sucked in his breath as he saw the liberties some of the men were taking with the women.

Grinning, Queenie swept her hand around in an expansive gesture. "Take your pick, boys. I believe in showing the merchandise. Not like some sporting

190

houses that keep the charms hidden until the transaction is made."

Two things struck Kevin—the girls were mostly young, lovely, and as yet relatively untouched by their profession, and they were of all nationalities. He saw Orientals, Indians, Spanish. But among them were no black women.

Brian was speaking to Queenie, "I'd like to take you on, Queenie."

The woman's dark eyes snapped with fire. "My days of working on my back, pissant, are long over." Then she bellowed laughter. "But I reckon I should thank you for the compliment. Hell, I'm old enough to be your ma! Or maybe . . ." Her gaze grew intent. "Is that what strikes your fancy, bedding down with your own ma?"

Brian's face went brick red. He gave her a venomous look, marched across the room, and reaching down for the hand of a dainty Oriental girl, yanked her to her feet. He started toward the staircase, veering aside to pick up a bottle of whiskey from a side table.

Queenie gazed after him thoughtfully. Turning, she said, "That one your brother?"

Kevin answered, his voice sounding rusty, "Yes, he's my brother."

"He gives off a smell of trouble. I just hope he don't cause a fuss. I won't stand for that. Jim can be mean as Satan himself when I turn him loose."

Hank hadn't taken his eyes off the couches crowded with girls since they'd entered, but as she talked, he had given himself a shake, as if coming out of a trance, and now crossed toward one of the couches, almost stumbling in his eagerness. Kevin stood rooted to the spot. He was excited and embarrassed at the same time.

Queenie said gently, "Your first time, huh?"

Kevin nodded mutely.

Her smile was understanding. "Don't fret it. I've got a special girl for times like this. She'll take care of you real good."

She took Kevin's hand and led him across the room. Halfway down, she stopped before a dusky woman with long black hair, which was parted behind her head and hung down over her shoulders, covering her breasts like folded wings. Kevin dimly noted that she seemed a little older than the others, but his gaze was riveted to that dark, veed mystery at the nexus of her thighs, scarcely concealed by the diaphanous bit of silk. His face flushed, his ears buzzed, and to his agonizing embarrassment, he felt himself getting an erection.

Dimly, he heard Queenie's voice: "Lola, the first time for this one. Take good care of him, huh?"

"Certainly, Miss Queenie."

The woman stood fluidly, giving her long hair a shake. It flowed like water back over her shoulders, and her full breasts rose proudly. They seemed to come at him threateningly, and Kevin swallowed past his dry throat and took an involuntary step backward.

Smiling gently, she took his hand. "Come with me."

He followed her, deaf, dumb, and blind to anything else in the room. They went up the stairs side by side. A haunch rubbed against his thigh, and it burned like flames through the material of his breeches.

Upstairs, the narrow hall was dimly lit, the carpet deep and red, and their footsteps made only a whisper of sound. Doors beyond counting lined the hall on each side. From behind one Kevin heard a muffled yelp of joy. From another a giggle. And from yet another a groan like some night creature in pain.

Then Lola stopped at a door, opened it, and went in. It was lit by candle flame as pink as her flesh tones. Kevin stood frozen, his gaze following the graceful movement of her buttocks.

She faced about, smiling. "What's your name, sweetie?"

He finally found his voice. "Kevin."

"That's a nice name, I like it. Come on in, Kevin."

Her low voice reminded Kevin of the cooing of doves. He went into the small room, stumbling in his haste. She laughed, patted his cheek, and went past him to close the door. Facing him again, she shrugged her shoulders, freeing her breasts, and then stripped away the wisp of material at her hips.

She came to him. Framing his face between her hands, she kissed him. A perfumed mist came from her, heavy with the scent of musk, dizzying Kevin's senses.

Her mouth still on his, her nimble fingers worked on the buttons of his shirt. The shirt off, she pushed him gently onto the bed, pulled off his boots, then tugged his breeches down and off.

"Oh, yes! Oh my yes, you're old enough," she said with uneven breath.

One small hand closed around the jut of his erection, and she swung her head back and forth. The strands of hair brushed across his organ. The sensation thus created was almost more than he could bear, and he groaned aloud.

He was wild with need, but with no knowledge of exactly how to proceed. Lola seemed to sense this, and in a blur of supple motion, she was on her back on the bed, and Kevin was kneeling between her raised, spreading knees. An instinct as old as man drove him toward the center of her. A whimper came from him when he couldn't seat himself.

"Let Lola do it, sweetie."

Without using her hands, with a hitch of her hips, she took him inside her, and Kevin was sheathed in heated flesh as sweet as honey, as slick as silk, and he was drowning in sensation. As he drove into her, Lola gasped in delight, fingers dancing along his shoulders. Her lithe body whipped, and her inner muscles contracted rhythmically around his plunging organ.

193

Were sportinghouse girls supposed to receive pleasure from coupling with their customers? Or was her passion feigned to make him think that . . .

Kevin groaned aloud as his pleasure broke. He shuddered, his ecstasy so intense as to be almost painful. He muttered, "I . . . I couldn't wait!"

"You did fine, sweetie. The first time, it happens that way." Her hands stroked his back. "The next time, it'll last longer. I'll see to it."

When he rolled off her onto his back, gasping for breath, heart thudding like hammerblows, he raised his head and gazed down at his softening organ retreating into its nest of pubic hair. The next time?

Lola laughed softly, and, as though reading his thoughts, said, "Just rest for a little. That staff of yours'll stand at attention again, you'll see."

She went away for a moment, and Kevin lay back. He was drowsy, awash with wonder and remembered pleasure. Then she was back, with a basin of warm water and a soft cloth. She laved his loins and thighs, and his manhood. It was a pleasant sensation, not erotic at first; yet it wasn't long before he took note of a stirring by his member, and soon it was standing again.

Lola made her cooing sound. "See, didn't I tell you?" she crowed. "He's returned to duty!"

Before he fully realized her intent, Lola rose and was astride him, head arched back, strands of that long black hair flailing his legs and thighs like a silken whip.

Kevin shivered with pleasure. At long last he knew passion's delight, and a thread of fear weaved its way through his mind. Would he become a slave to sensuality, like he had begun to suspect had happened to Brian? In quiet moments of reflection with his mother, she had often told him that a person should not be swayed by too great a passion, lest it deprive its victim of the ability for rational thought . . .

And now that had happened to him, as all thought

194

was blotted out by the onslaught of his orgasm, and the next sound he was really aware of was Lola's sobbing breath in his ear, and the warm, slippery length of her body lying next to his.

A door slammed violently in the hall, and a drunken voice shouted, "Goddamn you, nigger Jim! You ain't throwing me out of here! I've paid, and I won't allow it! Get your black hands off me, or I'll clobber you, damned if I won't!"

17

Kevin frantically began scrambling about for his clothes, his ears attuned to the sounds of scuffling in the hall.

From the bed Lola looked at him with lazy eyes. "What's the hurry, sweetie? Don't worry about a little fuss; Jim will handle matters. Queenie believes in keeping a proper house."

"That's my brother out there."

"Then I'd advise you to keep your nose out. Jim's a rough booger. You butt in, you may end up with a broken head."

Into his clothes, Kevin hurried from the room without another look at Lola. He was just in time to see Brian, in the grip of the towering black man, aim a knee at Jim's vitals. Jim twisted aside at the last instant, and cuffed Brian alongside the head. Brian flew backward, crashing against the wall. It wasn't until then that Kevin realized that his brother was naked, without a stitch.

He hastened over to kneel beside him. Brian stank of liquor and vomit. He was dazed, mumbling to himself; there was an eggsized lump on his head, and a cut made by his head striking a sharp corner.

Kevin swiveled on one knee as he heard a door bang open behind him. The girl Brian had taken upstairs stood there, a wrapper around her. She had a bundle of clothes on her arm.

"Here's the asshole's clothes!" She was crying as she threw them at him.

"Now, you know Miss Queenie don't like her girls using bad language," Jim said, mildly reproving.

"But what did he do?" Kevin asked in bewilderment.

"He beat me, cause I wouldn't . . ." She broke off, dabbing at the tears in her eyes; Kevin saw the red marks on her face, and one eye was swollen shut.

Now his attention was distracted by Jim, who moved him gently aside, and scooped Brian up in his arms.

Kevin cried, "Wait! What are you doing?"

"This one goes out, boy," Jim said.

"But not like that! Wait until I get some clothes on him!"

"That you can do outside. He goes now."

Jim was already striding toward the head of the stairs, Brian cradled as easily as a babe in his arms. Hastily, Kevin scrambled around, collecting Brian's clothes. Now another door opened, and Hank Lyons ran toward him, cramming his shirt into breeches.

"What's wrong, Kev? Was that Brian?"

"Yes. He created some kind of a rumpus, I guess." Kevin stood up with Brian's clothes and started down the stairs.

Hank was right on his heels. "Goldarn it, I was fearful he'd do somethin' like this! That brother of yours is a wild'un, Kev. Did you know that?"

They reached the entryway too late to save Brian from being tossed out. Jim stood in the open door, arms crossed over his broad chest. He stepped aside for them to exit.

In his deep, rumbling voice he said, "Miss Queenie says that you three pissants ain't to never come back here."

From outside Brian mumbled, "Who'd want to come back to this chickenshit place?"

As Kevin and Hank stepped outside, the big door closed with a slamming sound of finality.

Brian was reeling around, feeling his head. Kevin was grateful for one thing—the street they were on was empty. But he also realized with a lurch of dismay that it was very late, probably long after midnight. Sean and Joe Lyons were likely already back at the hotel. If they were, and knew that the boys weren't back in their rooms, Sean's anger would be awesome.

Kevin sorted through Brian's clothes and held out his drawers. "Here, put these on before somebody sees you in your bare ass."

Brian shoved him away, and lurched toward the door. "I'm going to show these bastards they can't beat on me and get away with it!"

Kevin seized him by the arm and spun him around. Through gritted teeth, he hissed, "You're going to get into your duds and we're going to scamper back to the hotel. You've caused enough trouble for one night, Brian! Daddy is probably back at the hotel right now. If he finds out what has happened, he's going to be as sore as a bear with a sore paw!"

Brian sobered, staring at Kevin blearily. "Jesus! You think Daddy is back? I didn't know it was that late . . ."

"It's that late. Now, get dressed."

With Kevin and Hank assisting, Brian got into his clothes. While not completely sober, he was reasonably coherent now.

As Brian buttoned his shirt with clumsy fingers, Hank asked him, "What brought all that on in there?"

"Huh?" Brian blinked, then began to grin. "Ah,

198

that little twit got prissy all of a sudden. I wanted her to . . ."

Kevin clapped a hand over his mouth. "We don't need to hear all the details."

"I do, Kev," Hank said.

Kevin whirled on him. "Well, I don't! You can get all the juicy details some other time. Now, let's go!" Seizing Brian's arm, he hustled him along the deserted street.

Brian went quietly enough now. He suspected that he was sick, and this was confirmed when he suddenly clapped both hands over his mouth, and turned aside to heave repeatedly. The sickening odor of vomit hung about him like a cloud as they continued on.

Entering the hotel, Kevin was relieved to see that there was nobody manning the desk. He started to hurry Brian onto the stairs, when there was a stirring from the alcove off to one side, and Sean's voice said, "Brian? Son, is that you?"

Kevin's heart lurched, then began to beat wildly. It had been too much to hope that they would get away with it. As their father neared, Brian ducked his face to one side, and tried to bolt past Sean toward the stairs. He stumbled, almost lost his balance, and Sean caught him by the shoulder, steadying him.

"Where have you lads been? Joe and I returned and found you weren't in your rooms. I've been worried sick. Joe has been after me to go to the constable's office . . ." As he spoke, Sean was turning Brian toward him, and he froze as he saw the blood-matted head, the swelling cheek, and the vomit-splattered shirt. "What on earth happened to you, son?" Then his nose wrinkled. "Lord God Almighty, you stink of liquor and puke!"

Hank began to chatter, "We been to a sporting house, Mr. Moraghan. Brian here caused a ruckus, and we got thrown out on our tails. The houseman there, a buck nigger, roughed ol' Brian up a little . . ."

199

Sean's face settled into cold, angry lines, and without warning he backhanded Kevin across the face, sending him reeling against the desk.

In a low, furious voice Sean said, "This is your doing, I know that. It's what I would expect from you!"

The blow to his face hadn't hurt nearly as much as the blow to his feelings. Kevin was accustomed to similar reactions from Sean, and had long recognized that it was unfair, but this, this was uncalled for! Once, he had tried to discuss this with his mother, and she had lamely explained that it sometimes happened that a father favored his firstborn over the second son; yet Kevin was able to recognize it for the weaseling explanation that it was.

Brian was speaking, ". . . no, Daddy. It wasn't Kevin's doing. The whole thing was my idea, and it was my fault that we got tossed out."

Joe Lyons, who had been listening quietly, laughed uneasily. "Sean, it's not all that bad. They're growed boys, or pretty much so. High time they learned what their peckers are there for."

Sean's furious gaze was still on Kevin, and he didn't seem to hear. At least, Kevin thought, Brian was man enough to shoulder the blame for his escapades—and had done so in the past. Yet this did little to heal the wound that Sean had reopened in Kevin.

Now Sean wheeled on Brian. "You're a disgrace to the Moraghan name! Pray to the Almighty that your mother never learns of this. I would be ashamed to tell her. Go up to your room now. We leave at first light in the morning. I had planned for another day or two in New Orleans, but now we go home, our heads hanging in shame!"

Sonny Danker had found a good vantage point overlooking the trail that the Moraghans would have to take returning from New Orleans. Most of the land around was flat farmland, but in one spot, for about a quarter of a mile, the trail went through a narrow defile, with banks rising on either side, but not too steep. A moss-grown cypress grew tall on the east side of the defile, and here Sonny had struck a cold camp. From where he was he could see the far end of the ravine, and that would give him plenty of time to mount up and ride down on them. Following the hog drive afforded him ample opportunity to observe the five in secrecy, and he knew they only carried two weapons, both toted by the older Moraghan: he had a Colt rammed into his belt and a rifle in a scabbard on his horse.

Sonny had no fear of a group with only two weapons. He was counting on the surprise and shock of his appearance to give him enough time to gun down the Moraghan boys and ride off before Sean could react sufficiently to pose a real threat. After all, the elder Moraghan was old now, in his forties, and probably getting soft in his old age. He'd be nothing like the coldly implacable man who had walked down into the gully on that terrible long-ago day to gun down Lem and Jed. Coming out of the sun that afternoon, Moraghan had loomed up like something out of a nightmare, terrible in his wrath, and Sonny had pissed himself. Since that day he had never faced an antagonist so terrifying, and he had never been really scared again. But, observing Sean from concealment, Sonny was confident that the man had become slower with age—he was no longer something to fear.

It did not escape Sonny's notice that, riding down on the Moraghans from his place of hiding would parallel that dreadful day, except that he would be mounted where Sean had been afoot. It was a fitting touch; Ma would take delight in that.

Sonny settled in for a long wait. It was dull, boring; yet he was accustomed to that. Practicing his trade over these past few years, he had learned the patience of a red Indian. In fact, he had come to relish the

201

waiting. It was something like the anticipation of coupling with a woman, for in the moment of the kill he experienced an ecstasy akin to sexual climax. There had even been times when he came in his breeches. Oddly enough, whenever that happened, across his mind's eye always flitted the memory of that time when he had pissed himself on seeing Lem and Jed die.

He didn't know how long he would have to wait, but he was sure that the Moraghans would remain in New Orleans a few days after the sale of their herd of porkers. Consequently, he was caught by surprise on the afternoon of the third day of his vigil when he saw them entering the narrow ravine, riding single file. He squinted and saw at once that he was fortunate in one respect—the two Moraghan boys were riding in the forefront, the one named Brian first. Sean Moraghan was third in line.

Sonny retreated to his horse, glad that he'd had the foresight to keep him saddled. He tightened the girth under the animal's belly and mounted up. Taking the Colt from its holster, he spun the cylinder, checking to see if it was fully loaded. Then, the Colt cocked and ready in his right hand, he kneed the horse to the lip of the ravine, and waited until the first Moraghan was about thirty yards distant.

Then he sent the horse plunging down the slope. The bank was not too steep, so there wasn't much risk of a broken leg. Sonny kept his gaze riveted on the boy on the lead horse. He chortled with glee. The boy was dozing in the saddle, head down. Like potting a sleeping sage hen!

Gaining the bottom of the ravine, Sonny reined the horse in, facing south. He raised the gun, taking dead aim.

Sean still seethed with a quiet, cold rage. What the boys had done the night before had been inexcusable! Not so much visiting a sporting house. After all, they were at an age when their blood ran hot. Sean could well remember the misery he had gone through at that age, his pecker at almost constant attention, and no way to relieve the sexual tension, so he could not find it in him to blame them too much for that. But for Brian to get drunk and cause a ruckus! It had to be Kevin's fault . . .

Yet neither Kevin nor Hank had been drinking, only Brian. Thus reasoned the logical part of his mind. He didn't want to listen to it, tried to shut it off, without much success. Brian was his own blood issue, while Kevin had bad blood in him. How many times had Nora scorned him for such reasoning? But it was true, Lord God Almighty it was true! How often he had wished that Kevin had never been born!

A chill of premonition passed over him. He had been staring ahead unseeingly, thoughts turned inward toward his torment. Now, puzzled, he shook his head to clear it, and at that exact instant, he heard a clinking sound up ahead—steel on stone. He craned his neck to see ahead, saw the horse and rider coming down the slope to the trail, and Sean knew with a clarity as cold as ice that the rider posed a deadly threat.

Even as he thought this, Sean was in motion. The trail was not really wide enough for two horses to walk abreast, but he forced his mount almost bodily forward, bumping Kevin's mule off the path. He shouted, "Brian! Son, watch out!"

He had a glimpse of Kevin's startled face, and then he was past, riding alongside the haunches of Brian's horse. Risking a glance ahead, Sean saw the rider had his horse directly athwart the trail now, and Sean saw the glint of sunlight on metal, as a gun came up to bear on Brian.

He surged half out of the saddle, his shoulder ramming into Brian's side, knocking him off his horse a split second before the gun roared. Sean heard the bullet whistle past, followed by a startled yelp from Brian as he struck the side of the ravine.

Sean, already snatching for the Colt in his belt, risked a second glance at the man up ahead. He caught a glimpse of a gaping face, but the other man reacted almost instantly, the gun barrel trying to track Brian still scrambling about on the ground.

Sean had his own pistol out now, bringing it up. The horse up ahead tossed its head at that moment, and all Sean could see was one arm and the Colt, cocked and ready to fire, glittering in the sunlight. He snapped off a shot at it.

Hard on the heels of the echoing gunshot, the gunman screamed in agony, and the Colt fell from his hand, clattering along the graveled slope. He stared stupidly at his right hand, at the gout of blood. Then his white face came up, and his gaze locked briefly with Sean's. His eyes had a strange, muddy look, and Sean knew that this was Sonny Danker—the muddy eyes could belong to no one else.

Instinctively, Sean aimed the Colt again, but he didn't fire; something froze his finger on the trigger. Their gazes remained locked for a long moment. Sonny Danker broke first, wheeling his horse about, and galloping it up the defile and around a curve out of sight.

Sean slowly lowered his gun, wondering why he hadn't killed the murderous bastard. He would only have to contend with him again in the future. He rammed the Colt into his belt, and turned his attention to Brian, who had gotten shakily to his feet, and stood leaning against the frightened horse.

Sean slid down and went to him. The others were crowding around now, voices yammering questions. Sean ignored them. "You all right, son?" He placed a hand on Brian's shoulder.

Brian looked up, managed an uncertain smile. "I think so, Daddy, aside from a few places where the skin is scraped off."

Sean nodded in relief, and raised his voice. "All right, you all stay here. I'm ridin' on ahead to see if that scoundrel has gone for good."

He rode cautiously, Colt drawn and ready, peering around every twist and turn of the ravine. There was no sign of Sonny Danker. The defile ended abruptly as Sean rode up a slight incline and out onto flatland. Far ahead he could see a dust cloud, and knew that it must be the fleeing Danker spawn.

As he reined in, Sean saw a bright splatter of blood on a nearby boulder, and he felt a sense of satisfaction. At least the bastard was wounded, hopefully severely, and likely would not venture back.

Sean was puzzled. Why, after all this time had passed, should the Danker family come seeking revenge? And then he recalled that tense moment back in the ravine, and he knew. Sonny Danker had been intent on killing Brian, and probably Kevin as well. The deviously evil mind of Ma Danker was clearly evident. She had purposely waited until both boys were, if not as old as her dead pair, at least approaching their majority. It would be a damnable, fiendish vengeance. Sean shuddered, contemplating life ahead of them without the boys, especially since Nora could bear no more children.

The irony of the fact that Kevin was Sonny Danker's nephew did not escape him. Naturally Ma Danker did not know that Kevin was of her blood, and never would know.

Sean sighed and turned his horse back down into the ravine. When he got the boys safely home, he would have to think about killing Sonny Danker. It was a prospect that appalled him; yet he and his could not live under the constant threat of danger from Sonny. Texas was far less lawless than it had been back when he had killed the Danker boys; yet Sean doubted that anyone would fault him if he killed their brother.

Sonny Danker rode hard for the rest of the day, and into the evening, rode as if the hounds of hell were nipping at his heels. If Moraghan came upon him now, he would be helpless to defend himself. His right arm was useless. The wound dripped blood continuously; it began to swell and the pain was excruciating.

He became light-headed from the pain and the fever that began to rage through him, and finally he had to slide off the horse under an oak. The night was cold, but he didn't have the energy to make a fire. He fumbled the blanket from where it was tied behind the saddle, and rolled up in it on the hard ground. He was shivering, and it was a long time before he went to sleep.

His sleep was troubled by nightmares. One persisted over and over. He stood on a treeless plain. Before him loomed a faceless man, a gun upraised and firing at him. Bullets struck him again and again, but Sonny would not fall, he *could* not fall, because behind him stood Ma, ranged on both sides by Lem and Jed, their graveclothes rotting to tatters, the flesh sloughed off their faces. Only their eyes were alive, burning like hellfire. Ma, face awful in its vengeful fury, was pointing a finger at the faceless man, and screaming: "Kill! Kill!"

The sun was well up when Sonny awoke with a scream dying in his throat. Sitting up, he looked wildly about, his heart hammering. In that first waking moment he was certain that Sean Moraghan stood over him, Colt aimed at his heart.

Sonny braced himself for the impact of a bullet. But there was no one. A jolt of pain up his arm brought his gaze down to the wounded hand. He almost fainted at the sight of it. The bleeding had stopped, but it was swollen, turning black. The bullet had gone all the way through his hand. He sent a message along his arm for the fingers to move. They hung still and lifeless, swollen like sausages. He knew nothing of medicine; yet he knew that the wound was bad. He moved it slightly, and a keening sound of agony erupted from him as bones grated together.

The first doctor he could find was in Saint Augustine, and by the time he reached there the hand was beginning to smell. The doctor, a grizzled oldster with a whiskey breath, frowned over the hand, fussing with it.

"How long back did this happen?"

"Several days. You're the first doc I could find."

"Well, I'll tell you something, Mr. Danker. Much longer and gangrene would have set in, and then you'd lose the hand. Fortunate you are that the bullet went all the way through. Now, I'm going to have to clean that wound, and it's going to hurt like the devil. Here, take a few pulls on this."

The doctor gave him a brown bottle of whiskey, and Sonny began to suck on it. In his fever and pain, he had eaten very little, and the raw liquor seized him immediately. He was quite drunk by the time the doctor began to probe at the hand, but even so, the pain blazed at him through the haze of alcohol. He screamed, screamed again, and passed out.

When he came to, Sonny was on a cot in the back room, his hand swathed in bandages. It throbbed, sending waves of pain up his arm. In a little while he went to sleep again. The doctor woke him up a second time, carrying a bowl of steaming potato soup.

"I think you'd better have a little of this. Strikes me you ain't been eatin' too well."

Sonny took the soup bowl in his good hand, and slurped it dry. The doctor started to leave the room, but Sonny stopped him.

"Doc . . . About my hand? Is it going to be all right?"

The doctor's glance slid away. "It won't have to come off."

207

A feeling of arctic cold crept over Sonny. "That ain't what I meant, goddammit! Don't weasel words with me, Doc!"

The doctor sighed, squared his shoulders. "Mr. Danker, I wanted to spare you until you're up and around, but if you insist . . . You'll never be able to use that hand again. The bullet cut at least three tendons, and smashed the bones in your hand. The bones have already begun to mend, crookedly true, and I could probably rebreak and set them properly. If you had come to me sooner . . . But it would have served no useful purpose. There's nothing I can do about the tendons."

Sonny sank back onto the cot, despair covering him like a gray shroud. But overriding all other considerations was his fear of what Ma would say. She would be furious enough at his failure, but this . . . She would be demonic in her rage!

The doctor was saying, ". . . look on the bright side, Mr. Danker. You've still got your life. Another day or two without treatment, and I couldn't have guaranteed *that*."

For two days Sonny sat in a low tavern on the outskirts of Saint Augustine from the moment it opened until it closed, drinking whatever was placed before him, smoking one Mexican cigar after another, awkwardly using his left hand. He would drink until his stomach could stand no more, eat something, vomit it up, then resume drinking again. Nothing going on around him registered—he was only interested in oblivion.

What would happen to him now? Without the use of his right hand? Not only was his livelihood gone, but he had made many enemies over the past few years. What if they came looking for him? He could no longer defend himself.

At the end of the second day, his money ran out, and the tavern owner refused to serve him anymore. There, that was an indication of things to come right there! Heretofore, no one would dare deny Sonny Danker food or drink, even if he didn't have a penny!

In the stream outside of town, Sonny washed and shaved away the week-old beard, then washed the clothes he was wearing and spread them across rocks on the stream's edge to let them dry. It wasn't from any desire for cleanliness, but if Ma even suspected that he'd spent two days drinking, she'd kill him!

Finally, reasonably clean, he rode on to the cabin north of Nacogdoches. It was awkward getting on and off a horse with his crippled arm in a sling, but he managed. When he rode up to the cabin, the children were playing in the yard. At the sight of him, they scampered away, and Ma emerged from the cabin.

As Sonny slid down, she came toward him, arms folded over her breasts. She looked at the bandaged hand, then jumped her burning gaze up to meet his eyes. "Did you kill the two Moraghan brats?"

"Ma . . . I been wounded," he said in a whining voice, holding the hand up.

"I can see that for myself," she snarled. "That ain't what I asked you. Are those brats dead?"

"No, Ma," he said sullenly, looking down.

"Well? Why not?" Her voice was a knife twisting, twisting in his vitals.

"Things went wrong. It weren't my fault. Their daddy got off a lucky shot. Ma . . ." He held out his crippled hand, weak tears starting in his eyes. "My hand is ruined. I'll never be able to handle a gun again!"

She slapped him stingingly across the face. Stunned, Sonny fell back a step.

"Poor Lem and Jed are aturning over in their graves. How can their souls ever rest in peace, knowing their murders ain't been revenged, like I promised them?"

"But Ma, my hand . . ."

"Shit! Your hand! What do I care about your hand, boy? You're no use to me anymore. Thank the good

209

Lord you blessed me with a pair of grandsons. I reckon it'll be up to them now, when they get big enough, and the good Lord sees fit to let me live long enough!" She turned and marched toward the cabin.

"Ma?"

She faced around, those muddy eyes burning. "You're no longer any son of mine. I want you out of my sight!"

From Sean's journal, December 4, 1853:

We returned in good order, with a fair profit from the hog drive. Joe Lyons happily talks of another next year, but I doubt that I will be interested. The profit realized was not that substantial, and my time will be better devoted to seeing to my affairs here.

I must confess, however, that Brian's behavior in New Orleans was most distressing, and I am reluctant to return to that City of Sin. How my Nora would hoot at that statement! She would claim that my priestly conscience, long dormant, is stirring again.

In retrospect, I suppose that Brian's conduct was not all that reprehensible. He is young, at that time of life when it is his nature to be heedless of consequences. But making a public spectacle of himself in such a manner! That is what I cannot condone!

But here, in our old cabin, in lonely solitude, my journal removed from beneath the hearthstone for the first time in a long while, I search my soul and know that what I am most sorry for is how I turned on Kevin. In my heart, I know that he was not at fault. Of the two boys, Brian is the leader. It galls me to admit this, but I know that it is true.

Is that why I have not told Nora of the episode? Is that why I cautioned both boys to keep mute

210

about it, and asked the Lyonses, father and son, to also keep their silence? Am I fearful of Nora's scorn if she learns that I once more turned on Kevin? He is not my son, God almighty knows, but he is Nora's!

I hope this is not the reason—that I merely wished to spare her the shame of knowing, but now, long after the midnight hour, I am not sure.

Enough, enough!

I could not avoid telling her of the attempt on Brian's life by Sonny Danker. I feared that, if I did not, she would learn eventually, and rage at me, and justifiably.

On our return, the knowledge that Sonny Danker had been mysteriously, and grievously, wounded was widespread.

This was good news, since it appears that my bullet shattered the scoundrel's hand beyond repair. That means that we will never again have to fear reprisal from the Danker clan. It is not beyond credence that Ma Danker might take matters into her own hands, but she is old now, not in the best of health, and as I told her on that long-ago day, she is in some respects like a rattlesnake. Without the fangs represented by her evil sons, she is rendered harmless.

There is, I understand, a growing brood of Dankers, but surely she will not pass her venom unto the third generation!

18

At fourteen, fifteen, and even into sixteen, Kate Lyons
hated the way she looked—long-legged and gawky
as a colt, all knees and elbows and knuckles. She
had been positive she would always be awkward and
unattractive.

Such was the strength of this conviction, that she
seldom looked into a mirror, and it wasn't until shortly
after her seventeenth birthday that she realized a
metamorphosis had taken place, almost overnight, or
so it seemed to Kate. What brought it to her attention
were the sudden bold glances from the boys, an occasional pinch on the rear, an accidental brushing against
her breasts, invitations to Sunday picnics, and the like.

When this realization dawned, she took a long look
in the mirror and saw a woman nearly grown, with
full breasts pushing forward, skin the color of fresh
milk, long, well-shaped limbs ending at the coppery
nest at the juncture of her thighs. Her hair was the
color of rust in the sun, long and flowing smoothly to

her shoulders. Her eyes were green, and her nose was rather small, but well-formed, over a generous mouth.

She ran the palms of her hands over the flatness of her belly and down her flanks. Her fingers were drawn irresistibly to the crease of her sex, stroking. A hot flash of pleasure radiated. Vaginal lips parted, she moaned, then stood straighter, forcing her hands down to her sides.

Kate had accepted none of the overtures made by the boys—except Kevin Moraghan. Being neighbors, their families fast friends, Kevin and Kate had naturally gravitated toward one another early on, and if Kate went to any function with a boy, it was always with Kevin.

She liked Kevin, liked him very much; it was even possible that she loved him. But wise beyond her years, Kate was not sure about the emotion of love. She liked Kevin's intensity, his clear intelligence, and he was handsome in a somewhat brooding manner. But now and again she was frightened by some of the dark moods that would descend upon him, especially the flashes of bitter resentment against his father.

She suspected that Kevin was in love with her. She knew that he was sexually attracted. More than once, when they had kissed or she had touched him, Kate noted his hardening response. This didn't frighten her. She was sexually aware, having lived around farm animals all her life.

And Kate was acutely aware of the sexual yearnings of her own body. Perhaps this was why she was uncertain about Kevin. In her dreams, in her sexual fantasies, the male was always Brian, never Kevin. In the dreams Brian was always naked, the outlines of his strong body vivid, his male organ rampant. This struck her as a little strange, since she had certainly never seen him naked; she had never seen any male without clothes, not even her father or Hank. She could only blame it on a particularly active imagination.

In any event, when Brian took her in the dreams, he was always laughing, overwhelming in his sexuality, and Kate would awaken with a warm seepage of moisture down below.

She felt a secret shame about the fantasies. Insofar as she knew, Brian had never looked upon her in that manner; she had scarcely spoken two dozen words to him, and never in private. But her shame came not from the dreams themselves, but from the fear she was somehow betraying Kevin by dreaming erotically of his brother.

Then came the night that she acted in a play put on by Nora Moraghan.

Nora's plays were always well received by the settlers along the river. The plays of Shakespeare she put on in the schoolhouse were given rapt attention, but of late years, the plays Nora wrote herself were by far the most popular. They were ,peopled by characters much like those in the audience, and the language spoken was the idiom used along the river. The thrust of the stories was less sophisticated than that of Shakespeare, the dialogue on a rural level, and the plots relatively simple: a pretty girl and her parents were being driven from their farm by various evil forces—the machinations of a scheming money lender; attacks by Indians and/or outlaws; the ravages of nature. The cast included the feminine lead, her parents, a handsome, dashing youth, the country bumpkin, a number of lesser roles. By the time Kate took a role Nora had gotten to the point where she had given her bumpkin character the name of Tobias—something about the name itself struck the audience as hilarious— and each new play pivoted around this same Tobias, no matter the plot.

Kate, an inveterate reader of anything she could get her hands on, thought the female lead was a rather silly, simpering character. With that sly grin of hers,

Nora said, "You're right, Kate dear. But she always triumphs, farm saved, getting the handsome lad, everything is hers in the end. That pleases the women in the audience, and the fact that the male characters in the play help her to get all these things, at least *seem* to, pleases the men. There's something you'll learn in time, Kate, since you're a smart girl . . . Most men see us as simpleminded, incapable of entertaining a serious thought of any kind. Hellfire and spit, so long as they cast us in that role in real life, most of us will be content to remain so."

"Does Mr. Moraghan look at you that way?"

"Sean?" Nora hesitated. "Not as much as most men, but he has spells when he does." A twinkle grew in her eye. "He's a man; how could I expect otherwise?"

Kate had reservations about acting in the play, about appearing before an audience, and she was cold and hot by turns as she waited to go on. Surprisingly, after she walked onto the stage and spoke her first lines, her nervousness vanished, and she forgot that people were watching her. Nora had told her in the beginning that she was a natural-born actress, and she began to believe it.

Due to the stupidity written into the role, she stumbled her way into one perilous situation after another; each time Tobias managed, in his bumbling way, to extricate her from danger, while the audience roared at his clownish antics.

It was only at the end that the stalwart hero saved her from being scalped by the villian, who was masquerading as an Indian. The hero slew the villian with his own tomahawk, untied Kate from the tree, and swept her into his arms, feigning a passionate kiss.

Just before the burlap curtain was drawn across the crude stage, Tobias strolled out, beaming. He said, "Bless you, my children," and stumbled over his own feet, falling headlong. The crowd roared laughter, and sent up a storm of applause as the curtain closed.

215

Nora hurried out and embraced Kate. "You were absolutely marvelous, dear! You'll be the toast of the valley. You'll have to do this again!"

Behind Nora, Kate saw Brian strolling onto the stage, that insouciant grin a white slash across his dark face. "Never thought you had it in you, Katie. Without you in it, that play would have been a bust."

"Kate *was* good, wasn't she?" Nora said. "But the others were good, too, up to what their roles demanded."

Sean came on stage in time to catch her remark. "Of course they were, sweet." He came over to kiss her. "I think it was your best play." He grinned fondly at Brian. "Don't pay any attention to this lout. What does he know about the finer things of life?"

Arm around his wife, he led her away. Kate was frowning. "Where's Kevin? He said he'd be here."

Brian said, "My brother has the grippe, and Momma made him stay home and in bed. She said she didn't want him hacking and sneezing, making a fuss during the play." He smiled lazily. "Reckon Kevin was going to walk you home?"

"He said he was."

"How about me? Will I do, just this once?"

To her dismay Kate felt her heart thumping wildly. Somewhat breathlessly, she said, "You don't have to put yourself out any, Brian. I can walk home alone. Pa and Hank were here, but they've already left, expecting Kevin to . . ."

"It won't be putting me out any." He was grave now. "It would pleasure me, Katie."

"My name is Kate, not Katie," she said tartly. "I hate being called Katie. It sounds condescending."

"Well, pardon me!" He made an elaborate bow, his eyes dancing. "Kate it is then."

He gave her his arm, and they went out the side door of the schoolhouse. The building had no facilities for changing costumes, and the performers wore them from

216

home. Kate remembered with amusement some of the weird costumes she'd seen converging on the schoolhouse when Nora was putting on a Shakespearean production. A stranger, coming upon them without warning, would have been flabbergasted.

Most of the people were gone now, and they strolled along in relative privacy. The Lyons's homeplace was about three miles north of the schoolhouse.

Brian said, "If I had known I was escorting you home, Kate, I would have brought along the buggy."

She shrugged. "I'm used to the walk. Kevin usually walks me home."

"Any secret place where you stop off on the way?" There was a sly note behind the query in his voice.

"If there was, would I tell you? Then it would no longer be secret."

"I don't think I'd be far off the mark in saying that my dear brother is not so bold as that."

Kate's thoughts flashed back to the time when her father and brother returned from the hog drive. They weren't back two days before Hank could hold still no longer—he told her of the excursion to the sporting house.

There was no artifice in Kate. In reply to Brian's question she said, "He was bold enough in New Orleans, wasn't he?"

Brian stiffened, drawing away from her. "I don't follow . . ."

She finally let her laughter go. "Oh, yes, you do, Brian Moraghan! I'm talking about the trip you, Kevin, and Hank made to a place called Queenie's."

He relaxed, smiling ruefully. "So you know. Old Hank couldn't keep his mouth shut, could he?"

"I very much doubt that Hank has ever managed to keep anything from me for very long."

He looked down at her, one eyebrow cocked. "Were you shocked?"

"Not particularly," she said judiciously. "I know

217

about men and their needs. I *was* a little shocked by the fracas you got into."

He shrugged. "I just had a tot too many, is all. No real harm done."

They walked on a few steps before Kate said musingly, "There is one thing that I do consider unfair."

"And what is that, my fair Kate?"

"Men can go to houses like that and pay to lie down with the women, and they're thought none the less for it. But if there were places like that for women, which there aren't, at least not in the States, how do you think a woman would be viewed if she went there?"

He recoiled, drawing a shocked breath. "A woman would never do a thing like that!"

"Why not?" she said challengingly.

"It's unheard of!"

"Sauce for the gander, or some such." She laughed softly behind her hand. "You see, you asked me if I was shocked. Now who's shocked?"

After a moment Brian began to smile, and looked at her appraisingly. "Viewed that way, I reckon you're right. You know something, Kate? You're somewhat different from other girls I've met."

"Why different? Just because I speak my mind? Other girls think these things, but don't dare voice them."

They walked in silence for a little. Finally Brian tentatively ventured, "A girl doesn't have to . . . Uh, visit a place like that. Not when she's pretty as you and some mature boy is available . . ." He stopped, evidently shaken by his own daring.

Kate wondered if she had gone too far. But what the dickens! She took a deep breath and said softly, "Meaning yourself, I gather?"

"Well . . . Yes." Then, in a rush: "I'm sure Kev is too bashful to venture anything. You're a pretty girl, Kate. The idea appeals to me, that it does!"

218

"I don't think you've spoken a dozen words to me before tonight."

"I admit that. So, I've been an idiot. I never said I was perfect."

"Aren't you forgetting about Kevin?"

"What about him?"

"Well, we have been . . . keeping company, in a manner of speaking."

"No particular reason to change that. That's up to you. Decide that for yourself."

"Then what you're saying is, we sneak off somewhere without anyone being the wiser, some secret place where you can mount me! Like a bull and a heifer." Her temper sparked. "At least a bull doesn't sneak around about it!"

He shrugged. "It's expected of a bull. And," his charming grin flashed, "it'll be far different from a bull, you can be sure of that." He sobered. "Look at it this way, Kate. Do you *want* people to know? Your father, for instance?"

"I can't believe we're talking like this!" She pushed a hand distractedly through her hair. "It would be bad enough if we were married."

"Oh, no!" He shook his head emphatically. "Not me, Kate. I'm a long way from thinking of marriage. I'm far from ready to be saddled with a wife and brats. If you're looking for a husband, forget it. I was thinking of a little fun. Remember? *You* were the one started this, with your talk of women visiting sporting houses."

She had to laugh. "At least you're honest enough about your intentions."

He halted, pulling her to a stop with a hand on her arm. "So, what will it be?" He gestured. "There's your place. Now, if we go any farther, your dad will see you, and it'll be too late."

She stared. "Tonight? You're talking about tonight?"

"When I see something I want, I don't dance around about it."

219

Now laughter poured from her, until she had to turn away to stifle it with a hand over her mouth. Finally getting herself in hand, she looked at him, and saw that infuriatingly smug grin on his face. Was he always this sure of himself?

She said formally, "Good night, Brian. Thank you for walking me home."

At least that wiped the grin off his face. He said coldly, "Good night to you, too, Kate," and wheeled away.

Kate stood for a little while, until the night had swallowed him up.

She wasn't angry at his boldness. After all, he was right—she had given him the opening. In fact, it rather intrigued her, and his blatant maleness was imprinted on her mindscreen long after he had vanished from her sight. How different he was from Kevin! It seemed impossible that two brothers could be so unlike by nature.

She had heard men whisper about certain women, that they gave off a smell of rut like a perfume. The same could apply to Brian. She had detected an odor of sex about him. Never mind that she had never smelled it on another man, and would have been totally unable to define it—some ancient woman sense passed down to her knew it for what it was.

Kate did not try to tell herself that she loved Brian, or ever would; she had the feeling that any woman who fell in love with him was doomed to regret it; yet the very thought of rutting with him, like animals in heat, dizzied her senses.

Shaking her head, she walked on toward the house, toward the light left burning for her. She knew that Pa and Hank would already be in bed, and was just as glad. She was afraid that her high color, or perhaps some odor of excitation of her own, would reveal her agitated state. Despite Brian's powerful physical attraction, she resolved not to let him have his way. It would be the worst mistake of her young life!

220

* * *

Their first rendezvous took place in the old cabin a half mile from the main Moraghan house—two weeks after Kate's performance in the play. She had not exchanged a word with Brian in the meantime, but that Sunday afternoon she had attended a church picnic with Kevin. Brian was there, by himself, and he caught Kate alone for a moment on the riverbank, while Kevin had gone to fetch her a glass of punch.

"Made up your mind yet?" he said with an amused gleam in his dark eyes.

For one of the rare times Kate dissembled. "Whatever do you mean?" she asked archly.

"Now that's not the Kate I saw the other night. You sound just like other girls along the river who'd rather play the coquet than do it." His glance skipped to Kevin, who was hurrying toward them with glasses of punch. "If that other Kate should come to the old cabin around midnight, I'll be waiting."

Kate wasn't sure she would accept the challenge until it was almost too late. She vacillated the rest of the afternoon and early evening, retiring to her room early. In the end the lure of a secret passion shared with Brian Moraghan was too powerful to resist. Both the men in her family retired early as was their habit, and she knew it would take something more noisy than her sneaking out to awaken them.

Heart beating wildly, palms moist and sweating, she left the house shortly after eleven and hurried along the river to the old Moraghan cabin. It was winter now, and the night was chill, a mist lying along the river, for which she was grateful since it would deter people from going out this late. She shivered, both from anticipation and cold. She had put on a long, everyday dress, sweeping the ground, with a shawl thrown over her shoulders, but in preparation for the inevitable, she had worn very little in the way of undergarments. Daring, quite daring

221

for a girl of her station in life, yet she suspected that Brian would merely think it sensible.

Kate had always despaired of the voluminous foundation garments a respectable woman was expected to wear, but never before had she been so bold as to venture out of the house without the complete outfit. The wind, finding its way up under her long skirt, was cold.

The cabin was dark, and no smoke emerged from the stone chimney. She wondered if Brian had already given up and departed. But at her hesitant knock, the heavy door swung inward, and Brian's whisper floated out to her, "Hustle in before you're seen."

He closed the door behind her. It was so dark inside his face was a blur. "Heavens, it's like the inside of a cave!"

"Don't dare show a light. Daddy would throw a conniption if he knew someone was in here."

"Not even a fire? It's icy in here."

"Can't risk chimney smoke, either." His chuckle was ribald. "Don't fret, pumpkin, I'll see you're soon warm. I brought along a couple of feather comforters."

He fumbled for her hand and led her across the room, drawing her down onto a comforter. He pulled the second one over her and stepped back for a few moments. From the sounds Kate knew that he was removing his clothing.

She was still shivering when he slipped under the top comforter with her. Brian was not an artful lover. He was direct and forceful—no time wasted in preliminaries. But she had guessed that about him, and in her heart she welcomed his directness. Dallying, protestations of love, would have cheapened it. This way, it was simply two healthy young animals taking their pleasure in each other, and that was the way Kate wanted it.

He shoved her dress up above her waist, chuckling

as his hands encountered warm flesh. "Nothing in the way, I see. Ah-h, I like that!"

"I thought you would."

An active young lady, spending much of her day in strenuous activities and a lot of time on the back of a mule or a horse, Kate had ruptured her hymen two years ago, so there was scarcely any pain, no bleeding, when she took him into her. She was tight, but anticipating pleasure, her body's lubrication caused her to experience little discomfort.

Brian grasped her hips in both hands, holding her off the dirt floor, and drove into her with vigor. In a very few seconds sensation raced along her nerve endings, and she drummed her pelvis blindly against him, a muted cry escaping her open mouth.

"You like that, Kate? Is it good?"

"Yes, damn you, yes!"

"Didn't I tell you?" His tone was gloating, and Kate had to smile to herself.

Kate lost her innocence with a moaning sound of ecstasy as her orgasm seized her, taking her out of herself, momentarily. When she was aware again, Brian was still, his panting breath hot on her cheek.

He moved to lie beside her, and Kate lay in a sort of daze, her mind lazily attempting to sort out the various sensations she had just experienced.

"Like I thought, you were a virgin."

Her head rolled toward him, and there was enough light for her to see his smile. "That pleases you, I expect. I've heard that men like virgins."

He shrugged. "It doesn't make all that much difference to me. I've pleasured myself with women of all ages, up and down the river."

"You're full of yourself, aren't you, Brian Moraghan?"

He chuckled. "Maybe. But not as much as you were full of me awhile ago."

223

She sat up, nettled. "I don't like vulgar talk!"

"Come on, Kate. Yes, you do. It tickles you deep down, to hear a man talk like that." His laughter was rich and full. "I'll bet old prissy Kevin never says anything you couldn't read in schoolbooks!"

Kate had to admit that he was right. His directness was refreshing; she was weary of men tiptoeing around earthy subjects with women. "But one thing I don't understand . . . Why do you always scorn Kevin when you talk about him?"

"Do I do that?" His voice sounded surprised. "I guess I didn't realize. I'll try to watch it. I love him; he's my brother. But enough of this talk." He took her by the shoulders and pushed her down onto the comforter. "We have better things to do."

Kate gasped as she felt the prod of his organ on the inside of her thigh. "Already? But I thought a man couldn't do it again so . . ."

"That shows how much you know about a man, pumpkin." He gave a shout of laughter. "Especially *this* man. And it'll be better for you this time, you'll see."

And it was.

The liaison thus begun in the old log cabin continued once or twice a week through the winter.

Kate was astonished at the depth of sensuality in her. She became a full and active partner in the relationship. Both took it for what it was—an enjoyable coupling. They never talked of love and marriage, which was fine with Kate. She wouldn't have believed Brian if he *had* proclaimed love, and would have hooted at the idea of marrying him. She was perceptive enough to gauge his character well. He was charming, full of rich humor, and—she suspected, without prior experience—a better-than-average lover; but he was also conceited, somewhat vain about his physicality, and incapable of being faithful to one woman for long.

224

In fact, she was sure, long before their affair was over, that he was bedding other women all the time. It was his nature. He saw nothing wrong in that, and neither did she. It was Brian's opinion that it was his duty to pleasure as many women as he possibly could, and they should look upon any relationship as no more than that and be content.

Kevin? Well, Kate was surprised at herself there as well. She experienced almost no guilt. After all, she wasn't betraying him in a sexual sense, since they had never been intimate. When this first occurred to her, she wondered if she was quibbling but decided in all honesty that she was not.

She was never seen in public with Brian, and when they did inadvertently meet, whatever verbal exchange they had was on an impersonal level. Once or twice, on these rare occasions, she caught a glint of mocking amusement in his eye, but he never talked of it, and neither did she. She and Kevin still went together to picnics and such, and on those outings, they behaved as always, and she could shove any thought of his brother back into a corner of her mind without a twinge of guilt.

So, the affair with Brian continued, without any cooling of the sexual passion that Kate could ascertain, through the winter and into spring, the time of rebirth and the stirrings of new life in the fertile earth, and she was pregnant.

The girls of her childhood had exchanged whispers to the effect that a girl could become pregnant if kissed by a boy during her menstrual period. Kate knew this was a myth long before the others did, and she was well aware of how a woman became pregnant. Her periods had always been as regular as the changes of the moon, and she suspected the truth after missing one period. She knew without doubt when she missed a second.

Now, too late, she railed at her stupidity. The times

when she had worried about becoming pregnant by Brian, she had dismissed from her thoughts. She didn't love Brian, nor did he love her, so how *could* she have the bad fortune to become pregnant? Foolish, romantic nonsense. Or so she concluded when the fact could no longer be denied.

What to do? All her life Kate had been able to make a decision and stick to it without regret, no matter how awry her judgment had been. But this predicament was totally beyond her experience. A pregnant girl without a husband was a creature to be scorned among the people about. They were not hard-core religionists as such, but there were some things beyond the pale, and a child born out of wedlock was one of them. When a man got a decent woman pregnant, he was expected to marry her at once, and Kate realized that she could probably force Brian into marriage. But did she want that? Did she want him for a husband for the rest of her life? The answer to that was no. He would come to hate her; they would hate each other.

The times Kate had cried since around the age of ten she could count on the fingers of one hand. She cried now, torn by indecision.

Perhaps that was the reason she did what she did. One night in the cabin, after they had made love, she found her eyes leaking weak tears, and she said, "Brian, I'm going to have a child. Your child, as if you could have any doubts."

He flung away from her. "How could you be so stupid?"

"Stupid? Brian, it's the natural course of events. When a man and a woman lie together, sooner or later the woman becomes pregnant. It must have happened to you before, the way you rut around."

"Sure, but always with . . ." He bit the words off.

"With women with soiled reputations and it didn't matter? Or . . ." She laughed without humor. "Or with

226

married women, who could lay the blame on their husbands?"

"Mostly that's the way of it, yes," he said sullenly. Now he turned to face her. "What do you expect me to do about it?"

"Nothing, not really," she said, knowing that it was true. "I'm not really sure why I even told you."

"But what will you do?"

"I haven't thought it through yet. But I'll manage."

"Maybe you could blame it on Kevin."

"That's a nasty thought. I would never do that! I think too much of Kevin for that."

He gestured helplessly. "But if Daddy ever finds out . . ."

Almost as if his words had been a conjuring-up ritual, the cabin door was flung open, and Sean Moraghan, carrying a lantern, stood framed in the doorway. "I thought I heard voices in here." He held the lantern high, his face registering shock as he saw his son and recognized the nude Kate on the comforters. "By the Lord God Almighty, what is going on here?"

His inopportune appearance had been so spooky that Kate had been paralyzed at first. Now she snatched up her dress and slipped it down over her head. A giggle broke from her, and it was difficult to maintain her dignity as she said, "I think it should be plain what. is happening, Mr. Moraghan. Or rather what *has* happened."

Kate waited fearfully for several days for the blow to fall, sure that Sean Moraghan would come to her father with his damning knowledge. Or, as an alternative, Brian would come to ask her to wed him, driven to it by his father's terrible wrath.

But nothing happened for three days. Then, on Sunday afternoon, Kate was down on the riverbank, staring pensively into the water, when she heard footsteps

227

behind her and looked around to see Kevin. His face was set in grave lines, and he seemed to be suffering from some emotional shock.

She sprang to her feet. "What is it, Kevin? You look terrible! What's wrong?"

In a grieving voice he said, "Brian ran away from home two nights ago. Nobody knows why or where he went. I would have come to tell you sooner, but Momma has been so broken up, and Daddy just walks around with a terrible face, not speaking to anyone . . ."

19

Since the Mexican War, the Texas Rangers had enjoyed a growing, sometimes lurid, reputation. Such fierce fighting men were the rangers that the Mexicans named them *Los Tejanos Diablos*—the Texas Devils.

They were legends in Texas long before 1854, when Brian Moraghan joined them. A tale was in circulation that Brian had heard many times—the story told of a town terrorized by a vicious, unruly mob. In desperation, the townspeople sent for the rangers.

A single ranger answered their plea for help. He was asked: "Where are the others? We need a whole company of rangers!"

The ranger drawled in reply: "Why? You've only got one mob, so I was told, and the captain thought one ranger could handle it easily."

Brian chose the rangers instead of the state militia because the rangers were paid $1.25 a day and the men of the Texas militia were paid nothing.

Brian left home with a fine horse and one of the

extra Colts his father had purchased since the Sonny Danker episode. Brian felt no qualms of guilt over this —he was a Moraghan, and he was entitled to his own. He knew that rangers were required to provide their own mounts and weapons. The horse had to have speed and "bottom," meaning endurance, the ability to carry a man and his equipment for days on end without quitting. The horse Brian rode was a descendant of the Spanish pony Sam Houston had given Sean at San Jacinto, with some mustang blood bred into him. There was no tougher horse than a Spanish mustang, able to live solely on grass and travel for long periods without water. Rangers were not allowed a string of horses, but only one, and that one necessarily had to be of the best.

Brian knew he also had to have a rifle. He had none as yet, but he had enough money with him to purchase a good rifle before he reached Corpus Christi, the state headquarters for the rangers.

He felt little guilt either about leaving a pregnant Kate Lyons behind; he had no intention of tying himself down with a wife and family. There was much of the world to see, much adventuring to experience, and he intended to experience it all. It had been in his mind for some time to leave home and join the rangers, and this had merely hastened his leave-taking. Not only did he not want a family, he had no desire to settle down yet to a life of hard, boring labor entailed by running the plantation. He realized that his father expected him to take over the reins eventually. . . .

His father.

Sean Moraghan had always been something of an enigma to Brian, a man of shifting moods. He could be warm, loving, and yet he could become almost cruel in his rages. These flare-ups had become more frequent of recent years, as Brian's escapades had multiplied. He knew that his father wasn't religious, neither of his parents were—at least they rarely attended religious

230

services, and there were no prayers said in their home, as was the custom in most of the houses along the river.

However, the Holy Bible was one of the books used in school to teach reading and to instill ethical values in the children. It struck Brian that his father, at certain times, resembled one of those old patriarchs spoken of in the Bible—those ancients whose wrath was awesome when they encountered evil in any form. Certainly, Sean was awesome when he punished Brian for wrongdoing.

The Sean Moraghan that Brian had seen in the old cabin the other night had been different. That Sean Moraghan had been chilling in his silent rage. He had stared at his son in silent contempt after Kate ran out, and had finally turned away without speaking a single word. It had been an apprehensive time during the next two days. Sean had avoided him at all times, and not one word had he spoken directly to him. Brian knew that this would not last; he sensed that his father would in the end insist that he marry Kate.

It was then that Brian knew he had to go, just pack up and go. It galled him to have to sneak away like a thief in the night; yet he realized that it would be a bad mistake to give any forewarning of his leaving. He also resisted any impulse to leave behind a note stating his intentions. He remembered the legend of Sean Moraghan tracking down and killing the Danker brothers, and it was not inconceivable that he could, if he knew Brian was joining the rangers, track him down and forcibly drag him home.

No, he had no regrets. Long had he been chafing at the restraints imposed on him at home. Now he was his own man, he could do as he wished, and nobody could say him nay. Riding along the road toward the Gulf of Mexico, he threw back his head and howled like a wolf.

* * *

231

Corpus Christi, in 1854, was not much of a town—a few houses strung along the bay. Its only industry was fishing, and even that was puny. A few wealthy folk from farther inland owned summer homes there, where they could find some relief from the heat.

Corpus Christi was the only town of any size in the area, and Brian understood that the rangers chose it for headquarters because their biggest chore was patrolling the border between Mexico and Texas, and by locating in Corpus Christi they were not too far removed.

It was early when he rode in. Eager to begin his new life, Brian asked directions to the ranger headquarters.

He was questioned by a sergeant, a leathery, tobacco-chewing individual of indeterminate age, with gray eyes hard as flint and a voice rough enough to grind cornmeal. He fixed those hard eyes on Brian and growled, "How old are you, son?"

"Eighteen, my last birthday." Brian tried to stand straighter. "Nineteen before long."

"Is that right now?" The sergeant spat at a spittoon by the low table he used for a desk. "I'd wager you're lying, but you're big enough. The question is, are you tough enough? In the rangers, we don't have military drill, no training. To be a Texas Ranger a man has to be able to fight before he joins up. On the other side, we don't have many officers, a man don't have to salute, follow any of that military horseshit."

"I'm tough enough," Brian said stoutly.

"Is that right?" The man's glance moved to the Colt on Brian's hip. "I see you got a pistol. We also have to provide our own rifle and a horse."

"I have both."

"But can you use them? Can you ride? And can you cook?"

"Cook?" Brian stared.

"That's what I said. When we're out in the field,

we don't carry along a man just to cook. A man has to prepare his own vittles or fight on an empty belly."

Brian, who had never so much as fried an egg, lied, "I can cook."

The sergeant eyed him dubiously. "We don't take much to city boys in the rangers. We like boys from farms or ranches, used to hard work, and not the easy life."

"I grew up on a farm, a plantation in fact, and I'm used to hard work."

"Then I reckon you'll do. Welcome to the Texas Rangers, Moraghan."

The man held out a leathery, callused hand, and Brian felt his heart give a leap of elation. He shook the hand.

"Some things we have to get straight first. Your duds mainly. I notice you ain't wearin' a hat . . ."

"I'll get one."

The sergeant flapped a hand. "Not so fast, Moraghan. Get yourself a stetson, high crown, and broad brim. Nothing floppy that'll fall down over your eyes when riding a horse at full gallop. A hat's important to a ranger. He uses it for drinking, for signaling, and to shade his eyes from the sun when napping. And those boots you're wearin' will never do. Clodhopper boots!" He snorted his contempt. "Get horse boots, pointed toes and high heels. Boots and hats, that's our main concern. We don't much care what a man wears in between, except nothing floppy. Nothing that will spook a horse, or get in the way of your handling your weapons, or a rope, or the reins."

"I'll outfit myself this afternoon."

The sergeant actually smiled for the first time. "You're a beaver, I'll say that for you. All right, Moraghan. Gather it all together and report back to me in the morning. I'll send you out with an old-timer to see how good you shoot. If you pass, you're a Texas Ranger!"

After making his purchases, which left him with
a thin poke, Brian rode along the beach to the edge
of town for a little target practice, especially with the
new rifle. He was glad he had been taught to shoot
early in life, and happy for all the time he had spent
hunting. He was good with a rifle, and a couple of
hours of practice familiarized him with the new one.

The Colt was another matter. The few times he had
fired it had been on the sly, when he had been able
to sneak off with it, and he had to be careful to re-
place the bullets he used, and equally careful to clean
it. Sean had once commented that he had a natural aptitude for handling guns, the comment accompanied
by an ironic, mysterious smile, and it would seem
that Brian had inherited his father's ability with rifles
and pistols.

After he tired of practice, Brian sat on the bluff
overlooking the gulf, knees drawn up. He had never
seen the ocean, and he found it fascinating, although
a touch frightening. It was close to dark when he
climbed on his horse and rode back into town.

The next morning he was grateful he'd taken the
time to practice, when he was escorted out of town by
a ranger named William Wallace, a towering, two-hun-
dred-pound Virginian. Even for a man of his great
size, Wallace's feet were all out of proportion, and his
boots were always well-worn before he bought a new
pair. He wore a thirteen boot, and replacements of
that size were expensive.

Bigfoot Wallace had long been a legend in the rangers, and Brian was somewhat in awe of him. It was
not known how many men he had killed in the pursuit of his duties. Yet Brian found him to be affable,
drawling, slow-moving.

They rode out of town along the sandy shoreline.
Finally Bigfoot Wallace called a halt, slid off his horse.
From his saddlebags he took several tin cans. Tossing

one in his hand, he drawled, "Want to be a ranger, do you, sonny?"

"Yes, sir."

"We don't go much for sirrin' in the rangers. Call me Bigfoot. Everbody else does. Now, I'm here to see how good a shot you are." His deepset eyes squinted at Brian. "How handy are you with Samuel Colt's invention?"

Brian started to lie, then swallowed and chose the truth. "I can shoot it, but at home I had to sneak it out of the house, so I ain't practiced too much."

"Honest, anyways. I like that. Thing is about shootin'; some old boys are born with the knack for it. Others now, they could practice until the cows come home, and never get it. Let's try a little game we call 'rollin' the can.' "

He tossed the can along the ground, sending it rolling toward the bluff. Wallace didn't wear a holster, but carried his gun jammed into his belt. He stood, hands at his sides, until the can had rolled halfway to the lip of the bluff. Then his right hand moved in a blur. The Colt, it seemed to Brian, was firing before it cleared his belt. Once, twice, five times, Wallace fired. Each bullet thunked into the can, sending it dancing and hopping along the ground, and the fifth bullet sent it sailing over the bluff to the beach below.

Wallace grinned lazily at Brian. "Your turn, sonny."

Taking a deep breath, Brian tried for a fast draw and almost dropped the gun. Finally, he brought it up and aimed it at the second can Wallace now sent rolling along the ground. Brian emptied the gun. Bullets kicked up spurts of sand. He hit the can once before it rolled off the edge, mostly of its own momentum.

Wallace whistled through his teeth. "I've seen better."

"Give me another chance," Brian said in dismay. "I know I can do better than that."

"I sure as shit hope so, sonny, and you'll get plenty

235

of chances." Wallace was methodically reloading the Colt. "That's what we're here for. Couple of things we have to clear up first. Now, a fast draw is necessary. Otherwise, you can get killed. Howsomever, *that* does come with practice. But the main thing is, you ain't got time to aim, sonny. Time you do that, you're a dead pigeon. A good shooter aims his pistol like he would a finger. Like this . . ." Wallace tossed another can a short distance away. "You got to learn to think of your gun as a finger and point it. Now, let's try her again."

With one shot he sent the can cartwheeling and nodded to Brian. This time Brian didn't try for a fast draw, but took his time, getting a firm grip, and as he swung the Colt up, he tried to think of it as his index finger pointing at the can. This time, he hit the can three times out of six, the last bullet sending it sailing into the waters of the gulf.

"At least you didn't have to kick it in, hoss," Wallace said dryly.

It was dim praise at best, and Brian swallowed his disappointment, but he was to learn in the coming days that when Bigfoot Wallace called a man "hoss," it carried the stamp of approval.

Wallace said, "Let's give that long barrel of yours a try. It looks spankin' new. Ever fired her?"

"It is new; I bought it on my way here." In another burst of candor, he added, "I fired it for the first time yesterday afternoon. But I've fired long guns at home."

From his saddle scabbard Wallace removed his own rifle. Brian noted that it was a Sharps, called the buffalo hunter's special. He knew it had an incredible range, and was deadly accurate up to 800 yards in the hands of a good shooter. Now, Wallace took an Indian arrow from his saddlebags. He walked about 40 yards to a palm tree and stuck the arrowhead into the trunk, the winged tip quivering.

236

Coming back to Brian, he hefted the Sharps. "Some advice, hoss. A long gun you *do* have to aim, you have to catch the sights."

He raised the rifle to his shoulder, holding it almost negligently. It didn't seem to Brian that he aimed at all before he fired. Brian watched in disbelief as the arrow 40 yards away disappeared! The rifle bullet had hit the feathered head, splintering the shaft, or maybe even driving it into the tree. Brian had heard of good shooters being able to do that. He desperately wanted to check, but feared that the big man would think his curiosity childish. Instead, he took out his own rifle.

Wallace studied it curiously. "One of them new Henrys, ain't she?"

"Yes, it is," Brian said proudly.

"One thing wrong with her, I understand. The bullet is its own cartridge case. Now, the purpose of a cartridge case is to keep the flame and gasses from spurting back into the shooter's face. I hear tell that some of them Henrys has scorched some noses pretty bad. Me, I'll stick with my old Sharps."

Already Wallace was walking toward the palm with another arrow. He drove it into the tree and strolled back. Brian took a deep breath, put the Henry to his shoulder, aimed down the barrel. He discovered that he was sweating, and before he could fire, he had to use his sleeve to wipe the sweat out of his eyes. Finally he fired, the rifle kicking back against his shoulder.

When the smoke cleared, he felt a tug of disappointment. The arrow was untouched. Wallace squinted at the tree and chuckled. "You missed her, boss, but it ain't too bad. About an inch to the right."

Brian stared hard at the tree. He couldn't see any sign of a bullet in the tree trunk, and wondered if the Virginian was hurrahing him. How could a man his age have the better eyesight? Again, he wanted to walk over and see for himself, but he didn't dare. Right now,

237

he was worried that Wallace would report back that he wasn't a good enough shot for the rangers.

As if reading his thoughts, Wallace clapped him on the shoulder. "You'll do all right, hoss. You've got the makings of a shooter. Right now, we ain't too busy. The greasers are whipped, for the second time, and most of the redsticks are quiet, so we'll just mosey out here ever day for a spell and get in a litttle practice."

Brian heaved a sigh of relief. "I'm mighty obliged to you, Mr. . . . Uh, Bigfoot, for taking the time and trouble."

"Not all that much trouble, hoss," the big man drawled. "Not for a man I take a likin' to. Now, suppose we have a snort, huh?"

Wallace took a brown bottle from his saddlebags and led Brian over to the meager shade of the palm. Brian stole a quick, furtive look at the trunk, and saw that Wallace was right—his rifle bullet was sunk into the tree an inch to the right of the arrow.

He hunkered down beside the ranger. Wallace gave the bottle to Brian, who took a hearty swallow of the liquor. It went down his throat like fire and he coughed.

Wallace slapped him on the back. "Powful potent, ain't it?" He took the bottle back and drank in a single swallow almost half of what was left.

Brian's attention was drawn to Wallace's hands. The one wrapped around the bottle almost swallowed it. Wallace, noting the direction of his glance, laughed.

"Big, ain't they?" he said comfortably. "Near as big as my feet. Helps to have big paws, howsomever, shootin', handling a Bowie, or just plain bare-knuckle fighting. A time or two, though, it came close to costin' me my life. I recollect one time, back in '42 it was." He paused to take another pull at the bottle, passing it to Brian.

"It was durin' the Mexican War. We Texans weren't doin' too well. The Mex forces, under the command

238

of General Adrian Woll, drove us across the Rio Grande, but we reorganized under Captain Jack Hays of the rangers. A real pisser, Coffee Jack. We rose up and drove them Mexicans back across the Rio.

"Captain Hays was smart, too. He stopped at the Rio Grande, sayin' it was one thing to fight off an invader on Texas soil, but another thing entire to venture onto foreign soil. But three hundred of us Texans was downright foolish. The Three Hundred elected Will Fisher as our commander, and set off in pursuit of the Mexican army. We arrived at a poor-ass adobe town called Mier. We attacked, hoping to take the place, but the Mex army arrived and killed some of us, takin' the rest as prisoners. The agreement was that we would be treated as prisoners of war and held near the Texas border.

"Seems us Texans hadn't learned the lesson of Goliad and the Alamo. Instead, they marched us south, to Matamoros, then Monterey. There, they turned us over to another Mex officer and herded us some hundred miles south to Haciendo Salado. Now, we had been talking of escapin' since the day we'd been captured, and we knew this was our last chance. At sunrise, we seized the guards, captured the ammunition stores, drove off the cavalry, and whipped the infantry. We had five dead and several wounded.

"We set out north for the Rio Grande. That was our mistake, right there. Some of us old hands might have made it, but most of us didn't know shit about survivin' in the desert, and that's what it was. A place that the Almighty had forgot, and left to the devil's devices. Maybe if we'd stayed on the main trails, we might have made it through, but our commanders were afraid that the Mexicans might find and recapture us. So, we set off across the desert and got lost. We had damned little food and water, and that was soon gone.

"We ate snakes and grasshoppers, dug into the

239

ground for wet dirt to moisten our mouths. Some were so damfool as to drink their own piss, and I reckon I don't have to tell you what *that* can do to a man!

"Well, the long and short of it is, the Mexicans finally found us. Five of us died, four got away and later reached Texas, and three was never heard from again. The rest of us was taken back to Salado in irons. Santa Anna, who was still runnin' Mexico, was beside himself. First, he said we was all to be shot, but this kicked up such a fuss from the Americans and from the British ministers in Mexico, that he relented a bit.

"Instead of all bein' shot, ever tenth man was to be shot! They dreamed up a bear of a way to pick that ever tenth man. They took a pitcher and poured in 159 white beans and 17 black ones. The suckers drawin' the black beans was to be shot at sunrise.

"Now my mammy didn't raise no fool. I watched real careful as them beans went into the pitcher. I noticed that the white beans went in first, and the black ones went in last. They didn't shake the pitcher, so I figured that the black beans stayed on top.

"So, I dipped way down to the bottom, and got me a white one! The trouble was," Wallace laughed uproariously, "my dad-blamed paw was so big I had trouble getting it into the mouth of the pitcher and down deep enough. And that's the way I came damned close to bein' shot, cause my hands are too big!"

Brian soon learned that Bigfoot Wallace was right— it was a time of relative peace for the rangers. He remained in Corpus Christi for over two months before a trouble spot developed. It would have been a boring two months, except for the ability of the Teaxs Rangers to find ways to amuse themselves. The means they could dream up to alleviate dullness were amazing, and fit right into Brian's way of life. The rangers loved games, and if none existed, they devised new ones.

They attended all horse races, betting heavily, and

if no races were available, they arranged racing events themselves, usually participating in them.

Cockfights were common. The Mexican people loved cockfights and so did the rangers. Brian soon became an afficionado, and was present whenever one took place. He had always loved to gamble, and now he could indulge in it without fear of neighborly or parental disapproval.

But what was most fascinating were the amusements the rangers devised themselves. Shooting matches were naturally commonplace, but other events were not.

Most of their games were played on horseback. One favorite was the "chicken tournament." In this game a chicken was the prize. There was always two groups of mounted contestants. They elected one rider to take the chicken and set off hell-bent for the opponent's goal. The riders on the other team tried to block him, ride him down, or take the chicken by brute force. It was a rough sport, hard on horses, risky to the participants, and always fatal to the chicken. Brian not only loved it, but excelled at it. He had been a fair horseman before, but after a month at their games, he became a skilled rider.

He was particularly skillful in the ring tournaments. In this sport small rings were suspended from posts, the number of posts varying. The player, using a long, pointed stick as a lance, rode at a fast pace down the line of posts, catching as many rings as possible on the wooden lance. Before long Brian became the reigning champion of this game. If a ranger caught half or more of the rings, he was considered good; yet it wasn't long before Brian was able to make a clean sweep. Soon, they handicapped him, adding more posts and more rings; yet more often than not, he snared them all.

The winner of each tournament was awarded a wreath of flowers. And this brought about the side benefit that most interested Brian. The tournaments were always attended by a number of local beauties, and it was the custom for the tournament champion to present the flower wreath to the girl of his choice, thus crowning her queen of the tournament.

This, in Brian's case at least, was seldom the end of it. The queen often ended up awarding him her sexual favors, and Brian not only became the best rider in the rangers, but he garnered a reputation as the best cocksman, a reputation he prized above all others.

He courted the women with his usual dash and flair, but as back home, he was far from discreet, so it wasn't long before he had several fathers, swains, and even husbands angry at him. He had already been challenged to a pistol duel, from which he emerged the victor, his challenger barely escaping with his life.

It was for this reason that he was just as happy when Indian trouble broke out along the Red River to the north, and his troop was called into action, under the command of Bigfoot Wallace.

They weren't on the trail long before Brian was damned glad he'd had some preparation for this. True, there hadn't been any formal training; yet the horseback games had toughened him physically, and he could easily hold his own with these hard-bitten, hard-riding Texas Rangers. Brian had a hunch that he would also be grateful for the daily gunmanship lessons under Bigfoot Wallace's tutelage.

The day before they left Corpus Christi, at Brian's last shooting lesson, Wallace had drawled, "I reckon I can tell you now . . ." He had clapped Brian on the shoulder. "You can hold your own now, pistol or long gun. Horses, you're a natural, the best I've ever seen. Women?" He guffawed. "Too bad you won't be runnin' into many up along the Red. Still pretty sparsely settled. Oh, might be a few squaws you can take on. But a word of warnin', hoss . . . You spread the blankets with some Indian wench, you better keep a wary eye peeled. Most of 'em hate white men. They might seem itchy to bed down with one of us, but you be careful, hear? Some of 'em have been known to take a knife to the blankets with them, and many an old boy has lost his pecker that way."

Laughing, Brian said, "I'll watch it, Bigfoot."

Brian learned that Captain Wallace had orders not to take prisoners, but to kill Indians, Comanche in this instance. The rangers liked simple orders.

The Red River, where the Comanche were on the warpath, was a long haul up from Corpus Christi, and the rangers rode hard. There were close to a hundred rangers, one of the largest groups to see action since the Mexican War. Fifteen mules, two supply wagons, and an ambulance accompanied them.

They rode from dawn to dusk, steadily eating up the miles. Brian settled into the life easily; he came to love it, in fact. There was only one lack that cramped his style—he still couldn't cook. He made out as best he could, stoically eating meat either undercooked or charred. He simply didn't have the patience for cooking. Leaving a rabbit cooking over his campfire, he would wander over to the next cooking fire and listen to the rangers yarning. He was endlessly fascinated by the yarns they spun—mostly lies, he suspected, but entertaining nonetheless. By the time he got back to his own supper, it would be burned.

Brian saw his first Indian reservation, on the Clear Fork of the Brazos, where his troop stopped off to pick up a number of friendlies—Indians to guide them across the Red. The rangers were not supposed to cross the Red River, which took them out of Texas, but they were tired of Comanche raiding and killing into Texas, then fleeing across the Red to sanctuary. Captain Wallace swore that this time they would put an end to that, once and for all. The Indians on the reservation were from friendly tribes, such as the Caddo, Nadarko, Waco, and others. They were willing to help defeat the Comanche because the latter were wild and warlike, and hated all reservation Indians. The Comanche raided into North Central Texas, killing Indians and whites alike; but the white settlers could not—or did not bother to—differentiate beween Comanche and friendly Indians, so remained hostile to all.

Three days after the ranger troop crossed the Red, two Indian scouts killed a buffalo and found two Comanche arrows embedded in the animal's hide. Scouting ahead, they found the Comanche encampment; the Comanche were over 200 strong. The scouts rode back to the main column of rangers and alerted Captain Wallace. Brian was riding nearby when the scouts came with the news.

Wallace grinned easily and drawled, "Well, gents, I reckon nobody is too upset by this news. You've all been spoilin' for a ruckus, so now you got one. Some 200 redsticks waiting to give us what for. All right, men," his voice became brisk, "make camp for the night. Get a good night's rest, 'cause we're gonna hit them about sunup in the morning!"

On the eve of his first combat, Brian found sleep hard to come by. He lay on his blankets, staring up at the glitter of a million stars, his thoughts circling endlessly but always coming back to the morning. He had never given much thought to the possibility of his own death, but he knew that no matter how good a horseman, how good a shot he was, a random arrow or a bullet could end his life in a second.

Did he have any regrets? His answer to that was prompt—none. Some people might look upon his fleeing home with disfavor; yet it was understandable to Brian in the context of the circumstances. Would he be missed at home? Nora Moraghan would grieve—he never for a moment doubted that, but would his father? Or was Sean so incensed by what he had done to Kate, and by his subsequent flight, that he would greet the news of his eldest son's death with a stony countenance?

244

And Kate . . . He counted back. She had been pregnant six months now; three more months, more or less, and he would be a father. If he were to die tomorrow, would he, in the last instant of his life, regret that he had never seen his son? Again, in all honesty, he could say that he would not. Brian had long thought parenthood an accident, and his own contretemps with Kate gave him no cause to change that opinion.

"What the hell am I worried about?" he said aloud, laughing. "I'm indestructible!"

Startled at the sound of his own voice, he glanced around. His voice had disturbed no one; all he could see were the unmoving mounds of sleeping rangers.

He turned over and went to sleep.

Shortly before sunup the next morning, the troop of rangers charged out of the trees on the ridge above the Indian village, and raced down among about 50 lodges, yelling and firing.

The Comanche, clearly caught unaware, staggered out of their lodges to be shot down one by one. One Comanche, emerging from a tepee just as Brian rode past, sprang off the ground with amazing agility, and to Brian's utter amazement, he landed on his mount's back, facing him. The Indian was naked except for a breechclout, and he was rank with the odor of grease. His fierce eyes blazed into Brian's. So startled was he by it all, riding along with the savagely grinning face inches from his, Brian almost lost his life. He had failed to note the tomahawk in the hand of the Comanche! He saw it out of the corner of one eye just in time and brought his left hand up to fend it off. The tomahawk struck his arm a glancing blow, numbing it, but he managed to fasten his fingers around the Indian's wrist.

He had been riding among the lodges firing his rifle, and, again belatedly, he realized that he had lost the rifle when the savage vaulted onto the horse.

His mind finally functioning again, Brian groped desperately for the Colt on his hip. Thumbing the hammer back, he brought it up and fired directly into the face of the Indian. The face disappeared, leaving a red mass of bleeding flesh, and then the Indian was gone, falling free. Brian reined in his horse, wheeled him about. The Comanche, tomahawk still clutched in his hand, lay sprawled in death.

Brian saw his Henry lying a few feet farther on. He slid off the horse, started to detour around the dead Comanche, but his gaze was drawn to it, and he saw the hole his bullet had made in the back of the Indian's head. The exit hole was rimmed with gray matter, and Brian had to turn aside and puke.

On one knee, still wracked by spasms, he suddenly remembered Sean telling of the Battle of San Jacinto, and how he had vomited after killing his first man. At the time Brian had been contemptuous of his father. The man he had killed had been not only a Mexican but an enemy. So why puke? And this man, this man he had killed, was not only an Indian but an enemy.

Brian grinned weakly to himself. That once, at least, you were right, Daddy.

"Draw first blood, hoss?"

Brian looked up into Bigfoot Wallace's smiling face. He got to his feet quickly, swiped at his mouth. "I'm sorry . . ."

"Nothing to be sorry for. Hell, I puked my supper when I killed my first. Course . . ." The Virginian chuckled. "That was so far back I can hardly remember."

Wallace raked the area with a glance. The Indian lodges had all been fired, and the ground was strewn with Comanche dead. In the distance Brian could see four rangers on horseback, giving chase to two fleeing Indians.

Bigfoot Wallace nodded in satisfaction. "Looks like it's all about over. Not bad, considerin' we lost only five men dead, plus two Indian scouts, and we got a few wounded. I figure we got a hundred or so dead Comanche. No prisoners to feed and take care of, either."

Wallace rode his horse to the edge of the village. Brian retrieved his rifle. And now, weaving his way through the Indian dead, he noticed that many were women and children, and his stomach rebelled again.

Fixing his gaze resolutely on his horse grazing at the edge of the Indian encampment, he strode on. He recalled what one ranger, an old Indian fighter, had told him on the way: "When you fight redsticks, young feller, you kill squaws, children, the whole kit and ka-boodle. That may strike you as rough, but any papoose you leave alive will only grow up and have to be killed another day, and no telling how many white scalps he'll take before that. The squaws . . . Well, let them live and what happens? They breed like rabbits. Naw, when you go after Injuns, kill ever one of 'em. It's the only way."

At the time Brian thought the man's words made sense, but the actual fact, seeing women and children dead, even some with dead babies in their arms, was something else again. Well, he had wanted excitement and adventure. To attain that, there evidently was a price to pay. If they remained here long enough fighting Comanche, Brian was confident that he would become hardened to it.

His group of rangers did remain along the Red River for six months. Orders had come from the governor's office that the Comanche were to be kept north of the Red, in any manner necessary. Bigfoot Wallace and his troop of rangers patrolled the Red, occasionally engaging in both minor and sometimes fierce skirmishes with the warring Comanche.

So Brian did become accustomed to killing Indians, and he had killed at least a half-dozen at the end of the six months. But they were all warriors, Comanche in fighting regalia, and although the rangers ventured across the Red a number of times to attack Indian villages, Brian was always careful to shoot above the heads of women and children.

During the extended campaign, he became almost as dark from exposure to the sun as the Indians he fought; he gained an inch in height, and lost five pounds in weight, becoming as hard and tough as rawhide.

When orders came to return to Corpus Christi, Brian was more than ready. During all his time on this frontier, he had seen a mere handful of white women, and they were all middle-aged or older. Remembering Wallace's advice, he at first steered clear of Indian women, but finally the enforced celibacy proved too much. Since the men often camped near an Indian reservation, there were any number of comely and available squaws.

He found them surprisingly passionate lovers, and not a one offered him any harm. He concluded that Wallace had been joshing him. Of course his blanket mates were all from the reservation tribes, and it might have been a different matter had he bedded down with a Comanche.

At any rate, he was just as happy to return to civilization. Always a fastidious man, Brian found the Indians' eating habits distasteful, and they were not known for cleanliness. Their lodges crawled with parasites, and the air in a closed lodge was foul due to various cooking odors.

Brian had been gone from home close to a year when he rode again into Corpus Christi with the rangers. The news awaited them that another period of peace with the Indians was anticipated by the state government, and the word was that the rangers were going to be reduced in number.

It was explained to Brian that this was nothing new in their experience. It had been occurring since the Mexican War; the official thinking was that the rangers

248

were not needed in times of peace, at least not in such numbers, and constituted an unnecessary drain on the state treasury.

Bigfoot Wallace shrugged. "Course it won't last, hoss. The minute the redsticks get rambunctious, they'll be callin' on us, and screamin' for recruits. It's something we old-timers are used to."

"But what exactly does it mean? To me, I mean?"

"It means, hoss, since you're one of the newer members, you'd be one of the first to go. But I got a favor or two owed, so if you like, I'll see to it that you stay in."

Brian started to accept the offer, then hesitated. He had joined the Texas Rangers mainly to escape the tedium of his life at home, but if the rangers were about to settle down to a peaceful existence, it could become dull too.

He said slowly, "Let me think about it, Bigfoot. I'll let you know."

"Sure, hoss."

That afternoon, as he was about to enter a tavern, there was a call. "Hey, Moraghan! Brian Moraghan!"

He faced about warily, remembering the disgruntled husbands and lovers he had left behind before departing for the Red River. He didn't immediately recognize the man getting off a horse and striding toward him. He was tall, shambling, his face shadowed by a wide-brimmed cowboy hat. The man peered from under the hat. "It *is* Brian Moraghan, ain't it?"

"Yes, I'm Brian Moraghan . . ." Then he recognized the man. Harvey Simpson. Simpson was a fiddle-foot who had lived around Nacogdoches for a time, but the wanderlust had seized him a few years back and he had meandered out to West Texas where he became a cowpuncher. Brian had seen him last two years ago when he'd come through with a trail herd of cattle bound for New Orleans.

"Hello, Harvey. How are you?"

"I'm fine, Brian," Simpson said heartily. "But what are you doing here in Corpus Christi, so far from home?"

"Oh, I joined the rangers about a year ago." Apparently, Simpson had no inkling of the circumstances under which Brian had left home so suddenly.

". . . passed through your home territory just last month. You been gone a year; reckon you ain't seen your niece yet."

"Niece?" Brian blinked.

"Yep, your brother Kevin, and that old girl he married, Kate . . . What was her name before she married? Oh, yeah, Joe Lyons's gal . . . Anyways, she gave that brother of yours a daughter not too long back." Simpson winked. "Guess old Kev got in there a little early. Way I get it, they had a six-months' baby!"

20

When Sean learned that Kate Lyons had consented to
be Kevin's wife, he felt scorn for her. What kind of
woman was she who would copulate with Brian, then
marry his brother when he left hurriedly? And then
when he learned that Kate was pregnant, he knew that
the child had to be Brian's, and he felt more scorn
for her.

He even felt a stirring of compassion for Kevin.
Poor sod, poor fool! No, not a fool, because Kevin,
whatever else he was, was far from stupid, and he had
to know that the coming child was not his.

The knowledge was a terrible weight on Sean's mind.
To know that his first grandchild, from Brian's seed,
was soon to come into the world, and never to be able
to accept the child for a true Moraghan, was hard to
endure. For a time he considered going to Kevin with
the truth, and offering to take the baby into his own
house after birth, and raise it as his own true grand-

child. When Kevin had announced his marriage to Kate, Sean had offered to let the newlyweds farm the old Ty Reynolds place to the south, and also offered to build them a house to live in. Everyone had tongues wagging over the generosity of the gesture—except Nora, who had guessed it all.

"You're happy to have a chance to get Kevin out of the house. You think I don't know that?"

"For once you could be wrong about me," he said stiffly. "Since Kevin is your son and not mine . . ."

"And you're never going to let me forget that, are you?"

He went on as if she hadn't spoken, ". . . I consider that I'm doing well by the boy."

"I notice you aren't giving him title to the land, and you're saving this house and land for Brian, when he comes back, of course."

He was plunged into gloom. "*If* he ever comes back."

Immediately contrite, she said, "I'm sorry, darling. As your son, Brian is entitled to the homeplace, I can't contest that. And don't worry about him, Brian is well able to take care of himself. Wherever he is, he's safe and sound. I'm sure of it. I have this feeling. If he wasn't all right, I would know about it. But I'm puzzled as to the reason he just up and took off like that. Brian is impulsive, but to do something like that!"

Sean could have told her, of course. The boy had been fleeing from his sins. In a way, Sean felt responsible for Brian's abrupt departure. If he had only said something that night in the cabin, let his rage wash over the boy, Brian might still be there.

Yet his outrage had been total, and he hadn't trusted himself to speak, afraid that he would say something that would drive Brian away forever. He had wheeled away, determined to let his anger cool for a day or so before he spoke his mind. After all, Brian was too

252

old to take the strap to, and it was hardly a whipping offense anyway.

But before he judged he was calm enough to talk rationally, it was too late—Brian was gone. Brian, the light of his life, the son who one day would take over the reins of Moraghan Acres, was gone!

For her part, Nora suspected that Sean knew the reason for Brian's flight. Yet she also knew that it must be something pretty dreadful, in which case it would be useless to query Sean about it. He had few secrets from her, but those that he did have could not have been wrung from him by even the worst torture.

Her grief over her older son's running away was alleviated somewhat by Kevin's announcement that he was marrying Kate Lyons. He was young, only just eighteen, and some months younger than Kate, but men and women in this country married young. And when Nora learned that the newly marrieds would be living on Ty Reynolds's old place, she was just as glad. They would not be so far away that she couldn't visit them at any time, and Kevin, at last, would be out of Sean's immediate presence. She understood Sean's feelings toward Kevin, which did not mean that she was happy about it; yet she recognized that it would probably always be that way. Perhaps some of Sean's animosity might diminish if Kevin wasn't always around to remind him of how he came to be.

She was more than a little surprised when Kate announced, one afternoon not too long after they had settled in, that she was pregnant. They were living in a rough lean-to until the house could be built. The elders had offered to house the couple until the new house was finished, but Kevin had reacted rather strangely, Nora thought, claiming that they wished to be by themselves. Sean had barely managed to conceal his relief.

Kate and Nora were having tea alone, Kevin out supervising the carpenters at work on the house. The first thought that popped into Nora's mind, on hearing Kate's news, was that this was the reason they had wished to live by themselves. Since they had only been married a month, there was no way the baby could be passed off as being simply premature, and being under the Moraghan roof with a bastard baby growing in Kate would have been awkward.

Her second thought brought an involuntary smile to Nora's face. So now we have another bastard baby in the Moraghan family! Yet Sean couldn't complain about this one, since the legal father was present, and Brian had also been, strictly speaking, a bastard. What was it with the Moraghans? Did bastardy run in the family? She laughed aloud.

Kate arched an eyebrow. "You look upon it as humorous, Nora? I should think you would be scandalized!"

"Dear Kate, no!" She touched the girl's hand. "I'm happy for both of you. Although I fear I may feel old, old," she pulled a face, "having a grandchild come along."

Kate's eyes came alive with humor. "Nora, I don't think you'll ever be really old, not even if you live to be a hundred." A shadow crossed her face. "But I'm afraid that folks will snigger behind my back at having a baby this soon."

"Hellfire and spit, don't fret about what people think or say. It's none of their business. If they didn't have *that* to gossip about, it would be something else. And there's one benefit to being a Moraghan. People may talk among themselves, but few will dare say anything to your face."

Kate said hesitantly, "Do you think . . . How will Kevin's father look upon this? I know Kevin is dreading him finding out."

It was on the tip of Nora's tongue to tell Kate

about Kevin's true parentage, but she stopped herself at the last instant. Instead, she said, "I'll let you in on a little family secret, Kate. Don't ever tell another living soul, not even Kevin. I was several months' pregnant with Brian before Sean and I got married."

Kate gasped. "You're not serious!"

"Oh, dead serious. So don't think that your situation is unique. With more men than women on the frontier, it happens more often than not. It's fortunate you are that Kevin was willing to wed you. Many times the man just ups and takes off for parts unknown."

Nora was puzzled by Kate's sudden expression of anguish, as quickly hidden. Nora said, "Now I'll have to get busy and write an entertainment featuring a pregnant woman, so you can play the role."

Nora told Sean about Kate's pregnancy at supper that evening.

They were eating in the new dining room. When building the house, Sean had constructed it so that additions could be made from time to time, and additional rooms wouldn't have a tacked-on appearance. The new dining room was spacious, built facing the river, with wide bay windows that could be opened to catch a breeze, when there was one. The new expense had shocked Nora's frugal soul—she still had difficulty adjusting to the fact that they were wealthy now and could afford anything within reason. Yet she had to admit that she was slowly accepting, and enjoying, more leisure time allowed her by a household of serving people. For instance, she no longer cooked, and even now their supper was being served by María, their maid from one of the few Mexican families along the river. The irony of it didn't elude her—a serving-woman and a cook now that both boys were gone, only she and Sean left in the house.

When told of Kate's condition, Sean looked thunderstruck. Then, in a voice muted with anger, he said, "Lord God Almighty! I should have known!"

"Known what, darling? How could you have known that Kate was pregnant, when even I didn't know until today?"

He gave a start. "Oh! That isn't what I meant . . ." He broke off again, staring out the window at the river below, a strange look on his face.

"Sean?"

His glance moved back to her. He sighed, his expression guarded now. "What I meant was, I should have known that Kevin would do something like this, getting a girl with child and having to marry her."

"Hellfire and spit! I reckon you'll always think the worst of Kevin, won't you? I hoped that when he was out of the house . . ." She leaned forward. "You have a short memory, Sean. You got me pregnant before we wed, and you a celibate priest yet!"

He winced. "That's a low blow, Nora."

"Is it now? Why is it any different from Kevin now?"

He said stiffly, "You were a party to it, as I remember."

"I was. I don't deny it, and I'm not ashamed of it. I haven't regretted it for a moment . . . Except when you're being so damned unreasonable! Sean, if you make either Kevin or Kate ashamed of this, I'll never, never forgive you!"

"I can't help the way I feel, Nora. Wait now!" He held up his hands, palms toward her. "I have no intention of causing them any discomfort. That, I promise you."

Mollified, she leaned back. "The thing that surprises me, is Kevin being bold enough for this. He's so shy. Brian now, it wouldn't have surprised me."

Again, Sean got that strange, inward look.

"Sean? What are you thinking?"

All of a sudden, his face was transformed with a

smile of dancing mischief. "I was just thinking that we Moraghans seem to have an affinity for bastardy, don't we?"

She laughed in delight. "Sometimes, we really *are* of one mind! That very same thought came to me when Kate told me." She sobered. "*We* Moraghans, you said. Does that mean you've finally accepted Kevin as one of the family?"

His face went still and cold. He threw down his napkin and left the room without a word.

The thing that his parents did not understand, was the depth of Kevin's love for Kate Lyons. Kevin knew about the intensity of first love; yet he was positive that it went far beyond that. With that sensitivity of his for the feelings of others, he knew that Sean didn't, for whatever puzzling reason, love him in the way a father should. Nora loved him, of course, but somehow it didn't compensate. With Kate, he would have someone of his own, someone who would love him without question—at least that had long been his hope.

He was far from sure about this, on that day, nearly six months back, when she told him about the coming baby. It was a lazy Sunday afternoon, and they were strolling hand in hand along the river. Kevin had long determined to ask her to marry him on his eighteenth birthday, which was still some months distant, but something about her strange behavior of late—quiet, unusually pensive, often melancholy—prompted him to postpone it no longer.

Spring was well along and grass grew high on the riverbank. Bees hummed a drowsy song. Wild flowers bloomed, and butterflies filled the air with fluttering color. Kevin took out his handkerchief and spread it on the grass for her to sit.

She sat down gracefully, tenting her long skirt over her drawn-up knees. She stared dreamily at the swiftly flowing water.

257

"Kate . . ." He took her hand. "You must know that I love you."

She gave him a faintly startled look. Then her eyes became gentle, her mouth shaping a tender smile. "Yes, dear Kevin, I know. I love you, too. Lately, I've come to realize just how much."

"Well . . ." He cleared his throat. "I want to ask you to marry me. I know, I'm not yet eighteen," he said in a rush, "but I soon will be. I was going to wait until after my birthday, but . . ."

Her gaze clung to his face. "Why didn't you?"

"I don't know. It's just that . . . Well, these past weeks, there's been a change in you, and I was afraid if I waited, it might be too late."

"Yes, Kevin." She sighed. "There *has* been a change. I'm pregnant."

Kevin was hushed, his mind frozen. In the quiet the various sounds around him seemed louder. He fancied he could even hear the catfish swimming past. Then his thoughts went on apace, and intuitively, he said, "It's Brian, isn't it? That's why he left so suddenly."

"Yes, Kevin, it's Brian."

"Does Daddy or my mother know?"

"Your father probably will, when he learns I'm with child."

Kevin was silent for a little, staring unseeingly at the river.

"Kevin?"

"Yes?"

"Do you hate me now?"

He considered the question for some time before looking around at her. "No, Kate, I don't hate you. I could never do that. I love you as much as ever. But this changes a few things. We can't live at home now."

"I don't follow you . . ."

"After we get married, we can't live at home. We'll

258

have to find a place of our own." He smiled suddenly. "For you'll *have* to marry me now. The child must have a father. Brian, Brian would not take well to fatherhood, I suspect."

Kate shook her head, long hair swinging. "I would never marry Brian, no matter what. But Kevin . . . Do you still want to marry me after what I just told you?"

"Of course," he said simply. "If you love someone, you accept them for what they are."

"You won't feel like you're taking Brian's leavings?" At his wince, she took his hand, squeezed it. "I'm sorry, Kevin, but it must be spoken of."

He nodded with a sober face. "If you mean, I'd rather it hadn't come about this way, yes. I would have been happier if I had been the first man in your life. But it didn't happen that way, and . . . Well, Brian is Brian."

"And you still want to marry me?"

"I do, yes. Even if you don't love me. I'll accept you on those terms."

"But I do love you. You are the dearest, sweetest man in the whole wide world, and I love you. Don't ask me to explain Brian. I think I must have been temporarily mad. It was like, well, like I couldn't help myself."

Kevin nodded. "I've noticed that Brian has that effect on people. Even me. There have been times when he got me into scrapes that I would never have gotten into alone."

"Like the sporting house in New Orleans?"

He gave her a startled look. "How did you know about that? Oh . . . Hank told you, didn't he?"

"Hank told me. That was the first time for you?"

In an agony of embarrassment, he looked away. "I'm ashamed to answer a question like that, Kate."

"Why should you be? It's a perfectly normal thing, certainly nothing to be ashamed of. What I did was far worse. So, here we are, two sinners! What do we do about it?"

"Do? What do you mean?"

"We love each other, we have both sinned. So . . ."

Her meaning was clear, and Kevin found himself beyond astonishment at this surprising woman. His heart began to pound, his palms to sweat, and his organ stirred like a small animal in its nest.

Her smile tender and knowing, Kate framed his face with her hands and kissed him. Her mouth was soft and warm, and Kevin muttered as her tongue invaded his mouth. Her boldness was an aphrodisiac—not that he needed one.

The kiss itself was a welding, creating a oneness almost as close as the joining of their bodies. Their passions swept them along, and neither took heed of the fact that they were out in the open. It seemed such a natural thing that there was no need for darkness, no need for a place of concealment.

Although Kevin was still awkward, unsure, he was glad of the one experience. His hand went under Kate's voluminous skirts, his nerve endings electrified by the sleekness of smooth thighs. When his probing fingers encountered her mound, Kate sighed, pelvis leaping at his touch, and she whispered, "Wait, darling."

She pulled away from him, half-turning aside, and was back almost immediately, dress up around her waist, and Kevin touched the red, luxuriant fleece in wonder. Reverently he parted the pubic pelt and caressed the moist lips. Again Kate's hips arched.

Kevin's organ was swollen, throbbing against the tightness of his breeches. Kate raised a thigh and rubbed against the hardness.

"Inside me, sweetheart," she said huskily. "I want you inside me." Even as she spoke, her hands were busy at the buttons of his breeches. She extricated his engorged organ, and manipulated it for a moment, until Kevin feared he would explode. And then, without his ever knowing exactly how it came about, he was inside her, and they were together, moving as one.

Kevin's pleasure was intense. He thrust into her frantically, awkwardly. Kate murmured soothing sounds. She reached up and pulled his mouth down to hers, and corralled his wildness between her supple thighs.

His orgasm began, his loins convulsed mightly. He was afraid that it was too soon for Kate, but there was no holding back. Then a muted cry came from her. She took her mouth from his with a sound almost of anguish, her head rolling back and forth on the ground. Her hips arched, shuddering, holding him off the ground.

After a long moment she sighed and relaxed, still holding him inside her. Kevin rested gingerly on her, trying to sort out the various sensations he had experienced. Inevitably he compared it to the night in New Orleans. He had felt pleasure there, of course, but also guilt and some shame.

There was nothing of that this time. He felt only joy at the remembered pleasure. He said tentatively, "Kate?"

"Yes, dear Kevin?"

"Was it . . . good for you?"

"Oh, yes. Yes, yes!" She looped her arms around his neck and rained kisses on his mouth, nose, cheeks, forehead. "It was grand!"

"I was afraid," already regretting what he was about to say but seemingly driven to it, "that after Brian . . ."

"Hush!" She clamped her hand over his mouth. "I won't engage in a game of who is the better lover, you or Brian. It makes me feel lower than dog shit, Kevin Moraghan!" Those eyes blazed like green fire.

He drew back, abashed. He had seen flashes of

Kate's temper before and had been amused, but it was different directed at him. "I'm sorry, Kate. I didn't mean it that way."

"You didn't? Then how did you mean it? If I'm to marry you, I want your promise that this is the last time Brian's name will crop up in this regard. I don't care to go through life always on the lookout for his name to come up. It'll be like waiting for a bear trap to snatch at me!"

As she talked, she was busy arranging her clothes, pulling up, snapping fasteners. He tried to grab her hand, but Kate, still furious, eluded him. He said, "I promise, Kate."

"All right!" Then she became still, her eyes meeting his. She sighed. "I've noticed this before. You've always looked up to Brian too much, following his lead. I've often thought you were secretly comparing everything you do to what *he* would do, and finding yourself lacking. Well, I won't have it with *us,* you hear? Brian is Brian, and you're you, two different men, and it's time you realized that."

He thought for a moment, staring away. Slowly he nodded. "You're probably right. I can see that now. It won't happen again." He squared his shoulders and looked at her. "But you *will* marry me?"

She assumed a look of wide-eyed innocence. "Of course, my darling Kevin! I thought that was already decided . . . especially after . . ." she smothered a bawdy laugh behind her hand, "what just happened."

Yet, despite Kevin's resolves, when the baby was born—a girl they named Debra Lee, after Kate's maternal grandmother—he couldn't help but wonder, staring down at the red, wrinkled face cradled on Kate's shoulders, if the child would grow up to resemble his brother.

They were alone in the lean-to at the moment. Nora, who had come over to help with the birth, was outside washing out the things she had used. Kate, red hair around her face like a tousled halo, smiled wanly up at him. She had come through the ordeal well.

She saw the look and divined its cause immediately. "There's nothing yet to tell, you goose. But she does have my green eyes, and her hair is going to be red like mine. As for the rest, I think there's little cause for worry. She's a girl, and people tend to look for a resemblance to the mother. When a son comes along, and I will give you sons, dear Kevin, it will look like you. You can be sure of that."

Kevin leaned down to kiss her sweaty forehead. Her eyes closed and she drifted into sleep. Kevin went outside to where his mother stood by the fire waiting for a kettle of water to boil.

Hearing his footsteps, Nora straightened up, hands bracing the small of her back. "Congratulations, Daddy! I reckon eighteen isn't too young to be a father in this country."

"Thank you, Momma." He kissed her absently.

Nora ran her palm down his cheek. "Happy, son?"

"Very happy. I love Kate very much. Momma . . ." His glance strayed in the direction of the big house, too far away to see, but it sprang vividly into his mind's eye. "Where's Daddy? Why didn't he come?"

"He'll be over soon, Kevin." Her gaze dropped away. "You know how it is. Many times pregnant women seem to be near their time, but aren't. Sean said he'd wait until the baby is actually here, then he'll come see it."

Which was not what he said at all. "Why should I go see the bastard of a bastard?"

"Sean Moraghan, I've had about all of this I can take! You're going over to see that baby, if I have to drag you! Hellfire and spit, it'll be your own grandchild!"

But when she got home that evening and told Sean that he had a granddaughter, named Debra Lee, his face was still for a moment, and she sensed a sudden easing of the tension in him. He smiled slowly. "A granddaughter, is it? I'll have to go over in the morning and see her."

Nora, with one of her intuitive flashes, realized why he felt a sense of relief—he had a granddaughter, not a grandson. A girl didn't matter all that much to him. But if the baby had been male, the first Moraghan grandson, he would have had to whip himself into going to see the child.

For the first time Nora felt a stirring of pity for him, but she was careful to screen it out of her expression. It would never do to let him know; yet she could grasp the torment he was going through. Which did not in any way excuse his behavior, in her estimation. But Sean was what he was, and it would always be this way.

✕ They were at breakfast one morning a few months later when they heard hoofbeats approaching, followed by shouts from the servants.

Sean looked up from his eggs and ham. "I wonder who that could be at this time of the day?"

Nora started to get up. "I'll go see."

"No, sweet." He waved her back down, smiling faintly. "It's time you learned to accept the fact that we have servants. How would it look for the mistress of Moraghan Acres to go scurrying out to greet a guest?"

"Mistress!" she scoffed. "I'm not a mistress, certainly not of a plantation . . "

She was interrupted by María's entrance. The plump woman was all aflutter. She burst in on them, chattering excitedly in Spanish.

Nora's command of Spanish was far from good, and she said in annoyance, "María, what is it? Will you for heaven's sake speak English, so I can . . ."

Behind María, a familiar voice said, "What she's

264

trying to tell you, Momma, is that your wandering son is home."

Grinning, Brian strode into the room. He was burned black by the sun, his hair long, almost to his shoulders, and his clothes were worn and filmed with trail dust. To Nora, who sat rigid in shock, he looked several inches taller, and his already slender frame seemed leaner.

Brian's grin faltered. He said uncertainly, "Don't I get a welcome home?"

The spell was broken and Nora came to her feet, flying across the room to him. "Brian! Oh, my God! Yes, yes, you're welcome!" Her arms went around him, tears springing to her eyes. Her hands moved over him, plucking at his clothing, feeling him here and there, assuring herself of his reality.

Finally she stood back, dabbing the tears from her eyes. "Son, where on earth have you been?" She couldn't keep the scolding note out of her voice. "Running off like that, without any word in all this time! Whatever got into you . . ."

Noting that his gaze was directed past her, she turned. Sean was sitting at the table as though turned to stone. His face had gone quite pale.

Brian said tentatively, "Daddy?"

Sean shook his head sharply, and Nora tensed as she saw rage flicker in his eyes. Then it was gone, and he was smiling with delight, on his feet and striding toward them. "Son! Lord God Almighty, I was after thinking that I would never see you again!" He extended a hand, then changed his mind and embraced him. "Welcome home, boy!"

Sean's eyes were moist when they broke the embrace. Nora found herself babbling, "Brian, you look skinny as a scarecrow! You must not have been eating proper."

"With the rangers a man has to cook his own vittles, and you know I can't cook, Momma." Grinning

265

again, Brian scrubbed a hand down over a day's growth of beard on his face.

"The rangers! You mean you ran off to join the Texas Rangers?"

"Yep. I been up on the Red fighting Comanche."

"My goodness! Were you hurt? That sounds dangerous." Involuntarily her hand reached out to him.

"Naw, I didn't get a scratch. And talking of eating, I could stand a bite of breakfast. I rode all night to get here."

"María, scare up some ham and eggs for Brian!"

Brown face grinning widely, María said, "Si, Señora Moraghan. Si!"

"Come to the table, Brian," Nora said. "There's fresh coffee. You can have a cup while María fixes you something to eat."

At the table, after Brian had taken several sips of coffee, Nora leaned forward. "I still don't understand why you took off like that, without a word to us."

Brian directed a glance at his father. Sean's expression was unreadable, and then he gave an almost imperceptible shake of his head. Brian realized that he hadn't told Nora about finding him and Kate together in the old cabin, and he wondered why. Whatever the reason he was grateful. Realizing that Nora was waiting for an answer, he said lamely, "I reckon I was afraid you would try and stop me."

"I wouldn't have approved, of that you can be sure," she said dourly. "But you're a man grown, so I don't know how we could have stopped you."

Brian hid his face in the coffee cup, as another thought popped into his head. Nora was a very perceptive woman. Why hadn't she grasped the fact that Kate's child was his? It could well be that she did, subconsciously, but refused to acknowledge it to herself.

Cautiously he said, "In Corpus Christi I ran into Harvey Simpson. He told me something surprised the

266

hell out of me. Told me that old Kev married Kate Lyons, and they have a baby girl."

Nora's face lit up. "Oh, yes! A darling baby. They named it Debra Lee . . ."

María came in with a platter of ham and eggs, and Brian ate hungrily, scarcely listening as Nora rattled on. Knowing how frank Kate was, he was sure that she had told Kevin who the girl's true father was. How had Kevin taken to that? And would he, Brian, be able to brazen it through when the inevitable confrontation took place?

It didn't happen for a week. Brian knew that word had reached Kevin of his return, and he expected his brother over every day, but he didn't come. Brian was just as happy. He was kept busy telling his parents about his ranger experiences, and reacquainting himself with Moraghan Acres.

One day Sean asked him into his office. "You're nineteen now, son, a man grown. Do you think that you've gotten the restlessness out of your system, and about ready to settle down?"

Brian doubted that he was all that ready to settle down permanently, but he didn't deem it wise to say so. Instead he said, "I think so, Daddy. Why do you ask?"

Sean sighed, leaning back. "I'm not gettin any younger, Brian, and the way the plantation is growing, I'm going to need help running it. For instance, it's been in the back of my mind for some time to build a sawmill on the property. Texas is going to grow and lumber will be needed for building. Cotton has never been a dependable money crop; the price fluctuates too much, and we've got acres and acres of prime timber. I think that's what the future holds for us, for East Texas. But to get things moving, I need help. I've always intended that you would someday take over Moraghan Acres, anyway."

"How about Whittaker? Won't he resent taking orders from me?"

Sean frowned. "I'm thinking of letting him go. He's a slave man, and I don't hold with slaves—never have. He's never let up pestering me to buy slaves. Since I refuse, he takes it out on the Negro workers I hire. Behind my back, he abuses them. I should have let him go long ago."

"Daddy, I think you're wrong about slaveholding. The whole economy of the South depends on slaves, and much of Texas. Slave labor costs very little, aside from the original purchase price. Without slaves, who could operate large plantations?"

"I've managed quite well without them," Sean said. He studied Brian in some surprise. "I didn't know you felt this way, son. But I am pleased that you've been giving some thought to business matters." He ran his hand across his face. "You're mistaken about slavery, Brian. Building the foundation of an economy on slavery is building on sand. In the end it'll collapse into itself. It's not as cheap as most people seem to think, holding slaves. Not if their owner provides them with decent living conditions."

"It's not necessary to do that, Daddy," Brian argued. He gestured. "The nigger is little more than an animal, and should be treated as such."

"Son, I don't like talk like that," Sean said harshly. "The Negro is one of God's creatures, and is entitled to live whatever life he, as an individual, is capable of living, and in freedom, not in chains! It's against everything I believe in. God did not intend it that way."

"Unless a nigger is taught differently, he's happy the way he is. Besides, slavery is an old, honored institution, going back to biblical times."

"That doesn't make it right. There are many people in the Church who unfortunately agree with your viewpoint. We used to have quite heated discussions about this subject when I was in . . ." He broke off, clearing his throat. "When I was in school. It's a moral question that is beginning to trouble many people deeply. The last time Sam Houston was in Nacogdoches, we talked about this. He believes that it's going to eventually divide the country right down the middle, South against North. I'm forced to agree with him."

Brian shrugged. "People who argue against slavery are in the North. The way I get it, white folks up there, working in factories, the Irish for instance, our own people, are far worse off than our slaves in the South."

"Well, I'm dead set against it, and hear me good now! As long as I run Moraghan Acres, we shall never keep slaves!" He leaned back with a sigh, his troubled gaze on Brian. "But I respect your opinion, even though I don't agree with it. I respect your *having* an opinion. It's a sign of maturity that pleases me."

Leaving his father's office, Brian was pleased with himself, as well as surprised, for having such strong opinions. Not that he didn't believe firmly in the institution of slavery, but he hadn't realized that he had given it all that much thought. One thing he knew for certain—if the day ever came when he would be at the reins there, Moraghan Acres would be worked by slaves!

It could be awhile before that happened—Sean was not likely to turn it over to him anytime soon. But Brian knew enough about himself to realize that the power inherent in running a plantation of this size would be worth biding his time, and could help to alleviate much of the restlessness of his nature.

Heretofore he had always thought that he would have to share it with Kevin; now it was glaringly apparent that that would never happen. The break between Kevin and their father had widened. Brian grinned to himself. Getting Kate pregnant and her ending up married to Kevin had turned into an unexpected but definite advantage.

And that reminded him—he had to ride over and see his brother and sister-in-law. And niece. He had put it off as long as he could.

The following day he rode over alone, without telling his parents. He had no idea what might result from the meeting, and it was best he be by himself.

Kate was alone before the lean-to when he rode up, washing clothes in a kettle. Brian heard hammering, and he could see the new house going up a hundred yards away.

She heard him coming and stood up, brushing moist hair out of her eyes. Damnation, he thought; she's a pretty wench! Desire stirred in him, and unbidden the thought came to him—she had taken pleasure from bedding him once, so why not again?

He was disabused of this notion almost at once. Getting down from his horse, he strode toward her. "Kate," he said easily, "how are you?"

"I'm fine, Brian." Her face was devoid of all expression. "We got word you were back. Several days ago."

"Yeah, but you know how it is." He gestured negligently. "The folks and all."

"Indeed I do know how it is."

"I thought I should ride over and congratulate you. You and Kevin."

"For what, Brian?" she said evenly.

"Why, uh, on your marriage, and, uh . . ."

"Our daughter? Mine and Kevin's?"

So that's the way it's going to be, is it? he thought wryly; and so much for any thought I might have had of her slipping her drawers down again.

Forcing heartiness into his voice, he said, "Where is she, by the way?"

"In the lean-to. She's sleeping."

"Oh, well, if she's asleep . . ."

She regarded him gravely. "You sure that's the reason you don't wish to see her, Brian?"

"What other reason could there be?"

270

Now she was looking past his shoulder, and he could hear the pound of hurrying footsteps behind him. Kevin, of course. He wanted to turn in the worst way, but somehow he just stood there, a smile frozen on his face.

A hand descended roughly on his shoulder, spinning him around. Kevin was white with anger. "What are you doing here, Brian?"

"I came to see you, little brother, to offer you and Kate here my congratulations."

"We don't want your congratulations! Do we, honey?"

Kate said softly, "I can do just as well without them."

Kevin hit him then, flush on the chin. Brian saw it coming, but made no move to elude the blow. It sent him careening back, and he landed on his rump on the ground. Flashes of light danced before his eyes. He shook his head to clear it, saw Kevin standing over him, booted feet planted wide apart.

"You're not welcome here, Brian. This is Daddy's property, right enough, but so long as I'm living here, you're never to set foot on it. Is that clearly understood?"

Brian tried to grin. "Is this any way to treat your only brother?"

"You're no brother of mine. You forfeited that right over a year ago."

Part Three

1863

21

The Steamboat House stood a half-mile from the court-house square in Huntsville, surrounded by cedar, crepe myrtle, and fig trees shaded by an immense oak. In a hollow to the south were the squat buildings of the Texas State Penitentiary. The only other building in view was the Rawlings mansion, a smaller replica of Mount Vernon. From where he sat with Sam Houston, on the front gallery of the long, narrow building, Sean could see a panorama of rolling, orderly hills stretching into the distance.

The Steamboat House had been built in 1860 by Dr. Rufus Bailey, president of Austin College, across town. Dr. Bailey, decrying the lack of originality in most structures of Texas, had decided to remedy this condition. The result—the Steamboat House. It did indeed resemble a Mississippi steamboat. The narrow, two-story structure was surrounded by a gingerbread galley, with outside stairways leading from one deck of the

274

gallery to the other. The windows were of small panes of stained glass. The parlor was on the saloon deck upstairs, and the bedchambers had been made to resemble staterooms.

It was a bizarre place, and many said that it was a sign of Sam Houston's dotage that he should sell both his Raven Hill plantation and his townhouse in Huntsville, and rent such a crazy place to live.

Sean knew that this was far from the truth. Houston might be old, now past seventy; yet he was far from being senile. He was gray now, much heavier, and the leg wound received at San Jacinto bothered him considerably. Although more irascible than ever, his mind was sharp as a honed razor.

No, the sad reason for the sale of his plantation and his fine townhouse was poverty. The giant who had been a telling force both in Texas and the United States Congress, as well as a revered war hero, was destitute. Not only impoverished, but in disfavor with most fellow Texans for his long and bitter battle against secession.

But for all that, his spirit was unbroken, he still being the proud warrior that Sean now saw evidenced as a group of gangling youths came along the dusty road. Seeing Sam Houston beside Sean on the gallery, they began to chant: "There's old Sam Houston, traitor to Texas! Traitor, traitor!"

A roar came from Houston. He lumbered to his feet and, ignoring the chill of the winter's day, he ripped his shirt open. "Dare you name me a traitor to Texas? Was it for this that I held fast at San Jacinto, to be branded a traitor in my old age?"

The youths scampered away in fright. The old warrior sighed heavily and sank back into the rocking chair. "I should not let them taunt me in such a manner, Sean. It all began when I ran against Harlan Runnels for governor back in '57, and that damned secessionist started his campaign of revilement." He chuckled. "It would seem that I should be accustomed to the charge by now, would it not, old friend?"

Sean was moved to say, "I think it a terrible thing, sir, and I don't blame you for being disturbed. Lord God Almighty, that anyone should call *you* a traitor to Texas!"

"Ah, well, with this damnable war, blood runs hot, in the name of secessionism and patriotism. I am only on the sidelines now, Sean." He sighed again. "Forgive me for not offering you a tot of Tennessee whiskey. But my dear Margaret finally had her way, and saw to my conversion into her beloved Baptist church. Now I am forbidden my spirits." His laughter rumbled. "Lord, Lord, how that conversion astounded people, friends and enemies alike. I well recall what a religious journal, *America's Own,* had to say on that momentous occasion. 'The announcement of General Houston's conversion has excited the wonder and surprise of many who have supposed that he was past praying for.' " He slapped a knee. "I can well imagine their shock. I recall a remark I made when I read that journal. I said that I hoped all my sins were washed away in that baptism in Rocky Creek, but if they *were* all washed away, the Lord should help the fish down below!"

Sean was silent for a moment. He very much doubted that the general's wife had gone so far as to forbid him from keeping liquor in the house. More likely, the reason was their genteel poverty, and Sam Houston's pride would not let him admit to that fact.

Sean stirred. "This war is a terrible thing, and wrong, all wrong. I saw it coming, as I know you did, sir."

"I did indeed, Sean," Sam Houston said gloomily. "I warned against it at every opportunity. I made speech after speech against secession, and met only hostility."

"I know," Sean said. "I was in Galveston on that February day in 1861, when you made one such speech."

276

They both fell silent, and remembering that day, Sean was moved close to tears. It was by coincidence that he had been in Galveston that day on business. Learning that Sam was to speak, he hurried to join the throng before the Tremont House. Waiting, the crowd was sullen and restless. There was to be a statewide vote on secession shortly.

As Houston, still straight as an arrow and magnificently self-possessed, strode out onto the balcony before them, a wave of hostility almost palpable rose against him.

The regal figure faced the crowd into silence, then began to speak in that sonorous voice. "Some of you laugh and scorn the idea of bloodshed as the result of secession. But let me tell you what is coming. Your fathers and husbands, your sons and brothers, will be herded at the point of a bayonet. You may, after the sacrifice of countless millions of treasure and hundreds of thousands of lives, as a bare possibility, win Southern independence, but I doubt it. I tell you that, while I believe with you in the doctrine of states' rights, the North is determined to preserve this Union. They are not a fiery, impulsive people as you are, for they live in colder climates. But when they begin to move in a given direction, they move with the steady momentum and perseverance of a mighty avalanche, and what I fear is, they will overwhelm the South. . . ."

At the end of his speech, Sam Houston was the target of jeers and catcalls. A man standing near Sean took a handkerchief from the lady with him and waved it daintily. In a loud, scornful voice he said, "I will be able to wipe up every drop of blood ever spilled over secession, with my Betsy's handkerchief!"

"And I," proclaimed the man next to him, "now offer to *drink* every drop of blood spilled!"

Not too long after the Galveston speech Texas voted an overwhelming 76 percent for secession, and now, as Sam Houston had predicted, the sons and fathers of

Texas were shedding their blood. Fighting on Texas soil was sporadic, but Texans were losing their lives in other southern states.

Not long after Texas joined the Confederate States of America, all Texas state officials were called upon to take the oath of allegiance to the Confederacy. On the day Governor Houston was commanded to take the oath, he sat in a chair in the basement of the capitol building. The officer of ·the gathering upstairs summoned the governor three times to come forward and take the oath. Three times the call rang out: "Sam Houston! Sam Houston! Sam Houston!" Governor Sam Houston never moved.

The following day he resigned as governor of Texas. "I love Texas too well to bring civil strife and bloodshed upon her . . ."

And now he sat there on the gallery of the Steamboat House, aging and destitute, and almost a forgotten man by his fellow Texans.

Sean said, "In a way it appears that the secessionists may be right, sir. The tide of battle seems to be going in favor of the Confederacy."

Sam Houston stirred, grunted. "Not for long, Sean, not for long. Mark my words well, it is all an illusion. It is a matter of numbers, and industrial capacity. The Northern armies will grow apace as more and more men are called into service. And the South is agricultural, by nature, inclination, and necessity. The factories of the North can make the weapons, and they control the railroads, and to a great extent the sea-lanes. The economy of the South rests on the production of cotton, rice, and the like. What do we know of weaponry?"

"I'm sure you are right, sir. Unfortunately much Southern blood will be spilled before that fact becomes clear to all."

"I greatly fear that the blood of my own family will be spilled, also. I suppose you know that Sam, Jr., is

278

fighting. He was felled at the Battle of Shiloh, and we were informed that he was missing in action, assumed killed. What a sad day that was for my dear Margaret and myself! It was like Lazarus resurrected when he appeared on our doorstep, sorely wounded but alive. Now he has recuperated and returned to the battlefield. I would have preferred he remain at home, but he is determined."

"I know," Sean said. "My son, Brian, is itching to go. So far I have managed to keep him home, short of tying him to the bedstead. But I don't how how much longer I can restrain him. The recruiters have been scouring our part of the country."

"He's married now, I believe."

"Yes, he's married five years, and has two children, a boy and a girl."

"Ah, yes, nothing so delights a man in his late years as grandchildren. And your other boy? Kevin, is it?"

"Kevin is married and has two children, also a boy and a girl. Brian is living at home, gradually taking over the management of the plantation. Kevin is farming the place next to my original acreage, the land Ty Reynolds willed to me the night he died. You remember Ty?"

Sam Houston nodded. "Yes, I remember. And your Kevin . . . Is he aching to get into battle?"

Sean said slowly, "No. Kevin, surprisingly, tends to agree with me. His sympathies do not lie with the Confederacy, and he says he will never fight for it." He smiled wryly. "We have belatedly learned to keep our sentiments to ourselves. Even so, our feelings are well-known along the river, and we are shunned by many of our neighbors."

"And does that bother you?"

"I would be less than truthful if I said it did not. It bothers me a great deal."

"A man with honor must stand up for his convictions."

279

"I agree. You certainly have, sir, and I am confident history will honor you for it." Sean smiled. "I believe it doesn't bother Kevin much. He is a private person, and not much swayed by criticism from his fellowman." Sean felt a pull of astonishment. A compliment to Kevin? If his mind had ever shaped one, he had certainly never voiced it. Nora would be pleased if she could have heard him!

Early the next morning, Sean left for home. Moving along at a fast clip in the buggy, his thoughts were melancholy. The conviction had been growing in him during the two-day visit with Sam Houston that the general was a dying man. He had awakened with a start in the still hours before dawn with a vivid image in his mind of General Sam Houston dying in the bed in the next room. At first Sean tried to dismiss it as the illogic of a dream, but now, he knew that he would not be surprised to receive the news any day.

The countryside was gray and stark with winter; withal, it was a peaceful scene, little indication that men were dying on battlefields not far distant. At least Texas would seem to be spared the ravages of war this time. It would be little consolation, however, if Brian was swept up in the conflict, laying down his life for a cause in which his own father did not believe.

And then, coming slowly toward him, were two figures in tattered gray uniforms, one supporting the other. As Sean's buggy drew closer, he saw that both had been wounded. One had an arm missing at the elbow, and the other one was missing a foot. Sean slowed as he drew abreast of them, about to speak—he knew not what.

They met his gaze, and their eyes were dull, lifeless, filmed with remembered anguish, and Sean flicked the reins, startling the horse into a trot. What could he possibly say to them? His eyes were moist as he rode toward home.

When war first came, Nora had thought of discontinuing her entertainments, but she found that the people along the river did not wish her to do so. So, she continued staging a new Tobias comedy-drama once a month in the schoolhouse. The people badly needed something to distract their thoughts from the fighting in the east.

Nora appreciated this; yet it nagged at her conscience that she, and others, should be enjoying themselves, however briefly, while their sons and husbands died.

She was of a like mind with Sean about slavery, but she had never given that much thought to it. She had not been raised on a plantation, and her parents had not been able to afford a house slave; so she had never had any personal experience with slavery. It was a book that really awakened her consciousness to the demeaning institution, a book that many were to say, in time to come, was a large factor in bringing about the War Between the States—*Uncle Tom's Cabin*. Nora read the Harriet Beecher Stowe novel not long after its publication in 1852, and had been moved by it, although recognizing its melodramatic sentimentality.

And it was this same book that finally turned most of the river people against the Moraghans. To be more accurate, the play which derived from the novel.

Nora had purchased a copy of the play some time back, with the thought in mind that she might stage it. She finally made up her mind to do it. It was probably the most daring act of her life, but she felt that it was her duty, and once Nora had reached a decision of such nature, she let nothing deter her.

She did, however, observe some caution—or deceit, as was later charged. She told no one of her plans, except those who were to act, and she was careful to select people who sympathized with the sentiments expressed. For instance, she didn't tell Brian of her inten-

281

tions. Nor Sean. Even though her husband agreed with the play's message, she knew he would be against her staging it.

Nora would have preferred black people portraying black people, but that simply was not possible. The few free blacks along the river had melted away when the war began, and the only blacks left behind were slaves.

So, for the pivotal roles of Uncle Tom and Eliza, she used Kevin and Kate, blacking Kate's face and hands with charcoal. It was the first time Kevin had played a role in one of his mother's entertainments, and he was skittish about it. If not for his strong sympathy with the theme, he would not even have considered it.

Except for the members of the cast then, no one along the river knew what the play would be about. Nora rarely advertised her entertainments anyway, just announcing the titles, and she practiced a subterfuge on this occasion. On the community bulletin board outside the schoolhouse, she posted a notice that this Sunday's performance would be titled: *Life Among the Lowly*. This was the subtitle of the book, and Nora was sure that few if any in the area were that familiar with the Harriet Beecher Stowe work. And in that, she was correct—not a soul in the audience prior to the performance had any suspicion of the drama's true nature.

Kevin had been dubious from the beginning. "Daddy is not going to be happy with you about this."

"Your father has never dictated to me as to the content of any plays I put on."

"Momma, you know this is different. None of your plays have involved a political issue before. And Brian . . . Brian will be furious!"

"So, he will be furious. He doesn't tell me what to do, either. Why are you so concerned about Brian?" She looked at him curiously. "You haven't spoken a civil word to him since I don't know when."

Kevin's color rose. "I'm not concerned about Brian

282

as such. I'm only worried about how he might take it because of you."

"Why? You think he'll thrash me?" She patted his cheek. "He won't approve, I well know that, but then we don't see a lot of things the same way, Brian and me. He might rant and rave, like he has when we've disagreed in the past, but I doubt it'll go beyond that."

Kevin was grim. "He's pretty rabid on the slave question, Momma, you know that."

Nora smiled. "Yes, I know. But so are a lot of other people. Who knows, maybe the play will cause them to see the light."

"No, Momma. There is no way that will happen, not with Brian."

At that very moment the subject of their conversation was engaged in his favorite activity. In the upstairs bedroom he shared with Anna, he was inside his wife, thrusting lustily, and Anna thrashed under him, stifling her cries with the corner of a pillow slip crammed into her mouth. Sean was in Huntsville, visiting Sam Houston, and Nora was at the schoolhouse, rehearsing her new play, so they had the house pretty much to themselves.

Brian said, "Why don't you take the pillow out, pumpkin? I like to hear you carry on a little. The folks ain't around to hear."

Anna shook her head. She gasped out, "The children . . . Just down the hall . . . They can hear."

"Doesn't matter. They're too young to understand."

"Children . . . understand more than parents think. Even Mark and Betsy, young as they are . . . Ach, God! Yes, Brian, yes! YES!"

In Anna Stressemann, Brian had finally found a woman with a sexual appetite to match his own. She was just as uninhibited about it as he, and never reluctant to let him know how much she enjoyed his love-making. Of course, Kate had enjoyed a good romp, but she had always remained her own woman and, even in her most passionate moments, Brian had always had the unsettling feeling that a part of her was reserved, was even slightly amused at her own antics. Not so with Anna, there was never the slightest doubt that she was wholly involved—body, mind, soul.

Anna was a big woman, voluptuous and blonde, with bright blue eyes misty with worship whenever she looked at Brian. The daughter of the owner of the general store at Bunker's Landing, Anna was half German, although born in America.

For a long time Brian had resisted all hints from his folks that he should get married and have children, and he doubted that he would have married when he did, if he had not found Anna. Certainly he would never have married a woman like too many along the river—giggling, empty-headed, and born into the world with a built-in chastity belt, and a firm conviction that sex was dirty.

Sean Moraghan had been dubious when Brian brought Anna home as his wife, and even the usual warm, loving Nora had been somewhat reserved. But ten months after Anna became Mrs. Brian Moraghan, she gave birth to a boy, and that was all it took. The boy had his father's handsomeness and his mother's blond locks and blue eyes, and from that moment on, Anna was a Moraghan, all reservations swept aside.

Brian didn't know about loving her, but he sure as hell loved to bed her. She kept him so well content that he never (well, hardly ever) availed himself of the favors of other women. He didn't even mind the two children, and took a measure of pride in being a father.

During the past two years, he had assumed a large part of the management of Moraghan Acres, but Sean wasn't fooling him a bit there. His father hoped that being kept busy running the plantation would stifle Brian's yearning to join the Confederate army.

284

Anna was speaking. Brian turned to her, placing his hand on that plump stomach, long fingers marching across her abdomen in what Anna called their "grasshopper dance." "What, pumpkin?"

"Now stop that," she struck at his hand, "and listen to me!"

He stilled his hand. "All right, dumpling, I'm listening."

"You've never said if you're going to see your mother's play Sunday night."

"Hell, I don't know. I suppose." He grunted. "The way Kevin feels about me, I don't know how he'll appreciate my being in the audience watching him. But since Daddy will be back from Huntsville, he'll expect us to go, and would be upset if we didn't . . ." As Anna started to speak, he sad, "Now just hush up, Anna. If you're going to ask me for the hundredth time why me and my little brother don't get along! I don't know what it is with him. It *is* him, you know. I'm perfectly willing to kiss and make up, whatever there is to make up. But he's got a broomstick up his ass about me, and nothing can be done about it. One thing I can't figure," he frowned in thought, "is how come he's appearing in one of Momma's entertainments. He's never done it before. For that reason alone, I wouldn't miss it."

His dancing fingers skipped down to her pudenda, and he ran an index finger inside her.

Anna gasped, her body leaping. She struck halfheartedly at his hand. "Now you stop that, Brian!"

"Why?" he asked innocently. "You know you love it."

It was a difficult play to stage, and the facilities offered by the little schoolhouse were severely limited. It was also a lengthy play, and Nora had eliminated a few of the minor characters, not only for brevity's sake, but because it was difficult enough to fill the roles when it was found out what the drama was about. She also

285

eliminated some of the more difficult scenes; but one, scene six, the climactic scene of act one, she refused to cut. It was absolutely vital to the play's message, and the most difficult to stage—Eliza crossing the ice in full flight, carrying Harry.

In it the scenery was supposed to represent the Ohio River, filled with floating ice. Nora improvised, using cotton bales to represent the ice floes, with ropes attached, leading off into the wings, pulled by whoever was handy, so that they seemed to be moving.

It was a spectacular scene, and drew gasps from the audience. The crowd had been quiet, if restless, so far, clearly disappointed that what they were seeing wasn't another comic tale featuring Tobias, and just as clearly puzzled.

Up to that point the thrust of the play wasn't too clear, but it soon became so, and here and there rose mutters of anger and outrage. People began to leave. Nora had anticipated a number of defections; yet to her dismay it soon became a mass exodus. By the time the last scene was played, only a handful remained.

The final scene was almost as difficult to stage as Eliza crossing the ice, and Nora was quite proud of the way she had handled it. Uncle Tom had just died, and this last scene depicted Eva, robed in white, on the back of a snow-white dove, with extended wings, as if soaring up to heaven. Her hands were held out as if in benediction over Uncle Tom and St. Clare, both kneeling on the stage and staring up at her.

With much ingenuity and at a drain on her purse, Nora had rigged up a sort of swing suspended from ropes hung from the rafters, and had devised a large paper dove, tacking it onto the audience side of the swing. Nora's pride in her achievement was in tatters as the final curtain closed, and there was a deathly silence from the half-dozen people left.

Kevin got up from his kneeling position and came to her, hands outstretched, his blackened face solemn.

"I'm sorry, Momma, but I did warn you that this might happen."

Kate strode on from the wings. "Never you mind, Nora," she said stoutly. "I think it was a hell of a job you did, absolutely marvelous! Sentimental as it is, this play has something to say, and I can't think of people any more in need of the message than the rabble here tonight." She took Nora's hand. "What did you tell me once about another matter? People will always gossip about something!" Her smile was forced. "And you told me then that the Moraghans are impervious to gossip!"

"I doubt that is going to hold true in this case," Nora said wanly. "I expected some hostility but not this." Then her spirit surged back. "Well, I can weather it . . ."

"That's a selfish viewpoint, Nora." It was Sean, striding in from the wings, his face a thundercloud. "You've brought down the wrath of the whole community upon us. What's even worse, you were deceitful about it. You did this behind my back, Nora!"

"Since when have I discussed my plays with you? When I first started, you said you were too busy with plantation affairs to be bothered; you'd prefer to attend as uninformed beforehand as the others in the audience . . ."

"But this, Nora, *this* was far from one of your entertainments!"

The curtain was violently agitated for a moment, as if some rampaging animal was trapped in its folds, and then it was shoved up and a red-faced Brian ducked onstage, followed by Anna.

"Momma," he roared, "what could you have been thinking of? You've disgraced the Moraghan name! Taking up for the niggers and defying the Confederate cause! It's near to treason, and you've brought shame upon us!"

"Speak for yourself, Brian Moraghan!" she said an-

287

grily. "I don't believe in your Confederate cause and never have! You well know that!"

"What you believe in our home and even what you speak out against in private is different from putting on this treasonous play!"

Kevin said, "I stand with Momma, Brian. As does," he drew Kate into the crook of his arm, "Kate. We don't feel shamed."

Without even looking at him, Brian made a dismissive gesture with one hand, as contemptuous as swatting at a buzzing fly. His anger abating somewhat, he said heavily, "There is only one way I can hold my head up along the river, after this night. I'm going to do what a real man should have done long ago. I'm going to fight for my country. You, Momma, Daddy, may not consider the Confederate States your country, but I do, and by God, no one of our neighbors is going to be able to say that Brian Moraghan is too cowardly to fight!"

Sean went pale with dismay. In a choked voice he said, "No, son, no! I know you're upset and angry, but don't do anything hasty."

Brian shook his head like a gored bull. "You can't talk me out of it any longer, Daddy. It's my duty and I'm going!"

"Your duty!" Nora said witheringly. "Your duty is here with your wife and little ones. It's a foolish thing you'll be doing!"

"Foolish, Momma? What you did here tonight, *that's* foolish!"

"That's not the whole of it, Brian," she said with flashing eyes. "You like to go off adventuring. It's just like when you ran off and joined the Texas Rangers. You have a responsibility here, not of fighting, likely to be killed, in some silly war that has nothing to do with us!"

"It has everything to do with us. If you can't see that, I feel sorry for you, Momma!"

"Go then," she flared, "and be damned to you, Brian Moraghan!" Face ashen, trembling with anger, she turned her back on him.

Sean took a step forward, said in an uncertain voice, "Son, I forbid you to go."

"Forbid? You forbid me, Daddy?" Brian laughed harshly. "I will be gone in the morning, and don't try to stop me!" He took Anna by the arm. "Come on, Anna, let's go home."

They all stood in strained silence after Brian and Anna had left. Sean looked gray and old, somehow shrunken. He directed a glance at Nora, took a hesitant step toward her, then faced about and walked off the stage with a heavy step.

As his footfalls died away, Nora began to cry helplessly, tears running in eerie silence down her cheeks. Kevin and Kate moved forward wordlessly to comfort her.

From Sean's journal, February 6, 1863:

Since Brian's stormy departure, all spirit has left me. I perform only what work is absolutely necessary. I spend most of the daylight hours in the office, the door open, staring at the river below.

At night, I retire shortly after supper and sleep like the dead. Nora and I speak only when necessity requires it, and we carefully avoid speaking of Brian.

Brian's prediction has come true. The people along the river shun the Moraghans. In the first two months following Nora's production of *Uncle Tom's Cabin*, we have not seen a single one of our neighbors.

This does not trouble me overmuch. My mind is too full of Brian. The boy has disappointed me many times, but this blow is so unexpected, so cruel, that I do not know if I can ever forgive him.

I feel lost and alone, and old, so damned old!

From Sean's journal, August 4, 1863:

My spirit is at a low ebb. News has filtered in
from Nacogdoches. Sam Houston is dead! He died
of pneumonia in the Steamboat House. He died
with the words "Texas, Texas!" on his lips.

I grieve for him as I have never grieved for a
fellowman. The general's death marks the passing
of an era. The death of greatness always dimin-
ishes all of us.

It strikes me, in this moment of despair and
grief, that it foreshadows my own imminent death.

22

Using his left hand, Sonny Danker drew and fired, the movement carried out with rattlesnake speed. The Colt roared and bucked in his hand. He emptied it, and every bullet struck home, sending the tin can hopping into the air until it was more sieve than can, and when the last bullet struck the can, it was over 40 yards away.

Sonny sighed, the lower part of his body relaxing. A rush of blood heated his groin, and even his bowels felt loose and soft, as if he'd just voided them.

The sun poured down, and sweat beaded his brow. He swiped at it with his gloved right hand. No, not a hand—a thing, a useless claw, kept hidden from the world by a black glove.

He owed that fucking Irishman, Moraghan, for that, and for the past eight years spent in limbo. Since that day in the ravine, hate had grown in him, festering, burning, gnawing, until at times it threatened to destroy him.

He forced calmness into his mind, walling off the hate until the time came to put it to use—a mechanism he had devised to retain his sanity, although at times he wasn't quite sure he had been entirely successful. Time and time again, over the past few years, sober or drunk, across the lunar landscape of his mind had danced that nightmare he'd experienced that first night, when, sorely wounded and delirious, he had dreamed of Ma and the boys and the faceless man firing at him over and over. The faceless man, of course, was Sean Moraghan. It could be no one else.

He sank down in the scanty shade of a mesquite tree, the emptied Colt still in his hand. He was in North Central Texas, near the Clear Fork of the Brazos. The land was flat, mesquite-dotted, and barren, baking in the summer heat; heat devils dancing in the distance like constantly reshaping demons.

Sonny longed for a drink; he felt the need deep in his bones. He tilted the canteen up and drank tepid water until his belly hurt. For almost a decade he had drifted across Texas, in an alcoholic haze, scrounging for a dollar when and where he could—robbing, stealing, murdering, but never with a gun.

He had hefted a gun in his hand for the first time over a year ago, and had not taken a drink since. Over the years in his wanderings, he had returned to the shack north of Nacogdoches perhaps a half-dozen times, and every time Ma had driven him away. Ma had dried up into little more than skin and bones, kept alive by the hate that blazed in her sunken eyes—a hate that was now about equally divided between the Moraghans and her own son.

He became a derelict, wandering across the face of Texas, crawling into a bottle every time he could get his hands on one. Even now he had no clear idea of what had finally started him on the road back. Perhaps some buried instinct for survival, a vestige of pride, hope of regaining a measure of respect in Ma's eyes, a burning desire to avenge his crippled hand—a combination of these factors, and perhaps something he couldn't put a name to.

For whatever reason, Sonny woke up one morning over a year ago, sick, hungover, every nerve in his body craving a drink, and decided he had one last chance. He hadn't drunk a drop since.

It had been a battle he would never have thought himself capable of. His nerves were shot; physically he was a wreck—bloated, hands palsied, muscles deteriorated. For the first time in his life, Sonny turned to physical labor. He took any job he could find, no matter how menial, how degrading, and the harder the labor the better. There weren't all that many jobs available for an ex-gunfighter with one hand. But slowly, he rounded into shape. His body became lean and hard, his alcohol-soaked brain began to function again, and his nerves steadied.

That was when he bought a Colt, a gun belt, a rifle, and began to spend every minute he could spare practicing. At first he despaired of ever mastering the pistol with his left hand. But the forgotten skills came back to him. In one respect he was fortunate. Forced to use his left hand exclusively for so long, it had grown stronger, quicker, and now Sonny knew without the least doubt that he was better with a gun than ever, even better then he had been with the right. With the rifle he was only fair, and Sonny realized that he would never be able to handle a rifle as well as he once had.

But he was satisfied. He no longer had to fear any man at close range.

He lit a Mexican cigar, drew on it contentedly. Now he could face Ma with pride, his own man again. Now he could down the Moraghans. And no matter what Ma said, he was going to see to it that Sean Moraghan died along with his two sons. Before it hadn't been personal with him, not really. Now it was.

* * *

293

Two weeks later he rode into the clearing before the shack north of Nacogdoches. The children playing in the yard—some half-grown now—stared at him warily. They were dirty, unkempt, and half-wild, and their own father was a stranger to them. Of course, Sonny reflected wryly, he wasn't father to all of them.

They scattered, fleeing around behind the shack. One stuck his head inside long enough to call something, then hurried to join the others.

Molly appeared in the doorway. Close to thirty now, her once-ripe figure had become blowsy; she was a slattern in appearance, and in behavior as well, Sonny knew. She said nothing, just lounged against the door jamb. A spark of contempt flared in her dull eyes.

Sonny dismounted, strode confidently toward her. He said, "I'm home, Molly, home for good."

Crossing her arms over her breasts, she said sullenly, "Don't be expectin' tears of joy from me, and if you're lookin' for liquor, we ain't got none."

"Where's Ma?"

"She don't want to see you, Sonny."

"She's my mother, bitch, not yours! So suppose you call her."

Molly didn't move.

Sonny hit her across the face with his withered hand. At least it was good for that; there was scarcely any feeling in it.

Molly cried out, shrinking away. It finally seemed to register on her that this was not the drunken lout who drifted by from time to time. Eyes leaking tears, she said, "She's dyin', Sonny. Ma's dyin'!"

A feeling of cold seized Sonny. "You're lyin'!"

"She is, Sonny. The doc says . . ."

He shoved her out of the way and plunged inside. It was dim, the shutters closed. The heat was stifling, and an overpowering stench made him gag. He recognized it as the smell of decay, of sickness—the seductive, sweetish odor of death.

294

Sonny bellowed, "Ma! Where are you? I'm sober and I'm home for good!"

He heard the mutter of her voice from what he knew was the shack's only bedroom. "You see, bitch," he roared, "she knows me. She ain't dyin'!"

Yet, when he had hurried into the room and dropped to his knees on the pallet beside her frail form, Sonny knew that he had been mistaken.

In a cracked voice she said, "Lem? Is that you, boy?"

"No, Ma, it's Sonny." He took her hand. It was hot, dry as scorched paper, fragile enough to crumple in his grip.

"Don't you worry none, Lem," that cracked voice continued. "We'uns will get our own back from them Moraghans. Shit, ain't no passel of Irishers can get the best of the Dankers."

"That's right, Ma, I'll take care of the Moraghans," he said fervently. "If it's the last thing I ever do, I'll take care of all of them."

"You'll . . ." The glaze cleared briefly from the fevered eyes, and she snarled, "You're not Lem! You're Sonny. Drunken, worthless Sonny! Shit!" She pulled her hand from his grasp. "You're no good to me."

"No, Ma, no! I'm as good as new. See?" He drew the Colt, faster, he was certain, than he'd ever drawn in his life. He held the gun up for her to see.

But her head had already fallen back onto the pallet, a gray film like a curtain falling across her eyes. From the sunken mouth came a garbled mutter of nonsense.

Heavy with frustration, Sonny got to his feet, reholstering the Colt.

From behind him, Molly's voice taunted, "See? I told you she was dyin'."

"You're a stupid bitch, Molly! Ma will be as good as new in a few days, soon as she realizes that I'm here and back in the saddle."

"What saddle? You look like the no-good drunken bum you've been for years."

"Drunken bum, am I?" He rounded on her, pulling the gun again. "If anyone's a bum, it's you, layin' on your back for ever' man that passes by."

"What was I supposed to do?" she yelled. "You been no good to me!"

As Sonny advanced, she retreated into the other room.

He poked the gun against her belly. "How'd you like this shoved up your snatch?"

"You'd have to do it that way. You ain't any good the regular way!"

Past her, Sonny could see the semicircle of children, listening avidly.

"Shoo! Scat, get the hell out of here, you brats."

He moved toward them, flapping his hands, and they scampered outside. He slammed the door, securing the wooden latch.

Sonny turned about, unbuckling his trousers. "We'll see how much of a man I am."

Her eyes widened, and she backed a step, gazing on his groin. He was on her in two strides and bore her down onto the packed dirt floor. He shoved her skirt up and went into her with a brutal thrust. Molly came alive under him. Sonny pounded at her like a hammer until he burst inside her.

Molly gave a satisfied sigh. "Reckon I was wrong, honey babe. You're still some man."

Lying on his back, gasping for breath, Sonny cast his thoughts back, and he realized with some astonishment that he had not had a woman since his hand had been crippled; he had not even felt the need for one. His member had been as withered and useless as his hand.

He kept the children outside all night and took Molly time after time on the dirt floor. When daylight seeped into the shack and Sonny went in to check on Ma, she was dead—the cold, sightless eyes staring accusingly into his.

Yet, Sonny felt little guilt. Instead, he experienced a

sort of sullen anger at her. For close to a decade she had lived, while he was more dead than alive, and now, now that he was a whole man again—or close enough to it—she had failed him, dying at his moment of triumph.

Alone, leaning on a shovel behind the shack after filling in her shallow grave, he said, "I'll still take care of the Moraghans, Ma, you can be sure of that, but you should have stayed around to see it. It won't be the same without you."

Kevin Moraghan dismounted and strode onto the porch, where Nora sat alone, rocking.

"Momma."

"Hello, son."

He stooped to kiss her cheek. It was August and East Texas sweltered in an enervating heat wave.

He dropped into the rocker next to hers. "Where's Daddy?"

"He's back in that office of his." She gestured with the straw fan. "Just like he's been for months now. Just sitting and staring at nothing."

Kevin sighed. "He's still at it, is he?"

"Kevin, he hasn't done any constructive work since Brian left. I thought he'd come out of it eventually, but he's been worse since General Houston died. I'm beginning to worry about him. There have been other times when circumstances were bad, like when Brian ran off to join the Texas Rangers, but Sean always managed to snap out of it. I think it's not only because Brian defied him, but he feels betrayed, his son going off to fight for a cause neither of his folks believes in."

Kevin's smile was sour. "Yet folks along the river shun me for a coward and hail Brian as a hero. I think they might even look upon me with more favor even if I'd gone off to fight for the North."

Nora's face clenched with alarm. "You have no such foolish notion, do you, Kevin?"

297

"No, Momma. And no matter what folks think, it's not because I'm afraid to fight, although I am. Only a fool wouldn't be. But I not only don't believe in the Confederate cause, I think this whole war is insane."

Nora smiled faintly. "My two sons, so different. One foolhardy, reckless, disregarding consequences. The other cautious, thoughtful, always looking before leaping."

"Does that aggravate you, Momma, that we're not more alike, Brian and me?"

Her face went blank, as empty of expression as a wiped slate. "No, Kevin dear. You may be sure that it does not. At one time, it might have, but not after this. If you were like Brian, I might have *two* sons gone off to die. The siege of Vicksburg is over, so we hear, the North victorious. Why don't we get word of Brian?" Now her face spasmed, and a tear escaped each eye to trickle down the side of her small nose.

"Ah-h, Momma! Don't!" he said in anguish. "Brian will be back. He's a survivor, Brian is."

She swiped at the tears and said angrily, "Hellfire and spit, I'm sorry, Kevin! I'm not a crying woman, you know that!"

"I know, Momma. I don't think I've seen you weep over a half-dozen times."

They sat in silence for a few moments, Nora rocking, Kevin stock still, feet planted solidly on the porch floor.

Nora was the first to speak. "How's Kate? And the little ones?"

"They're just fine, Momma. Kate sends her regards."

"I don't see much of my grandchildren, not even Brian and Anna's wee ones," Nora said wistfully. "When Anna and hers come for a visit, Sean takes one look and stamps off. Reminded too much of Brian, I reckon."

"I'm sorry, Momma. We'll try and come over more often. But you must admit that me and mine have never

298

been welcomed cordially by Daddy. Which reminds me . . . I'd better go back and speak to him." He got to his feet.

"Kevin . . . Son, be kind to him."

"Kind?" Kevin's voice rose. "Do you ever tell him to be kind to *me?*"

"I know, I know. But for my sake."

He sighed. "Of course, Momma." He laughed softly. "He always frightens me too much to be anything else."

He strode down the porch. Nora stared after him, her face melancholy. Unconsciously, she began to rock faster.

But Kevin was astounded by the reception he received.

He found Sean at his table-desk, staring down at the river, and unaware of his arrival. Kevin studied him for a little. Sean's tall figure had grown thinner, that thick hair, once so black, was streaked with white, and new lines had etched his face on either side of that dominating nose, like deep parentheses.

How old was he now, Kevin wondered. Why, he was past sixty! Kevin had never thought of Sean Moraghan as old, nor frail and vulnerable, as he certainly appeared now.

Feeling suddenly guilty for his secret scrutiny, Kevin cleared his throat. "Daddy?"

Sean turned his head slowly, and smiled, a slow, sweet, sad smile that wrenched at Kevin's heart.

"Kevin . . . It's happy I am to see you, son."

At the totally unexpected word, the first time in his life that this man had ever called him son, Kevin felt tears start in his eyes. He swallowed, blinking back moisture. It was a moment before he trusted himself to speak. "How are you, Daddy?"

"I don't know how to answer that. I've always had a zest for life. But no longer. It's gone. There's only one color to the world, gray. I'm ashamed to say this, but it is the truth. And I'm sure that your mother"—a wintry smile—"hàs lamented about this to you."

"I know, Daddy, and you have to snap out of it." He came on into the room. "You can if you'll only make the effort."

Sean was shaking his head. "I don't know. Something seems to have gone out of my life . . ."

"What? Brian?" Kevin said brutally. "He will be back; he always comes back. But even if he doesn't, what about Momma? Forget about me, but how about your grandchildren? How about Moraghan Acres? Are you just going to say fuck everything, and everybody, now that Brian has gone away?"

Face reddening, Sean roared back. "How dare you, sir! How dare you use such language to me?"

"I calculate that I have little to lose. Either it'll shock you out of that chair, or you'll just hate me even more than you already do."

Shaken, Sean stared. "Hate you? I don't hate you!"

"No?" Kevin's short bark of laughter burned with bitterness. "You've surely never loved me."

"But of course I love you, Kevin! You're my . . ." Sean broke off with an astonished look. "I have never given you any cause to think that I don't love you."

"You've never given me any cause to think that you do, either."

"You believe that? All these years you've been thinking that I hate you? Lord God Almighty, Kevin, I'm more sorry than I can say. What can I do to make it up to you?"

It was on the tip of Kevin's tongue to retort that it was too late, but the words were never uttered. He would only hurt Sean, and to no purpose. Besides, it wasn't too late, he realized with astonishment. All these years he had longed to hear this man express his love, and now that he had, Kevin, again, was dangerously close to tears.

300

In a choked voice he said, "Daddy, there's nothing you need do to make it up, now that I finally know you love me." He swallowed, firming his voice. "If you wish to do something to please me, get your ass out of that chair and start seeing to Moraghan Acres! It's falling apart!"

Again Sean looked startled, then outraged, and then he was roaring with laughter. "By God, you're right, much as I hate to say it! It *is* time I was stirring my ass. One thing . . ." He came to his feet. "You have to help me, son. If you'll promise to do that, I promise to try."

Now it was Kevin's turn to be startled. "Me, Daddy? You want me to help you run Moraghan Acres?"

"Of course. Who else?"

Kevin was silent for a moment, studying the older man. Sean's face was open, guileless; yet there was more fire in his eyes than Kevin had seen in a while. Kevin said, "How about my place? I'll soon be ready to start picking cotton."

"That's part of Moraghan. Before I turned it over to you, *I* ran that too. Surely, together, we can do as much."

Kevin started to shout out his assent, then restrained himself. "You say the two of us . . . Who'll have the final say-so? If it comes down to taw, one of us has to have the final word."

Sean narrowed his eyes, standing tall. "I will, of course."

Kevin shook his head, said stubbornly, "No, Daddy. You've shown no interest for too long. I know more about what's going on than you do."

"Why, you insolent young snot! How . . ." Sean broke off, eyeing him shrewdly. A tiny smile tugged at his mouth. "By God, I believe you mean it," he said in grudging admiration.

"I do mean it. Be sure of that, Daddy."

Sean seemed more amused now than angry, but there was no scorn in his amusement. "Then we'll have to

301

see, won't we?" He cocked his head. "If you're to become overseer, maybe you and Kate should move in here." A shadow of melancholy crossed his face. "Lord knows, there's enough room nowadays."

Kevin considered, sorely tempted; yet he had the feeling that it would be a mistake. Right now, this moment, he had an edge, one that he would never have anticipated, but under Sean's wing, he could easily slip back into being dominated. He said slowly, "I think not, Daddy. Kate and I are quite happy where we are."

"Suit yourself." Sean shrugged negligently, but Kevin had the fleeting impression that he was sorely disappointed. Again he wavered, but before he could speak, Sean went on, "When shall we start? In the morning? I haven't been in the saddle in so long, my ass will probably be sore as a boil at the end of the day."

"Why not now?"

"Right now?"

"Why not? There's still several hours of daylight left. Unless you don't feel up to it?"

"Up to it! Lord God Almighty, I'm not in my dotage quite yet," Sean roared. He reached for his planter's hat and clapped it on his head. "Let's go!"

Together, they went through the dog run and onto the front porch.

Nora reared up in the rocker, gaping at them. "Where are you two off to?"

"Taking a little canter over the plantation to see how things are coming on." Sean threw an arm around Kevin's shoulders. "Kevin says I've been lax, letting things go, and he's going to show me."

"Holy Mother of Jesus," Nora said in awe. "I can't believe I'm hearing right."

"What's so hard to believe, woman?" Sean growled. "You've been nattering away at me. Who better to straighten things out than our son?"

"*Our* son, is it?" she said dryly.

"That's what I said."

Kevin glanced from one to the other, bewildered. "What's this all about, Momma?"

"Never mind, son," Sean said quickly. "Sometimes, your mother is a little dense. Come on, let's ride out."

As they went down the steps and toward the stable, Nora whispered to herself, "God willing, you never will find out, Kevin." For the first time since she had wed Sean Moraghan, Nora crossed herself and glanced heavenward. "Thank you, dear Lord. I don't believe it, not yet, but thank you anyway. Hellfire and spit, another miracle such as this and I might even regain a smidgen of my faith!"

23

"Hey, Johnny Reb, is it true what I hear about your women? I hear tell that even the married ones with kids are virgins. I hear tell it's a high crime to diddle a white gal, even your own wife."

"You keep your dirty mouth shut, Yank! We respect our women down here in the South!"

"I hear tell you Rebs diddle the colored gals, the only diddling you get."

"We call it poontang and it comes free. Not like up north where you shitheads have to pay for it, even the nigger gals."

"Be a freezing day in hell before I pay for it, Reb. Course, that's why we're fighting, ain't you heard? So we can get all that nigger poontang we want. Could be we might service a few of your white gals while we're at it."

"I told you to keep your filthy tongue still. I'm acomin' after you, Yank, and tear it out by the roots."

"Come right ahead, Reb, come right ahead. I'm ready for you."

Another voice chimed in. "Goddammit, don't we fight each other enough other times? Can't you two act peaceful for at least a few minutes?"

Leaning on his rifle in a zigzag trench a few yards away, Brian Moraghan marveled. *This* was war? Now that the siege of Vicksburg was under way, it was not uncommon for the soldiers, deadly enemies by day, to fraternize by night. Brian could not bring himself to do so, it was not right, dammit!

The whole war, at least his part of it, was not going the way he had envisioned it. He had joined up, afire with zeal, ready to do battle, to fight or die. To fraternize with the enemy in such a manner struck him as close to treason. Yet neither side seemed to think it amiss. True, the officers on both sides frowned on the practice, but an effective grapevine was in operation— when an officer was approaching, word always preceded him, and the soldiers who had ventured out of the trenches scrambled back in time.

When Brian enlisted, he and a number of other recruits were rushed to join the Seventh Texas at Vicksburg. There had been no time for adequate combat training; in that respect Brian was better off than most, the campaign with the Texas Rangers standing him in good stead.

The men of the North had early recognized the strategic importance of the taking of Vicksburg. Capture Vicksburg and they gained control of the Mississippi. But so long as Vicksburg was in Confederate hands they were stymied. By late 1862, the Federals had control of the great river from New Orleans to Port Hudson, in Louisiana, and from its northern sources down to Vicksburg. But while the Confederacy held the 130-mile stretch of the river between those two points, it could maintain communication

305

with the western third of the new nation, allowing free access to supplies and reinforcements. In addition, with that portion of the Mississippi in Southern hands, they could prevent normal river traffic between New Orleans and the northern reaches of the river.

According to a story in circulation. President Lincoln, during the early part of the war when things were going badly for Union troops, had studied a map and made the comment: "See what a lot of land these fellows hold, of which Vicksburg is the key . . . Let us get Vicksburg and all that country is ours. The war can never be brought to a close until that key is in our pocket."

The South had recognized this fact as well, and had started fortifying Vicksburg shortly after the fall of New Orleans, anticipating an all-out assault on the river-bluff town. First, they built batteries below the town overlooking the river approach from the south, and then guns were mounted above the town, on the bluff, making Vicksburg almost impregnable to an attack from the water. It was not without reason that Vicksburg became known as the Gibraltar of America, for in addition to what men could do, nature seemed on their side. The ground to the north was low and swampy, often underwater from the flooding Yazoo River, and made impassable for an army.

The new commander of the Union army, Ulysses S. Grant, recognized the necessity of capturing Vicksburg, and he began to move toward the town in late 1862. His movements were slow, almost tentative at first, as he captured town after town to the north and the east, consolidating his position each time before moving on.

By the time Grant was ready to move on Vicksburg, the elements were against him. Winter runoff from the north and spring rains had brought the Mississippi to flood stage, and the lowland north of the Vicksburg bluffs was several feet underwater. Grant used the time to condition his troops and to add reinforcements, the number under his immediate command swelling steadily.

The Confederate troops at Vicksburg numbered some 40,000 men, and were under the command of Lieutenant General John C. Pemberton. Expecting Grant's assault on Vicksburg, General Pemberton had been steadily fortifying the town, but all his pleas for additional men went unheeded by the Confederate high command. After all, intelligence had informed him that Grant had only around 25,000 men, so he was outnumbered almost two to one.

But by the time Brian joined the Seventh Texas at Vicksburg, not long before the siege began, Grant's troops had more than doubled.

The first action Brian saw was during the Battle of Raymond, a town east of Vicksburg. Word had reached General Pemberton on May 11 that Grant's forces were moving on Raymond. Convinced that it was a feint, that Grant's main force was moving toward Big Black Bridge farther north, he had wired General John Gregg to strike the Federal flank and rear as they turned north. Brian had been sent in, along with several other Texas recruits, a few days before to help shore up the Raymond defenders.

Early on the morning of May 12, scouts informed General Gregg that a small Union force was marching up the Utica road. With Pemberton's wire in mind, Gregg at once moved his 3,000 men in to attack. The battle was long over before it was learned that the "small vanguard" of Union troops actually numbered 10,000.

The Seventh Texas was held in reserve, then finally sent in against the flank of the Twentieth Ohio. The battlefield was a bowl of dust and smoke, and a hell of a noise deafened Brian's ears as his unit charged, screaming the Rebel yell until they were hoarse.

They were very much outnumbered; that became obvious to Brian at once, but the Texans fought like demons. Heedless of personal danger, they began to drive the Union soldiers back by the very ferocity of their attack. Twice men in blue emerged from the dust and smoke like apparitions, and Brian coolly took aim and fired. Both times the bullets hit their mark, driving the soldiers back and out of sight.

The Yankees gave ground foot by foot, and Brian sensed victory. A puff of wind blew the air around Brian clear for a moment, and a cavalryman spotted him. The horseman fired and missed. With a curse he threw his rifle away, drew his saber and rode his horse directly at Brian. His own rifle empty, Brian stood his ground, desperately trying to reload. When he realized he wasn't going to reload in time, he threw himself to one side. The charging horse struck him a glancing blow, knocking him to the ground. Brian hit the ground rolling. He snatched at the pistol in his holster, and came up on one knee. The cavalryman had turned his horse and was thundering back.

Brian leveled the pistol and, waiting until the man's contorted face loomed large in his sights, he fired. The cavalryman arched high and back, as though slammed into a wall, and then fell away. The horse reared, screaming, and ran on, riderless.

And then from out of the battle murk charged another horse. Astride it was a Union general, with a thick flowing mustache. In his right hand he brandished a saber, and from his mouth came a yell as piercing as that of an eagle.

For a moment Brian thought he was riding at him. Before he could collect himself and fire, the general rode on, still yelling and waving the saber, disappearing into the dust and smoke.

In that moment the tide of battle began to turn. Union soldiers, who had been steadily falling back,

308

turned like cornered animals and fought fiercely. Several more times Brian saw the same general riding up and down the Union lines, verbally lashing his men into a frenzy.

The Confederates gave ground grudgingly at first, but soon they were in a complete rout. Late in the afternoon the order came down from Gregg—withdraw through Raymond, and bivouac on high ground beyond Snake Creek.

The bone-weary, discouraged Rebels straggled back through Raymond. Under the stately, shady live oaks along the streets the ladies of Raymond had spread out a picnic—a feast for Gregg's soldiers on their "return from victory."

The ladies lined the streets and watched sadly as the men trudged past. Brian was the only one to break ranks. Grinning, he stepped over to a comely belle in crinoline. "Pumpkin, how thoughtful of you. Brian Moraghan, of the Texas Seventh, at your service, ma'am." He swept off his cap and bowed.

The lady hid her blushing face behind a fluttery fan. "Katherine Lee, sir."

"Moraghan!" bellowed a voice from Brian's troop. "Goddammit, you get back in line, or you'll be on report! By God, you will, sir!"

"Sorry, pumpkin," Brian said with his flashing grin. "Duty calls." He leaned close to whisper, "Maybe I can sneak back in tonight, and we'll have us a high old time. How does that strike you?"

The fan fluttered. Eyes cast down demurely, she whispered back, "I'll be at the bandstand at nine . . ."

"Moraghan!"

Brian scooped a drumstick from the mound of fried chicken on the picnic table. Winking at the girl, he hurried back into line, gnawing on the chicken leg.

But there was no opportunity to sneak back into town that evening—the Union army occupied Raymond before sunset.

The Confederate forces retreated toward Vicksburg, and the Battle of Raymond was the last big battle Brian actively participated in. He was not in the battle for Champion Hill, which the Confederates also lost. He had found a willing maid in town, below the hill, and was dallying with her. For once he regretted that he was with a woman, since he felt, irrationally he realized, that the battle for Champion Hill might have been won had he been in the thick of it. To his astonishment and chagrin, Brian discovered that his absence was not even noticed, such was the disorganized state of the Confederates after another crushing defeat. He almost spoke out in indignation against this slight. Caution finally prevailed; he should consider himself fortunate that he wasn't court-martialed for desertion.

Shortly thereafter the ring began to tighten. They dug in, digging the zigzag trenches, and reinforcing their battlements. The Union army attacked again and again but was thrown back each time. The loss of life was heavy on both sides, but Brian sailed through all the Union attacks unscathed. He saw nothing unusual in this. After fighting the Indians along the Big Red, he was convinced that he was invincible, and this conviction was only strengthened as he helped to repel the Federal attacks. In fact, he was outraged that Pemberton did not give orders to counterattack. It was a purely defensive struggle now, and in Brian's view a Southern victory could never be won with such tactics.

By June 18, General Grant had established a firm base across the Yazoo River, and his army now tripled the Vicksburg defenders in numbers. Grant's lines ran from the Yazoo to the lowlands along the Mississippi above the city of Vicksburg to the banks of the river to the south. The Yanks had twelve miles of camps, trenches, and gun emplacements on the hills and ridges around the town.

The supply of food and ammunition to the defend-

310

ers of Vicksburg was shut off almost completely, and the men began to suffer from sickness and malnutrition. Brian overheard one officer complain bitterly: "We're so tightly cornered I doubt even a cat could slip out of Vicksburg without being discovered."

General Pemberton seemed content to settle back and wait for the next assault, keeping the loss of life at a minimum. And now the Union army also seemed content to wait, fully realizing that time was on their side.

The waiting was hard. Food became so scarce that both the citizens and the soldiery were reduced to eating mule meat and pea bread. There were no medical supplies for the wounded and the sick. Water became so precious that guards were posted at the few wells to ensure that the water was used only for drinking purposes. The people of Vicksburg burrowed underground into the perpendicular banks that cut through the ridges. To escape the constant Union bombardments, many lived in caves.

Brian was amused to see that some cut one or more rooms out of the embankments, carpeted and furnished them with tables, beds, and other furnishings.

The waiting was even harder for Brian than most of the soldiers, who seemed just as happy to be spared active combat. Never one to suffer inactivity gracefully, Brian chafed during the siege. Many times he itched to rush down the hill from where the Seventh Texas was entrenched, charge the Yank lines on his own. On this warm June evening, listening to the exchange between the Yankees and his own comrades, the urge was strong.

"Hey, Yank! I got some good Virginny leaf I'll trade you for some grub."

"Sure, Reb. I'll swap you . . ."

"You'd better not, Samuel," said another Yankee voice. "You know what Cap said . . . No trading vittles

311

with the Rebs. Shit, we're trying to starve them out! How can we do that, if we swap grub with 'em?"

"Sorry, Johnny Reb. Looks like we can't swap. Tell you what, I've got a week-old newspaper. How about I trade you that for your tobacco?"

"Shitfire, Yank! What do I want with a Federal newspaper?"

From Brian's right came a carrying whisper. "You birds better get back into the trenches. Officer coming!"

On a cloudy and very warm day, June 27, the fortieth day of the siege, Brian walked through Vicksburg. It was a depressing sight. It struck him that the town looked much as it would if devastated by some terrible plague. The streets were mostly deserted, except for hunger-pinched and wounded soldiers, and a few delicate women and small children peering wistfully at Brian out of bruised and sunken eyes. Those soldiers lying in the streets were covered with vermin and filth. Dogs howled and cats yowled their mournful cries, as though it were night instead of midday. Rats scampered unafraid around Brian's boots, running in packs into side streets and alleyways in a search for sustenance.

The houses were mostly in ruins, battered and rent by shellfire. Streets were barricaded by earthworks, and manned by civilians armed with pitchforks, shovels and even lengths of two-by-fours.

The few stores that remained open had a desolate look about them. Brian peeked into a few and saw that their shelves were mostly empty, and what goods were for sale were posted with outrageous prices.

What saddened Brian more than anything was the condition of many of the palatial homes he saw—already crumbling into ruin, the walks demolished by mortar shells, flower beds trodden and neglected. Some houses had been stripped of lumber for firewood. Even a graveyard Brian passed had been desecrated. The

312

fence was down, and wagons were parked around the graves. Mules trampled the sacred mounds, and men used the tombstones for tables for their scanty meals.

Yet, here and there, in incongruous contrast, some fine homes stood untouched, shining and proud in their splender, as though enjoying protection from some divine power.

Brian stopped in one of the stores downtown and parted with some of his little remaining money for a mug of beer. In a grumbling voice he said, "This is downright robbery, storekeeper, the price you're charging. Whyn't you wear a mask?"

The storekeeper merely shrugged and turned away. Brian resisted an urge to smash the man in the face. He drank from the mug, made a face. The beer had the flavor of warm horsepiss. He drank it down nevertheless and left the store. Outside, he debated briefly whether he should pay a call on his paramour. But it would do him little good in the daytime. She was living in one of the hillside caves with her family and would likely be unwilling to take a daylight stroll with him. She was an emptyheaded girl anyway, and Brian had no patience for small talk with her, or her folks.

He turned back up the hill toward the Seventh Texas lunette. Still restless and reluctant to return to his regiment and the boring inactivity, he swung left abruptly and walked toward the edge of the bluff. The weary men manning the cannon on the cliff paid him little heed. Finally he stood looking toward the Yazoo, still swollen from the spring rains, as it poured into the Mississippi.

Looking to his right, he saw the figure of a man slumped against a ruined cannon, its muzzle wrenched skyward, aimed at the sun. The man in the gray uniform was also staring out over the river. He was bareheaded, black hair skimpy on his head, with a full beard hanging almost to his breastbone. With a start Brian recognized him—General John C. Pemberton, the man in charge of the defense of Vicksburg. The man responsible for the gutless inactivity that Brian knew could only lead to the eventual surrender of Vicksburg.

Anger spurted through him, and without further thought he strode over to plant himself in front of the officer. "General Pemberton?"

Pemberton looked around, blinking in an effort to focus. "Yes, soldier?"

Brian said harshly, "How much longer are we going to hold still like this, penned here by the damned Yanks like a herd of sheep?"

General Pemberton blinked rapidly. Red color flooded his face, and he came erect, ramrod-straight, his very beard seeming to bristle with outrage. "How dare you, sir! Do you know who I am?"

"I do. You're General Pemberton, the man responsible for us squatting here, slowly starving, instead of driving off the Yankees."

The sunken eyes blazed. "Of all the brazen impudence! Do you know that I can have you court-martialed for such insolence?"

"I reckon you could." Brian shrugged. "Better that than sitting here on my dead ass until I rot. At least a court-martial would stir up some action and give me a chance to speak my mind."

"You're not even an officer! Rank insubordination, sir!" The general's gaze raked Brian fore and aft. "What is your name, soldier? And regiment?"

"Brian Moraghan. The Seventh Texas."

"Ah, yes. You're a Texan." A tiny smile tugged at Pemberton's mouth and was quickly gone. "Moraghan, Moraghan . . . the name is familiar. You fought at Raymond, I believe, and I hear they call you the Wild Man from Texas."

Brian said stiffly, "I was in the Battle of Raymond, yes, sir."

"I honor your valor and fighting spirit, young man,

314

but that does not give you the right to confront me in this manner."

"Perhaps not, General Pemberton, but I did join up to fight, and not hide in a trench."

"I owe you no explanation, soldier, but I will clarify matters for you. You are entitled to that much. We are completely ringed by Grant's men, and outnumbered probably four to one. To try and break through the Union lines would not only be disastrous for my troops, but would leave Vicksburg undefended, and the town is vitally important to our cause. So long as we hold it, we control the Mississippi."

"General, I know little of military strategy. Conceding that you are right, we are going to be starved into submission sooner or later. Sooner, from what I have seen today. So Vicksburg falls, anyway."

"That is true, sir, much to my regret." General Pemberton sighed. "We can only hold fast as long as we are able, hold off the enemy as long as possible."

"If you will pardon me, General," Brian said boldly, "I cannot agree with that attitude."

General Pemberton stiffened, eyes flashing. Then he smiled tiredly, shrugging. "If one of my officers heard that remark, I would have to order you shot. I would have no choice. But since I am forced to agree with your reasoning—and this is only between us—I do nothing. For a West Point officer to listen to an enlisted man is rank heresy. But I have listened to everyone else and it has gained me nothing. So, Brian Moraghan from Texas, what do *you* suggest as a course of action?"

Caught by surprise, Brian hesitated, then said forcibly, "I would send for reinforcements, sir. Have them come in behind the Yankees. Strike them by surprise from the rear and shatter the blockade!"

"Send for reinforcements?" Pemberton laughed harshly. "Do you not think I have tried? I have sent courier after courier, urgently requesting reinforcements, aid of any kind. My requests have either been

315

ignored, or what replies I have received claimed that men could not be spared. I think that General Lee and others in command do not truly grasp the desperate straits we are in. Now," he shrugged again, "it is too late. A rat could not slip through the ring Grant has drawn around Vicksburg."

"If I know the procedure, I doubt that the couriers you sent have seen much combat, General Pemberton. A man who has fought the Yankees might be more convincing."

Pemberton's smile was wry. "A man like yourself?"

Brian's head went back. "Yes, sir! I'm sure I could convince them. At least I would feel that I am *doing* something!"

"Ah, such fire and zeal. How I wish that more . . ." Pemberton broke off, eyes filled with pain. Then he squared his shoulders, his gaze probing. "There is great risk involved, you must realize that."

Brian nodded. "I understand the risk, sir."

"My officers tell me that no one can get through the Union lines."

"I can do it," Brian said confidently. "I've fought Indians. I've snuck in and out of their camps, and it's said an Indian can hear a leaf drop a mile away."

Pemberton sighed. "Perhaps, if you could find General Johnston and convince him of how dire our situation has become. Tell him that we cannot hold out much longer. My own officers are all advising surrender, and I am informed that General Grant's forces are increasing daily and am convinced that we can expect a big push by the enemy any day. When that happens, they will undoubtedly overwhelm us by superior numbers. Inform General Johnston . . . No, I will compose a note for you to deliver. When will you go?"

"Tonight."

Pemberton stared. *"Tonight?"*

"Why delay? With the threatening weather, it will be dark. The best way, I figure, is to swim the Yazoo . . ."

"My God, sir, you will be penetrating the very heart of the Union lines!"

Brian said cockily, "Then I figure that's where they'll be least expecting me. They'll likely be the most careless there."

At three o'clock in the morning Brian wormed his way to the flood-extended banks of the Yazoo River. The lowlands were obscured in a misty fog, visibility about three yards—perfect for his purpose. He had carefully worked his way through the no-man's-land between the Confederate lines and the river. Through a momentary break in the fog he had seen the Yank campfires to the other side, and he knew that often patrols probed across the river. So far he had encountered none, and it was his hope that the fog would keep them confined to camp.

The Yazoo was twice as wide as normal. He hesitated, debating his course of action. He knew the main channel would be quite deep, and he would be forced to swim. He had left his rifle behind and was armed only with his pistol. But if he was forced to swim, not only would his clothes become waterlogged, more than likely the pistol would get wet and liable to misfire if he was forced to use it.

With a sigh he divested himself of all his clothes except his drawers. Wrapping the clothes into a tight bundle, with Pemberton's message to Johnston and his pistol in the center, he lashed his boots to the bundle.

He slipped quietly into the water, wading for as long as he could, moving so quietly that he was confident he could not be heard over a few feet away. He waded until the water was up to his armpits, the bundle held high over his head. Then, holding the clothes out of the water with one hand, he began to swim on his side, using one hand and his feet to propel himself.

With the water higher than normal though the flood tide was receding, the current ran strong in the main

317

channel; yet he was able to make it across. He was a good swimmer; he had the childhood romps with Kevin in the river at home to thank for that.

When his feet touched bottom on the opposite shore, he remained crouched for an extended time, just his head and the bundle above water. His gaze scanned the riverbank. If any sentries had been posted, they weren't in evidence. There was no movement, no sound.

Cautiously he began to wade toward the bank. Shrubbery and trees grew thick right down into the water, and by the time he reached the undergrowth the water was still almost to his knees.

A furtive sound caused him to freeze. He began to fumble in the bundle for the pistol, but he knew with a lurch of dismay that he would never get it out in time.

"Going somewhere, Reb?" said a jeering voice.

A shadow darker than the surrounding shrubbery loomed up on his right, and reflected light from the river glinted off a rifle barrel. Brian thought of denying that he was a Confederate. After all, if he threw the bundle into the river, he would be left naked, with no identification on him. Yet he knew he would give himself away the instant he opened his mouth, and he'd be damned if he would play the sneak and deny his allegiance to the South.

Even as the thought passed through his mind, he acted. He threw the bundle as far out into the river as he could and bolted. At least the letter from General Pemberton would not be discovered, his mission revealed.

"Don't be a damned fool, Reb!" the voice shouted. "Halt, or I'll shoot!"

Brian ran on, bent over, trying desperately to zigzag, but the ankle-deep water and the underbrush made it difficult.

Then something slammed into his back with stunning force. He locked his teeth against a yelp of pain, and fell, facedown into the water.

24

Kevin was pleasantly surprised by the way in which Sean threw himself into the task of getting Moraghan back on an even keel. Things had deteriorated badly during the previous year.

For one thing, manpower was hard to come by since the war, even though they paid better than the prevailing wages for the area. Before the war began, a large part of their labor force was black, but when the war broke out, night riders had terrorized the Negroes along the river, hanging several, and the majority had then quietly packed up and left, heading north. The few whites left were either young and inexperienced, or too old to be accepted by the Confederate army.

Now most of their employees were Mexican; the Spanish people had learned that employment was both plentiful and lucrative, and had moved into East Texas in substantial numbers. Yet their employment also presented problems—the language barrier and their inexperience. A man needed little experience to plant, cultivate, and pick cotton, but Sean had long since directed most of the activity on Moraghan Acres toward the production of lumber. There were two sawmills on the plantation now, and men with some expertise were needed.

The felling of the trees and dragging them to the mills for conversion into lumber posed no great problem. Sean had brought in a couple of old-time loggers from Maine some years back and put them in charge of the logging operation. He paid them good wages and the felling of the relatively small trees of East Texas was child's play to them, after years spent logging in Maine's giant forests. Neither man had the slightest interest in going off to fight in the war, and remained in Moraghan employ. The laborers they needed to work with them required little skill and what little was needed could easily be taught.

The sawmills were a different matter. The man Sean had initially employed to run the mills was also a Yankee, and he had departed to join the Union army the moment the news of Fort Sumter reached him, leaving the sawmills without skilled supervision.

Kevin had always been fascinated by the operation of the sawmills—the pungent smells of freshly cut trees; the almost miraculous conversion of the unwieldy logs into lengths of lumber; the piercing whine of the steam-driven gang saws, the flashing blades sending off a glitter of light almost blinding. So he had spent much of his free time around the mills, absorbing many details of their operation, and was confident that he could train the unskilled Mexicans in the workings of the saws. He had not informed Sean of this until his aid was requested. As a result of no proper supervision and Sean's own disinterest, the production of the sawmills was at a low ebb.

Kevin, in an effort to solve the communications problem, was working with María for an hour every morning, before he rode out with Sean to inspect the sawmills. As a result, he could now manage enough stumbling Spanish to make at least the simple orders understood.

Every morning he and Sean rode to the sawmills. It was into fall now, the mornings crisp and smoky, the trees wearing their gold and brown autumn colors. There had still been no word of Brian, and even Kevin was beginning to doubt that his brother was alive. Vicksburg, where Brian had been with the Texas Seventh, had long since fallen to the Union army, and still no word of Brian. The war was not going well for the Confederacy, and Kevin expected any day to hear that it had reached a bloody conclusion. Even the most rabid Confederate sympathizers in East Texas wore glum faces nowadays.

Riding along one morning, Kevin said, "Now that picking is about over, Daddy, I can soon turn more attention to the mills." He sighed. "It was hardly worth raising a cotton crop this year. With New Orleans in Union hands and most foreign ships afraid to venture into Galveston harbor, most of my cotton is going to have to remain stored in Galveston warehouses."

Sean said, "Don't fret, son, you're not starving, like all too many in the South. As soon as this whole mess is over, the demand for cotton in Europe will send the price to the moon and beyond. You'll reap a good profit."

"You were wise, Daddy, in going into lumber instead of staying with cotton alone."

Sean, definitely more interested in Moraghan affairs now, waxed enthusiastic. "When this bloody conflict is over, Kevin, the demand for lumber is going to double, mark my words. Maybe even triple. When it's over, we're going to have settlers pouring into Texas. The South is going to be in chaos for years to come. Since we escaped most of the brunt of the war here, people are going to come in, hoping to find a new life. Towns are going to grow, and that means demand for building materials. I have this feeling that most structures built here will always be of wood, instead of brick and stone. It's cheaper, easier, and faster to build with."

"In that you're probably right."

"One thing, Kevin . . ." Sean twisted about in the saddle. "The supply of timber is not limitless. It's something I've been thinking about. Already we have cleared hundreds of acres of timber here on Moraghan. We should think of replanting behind the felling of trees. That way, within a few years we'll have a new growth of timber. Before the war, I rode through Tom Burns's acreage down south aways. He was one of the first to go into the lumber business, you know. He's cut down almost all of his trees and the land is bare as a baby's ass. In a few years his land will be almost worthless, even for planting crops since it will erode and wash away. The Lord made the earth plentiful, but man needs a little foresight or the land will be ruined forever."

Kevin was constantly amazed at this man—so many unsuspected facets and depths he had never seen. Now that they had grown closer, Kevin regretted all those lost years. He said, "That's an admirable thought, Daddy, and one I won't forget."

Sean acknowledged the admiration in Kevin's voice by a slight dip of his head. "All too often man is a greedy, ruthless creature, a despoiler, prone to ravage the earth and people as well to get what he wants *now*, with no thought or concern for the future." He broke off with a self-deprecatory smile. "Listen to me. I must be in my dotage, philosophizing like this."

Impulsively Kevin said, "Daddy, what were you before you came to Texas? You've spoken little of it. I know you're a well-educated man, but beyond that . . ."

He saw that cold, distant look come over Sean's

face, and he knew that he had gone too far. Yet he refused to apologize. He was this man's son, he was a Moraghan; it was his right to know what his roots were.

He stared resolutely ahead, and they rode for a little in a chilly silence. Then, as Sawmill No. 1 came into view, Sean kneed his horse close and touched Kevin's arm.

"Son, forgive me. Your curiosity is natural; I realize that, and I know I have never talked of the past. It's too painful for me. Perhaps, some day, I'll be able to talk of it to you. But for now, bear with me." His laughter was strained. "There is nothing of a criminal nature in my past. On that you have my oath."

Touched by the subdued tone of Sean's voice, Kevin nodded. "All right, Daddy. I reckon I can stand waiting a little longer."

As they rode on toward the mill, the high whine of the gang saw could be heard. Gouts of steam from the engine used to power the two flywheels poured out from under the roof. The sawmill was actually little more than a shed with a roof, open on two sides. The roof was needed to keep the cut lumber dry, and the sides were open to let the air in. It was hot work in summer.

They dismounted at the stream some distance away and tied the horses, then toiled up the slight slope, and stepped inside. Oscar Keller was the sawyer operating the gang saw, and also in charge of the six-man crew. Two men maneuvered the logs on and off the carriage of the saw, two men tended the boilers, and the other pair stacked the sawed lumber.

The gang saw was far from efficient. It was composed of six long, narrow, vertical blades that used an up-and-down reciprocating action. The blades were set a fixed distance apart on the carriage and sliced up every log identically, regardless of flaws. The saw

323

was inefficient for this reason, and also because the steam engine wasted energy overcoming the inertia on every stroke and return.

Kevin was unhappy every time he watched the saw in operation. He stood now, hands on hips, scowling at it.

Sean, aware of the cause of his displeasure, laughed and touched him on the arm. Raising his voice to be heard over the whining saw, he said, "I know, son. You long for one of the new circular saws. So do I, but you know that I have written, inquiring about them. None will be available until this damned war is over. All production of steam engines is occupied with making machines of destruction."

Kevin sighed. "I know, Daddy. All we do nowadays, it seems, is wait." He was sorry the instant the words were out. Sean turned his face away. Although he never talked about it any longer, he was still waiting for word of Brian. He had written numerous letters asking about his elder son, but what few replies he received offered no news of Brian, good or bad.

It was perhaps fitting that the letter came on the heels of the first norther of the season. It was a clear day but cold and windy, and Kevin was in the cotton field hurrying the picking along. Several acres of stalks laden with the snow-white bolls still remained to be picked. If it got cold enough, a sleet storm could hit, pounding the bolls from the stalks.

He was standing by the cotton wagon, weighing a picker's sack of cotton—the pickers were paid by the pound—when he saw Kate hurrying from the direction of the house. She waved and called out to him. There was something about her that bespoke trouble. With a cold feeling in his gut, Kevin turned the weighing over to the man next to him and hurried to meet her.

Seeing him coming toward her, Kate paused to wait for him. When he was within hearing distance, she said breathlessly, "Nora is at the house. A letter came about Brian."

"What is the news?"

"Not good, I fear," she said in a subdued voice. "Nora has the letter with her, but I haven't read it yet."

As they hurried toward the house, Kevin found his thoughts more on his wife than his brother. If Brian was dead, would Kate grieve for him? After all, Brian was the father of her daughter. They had rarely talked of Brian since that long-ago day when Kevin had knocked him down.

Nora was waiting on the veranda, sitting quite still in a rocker. Her eyes were dry, but her face was set in lines of grief. Without a word she handed a much-folded sheet of paper to Kevin.

The letter was from General John C. Pemberton. They had learned that Pemberton had been the general in command at Vicksburg. Sean had written to him some months ago, and had despaired of ever hearing.

Dear Mr. Moraghan: Sir, I hope you will pardon the long delay in this response to your query. Matters have been rather turbulent since that sad day back in July when I was forced to surrender Vicksburg to General Grant, and your letter was rerouted several times before it finally arrived in my hands.

Another cause for the delay was my desire to thoroughly investigate the matter of your missing son with every facility at my command. My investigation, I fear, has come to naught.

On June 27 last, not too long before it was my sorrowful duty to lay down arms against the enemy, your son volunteered for a dangerous mission. I was reluctant, but the brave lad was most insistent, so I finally acquiesced. I am not at liberty to reveal the purpose of the mission, but I

325

do feel compelled to inform you that there is a possibility that the tide of battle may well have turned in our favor should he have been successful.

Alas, such was not to be. He never reached his destination. Your courageous son seems to have vanished off the face of the earth. I have further bad tidings to report. A bundle of his clothing, with papers therein to substantiate their ownership beyond doubt, was washed ashore along the Yazoo River.

Beyond this, I know nothing of his fate. The Yazoo is a strong river at that period of the year, and I must warn you of the possibility that your son was drowned, or met his death by other means.

I shall pray to our Lord for his safekeeping, and commend him to you as a man of great courage and daring. You may be proud of your son, if that is of any comfort to you.

My condolences to you and yours, sir. I remain, General John C. Pemberton.

Still staring at the letter, Kevin found his eyes swimming with tears. Finally he looked at his mother. "How is Daddy? How did he take the news?"

Nora said stonily, "He is in that office of his again, staring down at the river. I found him after the messenger left, sitting there with that letter in his hand. I took it from him and read it. He will not talk of it, Kevin!" Finally she gave way to tears, burying her face in her hands.

Kevin felt helpless as a babe and could think of no words of comfort that wouldn't sound inane. Instead he said, "You stay here, Momma, and I'll ride over and see if he'll talk to me."

"Come along, Nora," Kate said. "I'll make a cup of tea. It's too chilly to sit out here, anyway."

Kevin saddled a horse and rode over to the main

house. He found Sean sitting in the usual place in his office.

At the sound of Kevin's footsteps, he slowly turned his head. His eyes were red and had a wild look. "Come to gloat, have you, now that Brian is dead?"

Kevin tried to overlook the injustice of the remark. "You don't know that he is dead . . ."

"I know! Lord God Almighty, I know!" he roared, slapping his hand down onto the desk. "And no weasel bullshit words from you will make me think any different!"

"I realize that you're broken up, Daddy, and not responsible for what you're saying . . ."

"I know exactly what I'm saying!"

"All right, Daddy. If that's the way it is, I'll leave now. I didn't come over here to be abused. I'll come back when you can talk more reasonably."

He was halfway through the dog run when he heard Sean's voice. "Kevin? Son, come back!"

Kevin hesitated, tempted to just keep going. But finally he turned back. He put his head into the room without speaking.

"Kevin . . ." Sean paused, scrubbing a hand down across his face. "Will you be over in the morning, for our usual inspection ride?"

"Ride over in . . .?" Astonishment rendered him speechless. In the end he merely bobbed his head in reply and left quickly.

When he came over the next morning, he half expected Sean to have changed his mind. Yet he was waiting on the steps of the veranda, in riding gear, his horse already saddled. In the doorway behind him stood Nora. She shook her head, spread her hands in a helpless gesture.

"You're late, son," Sean grumbled, and came down the steps to mount up.

"I'm sorry, Daddy. We're just finishing up picking, and I had to . . ."

"I've told you and told you, lumbering is more important than cotton."

Kevin marveled as the day wore on. Sean seemed to be a man possessed, driving himself harder than ever. Neither by word nor expression did he express any grief over Brian.

From Sean's journal, September 20, 1863:

I try not to brood on Brian's death. I know that my sweet Nora and Kevin think this strange of me. But if I allowed myself to dwell on it, I would go mad. Dear God, of this I am positive!

The only solace I have is losing myself in work. I seem to be in a fever these days, driving myself in a frenzy of work, so that I am so weary by the time evening comes that I sleep the sleep of the dead. At strange times I find myself longing for death. It would be a welcome surcease from grief.

I must not think such thoughts. It is an offense against God.

Oh, Brian, my son, my son! How can I continue my life with the knowledge that my own issue, my own flesh and blood, is gone from this earth?

Such thoughts do Kevin a grave injustice, I know. I have come, if not to love him as I would my own son, at least to respect and admire him. We have grown quite close, and I do sorely regret the doubts I had of him for all those years. Search as I may, I can find none of the Danker traits in him.

Perhaps my Nora is right. Perhaps upbringing is of more importance than blood. If such be the fact, the responsibility for the admirable man he has become belongs solely to Nora. God knows, I ignored him shamefully for so very long. Worse,

I scorned him. I found fault where it did not exist. Lord willing, I must endeavor to make it up to him, in the time I have left on this earth.

My estate is given into Brian's hands in my will. It was only fitting, not only because he was of my own flesh and blood, but also because he was the older. It has long been the custom that a man sees to it that his eldest inherits.

Now that has changed. Brian has gone from my bosom, and I must, in all conscience, consider Kevin as the rightful heir to Moraghan Acres.

Soon, I must journey into Nacogdoches and consult with Stony about changing my will, making Kevin my heir. I do not feel adequate to the task at present. Certainly before Christmas and the New Year.

Regardless of how much I endeavor not to, my thoughts always return to Brian.

I have long since fallen out of the habit of prayer, but now each night, when I lay me down to sleep, I pray for your immortal soul, my son.

Sonny Danker had been disconcerted when he learned that the older Moraghan boy had gone off to war. When he found this out, he decided to bide his time and wait for him to return. He wanted to kill all three Moraghans at once.

Consequently, when word spread across East Texas that Brian Moraghan was dead, Sonny was elated.

Now he could make his long-awaited move. He had spent most of his time around the shack since Ma's death, practicing daily with his guns, honing his skills. Three times, he had left briefly on assignments to earn money to live on. Word had spread in certain circles that Sonny Danker was for hire again and was the deadly killing machine that he had once been, and jobs came his way once more.

Sonny had amused himself teaching his oldest son,

Tod, how to handle a gun. Tod was sixteen, big for his age, and eager to follow in his father's footsteps. Sonny was not surprised to learn that the boy took to guns. He was *his* son, wasn't he? He had no doubt of that; Tod, the firstborn, had been whelped long before the hand was ruined and Sonny began his wanderings. In those days Molly had been well taken care of in the blankets, with no inclination to wrap her legs around another man.

Heretofore, Sonny had taken little interest in the numerous brats swarming around the shack, but it tickled his fancy that Tod wished to follow in his old man's footsteps. Sonny had heard other fathers talk of their sons carrying on after them. Of course, he had no one to brag to—Sonny had never made friends easily, and had never cultivated them. He had heard too many stories of men of his profession being gunned down, usually from ambush, by fast friends. The temptation was always there, the lure of getting the rep of being the one who had killed Sonny Danker. Sonny was a loner, and preferred it that way. Still, the fact that he *could* brag about Tod pleased him. Maybe, just maybe, they could ride together in time. In tandem, they could make a fearsome pair, and no man would dare come at them face to face.

But from the moment Sonny learned of Brian Moraghan's fate, all his time and thought were devoted to devising the best way to accomplish his, and Ma's, purpose.

He began to stalk the last two Moraghans. He watched them for over a month before he acted. He learned that the pair of them conducted an inspection tour of the plantation every day of the week except Sunday, devoting most of their time to the two sawmills. He took careful note of the fact that they rode without sidearms, only a rifle in the saddle scabbard on the old man's horse. If they had ridden out loaded down with guns, it wouldn't have changed Sonny's

330

mind, but it would have altered his plan. This way, with just the rifle to contend with, it made everything easier.

He noted that there were any number of places along the trails they rode where he could ambush them, shoot both men off their horses, but Sonny didn't want that. They had to *know* who brought about their deaths—certainly the older man had to know. He thought of stepping out on the trail in front of them, and leveling down on them. Yet there was always an element of risk involved in that; horses were unreliable and could suddenly shy just enough to throw his aim off. That had happened in the defile down in Louisiana on that day long ago.

He finally decided that the ideal spot for the gun down was just outside the first sawmill they visited regularly. They always tethered their horses about fifty yards distant, at the bottom of the slight slope, and toiled up to the mill; the high whine of the saw seemed to spook the horses. And halfway up that slope was a large stump, which made an ideal place of concealment. If he hid behind the stump and stepped out with gun already drawn, he could shoot them down, and be on his horse and away before anyone in the sawmill would be the wiser. The whine of the saw would drown out the sounds of any gunshots to those working at the mill.

So, on a clear, chill morning in late November, he rode to the sawmill, and tied his horse off in a copse of small trees not too far from the stump. Since the Moraghans kept to a fairly regular schedule, Sonny knew that he was in advance of them by at least an hour.

He stationed himself behind the stump and settled down to wait. His breath smoked in the cold air, and he jammed his left hand into the pocket of his wool jacket to keep it warm.

He longed for a cigar, but there was a risk, however slight, that the smell might drift on the stiff breeze to his approaching victims. The little Mexican cigars smelled to high heaven.

"I think it'll freeze tonight, Kevin," Sean said. "Good hog-killing weather. Maybe we'll butcher those shoats soon."

"That sounds like a good idea, Daddy." Like most of their conversations of late, Kevin thought glumly: the weather, the price of cotton and lumber, hog-killing time—anything but Brian or anything touching on Brian.

They forded the small stream at the bottom of the slope. Across the other side they reined in their mounts and got off, tying the horses to the live oak stretching its limbs out over the water. Frost had long since killed any graze, but the horses had access to water.

They began walking toward the mill. The smell of sawdust hung heavy in the brisk morning air. Kevin tilted his head back and took a deep breath.

He heard Sean's incredulous whisper: "Lord God Almighty!"

Kevin snapped his head down. Standing athwart the trail about fifty yards ahead was a slim man in dark clothing. Sunlight glinted off the gun in his left hand. His right hand, sheathed in a black glove, hung by his side. Recognition was slow in coming. And then he had it—Sonny Danker!

"It's finally come down to it." Danker's voice curled like a whip across the distance separating them. "Remember Lem and Jed? Remember this hand?" He raised and lowered the gloved hand. "All your doing, you Irish fucker. I swore to Ma that you'd be paid back, and now it's time."

Sonny Danker's face wore the look of a grinning skull, and his eyes had a maniacal snap. The sound of the Colt cocking was loud in the still morning. "The

332

brat first, Moraghan. The last one left to you. He goes first, I want you to watch him die!"

The Colt swung up, centering on Kevin, who stood like a statue, his mind frozen. The danger was there, it crackled like a current between them, but he seemed unable to move. The situation was so unreal as to be unbelievable.

"No! Dear God, no!" The words were wrung from Sean's throat like a scream of agony. He gave Kevin a mighty shove, sending him crashing to the ground, and threw himself into the path of the bullet as Danker fired.

The slope was not steep, but such had been the power of Sean's push that Kevin tumbled over and over two-thirds of the way to the stream before he could stop and scramble around on his hands and knees to look back.

His heart skipped when he saw Sean sprawled on the ground. His gaze jumped to Danker, looking tall and threatening now, with the rising sun directly behind him. He saw the gun in the man's hand pointing at him, and Kevin threw himself to one side and rolled on down the slope as the pistol cracked. The bullet kicked up dirt only inches from him.

He forced all concern for Sean out of his mind and concentrated on surviving the next few moments. This second roll brought him within a few feet of the tethered horses. Sean's horse whinnied in fright, rearing as another bullet whined off a rock nearby. Kevin scrambled on his hands and knees beneath the sharp hooves pawing the air.

He came to his feet on the opposite side of the horse, clawing for the rifle in the saddle scabbard. Just as his hands closed around the butt, the Colt cracked again. The bellow of the animal was womanish. The horse shuddered and began to fall. Kevin scrambled out of the way as the animal thudded to the ground, then threw himself flat behind the still thrashing horse. He risked a peek over the prone animal, and saw that Danker hadn't moved.

Then Danker said, "May as well show yourself, Moraghan. You're a dead man any way you cut it. Your old man is dead; you're next!"

He fired, and Kevin ducked down. The bullet whipped past overhead.

He looked at the rifle gripped in his sweaty hands. It was a .44-caliber Henry that Sean had purchased last year. It had lever action, firing fifteen shots. Unlike Brian, Kevin had never developed any special affection for guns; he had never practiced with a pistol, but he had hunted on occasion with a rifle. A terrible shooter, he had never tried to improve, but at least he knew which end to point when firing.

He took a deep breath, gathered himself, and came up from behind the dead horse, firing, levering the rifle as fast as he could. He charged up the slope, zigzagging from side to side.

Clearly the suddenness of his move had caught Danker by surprise. For all the good it did him—Kevin hadn't counted the shots, but he had gotten off several —and the man with the Colt stood untouched.

Kevin charged on, firing. He saw a puff of smoke from the Colt, and something struck his left leg like a club. The leg gave way under him, and he fell headlong. He tried to get up and fell again. The leg was numb, useless.

Looking up, he saw Danker standing perfectly still. He was grinning savagely. Then his mouth opened in a laugh. A silent laugh. At least Kevin could hear nothing. Then he realized that all the gunfire had momentarily deafened him.

With a superhuman effort he came to his feet. He was close enough now to see a look of astonishment, tinged with fear, cross Danker's face. Danker shouted, "Damn you, you're dead! Die, you fucker!"

The words reached Kevin's ears as a whisper, and even before the last word was out, he levered the rifle and fired, fired as the pistol in Danker's hand bucked. Again, Kevin felt the impact of a bullet, this time in his left shoulder. He began to fall. But he saw Danker go stumbling back, and as Kevin hit the ground, he managed to twist his head up far enough to see the other man flat on the ground on his back, unmoving.

Kevin let his head fall again, his cheek grinding against a stone. He had never been so weary, and pain throbbed in his leg now, and his left shoulder. He could see the shoulder. Blood was spreading on his shirt, like a scarlet inkblot.

It took a great effort to raise his head. A wave of dizziness took him, and everything went wavery, like a scene viewed underwater. He blinked furiously, and finally could see enough to locate Sean's body, lying still where it had fallen.

Leaving the Henry behind, Kevin began to crawl toward Sean.

Sean's consciousness had faded in and out, and he had heard the crack of the Colt several times, followed by the booming of the rifle, and knew that Kevin was still alive. He wanted to rise and shout to them that they were uncle and nephew, that it was a sin to kill each other. He could not move, and when he tried to speak, his words were only a whisper.

Now there was only a silence, a terrible silence. "Kevin? Son, are you all right?" His lips shaped the words; yet he knew they were not voiced. The pain in his chest was almost unbearable. With an effort that dimly surprised him, he raised his hand to his chest to make the sign of the cross. "Our Father who art in Heaven, forgive me. Forgive me, Father, for I have sinned . . ."

He felt a touch on his face. "Daddy?"

Sean opened his eyes to see Kevin's face hovering

over his. In a burst of strength he managed to say, "Kevin? Are you . . .?"

Kevin nodded. Tears stood in his eyes. "Yes, Daddy. I'm all right. Sonny Danker is dead . . ."

"Ah, son, son! Danker was . . . He was your . . ."

"Don't try to talk, Daddy. I'll get help from the mill."

"No use . . . Tell Nora . . ."

Again, he tried to make the sign of the cross, and his hand fell nervelessly to his side, and Sean Moraghan was no more.

25

It was a cold day when they buried Sean Moraghan.
The ground around the grave dug into the hillside
overlooking the river had a light dusting of snow.

Nora was astounded by the outpouring of mourners.
Considering the hostility toward the Moraghans among
their neighbors, she would have thought that most of
them would have stayed away. But the schoolhouse,
where the local preacher had delivered the eulogy,
had overflowed, and even now, as they stood by the
grave, like an open wound, she could see horses and
buggies still coming from both directions along the
river road. People had come from as far away as Nacogdoches and Huntsville. It was out of respect for
Sean, she knew, but she also suspected that the report
of Brian's death had something to do with it. That
had drained away much of the hostility, and the violent death of Sean coming on the heels of that news
had aroused general sympathy.

Nora had debated long and hard about revealing

Sean's Catholicism and about getting a priest in from Nacogdoches, but she had finally decided against it. To her knowledge, Sean still thought of himself as a failed Catholic on the day of his death, and somehow, as strange as it might strike most people, Nora felt that to declare him a Catholic after his death would be the worst form of sacrilege.

As the preacher droned on at length with the graveside service, Nora glanced to her right. Kate stood beside her, hovering close, Nora suspected, to support her in the event she needed it. But Nora had existed in a sort of calm since Sean's death, and had yet to give away to tears. She had heard that there was a phenomenon associated with violent storms at sea, wherein the storms carried a core of eerie quiet as they traveled. The eye of her own storm would pass, she knew, and she would break; yet she was determined that it would not be in the presence of others, not even the members of her own family, but in the privacy of her bedroom. No . . . in her and Sean's bedroom, and at that thought, the storm threatened. Resolutely she held it at bay, and let her glance move on.

Kevin, his leg and shoulder swathed in bandages, sat in a camp chair on the other side of Kate. His face had a white, haunted look, and Nora knew that he blamed himself for Sean's death, and no amount of reassurance had so far swayed him otherwise. Ranging on either side of the chair were their two children. Debra Lee, almost eleven, was showing signs of growing into a great beauty. She had Kate's bold good looks and some of her unexpected humor; yet she was headstrong, and Nora feared that she might have a wild streak. Michael, now eight, more favored his father—dark, thin, and very intense. Clearly baffled by what was happening, Michael hovered on the verge of tears.

Nora sighed, looked to her left. Anna had been pin-

338

ing, since the news of Brian reached them. She had lost several pounds, and her clothes hung loosely on her normally voluptuous figure. Her eyes were often red, and even now she was weeping softly; but Nora didn't know whether it was for husband or father-in-law. Her pair stood on either side of her, their hands in her tight grip. Brian's two were more boisterous than Kevin's children, except possibly Debra Lee. There was a rivalry between Mark and Betsy and Debra Lee, at times blazing into open antagonism. Debra Lee competed with them in everything—schoolwork and at play. Since she was an unusually bright child, she almost always bested them at schoolwork; yet she even got the better of Mark occasionally in physical activity.

The girl always made sure that her parents and grandmother knew of these occasions, since she ran home and reported at length.

Nora came to herself with a start when she heard the first thump of dirt on the pine coffin. While her attention had wandered, the preacher had finally finished, and two men with shovels were filling in the grave. Already people were milling about, forming small groups, shooting curious glances her way. Nora furtively scrubbed a tear from her eye, and mentally prepared herself for the coming ordeal. There was food and drink aplenty at the big house. Kate had worried as to whether her mother-in-law was up to it, but Nora knew that it would be viewed as rather odd if the usual after-burial gathering did not take place. She smiled inwardly as she remembered the boisterous Irish wakes back in Tennessee. Sean had once commented that a festive wake gave the mourners the opportunity to celebrate their relief that they were alive, whereas the one they mourned was dead.

Resolutely she faced away from the gravediggers and accepted with an appropriate face the condolences of the mourners as they filed past. She noticed one hanging back—a young man, probably in his mid-twenties. His eyes were dark, glowing under deepset, heavy black eyebrows. His hair above a high forehead was black as pitch. His was a very expressive face. He was dressed in funereal black, with a sober white shirt, a black string tie, and held a flat-crowned black hat over his heart with one long-fingered hand.

Nora couldn't remember ever seeing him before, and was mildly curious about his presence here. He waited until the others had moved off, then approached, dipping his head. In a deep, melodious voice, he said, "My condolences, Mrs. Moraghan. I don't believe we've met, but I knew your husband well. I am Stonewall Lieberman."

A Jew? Here? She hadn't known there were any Jews in East Texas. There had been a few back in Tennessee, but they were a race apart, mostly storekeepers or professional people, and she had known them by name only. "Thank you, Mr. Lieberman. You say you knew Sean?"

"I did. A fine man, Mr. Moraghan," he said with a mournful face. "I am an attorney with a practice in Nacogdoches. Mr. Moraghan came to me a week after I hung out my shingle . . ."

"Whatever for?" she asked in astonishment.

"He did me the honor of allowing me to draw up his last will and testament. He was my first client and I shall never forget him for that reason alone."

"That's odd," she mused. "Sean didn't tell me of this." A spark of anger brought her head up. "Hellfire and spit, why wasn't I informed of this?"

The lawyer's face flamed and he looked away in an agony of embarrassment. "I'm sorry, I thought you did know. Mr. Moraghan didn't take me into his confidence to that extent."

She managed a contrite smile. "No, I'm the one to be sorry. I had no cause to bite your head off;

340

it's not your doing." She tilted her head to one side. "Mr. Lieberman, is it? *Stonewall?*"

His embarrassment mounted. "Papa was a great admirer of General Stonewall Jackson."

Amused, Nora said, "Was he indeed?"

"My friends call me Stony."

"Stony?" In spite of the circumstances Nora was hard put to hide a smile. The name implied a stone face, and this man's face was a perfect mirror of his emotions. She felt a tug at her skirt and looked down.

It was Debra Lee. The girl's face was turned up. She wore a solemn expression, her eyes round as she stared at the lawyer. "Grandma?"

"Yes, child?"

"I am not a child." Debra Lee drew herself up with an adult dignity. "I am eleven, almost. Aren't you going to introduce me to the gentleman?"

"Eleven, is it?" This time Nora let her laughter go and was rewarded by startled, shocked glances from the mourners still within earshot. "This is my granddaughter, Mr. Lieberman, Debra Lee Moraghan. *Miss* Moraghan, this is Stonewall Lieberman, your grandfather's attorney."

A smile broke across Stony's mobile features, and he bowed slightly, said gravely, "A pleasure, Miss Moraghan."

Debra Lee, whose gaze had never left his face, took a step away from Nora and curtsied. Nora, remembering the girl in trousers and one of her brother's old shirts, had to struggle to keep from bursting into laughter again. If a girl ever deserved to be called a hoyden, it was Debra Lee. Nora had never seen her curtsy, and if asked, would have sworn she didn't know how. Now Kate called to Debra Lee, and the girl gave Stony a dimpled, flashing smile, and walked sedately over to her mother.

"A lovely girl, Mrs. Moraghan," Stony commented.

"You should have seen the little witch fighting with

her cousin a few days ago," Nora murmured, but with pride in her voice. "Will you be coming up to the house, Mr. Lieberman?"

"I believe not, madam. Business affairs demand my presence back in Nacogdoches. However, I do have legal business to transact with you and yours. To be specific, the reading of your late husband's will, but this is hardly the time for such matters. Would it be all right if I rode out again? Say, in two weeks?"

"That will do nicely, sir." Curiosity got the better of her. "I don't suppose you could reveal the contents of the will now? In a general sort of way, a summary?"

He frowned. "I'm afraid not. That would not be ethical on my part. A gathering of all relatives is required. Two weeks should give you ample time to inform distant relations. If that time is not sufficient, a further postponement may be arranged."

Although she had not met them and Sean had been laconic when mentioning them, Nora understood there were some distant relatives in Tennessee, though no parents and no siblings. To attempt to contact them would only result in uncovering Sean's leaving the priesthood. And that would stir up a scandal, which she was certain he would not have wanted. She shook her head, motioning. "All of Sean's relations are here today, except for," she swallowed, "for a son lost in the war."

Stony's face mirrored sympathy. "I am sorry."

"So, you see, there will be no cause for delay. I shall expect you two weeks from today, Mr. Lieberman."

East Texas winters were usually relatively mild. Snow seldom stayed on the ground for more than a few days. But the winter of 1864 was unduly severe. It snowed for two days after New Year's, and the temperature hovered around zero following the storm. Even the swift-running river was rimmed with ice.

Even with all the fireplaces roaring, the big house was chilly. Following Sean's death and funeral, Nora had taken to her bed with the grippe. Seldom sick, it made her cross and irritable. Kate had insisted on staying over and tending to her. Late in the afternoon of the third day of her illness, Nora demanded to be allowed out of bed. Over Kate's strenuous objections, she huddled before the bedroom fireplace, with a shawl around her shoulders.

Kate came into the room carrying a tea tray. She placed the tray beside the rocking chair and tucked the shawl around Nora's shoulders.

"Stop fussing so, Kate!" Nora snarled. "A proper wife would be home tending to her injured husband, instead of here with me!"

"Kevin is coming along just fine," Kate said with equanimity. "He is even getting about now.. And I don't know who is the grumpier, mother or son."

Nora said, more reasonably, "I'm sorry, dear. It's just that I hate being sick; you know that. I should be up and doing."

"Doing what? It's too cold to venture outside, and Lord knows you've got enough servants inside to . . ." There was a sound of commotion downstairs. Kate cocked her head, listening. "Now what? I'd better go see."

Kate left the room quickly. Nora, her head fuzzy from the grippe, was not even curious. She sipped the scalding tea, grateful as the steam cleared the stuffiness from her head.

She didn't bother to look around when the door opened again. She heard footsteps, then silence. She said irritably, "Well, what is it?"

"Nora," Kate said in a strange voice, "we have company."

"Tell them to go away. I'm not up to having company . . ."

"Momma?"

Nora's heart almost stopped at the sound of the voice she had resigned herself to never hearing again. With a cry she whipped her head around, the teacup thumping to the floor.

Brian stood grinning at her. He was terribly thin, gaunt. His hair was long, matted, and a heavy, unkempt beard covered the lower half of his face.

"Brian! My God, we thought you were dead!"

"Nah. You should know by now that I'm indestructible."

She held out her arms, and he loped across the room to fall to his knees beside the chair. Nora hugged him fiercely, tears stinging her eyes. Then she gave a strangled laugh. "Whew! Hellfire and spit, son, you smell as strong as a horse!"

"Sorry, Momma." He stood up. "I haven't been too close to water of late. It's too damned cold to wash in the rivers, and I've been hurrying to get home."

Kate had been cleaning up after Nora's dropped teacup. She said, "Sit down, Brian, and I'll pour you and Nora tea."

Grinning wanly, he perched on the edge of a chair. "I've been in a Yankee prison camp, Momma. Rough times. I damned near starved to death. Also, I was wounded in the back when they captured me, and that gave me some trouble, but I got through it all right. Three weeks ago, I managed to escape."

"But couldn't you have gotten word to us, so we would at least have known you were still alive?"

Brian accepted a cup of tea from Kate and sipped it. "I was naked as a skunk when they captured me, and I never told them who I was. Didn't want to give them the satisfaction. All they knew was that I was a Confederate. And getting letters out ain't all that easy, even if I had been so inclined."

"But you could have let us know *somehow!* Your father," she looked away, "all of us thought you were dead. It caused us a lot of needless grief."

Brian sat up, looked around. "Where is Daddy?"

"Sean is dead, son. We buried him over a week ago."

"What!" He jumped up. "You're joshing me, you must be!"

"I wouldn't josh about a thing like that. He is no longer with us."

"What happened?"

At that moment Anna burst through the open door, eyes wild. "María told me . . ." She skidded to a stop, staring at Brian. She swayed, as though about to faint, then collected herself, and ran across the room. "Dear God! Brian, Brian! You're alive!" She wrapped her arms around him, raining kisses on his face.

Brian, his gaze never leaving Nora's face, suffered Anna for a moment, then growled, "Not now, woman." He pushed her away and resumed his seat. "Tell me about Daddy."

Nora took a deep breath and told him what had happened. Anna stood back for a moment, biting her lip, tears flowing unchecked down her face. Then she sank down beside his chair, and hid her face against his leg. Brian ignored her.

Silence reigned in the room for several moments after Nora was finished. "Those goddamned Dankers," Brian finally said in an anguished voice. "They plagued Daddy all his life and I never did understand why."

Instead of enlightening him, Nora said, "The last one is gone now, except for some children left behind."

Brian came to his feet again, fists doubled. "I should ride over and kill them all, children or not!"

"No!" Nora said sharply. "There's been enough death!"

"You don't understand, Momma. It's like I learned in the rangers . . . When you're fighting Indians, kill women and children, too. If not, one of them may grow up and kill *you*. Who knows but what one of the Danker brats may come after us some day?"

"Hellfire and spit, son, I should think you've had enough of killing to do you awhile!"

Brian paced for a moment. Kate and Anna watched him, Anna still with that bewildered, hurt look on her face. Nora stared down at her clasped hands in her lap.

"Kevin!" Brian suddenly snarled. He socked a fist into his palm. "It's his fault, he should have watched over Daddy better. I bet he wasn't even," he sneered, "carrying a sidearm. A milksop, is what he is! Where is he, anyway?" He glared around. "Hiding away, afraid to face me?"

"Your brother almost lost his life as well. He was grievously wounded and can hardly get around."

"I'll see to it that he never gets around, by God, I will!" He started toward the door in galloping strides.

"Brian." Nora spoke quietly, but such was the icy tone of her voice it stopped him in his tracks. "If you do anything to Kevin, or even speak to him of blame, you'll leave this house forever. He blames himself enough as it is. Now, sit down and behave yourself for once."

They were all gathered in Sean's office for the reading of the will. Since Nora, now fully recovered from the grippe, had the uneasy feeling that it was going to be far from a social occasion, she thought the office a fitting place. Only the adults were gathered; the children had been shooed outside to play. Debra Lee had protested vociferously, demanding to remain by Stony's side, much to the attorney's red-faced embarrassment. Nora had never seen a girl, especially one so young, become so moonstruck so quickly.

Kevin had been brought over in a buggy. He was ambulatory now, but he was still suffering a great deal of discomfort. The greeting between the two brothers had been stiff, and Nora could only assume that Kate had told Kevin of Brian's outburst.

The lawyer read the brief will in a low, toneless

voice. He had already dispensed with the minor bequests to the household servants, and Nora had sent them away. Now only the immediate members of the family were present.

Stony cleared his throat, glanced at them, and resumed reading again: "To my dear Nora, loyal and loving wife, I bequeath the main house at Moraghan. The house will be hers for as long as she shall live.

"And to my elder son, Brian Moraghan, I bequeath Moraghan Acres, same to include the original grant, and the grant adjoining, which came to me through the offices of one Ty Reynolds . . ."

Kevin stirred, a mutter coming from him. Brian was smiling broadly.

Stony continued to read: "Also to my elder son, I bequeath the 640 acres near Beaumont, the acreage I received for serving in the Army of Texas.

"To my second son, Kevin Moraghan, I bequeath the 640 acres located in the Rio Grande Valley, which also became mine on the death of Ty Reynolds . . ."

Kate was on her feet, fists clenched. "Kevin might as well be disinherited! Years of hard labor, dawn until dark, he has devoted to improving Moraghan, and now he is being evicted, not even left title to the house he built!"

"Now, Kate," Brian said amusedly, "don't get all het up. Daddy built that house, if I remember correctly. Besides, nobody's kicking Kev out. He can continue to live there. Moraghan is a big place; he can help me run it."

In a choked voice Kevin said, "Become hired help, is that the way of it? Living off what crumbs you see fit to pass out?"

Brian shrugged. "Suit yourself. It's no skin off me. I think I'm being fair. Daddy left it all to me." His manner became smug. "I have the say-so now."

Kevin's face reddened, and he started to speak in anger, but Nora placed a quieting hand on his arm.

347

"Mr. Lieberman, there is a grave injustice here, surely you can see that?"

Stony Lieberman shifted, his face troubled. "I am sorry, madam. I have no choice but to interpret the will as written."

"But I'm sure Sean had it in his mind to change it!"

"That, I have no way of knowing. But he did not."

"How about *my* rights? I am his wife!"

"Mrs. Moraghan, the will is legal in every way. Unfortunately, under our legal system as it is today, a female's legal rights are severely limited. If you have in mind to fight it through the courts, I must advise you that, in my opinion, you will be wasting time and money."

"Come on, Momma," Brian said chidingly. "You've got a home for as long as you live. And I am the older son. It's the customary thing for the firstborn to inherit."

Stony said stiffly, "In that he is correct, madam."

"But it's not fair!" Kate burst out.

Nora turned to Kevin. "We'll fight it, Kevin. You and yours can move into the big house with me."

"And then what?" Kevin said angrily. "Live off Brian's charity? That I will never do."

Brian said carelessly, "I don't see that you have much of a choice, little brother."

"I have a choice. I will leave here; I will take my family and go. The acres in the Rio Grande Valley that Daddy saw fit to leave me . . ."

Brian laughed. "Only Mexicans and goats down there, the way I get it."

"Then I will raise goats! Better that than remaining here."

"Don't say that, Kevin," Nora said in dismay. "This is your home; you can't just pack up and leave."

"Let him go, Momma," Brian said with scarcely disguised contempt. "Poor little tad got his feelings all

348

hurt. We don't need him around, to have to listen to his whining."

Goaded, Kevin snapped, "Yes, I'm hurt! Goddammit, all those years I took a backseat to you. I thought Daddy didn't love me. But while you were away, we grew close. At least that's what I thought." His mouth took on a bitter twist. "But I reckon I was wrong in that."

Brian gestured. "If Daddy favored me, there must have been a reason. Did you ever think of that?"

"I've thought of it, yes, many times. And I finally decided it was because he was blind to your true nature. He said something not long ago about others, but it fits you like a glove, Brian." Kevin leaned forward with great difficulty. "You're a despoiler, Brian, a user, a taker. Other people mean damn all to you. You didn't even care enough about the members of your own family to let us know you were alive, instead of dead. And look what you did to Kate . . ." He broke off, darting a quick glance at Nora.

Face paling, Brian took a step forward. "You can't say such things to me, even if you are my brother! If you weren't laid up, I'd break your head open!"

"Come on, *brother!* Don't let that stop you."

"Stop it, just stop it!" Nora clapped her hands over her ears. "Hellfire and spit, you're brothers! And with Sean scarcely in his grave!" Belatedly, she took note of what Kevin had just said. "Kate? What did he mean about what Brian did to you?"

Kate was staring at Brian. She gestured tiredly. "It's nothing, Nora. Not important, not anymore."

With a grunting effort Kevin was levering himself to his feet. Upright, he said to Brian, "We'll be off Moraghan within the week." Supporting himself with an improvised crutch, he made his way outside.

As Kate started to follow, Nora said urgently, "Kate, try to get him to see reason! You can't just go!"

349

"I'm sorry, Nora." Kate's look was steady. "He can be stubborn when he's made up his mind. Besides, it so happens I agree with him. We can't stay here. Not now, perhaps not ever." She followed Kevin outside.

Brian took Anna by the arm. "Let's go round up the children, woman." At the door he paused to look back, his expression grim. "I'm sorry, Momma, sorry it had to happen. But it wasn't my doing; you'll have to admit that."

"Wasn't it, Brian?" she said softly. "I wonder."

He gave her a furious look and stamped out. Nora sat unmoving, staring at the door long after he was gone. She felt empty, used up, devoid even of grief. Within the month she had lost a husband; she had regained a son, and then lost another. With a start she realized that Stony Lieberman was speaking. "I'm sorry, Mr. Lieberman . . . What did you say?"

"I said, I'm sorry for your trouble, Mrs. Moraghan," he said wretchedly, his gaze down as he stuffed papers into his case.

Nora had to smile. "You're sure you're not Irish, Mr. Lieberman?"

He gave her a startled look. "I'm sure about that as I am about anything, but while growing up, I did live next door to an Irish family." He laughed self-consciously.

That's the first time I've seen him laugh, she thought.

Abruptly her spirit rose, her natural optimism coming to her rescue. After all, it was not unusual for brothers to squabble. She was intelligent, she should be able to think of a way to heal the breach. She studied the lawyer's bowed head. She had a strong suspicion that he was a very good lawyer. Scheming together, two clever minds at work, it was more than possible they could find a way to get around the terms of the will. In her heart, Nora knew that Sean had it in mind to do better by Kevin, so it was now left up to her.

350

She said, "Stony, I think we should get to know each other better. And what better time than now? You don't have to rush away, do you? Why not stay for tea? Or something stronger, if you prefer?"

Epilogue

The spring wagon pulled to a stop on the bank of the San Jacinto River, waiting for the ferry to cross over from the opposite side. The cumbersome Conestoga wagon drew up behind.

Kevin Moraghan craned awkwardly around to shout back to the driver of the Conestoga. "You wait here, Bertram. We won't be gone more than a couple of hours."

Kate, holding the reins, said, "Darling, you sure you want to do this? We've put a long day's trek behind us, and we should find a good campsite before nightfall."

"I'm sure," Kevin said curtly. "I haven't come all this far out of our way just to pass it by." He dredged up a tired smile. "Don't you see, Kate, it's something I must do. I'm hoping to understand Daddy better for doing this. I know it probably strikes you as foolish . . ."

Kate placed a hand on his knee. "If you feel you must do it, then it's not foolish, Kevin."

Sitting alongside her brother in the rear seat, Debra Lee gave an unladylike snort, quickly smothered behind her hand. She thought it was foolish in the extreme, but then she had been rebellious and out of sorts since they left Moraghan. The only home she had ever known, her grandmother, her friends—all were left behind while they went kiting off to a place nobody had ever heard of, and she vividly remembered her Uncle Brian saying: "Nothing down there but Mexicans, goats, and cactus. You'll be back, little brother!"

Debra Lee hoped so. Every night when they bedded down—out in the open, like animals!—she prayed that her father would change his mind and turn back. But with every passing day that seemed less and less likely.

Aside from leaving behind everything she knew, Debra Lee was in love, and every mile they traveled took her farther and farther away from her own true love. She sat up alertly at the end of the short ferry ride, as Kate guided the wagon off the ferry and onto a dusty deserted road.

After a short distance her father said, "Pull up here, Kate." He started to clamber awkwardly down from the seat.

Kate said, "I'd better help you, darling."

"No! I can manage. The rest of you stay here. There's nothing of interest to you here."

Watching her father fit the tree-limb crutch under his arm and hobble off toward a grove of trees along the river, Debra Lee could agree with *that* wholeheartedly. Even with the top over the spring wagon, it was hot and humid, and the air stank like spoiled fish. All she could see was stagnant water, a few trees, and grass high as her father's waist. If it was this hot now in winter, what would it be like in summer?

Debra Lee wasn't exactly sure why they were here. It had something to do with a long-ago battle in which Grandfather had fought. Was it possible that, after her father had seen what he had come to see, he would change his mind and they'd go back home? It was a small thread of hope.

Kevin hobbled into the grove of trees, and the scattering of tombstones. The men killed at the Battle of San Jacinto, and veterans who had died since of natural causes, were buried here. He wondered briefly if Sean would have liked to have been laid to rest here, and decided not.

Resting his weight on a high tombstone, he looked out across the field of tall grass through which the Texans had charged into battle that day. Aside from the graves, there was nothing to mark that crucial battle.

Why was he here? Kevin wasn't sure. It was a whim; yet it wasn't.

He closed his eyes and listened intently. At first, he heard nothing but the rustle of the trees in the faint breeze, and the chirping of insects. Then, as if from a great distance, he heard the roll of drum, the piping of fifes—"Come to the Bower." Voices shouted and muskets cracked and a roster sergeant thundered names: "General Sam Houston! Sean Moraghan . . ."

Kevin's eyes flew open, and he smiled sardonically at the flight of fancy. Of course he had heard nothing. Ghosts from the past, if such existed, drifted noiselessly through time and space.

And yet he felt a sudden, inexplicable lift of spirit. Sean Moraghan had talked rarely of his role in the battle, but he had been here, he had left his mark, and Kevin felt that it was a heritage more precious than land, more precious than wealth.

Sean and Nora Moraghan had arrived in Texas in a cart, with little more than the clothes on their backs, and four thousand acres of raw land, and from that acreage had carved a minor empire. Could he not do the same? True, he had only 640 acres, but it was a starting point.

He took a last look across the San Jacinto battlefield

354

and started back toward the wagon, glad that he had made the detour. His step was almost jaunty, considering the crutch, and his spirits were high. He should be almost healed by the time they reached their destination.

Debra Lee, watching her father return, knew instinctively that any hope they had of returning to Moraghan was dashed.

At the wagon Kevin threw away the crutch and hauled himself up onto the seat. "We can go now, Kate." His voice rose. "Rio Grande Valley, here come the Moraghans!"

As her mother expertly swung the wagon around and headed back toward Lynch's Ferry, Debra Lee rode with her lips set in iron determination.

Someday, when she was old enough, she would return to Moraghan. Her father might turn his back on what was rightfully his, but she was going to fight for her inheritance . . . and her love.

You'd better wait for me, Stonewall Lieberman, she said silently; or you'll be everlastingly sorry!

Kate flicked the reins at the horses, and the wagon picked up some speed, trailing a cloud of dust.

K.